She did a great deal he f... starting with the way she walked. She carried herself like a lady, like the women of his class, yet the sway of her hips promised something tantalisingly unladylike.

'I married Marcelline knowing she'd never give up her work,' Clevedon was saying. 'If she did, she'd be like everyone else. She wouldn't be the woman I fell in love ...'

'Love,' Longmore ...d. 'Bad idea.'

Cleved... ... 'One ... Love will come along and knock you on your arse,' he said. 'And I'll laugh myself sick, watching.'

'Love will have its work cut out for it,' Longmore said. 'I'm not like you. I'm not *sensitive*. If Love wants to take hold of me, not only will it have to knock me on my arse, it'll have to tie me down and beat to a pulp what some optimistically call my brains.'

'Very possibly,' Clevedon said. 'Which will make it all the more amusing.'

THE DRESSMAKERS SERIES

Silk is for Seduction
Scandal Wears Satin
Vixen in Velvet

Loretta CHASE

Scandal wears Satin

MILLS & BOON

Published in Great Britain 2014
by Mills & Boon, an imprint of Harlequin (UK) Limited,
Eton House, 18-24 Paradise Road, Richmond, Surrey, TW9 1SR

Excerpt from *Lessons from a Scandalous Bride* © 2012 Sharie Kohler

ISBN: 978 0 263 24603 2

009-0514

Harlequin (UK) Limited's policy is to use papers that are natural, renewable and recyclable products and made from wood grown in sustainable forests. The logging and manufacturing processes conform to the legal environmental regulations of the country of origin.

Printed and bound by
CPI Group (UK) Ltd, Croydon, CR0 4YY

Loretta Chase has worked in academe, retail and the visual arts, as well as on the streets—as a meter maid (aka traffic warden)—and in video, as a scriptwriter. She might have developed an excitingly chequered career had her spouse not nagged her into writing fiction. Her bestselling historical romances, set in the Regency and Romantic eras of the early nineteenth century, have won a number of awards, including the Romance Writers of America's RITA®.

Website: www.LorettaChase.com.

ACKNOWLEDGEMENTS

This book was made possible by the support of: my insightful and inspiring editor, May Chen; my indefatigable agent, Nancy Yost; my witty and fashion-wise friend and blogging partner, Isabella Bradford, aka Susan Holloway Scott; my patient French adviser, Valerie Kerxhalli; my loyal, funny and crazy sisters, Cynthia, Vivian and Kathy; and, most especially, my brainy and brave husband, Walter, a hero every single day.

Scandal wears Satin

Prologue

Observe his fierce, fighting-cock air; his coal-black gipsy curls; his aristocratic (not to call it arrogant) expression of countenance—never laid aside, whether he is smiling on a fair dame or frowning on a fawning dun.

—*The Court Magazine,*
"Sketches from Real Life," 1835

London
Thursday 21 May 1835, early morning

The trollops knew how to throw a party.

On Wednesday nights, after dancing or playing cards with Society's crème de la crème at Almack's, London's wilder set continued more eagerly to a very different assembly at the house of Carlotta O'Neill. On offer was a roulette table, along with other games of chance, as well as spicier games with the demireps who played ladies-in-waiting to London's current queen of courtesans.

Harry Fairfax, Earl of Longmore, was on the scene, naturally.

Carlotta's wasn't the sort of place his father,

the Marquess of Warford, would wish his twenty-seven-year-old son and heir to frequent, but heeding his parents' wishes, Longmore had decided a long time ago, was the fast and easy route to murderous boredom.

He was nothing like his parents, on any count. He'd inherited not only his great-uncle Lord Nicholas Fairfax's piratical looks—black hair, black eyes, and a tall, muscular physique usually associated with buccaneers—but Great-Uncle Nicholas's talent for Doing What He Was Not Supposed To.

And so Lord Longmore was at Carlotta's.

And she was draped over him, wafting waves of scent. And talking, unfortunately.

"But you're intimately acquainted with them," she was saying. "You must tell us what the new Duchess of Clevedon is really like."

"Brunette," he said, watching the roulette wheel spin. "Pretty. Says she's English but acts French."

"My dear, we could have found that out from the *Spectacle*."

Foxe's Morning Spectacle was London's premier scandal sheet. The high-principled Marquess of Warford called it disgusting tripe, but he read it, as did everyone else, from London's bawds and pimps on up to the Royal Family. Every detail it published regarding the Duke of Clevedon's new bride had, Longmore knew, been artfully crafted by the bride's fair-haired sister Sophia Noirot, evil dressmaker by day and Tom Foxe's premier spy by night.

Longmore wondered where she was this night. He hadn't spotted her at Almack's. Milliners—especially slightly French ones—had as much chance of receiving vouchers to Almack's as he had of turning invisible at will. But Sophia Noirot had her own mode of invisibility, and she was perfectly capable of inserting her elegantly curved body anywhere she pleased, in the guise of a temporary servant. That was how she dug up so much dirt for Foxe's scandal sheet.

The roulette wheel stopped spinning, one of the fellows at the table swore, and the wench acting as croupier raked a pile of counters in Longmore's direction.

He scooped them up and handed them to Carlotta.

"Your winnings?" she said. "Do you want me to keep them safe for you?"

He laughed. "Yes, m'dear, keep them safe. Buy yourself a bauble or some such."

Her well-groomed eyebrows went up.

Until a moment ago, when visions of Sophy Noirot sashayed into his mind, he'd assumed what Carlotta had assumed: that he'd soon disappear with her into her bedroom. She was supposed to be in Lord Gorrell's keeping, but he, while rich enough, wasn't quite lively enough to keep Carlotta fully amused.

Dependent on an allowance and gambling winnings, Longmore probably wasn't rich enough. But while he didn't doubt he possessed the necessary stamina and inventiveness to hold her interest, it occurred to him now that she wasn't likely to hold his for more than five minutes. Even by his careless standards, that hardly justified a large financial investment and the subsequent tedium of listening to his father rant about overspent allowances.

In other words, Longmore was tired of her already.

Not too long after abandoning his winnings, he took his leave, along with two of his friends and two of Carlotta's maids of honor. They found a hackney and after a short discussion, set out for a gaming hell with a very bad reputation, in the neighborhood of St. James's. There, Longmore could count on a brawl.

Bored with the conversation inside the coach, he turned to gaze out of the window at the passing scene. The sun rose early at this time of year, and though the window was dirty, he could see well enough. A drably dressed female carrying a shabby basket was hurrying along the street. Her pace and dress, along with the basket, made it clear she wasn't one of London's numerous streetwalkers but an ordinary female on her way to work at about the time her betters in the beau monde were going home from their parties.

She moved at a fast clip, but it wasn't fast enough. A figure darted out of an alley, grabbed her basket, and knocked her into the street.

Longmore stood, put down the window, opened the carriage door, and jumped out of the moving carriage, deaf to his companions' shrieks and shouts. After the first stumble, he quickly gained his balance, and charged after the thief. His prey was fast, darting this way and that. At a busier time of day, he would have soon shed any pursuer. But the hour was early, and hardly anybody stood in Longmore's way. He wasn't thinking, only running, in a blind fury. When the fellow sprang into a narrow court, Longmore never thought of ambush or danger—not that he'd care, had he thought about it.

The fellow was making for a door, and it opened a crack, its inhabitants expecting him, no doubt. Longmore got to him first. He grabbed the thief and dragged him backward. The door banged shut.

Longmore slammed him against the nearest wall. The man instantly crumpled and slid to the ground, dropping the basket. Though he couldn't be much damaged—these villains didn't break easily—he stayed where he was, eyes closed.

"I shouldn't get up again in a hurry, if I were you," Longmore said. "Filthy coward. Attacking *women*." Longmore collected the basket and cast a glance round the court. With any luck, dangerous accomplices would hurry to their friend's rescue.

But no luck. The area was quiet, though Longmore was well aware he was being watched. He sauntered out into Piccadilly.

He found the girl minutes later. She stood slumped against a shop front, weeping. "Never mind the bawling," he said. "Here's your precious goods." He fished some coins from a pocket and thrust those and the shabby basket into her hands. "What in blazes was in your mind, rushing on blindly without minding your surroundings?"

"W-work," she said. "I had to get to work . . . your lordship."

He didn't ask how she knew he was a lord.

Everybody knew the Earl of Longmore.

"Thieves and drunken aristocrats roaming the streets, looking for trouble, and you without a weapon," he said. "What's wrong with women these days?"

"I d-don't know."

She was shaking like a leaf. She was bruised and

dirty from her fall in the street. She was lucky that none of the scores of drunken louts on their way home from their debauches had run her over.

"Come with me," he said.

Whether too shaken to think or simply intimidated—he often had that effect, even on his peers—she followed him across the street to the hackney. His friends could have continued on: They were drunk enough. But they'd stopped to watch the fun.

"Everybody out," Longmore said.

They made noises of protest but they staggered out of the vehicle, all staring at the drab female. "Not your type, Longmore," Hempton said.

Crawford shook his head. "Standards dropping, I'm afraid to say."

Longmore ignored them. "Where were you going?" he said to the girl.

She stared at him, then at his friends, then at the tarts.

"Never mind them," he said. "Nobody's interested in your doings. We only want to get on to the next party. Where do you want the driver to take you?"

She swallowed. "Please, your lordship, I was on my way to the Milliners' Society for the Education of Indigent Females," she said.

"There's a mouthful," Crawford said.

"I work there," the girl said. "I'm going to be late."

She gave Longmore the direction, which he relayed to the driver, with strict orders to take the girl to her destination in half the usual time, or Longmore would find him and give him an excellent excuse for moving slowly.

He helped the girl up into the coach, slammed the door on her, and waved the driver away.

He thought about milliners.

One milliner, actually, a blonde one.

Leaving his companions to find another hackney, he continued on foot, on his own, the short distance to St. James's Street. To get to Crockford's, he had to pass White's Club on one side of the street, and a very little way farther down, Maison Noirot, lair of French dressmakers.

He passed the dressmakers' shop, walking slowly. Then he paused and looked back, up at the upper storeys where, for reasons that eluded him, two of the three Noirot sisters still lived.

He continued to Crockford's, where he proceeded to lose large sums for quite an interesting while before he started to win large sums.

When, after an hour or so of increasing boredom, he left Crockford's, it was still prodigious early by Fashionable Society's standards. Nonetheless, London was coming to life. People going up and down St. James's Street: a few vehicles but mainly pedestrians. The shops hadn't yet opened.

Maison Noirot, he knew, did not open until ten o'clock, though the seamstresses—a great parade of them these days—all marched in at nine.

Still, over the past few weeks he had acquired a general notion of Sophia Noirot's habits.

He waited.

Chapter One

For the last week, the whole of the fashionable world has been in a state of ferment, on account of the elopement of Sir Colquhoun Grant's daughter with Mr. Brinsley Sheridan . . . On Friday afternoon, about five o'clock, the young couple borrowed the carriage of a friend; and . . . set off full speed for the North.

—*The Court Journal*, Saturday 23 May 1835

London
Thursday 21 May 1835

Waving a copy of *Foxe's Morning Spectacle*, Sophy Noirot burst in upon the Duke and Duchess of Clevedon while they were breakfasting in, appropriately enough, the breakfast room of Clevedon House.

"Have you seen this?" she said, throwing down the paper on the table between her sister and new brother-in-law. "The *ton* is in a frenzy—and isn't it hilarious? They're blaming Sheridan's three sisters. Three sisters plotting wicked plots—and it isn't *us!* Oh, my love, when I saw this, I thought I'd die laughing."

Certain members of Society had more than once in recent days compared the three proprietresses of Maison Noirot—which Sophy would make London's foremost dressmaking establishment if it killed her—to the three witches in *Macbeth*. Had they not bewitched the Duke of Clevedon, rumor said, he would never have married a *shop-keeper.*

Their Graces' dark heads bent over the barely dry newspaper.

Rumors about the Sheridan-Grant elopement were already traveling the beau monde grapevine, but the *Spectacle*, as usual, was the first to put confirmation in print.

Marcelline looked up. "They say Miss Grant's papa will bring a suit against Sheridan in Chancery," she said. "Exciting stuff, indeed."

At that moment, a footman entered. "Lord Longmore, Your Grace," he said.

Not now, dammit, Sophy thought. Her sister had the beau monde in an uproar, she'd made a deadly enemy of one of its most powerful women—who happened to be Longmore's mother—customers were deserting in droves, and Sophy had no idea how to repair the damage.

Now *him*.

The Earl of Longmore strolled into the breakfast room, a newspaper under his arm.

Sophy's pulse rate accelerated. It couldn't help itself.

Black hair and glittering black eyes . . . the noble nose that ought to have been broken a dozen times yet remained stubbornly straight and arrogant . . . the hard, cynical mouth . . . the six-foot-plus frame.

All that manly beauty.

If only he had a brain.

No, better not. In the first place, brains in a man were inconvenient. In the second, and far more important, she didn't have time for him or any man. She had a shop to rescue from Impending Doom.

"I brought you the latest *Spectacle*," he said to the pair at the table. "But I wasn't quick enough off the mark, I see."

"Sophy brought it," said Marcelline.

Longmore's dark gaze came to Sophy. She gave him a cool nod and sauntered to the sideboard. She looked into the chafing dishes and concentrated on filling her plate.

"Miss Noirot," he said. "Up and about early, I see. You weren't at Almack's last night."

"Certainly not," Sophy said. "The Spanish Inquisition couldn't make the patronesses give me a voucher."

"Since when do you wait for permission? I was so disappointed. I was on pins and needles to see what disguise you'd adopt. My favorite so far is the Lancashire maidservant."

That was Sophy's favorite, too.

However, her intrusions at fashionable events to collect gossip for Foxe were supposed to be a deep, dark secret. No one noticed servant girls, and she was a Noirot, as skilled at making herself invisible as she was at getting attention.

But *he* noticed.

He must have developed unusually keen powers

of hearing and vision to make up for his very small brain.

She carried her plate to the table and sat next to her sister. "I'm devastated to have spoiled your fun," she said.

"That's all right," he said. "I found something to do later."

"So it seems," Clevedon said, looking him over. "It must have been quite a party. Since you're never up and about this early, I can only conclude you stopped here on your way home."

Like most of his kind, Lord Longmore rarely rose before noon. His rumpled black hair, limp neckcloth, and wrinkled coat, waistcoat, and trousers told Sophy he hadn't yet been to bed—not his own, at any rate.

Her imagination promptly set about picturing his big body naked among tangled sheets. She had never seen him naked, and had better not; but along with owning a superior imagination, she'd seen statues, pictures, and—years ago—certain boastful Parisian boys' personal possessions.

She firmly wiped her mind clean.

One day, she'd marry a respectable man who would not get in the way of her work.

Not only was Longmore far from respectable, but he was a great thickhead who constantly got in one's way—and who happened to be the eldest son of a woman who wanted the Noirot sisters wiped off the face of the earth.

Only a self-destructive moron would get involved with him.

Sophy directed her attention to his clothes. As far as tailoring went, his attire was flawless, the snug fit outlining every muscled inch from his big shoulders and broad chest and his lean waist and narrow hips down, down, down his long, powerful legs . . .

She scrubbed her mind again, reminded herself that clothing was her life, and regarded his attire objectively, as one professional considering the work of another.

She knew that he usually started an evening elegantly turned out. His valet, Olney, saw to it. But Longmore did not always behave elegantly, and what happened after he left the house Olney could not control.

By the looks of him, a great deal had happened after Olney released his master yesterday.

"You always were the intellectual giant of the family," Longmore said to the duke. "You've deduced correctly. I stopped at Crockford's. And elsewhere. I needed something to drive out the memory of those dreary hours at Almack's."

"You loathe those assemblies," Clevedon said. "One can only assume that a woman lured you there."

"My sister," Longmore said. "She's an idiot about men. My parents complain about it endlessly. Even I noticed what a sorry lot they are, her beaux. A pack of lechers and bankrupts. To discourage them, I hang about Clara and look threatening."

Sophy could easily picture it. No one could loom as menacingly as he, gazing down on the world through half-closed eyes like a great, dark bird of prey.

"How unusually brotherly of you," said Clevedon.

"That numskull Adderley was trying to press his suit with her." Longmore helped himself to coffee and sat down next to Clevedon, opposite Marcelline. "She thinks he's charming. I think he's charmed by her dowry."

"Rumor says he's traveling up the River Tick on a fast current," Clevedon said.

"I don't like his smirk," Longmore said. "And I don't think he even likes Clara much. My parents loathe him on a dozen counts." He waved his coffee cup at the newspaper. "They won't find this coup of Sheridan's reassuring. Still, it's deuced convenient for you, I daresay. An excellent way to divert attention from your exciting nuptials."

His dark gaze moved lazily to Sophy. "The timing couldn't have been better. I don't suppose you had anything to do with this, Miss Noirot?"

"If I had, I should be demanding a bottle of the duke's best champagne and a toast to myself," said Sophy. "I only wish I could have managed something so *perfect*."

Though the three Noirot sisters were equally talented dressmakers, each had special skills. Dark-haired Marcelline, the eldest, was a gifted artist and designer. Redheaded Leonie, the youngest, was the financial genius. Sophy, the blonde, was the saleswoman. She could soften stony hearts and pry large sums from tight fists. She could make people believe black was white. Her sisters often said that Sophy could sell sand to Bedouins.

Had she been able to manufacture a scandal that would get Society's shallow little mind off Marcelline and onto somebody else, Sophy would have done it. As much as she loved Marcelline and was happy she'd married a man who adored her, Sophy was still reeling from the disruption to their world, which had always revolved around their little family and their business. She wasn't sure Marcelline and Clevedon truly understood the difficulties their recent marriage had created for Maison Noirot, or how much danger the shop was in.

But then, they were newlyweds, and love seemed to muddle the mind even worse than lust did. At present, Sophy couldn't bear to mar their happiness by sharing her and Leonie's anxieties.

The newlyweds exchanged looks. "What do you think?" Clevedon said. "Do you want to take advantage of the diversion and go back to work?"

"I must go back to work, diversion or not," Marcelline said. She looked at Sophy. "Do let's make a speedy departure, *ma chère sœur*. The aunts will be down to breakfast in the next hour or so."

"The aunts," Longmore said. "Still here?"

Clevedon House was large enough to accommodate several families comfortably. When the duke's aunts came to Town on visits too short to warrant opening their own townhouses, they didn't stay in hotels, but in the north wing.

Most recently they'd come to stop the marriage. Originally, Marcelline and Clevedon had planned to wed the day after he'd talked—or seduced—her into marrying him. But Sophy and Leonie's cooler heads had prevailed.

The wedding, they'd pointed out, was going to cause a spectacular uproar, very possibly fatal to business. But if some of Clevedon's relatives were to attend the ceremony, signaling acceptance of the bride, it would subdue, to some extent, the outrage.

And so Clevedon had invited his aunts, who'd descended en masse to prevent the shocking misalliance. But no great lady, not even the Queen, was a match for three Noirot sisters and their secret weapon, Marcelline's six-year-old daughter, Lucie Cordelia. The aunts had surrendered in a matter of hours.

Now they were trying to find a way to make Marcelline respectable. They actually believed they could present her to the Queen.

Sophy wasn't at all sure that would do Maison Noirot any good. On the contrary, she suspected it would only fan the flames of Lady Warford's hatred.

"Still here," Clevedon said. "They can't seem to tear themselves away."

Marcelline rose, and the others did, too. "I'd better go before they come down," she said. "They're not at all reconciled to my continuing to work."

"Meaning there's a good deal more jawing than you like," Longmore said. "How well I understand." He gave her a wry smile, and bowed.

He was a man who could fill a doorway, and seemed to take over a room. He was disheveled, and disreputable besides, but he bowed with the easy grace of a dandy.

It was annoying of him to be so completely and gracefully at ease in that big brawler's body of his. It was really annoying of him to ooze virility.

Sophy was a Noirot, a breed keenly tuned to animal excitement—and not possessing much in the way of moral principles.

If he ever found out how weak she was in this regard, she was doomed.

She sketched a curtsey and took her sister's arm. "Yes, well, we'd better not dawdle, in any event.

I promised Leonie I wouldn't stay above half an hour."

She hurried her sister out of the room.

Longmore watched them go. Actually, he watched Sophy go, a fetching bundle of energy and guile.

"The shop," he said when they were out of earshot. "Meaning no disrespect to your duchess, but—are they insane?"

"That depends on one's point of view," Clevedon said.

"Apparently, I'm not unbalanced enough in the upper storey to understand it," Longmore said. "They might close it and live here. It isn't as though you're short of room. Or money. Why should they want to go on bowing and scraping to women?"

"Passion," Clevedon said. "Their work is their passion."

Longmore wasn't sure what, exactly, passion was. He was reasonably certain he'd never experienced it.

He hadn't even had an infatuation since he was eighteen.

Since Clevedon, his nearest friend, would know this, Longmore said nothing. He only shook his head, and moved to the sideboard. He heaped his plate with eggs, great slabs of bacon and bread, and a thick glob of butter to make it all slide down smoothly. He carried it to the table and began to eat.

He'd always regarded Clevedon's home as his own, and had been told he was to continue regarding it in the same way. The duchess seemed to like him well enough. Her blonde sister, on the other hand would just as soon shoot him, he knew—

which made her much more interesting and entertaining.

That was why he'd waited and watched for her. That was why he'd followed her from Maison Noirot to Charing Cross. He'd spotted the newspaper in her hand, and deduced what it was.

By some feat of printing legerdemain—a pact with the devil, most likely—*Foxe's Morning Spectacle* usually slunk onto the streets of London and into the newspaper sellers' grubby hands not only well in advance of its competitors, but containing fresher scandal. Though many of the beau monde's entertainments didn't start until eleven at night or end before dawn, Foxe contrived to stuff the pages of his titillating rag with details of what everyone had done mere hours earlier.

This was no small achievement, even bearing in mind that "morning," especially among the upper classes, was a flexible unit of time, extending well beyond noonday.

Curious about what was taking her to Clevedon House at this early hour, he'd bought a copy from the urchin hawking it on the next corner, and had dawdled for a time to look it over. By now familiar with Sophy's writing, Longmore knew it wasn't the sort of thing to take on an empty stomach. He'd persevered nonetheless. Though he couldn't see how she could have had a hand in the Sheridan scandal, that was nothing new. She did a great deal he found intriguing—starting with the way she walked: She carried herself like a lady, like the women of his class, yet the sway of her hips promised something tantalizingly unladylike.

"I married Marcelline knowing she'd never give up her work," Clevedon was saying. "If she did, she'd be like everyone else. She wouldn't be the woman I fell in love with."

"Love," Longmore said. "Bad idea."

Clevedon smiled. "One day Love will come along and knock you on your arse," he said. "And I'll laugh myself sick, watching."

"Love will have its work cut out for it," Longmore said. "I'm not like you. I'm not *sensitive*. If Love wants to take hold of me, not only will it have to knock me on my arse, it'll have to tie me down and beat to a pulp what some optimistically call my brains."

"Very possibly," Clevedon said. "Which will make it all the more amusing."

"You'll have a wait," Longmore said. "For the moment, Clara's love life is the problem."

"I daresay matters at home haven't been pleasant for either of you, since the wedding," Clevedon said.

Clevedon would know better than most. Lord Warford had been his guardian. Clevedon and Longmore had grown up together. They were more like brothers than friends. And Clevedon had doted on Clara since she was a small child. It had always been assumed they'd marry. Then the duke had met his dressmaker—and Clara had reacted with "Good riddance"—much to the shock of her parents, brothers, and sisters—not to mention the entire beau monde.

"My father has resigned himself," Longmore said. "My mother hasn't."

A profound understatement, that.

His mother was beside herself. The slightest reference to the duke or his new wife set her screaming. She quarreled with Clara incessantly. She was driving Clara to distraction, and they constantly dragged Longmore into it. Every day or so a message arrived from his sister, begging him to come and Do Something.

Longmore and Clara had both attended Clevedon's wedding—in effect, giving their blessing to the union. This fact, which had been promptly reported in the *Spectacle,* had turned Warford House into a battlefield.

"I could well understand Clara rejecting me," Clevedon said.

"Don't see how you could fail to understand," Longmore said. "She explained it in detail, in ringing tones, in front of half the ton."

"What I don't understand is why she doesn't send Adderley about his business," Clevedon said.

"Tall, fair, poetic-looking," Longmore said. "He knows what to say to women. Men see him for what he is. Women don't."

"I've no idea what's in Clara's mind," Clevedon said. "My wife and her sisters will want to get to the bottom of it, though. It's their business to understand their clients, and Clara's special. She's their best customer, and she shows Marcelline's designs to stunning advantage. They won't want her to marry a man with pockets to let."

"Are they in the matchmaking line as well, then?" Longmore said. "If so, I wish they'd find her someone suitable, and spare me these dreary nights at Almack's."

"Leave it to Sophy," Clevedon said. "She's the one who goes to the parties. She'll see what's going on, better than anybody."

"Including a great deal that people would rather she didn't see," Longmore said.

"Hers is an exceptionally keen eye for detail," Clevedon said.

"And an exceptionally busy pen," Longmore said. "It's easy to recognize her work in the *Spectacle*. Streams of words about ribbons and bows and lace and pleats here and gathers there. No thread goes unmentioned."

"She notices gestures and looks as well," Clevedon said. "She listens. No one's stories are like hers."

"No question about that," Longmore said. "She's never met an adjective or adverb she didn't like."

Clevedon smiled. "That's what brings in the customers: the combination of gossip and the intricate detail about the dresses, all related as drama. It has the same effect on women, I'm told, as looking at naked women has on men." He tapped a finger on the *Spectacle*. "I'll ask her to keep an eye on Clara. With two of you on watch, you ought to be able to keep her out of trouble."

Longmore had no objections to any activity involving Sophy Noirot.

On the contrary, he had a number of activities in mind, and joining her in keeping an eye on his sister would give him a fine excuse to be underfoot—and with any luck, under other parts as well.

"Can't think of a better woman for the job," Longmore said. "Miss Noirot misses nothing."

In his mind she was *Sophy*. But she'd never invited him to call her by the name all her family used. And so, even with Clevedon, good manners dictated that Longmore use the correct form of address for the senior unmarried lady of a family.

"With you and Sophy standing guard, the lechers and bankrupts won't stand a chance," Clevedon said. "Argus himself couldn't do better."

Longmore racked his brain. "The dog, you mean?"

"The giant with extra eyes," Clevedon said. "'And set a watcher upon her, great and strong Argus, who with four eyes looks every way,'" he quoted from somewhere. "'And the goddess stirred in him unwearying strength: sleep never fell upon his eyes; but he kept sure watch always.'"

"That strikes me as excessive," Longmore said. "But then, you always were romantic."

A week later

Warford, how *could* you?"

"My dear, you know I cannot command his majesty—"

"It is not to be borne! That *creature* he married—presented at *Court!*—at the King's Birthday Drawing Room!—as though she were visiting royalty!"

Longmore was trapped in a carriage with his mother, father, and Clara, departing St. James's Palace. Though court events bored him witless, he'd attended the Drawing Room, hoping to spot a certain uninvited attendee. But he'd seen only Sophy's sister—the "creature" his mother was in a snit about. Then he'd debated whether to sneak out or to hunt for an equally bored wife or widow. The palace was well supplied with dark corners conducive to a quick bout of fun.

No luck with the females. The sea of plumes and diamonds held an overabundance of sanctimonious matrons and virgins. Virgins were what one married. They weren't candidates for fun under a staircase.

"Odd, I agree," Lord Warford said carefully. Though he'd given up being outraged about Clevedon's marriage, he'd also long ago given up trying to reason with his wife.

"Didn't seem odd to me," Longmore said.

"Not odd!" his mother cried. "Not odd! *No one* is presented at the King's Birthday Drawing Room."

"No one but foreign dignitaries," Lord Warford said.

"It was a shocking breach of etiquette even to request an exception," Lady Warford said, conveniently forgetting that she'd told her husband to commit a shocking breach of etiquette by telling the King not to recognize the Duchess of Clevedon.

But it was up to the husband, not the son, to point this out, and years of marriage had taught Lord Warford cowardice.

"I could not believe Her Majesty would do such a thing, even for Lady Adelaide," Mother went on. "But it seems I'm obliged to believe it," she added bitterly. "The Queen dotes on Clevedon's youngest aunt." She glared at her daughter. "Lady Adelaide Ludley might have used her influence on your and your family's behalf. But no, you must be the most ungrateful, undutiful daughter who ever lived. You must jilt the Duke of Clevedon!"

"I didn't jilt him, Mama," Clara said. "One cannot jilt someone to whom one is not engaged."

Longmore had heard this argument too many times to want to be boxed in a closed carriage, hearing it again, his mother's voice going higher and higher, and Clara's climbing along with it. Normally, he would call the carriage to a halt and get out, and leave everybody fuming behind him.

Clara could defend herself, he knew. The trouble was, that would only lead to more quarreling and screaming and messages for him to come to Warford House before she committed matricide.

He thought very hard and very fast and said, "It was clear as clear to me that they did it behind the scenes, so to speak, to spare your feelings, ma'am."

There followed the kind of furiously intense silence that typically ensued when his parents were deciding whether he might, against all reason and evidence, have said something worth listening to.

"What with the aunts and all, the Queen would be in a fix," he went on. "She could hardly snub Clevedon's whole family—which is what she'd be doing, since the aunts had accepted his bride."

"His bride," his mother said bitterly. "His *bride*." She threw Clara the sort of look Caesar must have given Brutus when the knife went in.

"This way at least, the deed was done behind the scenes," Longmore went on, "not in front of the whole blasted ton."

While his mother stirred this idea around in her seething mind, the carriage reached the front of Warford House. The footmen opened the carriage door, and the family emerged, the ladies shaking out their skirts as they stepped out onto the pavement.

Longmore said nothing and Clara said nothing but she shot him a grateful look before she hurried inside after their mother.

His father, however, lingered at the front step with Longmore. "Not coming in?"

"I think not," Longmore said. "Did my best. Tried to pour oil and all that."

"It won't end," his father said in a low voice. "Not for your mother. Shattered dreams and wounded pride and outraged sensibilities and whatnot. You see how it is. We can expect no peace in this family until Clara finds a suitable replacement for Clevedon. That's not going to happen while she keeps encouraging that pack of loose screws." He made a dismissive gesture. "Make them go away, will you, dammit?"

Countess of Igby's ball
Saturday 30 May 1835

One o'clock in the morning

*L*ongmore had been looking for Lord Adderley for some time. The fellow having proven too thick to take a hint, Longmore had decided that the simplest approach was to hit him until he understood that he was to keep off Clara.

The trouble was, Sophy Noirot was at Lady Igby's party, too, and Longmore, unlike Argus, owned only the usual number of eyes.

He'd become distracted, watching Sophy flit hither and yon, no one paying her the slightest heed—except for the usual assortment of dolts who thought maidservants existed for their sport. Since he'd marked her as *his* sport, Longmore had started to move in, more than once, only to find that she didn't need any help with would-be swains.

She'd "accidentally" spilled hot tea on the waistcoat of one gentleman who'd ventured too close. Another had followed her into an antechamber and tripped over something, landing on his face. A third had followed her down a passage and into a room. He'd come out limping a moment later.

Preoccupied with her adventures, Longmore not only failed to locate Adderley, but lost track of the sister he was supposed to be guarding from lechers and bankrupts. This would have been less of a problem had Sophy been watching her more closely. But Sophy had her own lechers to fend off.

Longmore wasn't thinking about this. Thinking wasn't his favorite thing to do, and thinking about more than one thing at a time upset his equilibrium. At the moment, his mind was on the men trespassing on what he'd decided was his property. Unfortunately, this meant he wasn't aware of his mother losing sight of Clara at the same time. This happened because Lady Warford was carrying on a politely poisonous conversation with her best friend and worst enemy Lady Bartham.

In short, nobody who should have been paying attention was paying attention while Lord Adderley was steering Clara, as they waltzed, toward the other end of the ballroom, toward the doors leading to the terrace. None of those who should have been keeping a sharp eye out saw the wink Adderley sent his friends or the accompanying smirk.

It was the crowd's movement that brought Longmore back to his surroundings and his main reason for being here.

The movement wasn't obvious. It wasn't meant to be. Men like Longmore were attuned to it, though. He had no trouble recognizing the sense of something in the air, the shift in the attention in some parts of the room, and the drifting toward a common destination. It was the change in the atmosphere one felt when a fight was about to happen.

The current was sweeping toward the terrace.

His gut told him something was amiss. It didn't say what, but the warning was vehement, and he was a man who acted on instinct. He moved, and quickly.

He didn't have to push his way through the crowd. Those who knew him knew they'd better get out of the way or be thrust out of the way.

He stormed out onto the terrace. A small audience had gathered. They got out of his way, too.

Nothing and nobody obstructed his view.

Chapter Two

Adderley.

And Clara.

In a dark corner of the terrace.

Not so dark that Longmore couldn't see Adderley clumsily trying to help his sister get her bodice
back in place.

Her dressmakers had cut the neckline of her
white gown indecently low, which had already
allowed every gaping hound at the ball to see a
bit of the lacy thing she wore underneath. In the
process of groping her, however, Lord Adderley
had pushed her dress sleeves and corset straps well

down over her shoulders, practically to her elbows. By the looks of things, he'd contrived to loosen her corset as well.

When she slapped his fumbling hands away, Adderley moved in front of her to shield her, but he wasn't big enough. A fair-haired, blue-eyed beauty Lady Clara Fairfax might be. Petite she was not. As a result, her expensive underwear—not to mention a good deal of skin not usually on public view—was on display for any gawker who happened to be in the vicinity.

That included the dozen or so who'd drifted out to the terrace and were now circling like vultures over the carcass of Lady Clara Fairfax's reputation.

"Her maid will never get the creases out of those pleats," muttered the maidservant standing beside Longmore.

In a distant corner of his mind he marveled at anybody's noticing at such a moment something as trivial as wrinkles in Clara's attire. In the same distant corner he knew there was nothing to marvel at, given the speaker: Sophy Noirot.

That was only a distant awareness, though. The main part of his mind heeded only the scene in front of him, one he saw through a curtain of red flames. "I'll take the wrinkles out of him, the cur," he growled.

"Don't be an id—"

But he was already storming across the terrace, knocking aside any guests who got in his way—though most of them, seeing him coming, moved out of the way, and quickly.

He marched up to Adderley and punched him in the face.

* * *

"—iot," Sophy finished.

She swallowed a sigh.

She should have held her tongue. She was supposed to be a maidservant, and menials did not call their betters *idiots*. Not audibly, at any rate.

But that was the trouble with Longmore. He got in the way of everything, especially clear thinking.

She pushed away the first, emotional reaction and summoned her practical side, the one Cousin Emma had cultivated. A cousin by marriage, Emma was nothing like Sophy's vagabond parents. Emma was not a charming wastrel like her in-laws. She was a hardheaded, practical Parisian.

Practically speaking, this was a disaster.

Lady Clara was Maison Noirot's most important customer. She bought their most expensive creations and she bought lavishly, in spite of her mother's hostility. It was Lord Warford's man of business who paid the bills, and his orders were to pay promptly and in full, not to make fine distinctions among milliners.

Lord Adderley was bankrupt, or very nearly so, thanks to the gaming tables.

If Lady Clara had to misbehave with somebody, Adderley wasn't Sophy's first choice. Of the Upper Ten Thousand, he came in at nine thousand nine hundred fifty six.

Had Longmore been more intelligent, less impetuous, and several degrees less arrogant, she would have counseled him not to go barging in and kill his sister's lover. Since Lord Longmore qualified in none of those categories, she didn't waste her breath pointing out that murder would only complicate the situation and leave Lady Clara's reputation in ruins forever.

He was furious, and he needed to hit somebody, and Adderley deserved to be hit. Sophy was tempted to hit him herself.

This wasn't the only reason she didn't close her eyes or turn away.

She'd seen Longmore fight before, and it was a sight to make a woman's pulse race, if she wasn't squeamish, which Sophy most certainly wasn't.

The blow should have dropped Lord Adderley, but he only staggered backward a few steps.

Tougher than he looked, then. Yet all he did was hold his ground. He offered no sign of fighting back. She couldn't decide whether he was following some obscure gentlemanly code or he held strong opinions about keeping the general shape of his pretty face as it was and all his teeth in his head.

Longmore, meanwhile, was too het up to notice or care whether Lord Adderley meant to defend himself.

Once more he advanced, fists upraised.

"Don't you dare, Harry!" Lady Clara cried. She pushed in front of her lover to shield him. "Don't you touch him."

Then she burst into tears—and very good tears they were. Sophy herself couldn't have done better, and she was an expert. Crooning over her injured lover—who was on his way to a magnificent black eye, if Sophy was any judge—tears streaming down her perfect face, her creamy, amply-displayed bosom heaving, Lady Clara played her part to perfection.

Her ladyship would awaken, along with their baser urges, the sympathies of all the gentlemen present. The ladies, satisfied to have witnessed the downfall of London's most beautiful woman, would allow themselves to feel sorry for her. "She might have had a duke," they'd say. "And now she'll have to *settle* for a penniless lord."

Fashionable London still wasn't tired of repeating bits of Lady Clara's speech rejecting the Duke of Clevedon. One of the favorite bits was the concluding remark: *Why should I settle for you?*

For a moment, Lord Longmore looked as though he'd push his sister out of the way. Then he must have realized it was pointless. He rolled his eyes and sighed, and Sophy watched his big chest rise and fall.

Then he threw up his hands and turned away.

The crowd closed in, blocking Sophy's view.

No matter. Any minute now, the Marchioness of Warford would get wind of her daughter's lapse from virtue, and Sophy owed it to the *Spectacle* to be there when it happened. And at some point, she'd need to look more closely into a disturbing rumor she'd heard in the ladies' retiring room.

It was going to be a long night.

She turned away to look for a discreet route to the other end of the ballroom. Unlike the menservants, the maids were expected to remain inconspicuous. They were to keep out of the main entertainment rooms, and travel in the serving passages as much as possible or attend the ladies in the retiring rooms, where they repaired hems and stockings, ran back and forth for shawls and wraps, applied sal volatile to the swooners, and cleaned up after the excessively intoxicated.

She was deciding which of two doorways offered the best eavesdropping vantage point when Longmore stepped into her path.

"You," he said.

"Me, your lordship?" she said, her tongue curling round the broad Lancashire vowels. She was aware she'd forgotten herself a moment ago and spoken to him as she normally did, but Sophy was nothing if not a brazen liar, like the rest of her family. She looked up at him, her great blue eyes as wide as she could make them, and as innocent of comprehension and intelligence as the cows she prided herself on imitating so well.

"Yes, you," he said. "I'd know you from a mile away, Miss—"

"Oh, no, your lordship, it's no miss but only me, Norton. Can I get you something or other?"

"Don't," he said. "I'm not in the mood for play-acting."

"You're going to get me into trouble, sir," she said. She didn't add, *you great ox*. She kept in character, and smiled brightly, opening her eyes wide and hoping he'd read the message there. "No dallying with the guests."

"How the devil did he do it?" he said. "Why did *she* do it? Is she mad?"

Sophy scanned the area nearby. The guests were busy spreading the news of Lady Clara's lapse from virtue. Lord Longmore, apparently, was not so interesting—or, more likely, he was alarming enough to discourage anybody from even looking at him in a way that he might not like. Since he'd made his state of mind perfectly clear to the company, no one owning a modicum of sanity would care to try his temper further at present. Everybody would take the greatest care to see nothing whatsoever of where he went or what he did.

She grabbed his arm. "This way," she said.

If he'd balked, she would have had as much luck leading his great carcass along as she would a stopped locomotive.

But very likely the last thing he expected was to be hauled about by a slip of a female. Whether bemused or merely amused, he went along tamely enough. She led him into one of the serving passages. Since most of the servants were finding excuses to get near the principals of the scandal, she doubted anybody would wander through for a while.

Still, she looked up and down the passage.

Certain the coast was clear, she let go of his arm. "Now, listen to me," she said.

He glanced down in a puzzled way at his arm, then at her. "Here's one positive note. We've abandoned the Lancashire cow performance."

"Have you any idea what would happen to me if I'm found out?" she said.

"What do you care?" he said. "Your sister married a duke."

"I *care*, you—you great *ox*."

His head went back a degree and his black eyebrows went up. "Did I say something wrong?"

"Yes," she said between her teeth. "So don't say anything more. Just *listen*."

"Gad, we're not going to *discuss* this, are we?"

"Yes, we are, if you want to help your sister."

His eyes narrowed, but he said nothing.

"Believe me, I'm no happier about this recent turn of events than you are," she said. "Have you any idea how bad this is for our business?"

"Your business," he said.

He spoke quietly, but she knew he wasn't calm. The violence he held in check vibrated in the atmosphere about him. She understood why people scrambled out of his way when he bore down on somebody or something.

Violence wouldn't be useful at the moment. She needed to distract him—and for once, the truth would do well enough.

"Adderley is up to his neck in mortgages, and the moneylenders will own his first-, second-, and third-born," she said. "Leonie can tell you to the farthing how much he's worth, and if he's worth a farthing, I'll be amazed."

"I know that," he said. "What I want to know is how my sister ended up on the terrace with him. I know she's naïve, but I never thought she was stupid."

"I don't know how it happened," Sophy said. "I could have sworn she was only honing her flirting skills on him—on all of them. She's never shown signs of favoring anybody."

"You're sure of this?" he said.

She didn't like the tone of his voice. It boded trouble for Adderley. Much as she wished Adderley trouble, she couldn't let Longmore break him into small pieces, as he so clearly wished to.

"I've heard he can be very winning," she said. "And I know she's been feeling—"

"Oh, good. We're going to talk about *feelings*."

If she'd had a heavy object near to hand, she

would have hit him with it. He wouldn't feel it, but the gesture would make her feel better.

"Yes, we are," she said. "I'll spare you all the complicated whys and wherefores and come to the point. Lady Clara is feeling a little rebellious, and I daresay she was waiting for a chance to do something naughty when her mother wasn't looking. Apparently, Adderley saw his chance and turned a minor naughty into a major one. Apparently." She frowned. There was something wrong with that scene. But she'd have to work it out later.

The priority was the man standing a few inches from her. He seemed to have stopped breathing fire.

"I'll have to call him out, the swine," he said. "Which means going off into some dismal wood at the crack of dawn. It's the very devil on one's boots, morning dew, not to mention the fuss Olney makes about gunpowder on my shirt cuffs."

Sophy grabbed his lapels. "Listen to me," she said.

He looked down at her hands in the same puzzled way he'd looked at his arm before.

But his lordship was not the world's deepest thinker, and a great deal could be counted on to puzzle him. She gave his lapels a shake. "Just listen," she said. "You can't kill him in cold blood."

"Whyever not?"

Ye gods grant me patience. "Because he'll be dead," she said as patiently as she could, "and Lady Clara's reputation will be stained *forever.* Do not, I pray you, do *anything*, Lord Longmore. Leave this to us."

"Us."

"My sisters and me."

"What do you propose? Dressing him to death? Tying him up and making him listen to fashion descriptions?"

"If necessary," she said. "But pray, don't trouble yourself about it."

He stared at her.

"Whatever you do, do not injure, maim, or kill him," she said, in case she hadn't made everything perfectly clear. "The right uppercut was excellent. It expressed magnificently a brother's outrage—"

"Did it, by Jove. You wouldn't by any chance be composing your eulogy on my sister's reputation? The one to appear in tomorrow's *Spectacle*?"

"If I don't do it, someone else will," she said. "Better the devil you know, my lord. Only let me do what I can—and you go out and be all manly and protective of your womenfolk."

"Ah." His black eyes widened theatrically. "So *that's* what I'm to do."

"Yes. Can you manage it?"

"With one hand tied behind my back."

"I beg you to do it the usual way," she said. "Don't show off."

"Right." He stood looking at her.

"Yes," she said. "Time to go. Your mother will be getting the news any minute now if she hasn't already." She made a shooing motion.

He only stood, still looking at her in a very concentrated way, and she became aware of a heat and hurry within and a feeling of not being entirely clothed.

Oh, for heaven's sake. Not now.

"You need to go," she said. She tried to give him a push.

It was like trying to push a brick wall.

She looked up at him.

"That tickles," he said.

"Go," she said. "*Now.*"

He went.

Mere moments earlier, Longmore had been primed for murder.

Now he had all he could do not to laugh.

There Sophy was, in her demure housemaid's dress, the wide-eyed, stupid look fading when she lost her patience and called him an ox.

Then the darling had grabbed his arm, trying to manhandle him. That was one of the funniest things he'd seen in a long time.

Leave this to us, she'd said.

Not likely, he thought. But if it pleased her to think so, he was happy to please.

In this agreeable state of mind he sought out his mother and sister. Finding them wasn't difficult. All he needed to do was walk in the direction of the scream.

Only one scream before Lady Warford collected her dignity and swooned.

He arranged as graceful a departure as possible for his mother and sister. He acted all manly and protective, exactly as he'd been told to do.

He'd deal with Adderley later, he promised himself.

And then . . .

Why, Sophy, of course.

* * *

Warford House
Saturday afternoon

"Clara, how *could* you!" Lady Warford cried, not for the first time. "That *bankrupt*!"

She lay on the chaise longue of her sitting room, a tray laden with restoratives on the table at her elbow.

Clara had far greater need for restoratives than her mother did. She wished she were a man, and could solve her problems the way men did, by getting drunk and fighting and gaming and whoring.

But she was a lady. She sat straight in her chair and said, "What sort of question is that, Mama? Do you think I humiliated myself on purpose?"

"You did what you ought not to have done on purpose," Mama said. "Of that I have not the slightest doubt."

It hadn't seemed so very wicked at the time. Clara and Lord Adderley had been waltzing, and she'd felt dizzy. Too much champagne, perhaps. Or perhaps he'd steered her into too many turns. Or both. He'd suggested fresh air. And it was a thrill to slip out onto the terrace unnoticed. Then he'd said things, such sweet things, and he'd seemed so passionately in love with her.

And then . . .

Had she been alone at present, she would have covered her face and wept.

But that's what Mama always did. She wept and screamed and fainted.

Clara sat straighter, hands folded, and wished she could climb out of the window and go far, far away.

The door opened and Harry came in.

She wanted to leap up and run at him the way she used to do when they were children and she was frightened or brokenhearted about this or that: A robin's nest on the ground and the eggs broken. A sick puppy. An injured horse put down.

But they weren't children, and Mama was already using all the hysteria in the room. Harry had enough to cope with.

"There you are, at last!" Mama cried. "You must fight Adderley, Harry. You must kill him."

"That's a bit sticky," he said. "I saw Father as I came in. He told me the blackguard's offered for Clara." He walked to Mama and dropped a light kiss on her forehead. He straightened and said, "I should have killed him when I had the chance. But Clara got in the way."

What choice had she? She'd been afraid Harry would kill Adderley—a man who hadn't tried to fight back. It would be murder, and Harry would hang or have to run away and live in another country forever—all because she'd been silly.

It seemed more than likely she'd ruined her own life. She wasn't about to destroy her brother's as well.

"Mama, if Harry kills Lord Adderley, my reputation will be ruined forever," Clara said steadily. "The only way to mend this is marriage. Lord Adderley's offered and I've accepted and that is that."

Harry looked at her. "Is it?"

"Yes," she said. "Since Mama is too upset to stir, and I'm sure she isn't ready to go out in public, in any event, I wish you would take me to buy my bride clothes."

"Bride clothes!" Mama cried. "You think entirely too much about your clothes—and all the world knows too much about them. In my day, young ladies did not make public spectacles of themselves, advertising every stitch they wore. To have your chemisette described—in detail!—in a public journal, as though you were a courtesan or a banker's wife! You ought to be sick with shame. But nothing shames you. Small wonder you behaved last night like a common trollop. I blame those French milliners. If you set foot in their shop again, I'll disown you!"

"Gad, what difference does it make?" Harry said. "Unless Adderley meets with a fatal accident, she'll have to marry him, like it or not. She might as well have some frocks she likes now, since she's not likely to have many after the wedding."

"Adderley may take her in her shift," Mother said. "He's no better than a fortune hunter, and a vile seducer in the bargain. Oh, that ever I should see this day! A fresh-minted *baron*—swimming in debt, thanks to the gaming tables—and his mother an Irish innkeeper's daughter! When I think that she might have had the Duke of Clevedon!"

"I strongly advise you not to think about it," Harry said. "They'd have made each other wretched."

"And Adderley will make her happy?" Mama sank back on the pillows and closed her eyes.

"Clara will break him to bridle," Longmore said. "And if she can't cure his wild ways, who knows? Maybe he'll ride into a ditch or get run over by a post chaise, and she'll be a young widow. Do try to look on the bright side."

He ought to know this wasn't the best tack to take with Mama. She wouldn't know whether he was joking or not, and that would only add irritation to the emotional stew.

Clara took a more effective route. "I wonder what Lady Bartham will say when she hears I'm to be sent away without a trousseau, without so much as a wedding dress," she said.

Lady Bartham and Mama were ferocious social rivals. They pretended to be the dearest of friends.

A short, sharp silence followed.

After a moment, Mama sat up again. She wiped her eyes with her handkerchief and said, "My own wishes cannot signify. We must consider your father's position. I shall persuade him to let you have bride clothes." She waved the handkerchief. "But not from those French strumpets! You'll go to Mrs. Downes."

"Downes's!" Clara cried. "Are you delirious, Mama? She's closed her shop."

She caught her breath. She was supposed to be the calm one. She had to be, with a hothead brother and a hysterical mother. Luckily, her mother was too taken up with her own emotions to notice anybody else's.

"That was only temporary," Mama said. "She sent me a note yesterday, telling me she's reopened, thank heaven. You'll go to her. Your morals may be all to pieces, but you shall be clothed respectably."

"Very well, Mama," Clara said meekly.

Harry gave her a sharp look.

She gave him a warning one back.

Meanwhile, at No. 56 St. James's Street, the sisters Noirot were staring in disbelief at a tiny advertisement.

Today's *Spectacle* hadn't arrived until some time after the shop opened. The morning being unusually busy, they hadn't had time to do more than skim the papers.

At present, though, their more-than-competent forewoman, Selina Jeffreys, was on duty in Maison Noirot's showroom.

Having adjourned upstairs to Marcelline's studio, the three dressmakers huddled over her drawing table, gazes fixed on twelve lines of print in one of the *Spectacle*'s advertising pages.

Therein Mrs. Downes proclaimed herself delighted to announce that, having completed a short period of "refurbishment," she had reopened her dressmaking establishment.

Sophy had got wind of it last night at the party. She'd mentioned it to her sisters. They'd all hoped it was merely the usual idle rumor.

They had quite enough trouble as it was.

"Curse her," Marcelline said. "We should have been finished with her. She closed her shop. She said it was for repairs, but she dismissed her staff. I was sure she'd slither out of London like the viper she is."

The viper was Hortense Downes, proprietress of the shop known at Maison Noirot as Dowdy's. A few weeks earlier, she and one of her minions had brought them to the brink of ruin. But the sisters had played her own trick against her, thus exposing her to the world as a fake and a cheat.

Or so they'd thought.

Marcelline shook her head. "That business of stealing my designs ought to have finished her."

"She's blamed it on her seamstresses," Sophy said. "She's told her patrons she's dismissed the lot and hired all new staff."

"Plague take her," Marcelline said. "Who knew that Hortense the Horrible was clever enough to recover her reputation?"

"It's what I'd have done in her place," Sophy said. "Blamed the help. Cleaned house. And made sure to tell my clients the 'truth' of how I'd been a victim of ungrateful employees. Then I'd send my customers personal notes in advance of the public advertisement."

"This is very bad," Marcelline said. She looked at her sisters. "How much business have we lost because of me?"

Sophy and Leonie looked at each other.

"I see," Marcelline said. "Worse than I thought."

"Lady Warford is a formidable social power," Leonie said. "No one wants to shop at a place she's blackballed."

"But she dresses so ill!" Marcelline said.

"She doesn't think so and nobody has the courage to tell her," Sophy said. "Not that most of them are any more discerning than she is. They're like sheep, as we all know. She's a leader, and they follow the leader."

"And she hates me," Marcelline said.

"With a pure, white-hot hatred, the sort of feeling her kind more usually reserve for anarchists and republicans," Sophy said.

Marcelline began to pace.

"It wouldn't be nearly so bad if Lady Clara had got herself into trouble with the right man," Leonie said. "She could become a fashion leader in her own right, and she'd help us build a clientele with the younger generation."

"But she picked the wrong man," Marcelline said. She returned to her drawing table, pushed the newspaper aside, took up her notebook, and began sketching, in strong, angry lines. "Tell me the truth, Leonie."

"We're facing ruin," Leonie said simply.

No one said a word about Marcelline's husband, who could buy and sell the shop many times over out of his pocket change.

They didn't want to be bought.

This was *their* shop. Three years ago they'd come from Paris, having lost everything. They'd come with a sick child, a few coins, and their talents. Marcelline had won money at the gaming tables. That gave them their start.

Now she must feel as though she'd destroyed everything they'd worked for. All for love.

But Marcelline had a right to love and be loved. She'd worked so hard. She'd endured so much. She'd looked after them all. She deserved happiness.

"We've faced ruin before," Sophy said. "This isn't worse than Paris and the cholera."

"We've survived a catastrophe here as well," Leonie said.

"With Clevedon's help," Marcelline said. "Which we didn't like accepting. But we agreed because we hadn't any choice."

"And we made sure it was a *loan*," Leonie said.

"Which it now seems we can't repay," Marcelline said, her pencil still moving angrily. "We're so far from repaying it that we'll have to ask for another one. Or accept failure. Leonie was right, after all. We bit off more than we could chew."

Weeks ago, when the Duke of Clevedon had found them these new quarters, Leonie had warned that they hadn't enough customers to support a large shop on St. James's Street.

"We *always* bite off more than we can chew," Sophy said. "We came from Paris with nothing, and built a business in only three years. We set out to capture Lady Clara and we succeeded—although not quite in the way we intended. We wouldn't be who we are if we acted like normal women. I don't see why we should start acting normal now, just because our best customer made a mistake with a man, as most women do, or because her mother holds grudges. I for one am not going to lie down and surrender merely on account of a little setback."

Marcelline looked up from her sketching and smiled, finally. "Only you would call impending ruin 'a little setback.'"

"The trouble with you is, you're in love, and you feel guilty about it, which is perfectly ridiculous in a Noirot," Sophy said.

"She's right," Leonie said. "You married a duke. You're supposed to be thoroughly pleased with yourself. It's a great coup. No one else, on either side of the family, has done it, to my knowledge."

"Not only a duke, but stupendously rich," Sophy said. "Your daughter has actual, genuine castles to play in."

"So stop brooding," Leonie said.

"I'm facing failure," Marcelline said. "A gigantic, catastrophic failure—which that horrid Dowdy reptile will laugh at. That entitles me to brood."

"No, it doesn't," Sophy said. "She isn't going to laugh, and we're not going to fail. We'll think of something. We always do."

"We merely need to think fast," Leonie said. "Because we've less than a month until quarter day."

Midsummer: 24 June. When rents were due and accounts were settled.

Someone tapped at the door.

"What is it?" Marcelline called.

The door opened a crack, revealing a narrow slice of Mary Parmenter, one of their seamstresses. "If you please, Your Grace, mesdames. Lady Clara Fairfax is here. And Lord Longmore."

Chapter Three

There is certainly some connexion between the dress and the mind, an accurate observer can trace some correspondencies; and the weak as well as the strong-minded never cease to be influenced by a good or bad dress.

—*Lady's Magazine & Museum,* June 1835

It was sort of a brothel for women, Longmore decided.

The shop even had a discreet back entrance, reserved, no doubt, for high-priced harlots and the men who kept them.

A few minutes earlier, a modestly but handsomely dressed female had let them in that way and led them up a flight of carpeted and gently lit back stairs. Small landscape paintings and fashion plates from earlier times adorned the pale green walls.

He'd been in Maison Noirot's showroom, but this was another world altogether.

The room into which the female had taken them looked like a sitting room. More little paintings on the pale pink walls. Pretty bits of porcelain. Lacy things adorning tables and chair backs. The very air smelled of women, but it was subtle. His nostrils caught only a hint of scent, as though a bouquet of flowers and herbs had recently passed through. Everything about him was soft and luxurious and inviting. It conjured harem slaves in paintings. Odalisques.

He was tempted to stretch out on the carpet and call for the hashish and dancing girls.

The door opened. All his senses went on the alert.

But it was only the elegantly dressed female carrying a tray. She set it upon a handsome tea table. Longmore noticed the tray held a plate of biscuits. A decanter stood where the teapot ought to be.

When the female went out, he said, "So this is how they do it. They ply you with drink."

"No, they ply *you* with drink, knowing you'll be bored," Clara said. "Although I shouldn't mind a restorative." She flung herself into a chair. "Oh, Harry, what on earth am I going to do?"

Her face took on a crumpled look.

He knew that look. It augured tears.

He was taken completely unawares. She'd seemed perfectly well on the way here. Chin aloft and eyes blazing. He hadn't been surprised when she told him to take her to Maison Noirot. The meek act with their mother hadn't fooled him.

Clara was so angelically beautiful that people thought she was sweet and yielding. They mistook indifference for docility. She was the sort of girl who generally didn't care one way or another about all sorts of things. But when she did care, she could be as obstinate as a pig.

Since the Noirot sisters had got their hooks in her, she'd become extremely obstinate about her clothes.

He beat down panic. "Dash it, Clara," he said. "No waterworks. Say what's the matter and have done."

She found a handkerchief and hastily wiped her eyes. "Oh, it's Mama. She wears on my nerves."

"That's all?" he said.

"Isn't it enough?" she said. "I'm Society's big joke and I'm about to marry in haste and my mother does nothing but tell me every single thing I've done wrong."

"And this"—he swept his hand, indicating their surroundings—"will be one more thing."

"What's one more thing?" Clara said. "This, at least, will lift my spirits. Unlike a visit to that incompetent in Bedford Square Mama's so irrationally devoted to."

He'd taken her here because this was where she wanted to go . . . and it was where he preferred to go.

Maison Noirot was stupendously expensive, the proprietresses were seductresses (in the way of clothes) of the first order, it was extremely *French*, and, above all, it was Sophy Noirot's lair.

If a man had to hang about a dressmakers' shop, this was the place.

But there would be trouble at home for Clara. More trouble. "Our mother's going to kick up a fuss," he said. "And you'll bear the brunt of it."

"The clothes will be worth it," she said.

And this would be her last chance for extravagance in that regard, unless he found a way to dispose of Adderley and restore Clara's reputation at the same time.

He wasn't sure Clara wanted Adderley disposed of, but if she didn't she was either stupid or mad, which meant her wishes didn't signify.

He must have frowned without realizing, because she said, "It'll be fun for me, but I know you'll be bored to death. You needn't stay. I'll take a hackney home."

"A hackney?" he said. "Are you mad? I'd never hear the end of it." He laid a limp wrist against his temple, pitched his voice an octave higher, and in the put-upon tone his mother had perfected said, "How *could* you, Harry? Your own sister, left to a dirty public conveyance? Heaven only knows who's seen her, traveling the London streets like a shop clerk. I shall be ashamed to look my friends in the eye."

From behind him came the rustling of petticoats—and a stifled giggle?

He turned, his pulse accelerating.

Three young women—one brunette, one blonde, one redhead—regarded him with expressions of polite interest. The two latter had large, shockingly blue eyes. Only in the eyes did he detect any sign of the amusement he'd thought he'd heard, and it wasn't much of a sign.

It would be more accurate to say he detected it only in *her* eyes, since Sophy Noirot's sisters might as well have been shadows or a Greek chorus—or window curtains, for that matter.

They were all very well, each entertaining in her own way, and all quite good-looking, if not great beauties.

But she cast the others into the shade.

Why, only look at her. Pale gold curling hair under the frothy lace cap. Enormous, speaking eyes of deepest sapphire. A haughty little nose. A plump invitation of a mouth. A sharp, obstinate little chin. Below the neck . . . ah, that was even better. Delicious, in fact, despite the lunatic clothing style deemed the height of fashion.

"Duchess," Clara said, rising from her chair and curtseying.

"Pray don't 'Duchess' me," said Her Grace. "This is business. While on the premises, why do we not pretend we're in France, where you'd address a duchess as *madame*, much as one addresses a modiste. Meanwhile, think of me simply as your dressmaker."

"The world's *greatest* dressmaker," Sophy said.

"And that would make you . . . ?" Longmore said.

"The other greatest dressmaker in the world," Sophy said.

"Someone ought to explain superlatives to you," he said. "But then, I'm aware that English isn't your first language."

"It isn't my only first language, my lord," she said. "*Le français est l'autre.*"

"Perhaps someone ought as well to explain the meanings of *only* and *first*," he said.

"Oh, yes, please do enlighten me, my lord," she said, opening her extremely blue eyes very wide. "I never had a head for figures. Leonie always complains about it. 'Will you never learn to count?' she says."

"And yet," he began.

It was then he realized she'd drawn him away from his sister—who was moving with the other two toward another door.

"Where are you slipping off to?" he said.

"To look at patterns," said Clara. "You'll find it exceedingly tedious."

"That depends," he said.

"On what?" Sophy said.

"On how bored I feel." He looked around. "Not much entertainment hereabouts."

"Your club is only a few steps up the street," Sophy said. "Perhaps you'd rather wait there. We can send to you when Lady Clara is done."

"I don't know," he said. "I feel I ought to hang about and exert a calming influence."

"You," Sophy said. "A calming influence."

"Excitable women. Clothes. The possible rape and pillage of our father's bank account. A man's cool head seems to be needed."

"Harry, you know Papa doesn't care how much I spend on clothes," Clara said. "He likes us to look well. And I know you don't care what I buy. It was kind of you to take me here, but you needn't watch over me. I'm perfectly safe."

His gaze traveled over the three sisters, and lingered on Sophy. He thought hard and fast and picked his words carefully. "Very well. A man can think more clearly when he isn't surrounded by women, and I need to create an alibi."

She took the bait, her gaze sharpening. "Why?" she said. "Are you planning to murder somebody?"

"Not yet," he said. "You won't let me murder the bridegroom. No, I want an alibi for Clara, who isn't supposed to be here."

"Mama said I must go to Downes's," Clara said, "but Harry took pity on me."

"I took pity on *me*," he said. His gaze returned to Sophy. "I brought her here to prevent scolding, ranting, and sobbing, that's all."

"Then the least I can do in gratitude is give you an alibi," Sophy said.

He could think of any number of pleasing acts of gratitude, but this would do for a start.

"Not too complicated," he said.

She rolled her great blue eyes. "I know that."

"I'm a simple man."

"This is so simple, even a dolt could remember it," she said. "When Lady Clara returns home, she'll say that you were intoxicated and drove her here instead of to Downes's, drunkenly insisting this was the place."

"Oh, that's perfect!" Clara said.

"That will do admirably," he said. "She can say I stood over her and *made* her order sixty or seventy dresses, and a gross of chemises and . . ."

His mind went hazy then, and images of muslin and lace underwear strewed themselves about his brain, and somewhere in that dishevelment was a blue-eyed angelic devil, mostly unclothed. He waved a hand, waving the images away. Now wasn't the time. He was only beginning his siege, and he knew—he could always tell—he faced a very tricky fortress. All sorts of hidden passages and diversions and booby traps.

But then, if it were easy, it would be boring.

He continued, " . . . and all those other sorts of trousseau things. And when our mother regains consciousness, and demands that Clara cancel the order, Clara will appeal to our overly conscientious sire, who'll say one can't simply cancel immense orders on a whim."

Sophy folded her arms. Something flickered in her blue eyes. Otherwise, her expression was unreadable. "Good," she said. "Keep with that. Don't embellish."

"No danger of that," he said. "At any rate, it's easy enough to make it partly true. I've only to toddle into my club and drink steadily until you've finished bankrupting my father. Then, when I return Clara to Warford House, no one will have any trouble believing in my inebriated obstinacy."

He sauntered out of the sitting room.

He walked to the stairs and started down.

He heard hurried footsteps and rustling petticoats behind him.

"Lord Longmore."

She said his name as everybody else did, not precisely as spelled but in the way of so many ancient names, with vowels shifted and consonants elided. Yet it wasn't quite the same, either, because it carried the faintest whisper of French.

He looked up.

She stood at the top of the stairs, leaning over the handrail.

The view was excellent: He could see her silk shoes and the crisscrossing ribbons that called attention to the fine arch of her instep and her neat ankles. He saw the delicate silk stockings outlining the bit of foot and leg on view. His mind easily conjured what wasn't on view: the place above her knees where her garters were tied—garters that, in his imagination, were red, embroidered with lascivious French phrases.

For a moment he said nothing, simply drank it in.

"That was a beautiful exit," she said.

"I thought so," he said.

"I hated to spoil it," she said. "But I had an idea."

"You're a prodigy," he said. "First an alibi, then an idea. All in the same day."

"I thought you could help me," she said.

"I daresay I could," he said, contemplating her ankles.

"With your mother."

He lifted his gaze to her face. "What do you want to do to her?"

"Ideally, I should like to dress her."

"That would be difficult, considering that she hates you," he said. "That is, not you, particularly. But you as a near connection to the Duchess of Clevedon, and your shop as harboring same."

"I know, but I'm sure we can bring her round. That is, I can bring her round. With a little help."

"What do you propose, Miss Noirot? Shall I drug her ladyship and carry her, senseless, to your lair, where you'll force her into dashing gowns?"

"Only as a last resort," she said. "What I have in mind for you at present is quite simple—and no one will ever know you aided and abetted the Enemy."

"This is London," he said. "There's no such thing as 'no one will ever know.'"

"No, really, I promise you—"

"Not that I care what anybody knows," he said.

"Right," she said. "I forgot. But I *must not* be recognized."

"Does that mean a disguise?" he said.

"Only for me," she said. "I need to visit Dowdy's, you see, and—"

"And Dowdy's is . . . ?"

"The lair of the reptile, Horrible Hortense Downes, the monster who puts your mother into those dreary clothes. I need to get into her shop."

In her world, he knew, clothes were the beginning and the end of everything, and worlds were lost on the wrong placement of a bow.

"You're proposing a spying expedition behind enemy lines," he said.

"Yes," she said. "That's it *exactly*."

"Are you going to blow up the place?"

"Only as a last resort," she said.

He was quite happy to take her, even if she didn't blow the place up. He'd be happy to take her anywhere. But his promptly agreeing meant her prompt departure and he wasn't yet tired of looking at her ankles.

He pretended to ponder.

"It's only for an hour or so," she said. "That shouldn't disrupt your busy schedule."

"Ordinarily, no," he said. "But I've got this Adderley problem to work on, and that wants deep and lengthy cogitation."

"You do not have the Adderley problem to work on," she said. "Did I not tell you my sisters and I would deal with it?"

"It's not the sort of thing I want to leave to women," he said. "It could get messy, and I'd hate to see your pretty frocks spoiled."

"Believe me, Lord Longmore, my sisters and I have dealt with extremely messy situations before."

He met her gaze. In those blue eyes he caught a glimpse of something, unexpected and hard. It was gone in an instant, but it set off a sharp recollection of the men who'd pursued her and emerged from the experience damaged.

There was more to her than met the eye: that much he'd recognized early on.

"Let me think it over," he said. "Let me think it over in the cool depths of my club."

He continued down the stairs.

Two hours later

From the environs of White's famous bow window, where Beau Brummell had presided some decades earlier, a sudden buzz of excitement broke in upon a dull, drizzly afternoon. The noise gradually increased in volume sufficiently to obtain Lord Longmore's attention.

He'd settled in the morning room with *Foxe's Morning Spectacle* to review Sophy's story about last night's debacle. As regarded breathlessly dramatic style and fanatical attention to every boring inch of Clara's dress, Sophy had outdone herself. Clara had been "innocence cruelly misled," Longmore had appeared as a paragon among avenging brothers, and the dress description—dripping with an arcane French known only to women—took up nearly two of the front page's three columns. Her account had routed from said page virtually all the other gossip Foxe called news.

Longmore had read it this morning after breakfast. He saw no more in it now than he had then. It was unclear what good the piece would do Clara—unless it was simply the first step in a campaign. If so, he looked forward to seeing where it would lead.

After chuckling over Sophy's world's-greatest-collection of adjectives and adverbs, he moved on to the other gossip and sporting news. Thence he proceeded to the advertising pages at the back.

There Maison Noirot had taken over prime real estate, squeezing into obscure corners the notices for pocket toilets, artificial teeth, and salad cream.

That was when he discovered Mrs. Downes's announcement.

He was wondering about the connection between Sophy's need to be taken to her rival's shop and the advertisement when someone at the bow window said, "Who is she?"

"You're joking," someone else said. "You don't know?"

"Would I ask if I knew?"

Other voices joined in.

"Hempton, you innocent. Have you been in a coma during the last month?"

"How could you not have heard about the Misalliance of the Century? They talk of it in Siberia and Tierra del Fuego."

"But that can't be Sheridan's new bride."

"Not the elopement, you slow-top."

"You mean Clevedon?" said Hempton. "But he married a brunette. This one's a blonde."

Longmore flung down the *Spectacle*, left his chair, and stalked to the bow window.

"What now?" he said, though he could guess.

The men crowding the window hastily made room for him.

Sophy Noirot stood on the other side of St. James's Street. A gust of wind blew the back of her pale yellow dress against her legs and made a billowing froth of skirt and petticoats in front. The wind made a complete joke of the lacy nothing of an umbrella she held against the rain. The previous downpour had diminished to a light drizzle, and the misty figure glimpsed between the clumps of vehicles, riders, and pedestrians seemed like something in a dream.

The commentary at the bow window, however, made it clear she was not a dream, except in the sense that she was, at the moment, the starring player in every man's lewd fantasy.

Ah, she was real enough, wearing a scarf sort of thing that dangled to her knees—or where one assumed her knees must be, under all those yards of lace and muslin. Atop the golden hair perched a silly hat, dripping lace and ribbons and feathers. Longmore could see a sort of Dutch windmill arrangement of lace and feathers at the back of the hat when she bent to talk to a scruffy little boy. She gave him something, and he dashed across the street, dodging riders and vehicles.

Then she looked up, straight at the bow window and straight at Longmore.

And smiled.

Then all the men at the bow window looked at him.

And smiled.

And he smiled right back.

Longmore took his time. He finished his glass of wine, reread the advertisement, then called for his things.

He donned his hat and gloves, grasped his walking stick, and went out. The drizzle had dwindled to a fine mist and the wind had died down somewhat.

She had walked a little way up the street. She was watching the passing scene on Piccadilly. Every passing male was watching her.

He coolly descended the steps and strolled across the street to her.

"I should have thought you'd find an urchin nearer the shop to carry the message that my sister was ready to go home," he said. "Or why not send a servant or a seamstress? You had to come yourself? In the rain?"

"Yes," she said.

"I collect you had something particular to say to me, then," he said.

"I daresay I could have said it elsewhere," she said. "But this was a fine opportunity to show off my hat, which is my own design. I'm not a genius with dresses, like Marcelline, but my hats are quite good."

He eyed the hat, with its lace and windmill and whatnot. "It strikes me as demented," he said. "But fetching."

She dimpled, and his heart gave a lurch that astonished him.

"I sincerely hope it's fetching enough to weaken your resistance," she said.

"What resistance?" he said.

"To my scheme."

"Oh, that. Taking you to Dowdy's."

"I need to find out what they're up to."

"I should think that was obvious," he said. "They're out to crush the competition, as any self-respecting rival would do."

He started walking down St. James's Street, wondering what devious means she'd contrived to persuade him to do what he was going to do anyway.

She walked alongside him. "I know that," she said. "But I need to see exactly what we're up against: the old Dowdy's or something new, something we hadn't reckoned on. I need to see whether the place is the same and the clothes are the same."

"I suppose you'll be shocked if I say that all women's clothes look the same to me," he said.

"I wouldn't be shocked at all," she said. "You're a man. And that's the point of my asking you. I need a big, strong man in case I'm discovered, and run into difficulties with Dowdy's bullies." She paused briefly. "While we were fitting your sister, she happened to mention Lady Gladys Fairfax, and what a pity it was that we couldn't take her in hand," she said.

"Cousin Gladys," he said. "Don't tell me she's coming to the wedding."

"I don't know who'll be invited," she said. "But when Lady Clara spoke of her, I got the idea for a way to manage this."

They'd reached the corner of Bennet Street. He paused to check for carriages and riders turning off St. James's Street.

When the way seemed clear, he took her elbow and hurried her across. As soon as they reached the pavement on the opposite side, he let go of her. He still felt the warmth of her arm under his palm, and the warmth raced straight to his groin so suddenly that it made him dizzy.

The rear entrance to the shop was through a narrow court off Bennet Street. She waited until they'd turned into the court. Then she said, "Lady Clara says your mother will go to Dowdy's early in the week to order a dress for the wedding. Leonie can spare me from the shop most easily on Friday morning. Would you take me then?"

After the bustle of St. James's Street, the tiny

court seemed eerily quiet. He was aware of a scent, vaguely familiar, drifting about him. He drew a fraction closer and stared at the discreet door, pretending to think hard while he drank in the scent. Woman, of course, and . . . lavender . . . and what else?

He realized his head was sinking toward her neck. He straightened. "Bullies," he said. "In a dressmaking shop."

"Two great brutes," she said. "To deal with the drunks and thieves. Or so Dowdy claims. Personally, I believe she's hired the men to intimidate the seamstresses. You know, the way they keep them in brothels to—"

"That sounds like fun," he said. "And you'll be in disguise, of course."

"Yes."

"As a serving maid, I suppose."

"Certainly not," she said. "What would a serving maid be doing buying expensive dresses? I'm going to be your cousin Gladys."

Lord Adderley wasted no time in putting the notice of his engagement in the papers, but the news traveled through London in a matter of hours—faster even than the *Spectacle* could get it into print. By Monday his tailor, boot maker, hatter, vintner, tobacconist, and others who provided for his comfort and entertainment had once again opened their account books and allowed him credit.

He'd had a narrow escape.

Another week and he would have had to flee abroad. While peers could not be arrested for debt, they weren't immune to other unpleasantness, like having their credit shut off. All of his creditors seemed to have joined a cabal, because every single one, including all the shopkeepers, cut him off at the same time, two days before Lady Igby's ball.

The forthcoming nuptials put everybody in a more forgiving frame of mind.

He celebrated on Monday night with Mr. Meffat and Sir Roger Theaker in a private dining parlor of the Brunswick Hotel. They toasted one another throughout the meal. By the time the table had been cleared, wine had loosened their tongues—no matter, since there was nobody nearby to hear.

"A close-run thing it was," said Sir Roger.

"Perilously close," said Lord Adderley.

"Wasn't sure you'd manage it," said Mr. Meffat. "Watching like hawks, they were."

Lord Adderley shrugged. "As soon as I saw Lady Bartham settle in to gossip with the mama, I knew there wouldn't be trouble from that quarter for a while."

"It was Longmore who worried me," said Mr. Meffat.

Adderley resisted the urge to feel his bruised jaw. He'd had more reason than anybody to worry. He'd broken into a sweat, which he'd explained away to Lady Clara as excitement, to be so close to her, to hold her in her arms—all the usual rubbish, in other words.

He said, "I only needed a few minutes, and he was on the other side of the room. Still, it was your quick acting that saved the day."

It was Meffat's and Theaker's job to attract attention to the terrace without attracting too much attention. Not the most difficult job in the world.

One only had to say, "Wonder what Adderley's about on the terrace? Who's the female with him?"

One didn't have to say it to too many people. One or two would do. The drift terrace-wards would begin, and some others would notice, and follow, curious to see what was attracting attention.

Clara had been easiest of all to manage. Though no schoolroom miss—she was one and twenty, older than Adderley would have preferred—she was as ignorant about lovemaking as a child. All he had to do was keep her wineglass filled and whirl her about the floor until she was dizzy and whisper poetry in her ear. Still, one had to be careful. Too much wine and too much spinning and she'd be sick—on his last good coat.

"At least you got yourself a beauty," Theaker said. "Mostly, when their pa sets a big dowry on them, it's on account of being squinty or spotty or bowlegged."

"What he means is, mostly, they're dogs," Meffat said.

"I'm fortunate," Adderley said. "I know that. I might have done so much worse."

She was a beauty, and that would make the bedding and getting of heirs more agreeable. Still, she wasn't to his taste, a great cow of a girl. He liked daintier women, and he would have preferred a brunette.

But her dowry was enormous, she'd been vulnerable, and beggars couldn't be choosers.

"Bless her innocence," said Theaker. "She went just like a lamb."

"There's one won't give you any trouble," said Meffat.

* * *

Warford House
Wednesday 3 June

Clara kept her composure until she'd closed her bedroom door behind her.

She swallowed, walked quickly across the room, and sat at her dressing table.

"My lady?" said her maid, Davis.

A sob escaped Clara. And another.

"Oh, my lady," said Davis.

"I don't know what to do!" Clara buried her face in her hands.

"Now, now, my lady. I'll make you a good, hot cup of tea and whatever it is, you'll feel better."

"I need more than tea," Clara said. She looked up to meet Davis's gaze in the mirror.

"I'll put a drop of brandy in it," said Davis.

"More than a drop," Clara said.

"Yes, my lady."

Davis hurried out.

Clara took out the note Lord Adderley had sent her.

A love note, filled with beautiful words, the kinds of words sure to melt the heart of a romantic girl.

Of course the words were beautiful. They'd been written by poets: Keats and Lovelace and Marvell and scores of others. Even Shakespeare! He thought she wouldn't recognize lines from a Shakespeare sonnet! Either he was a complete idiot or he thought she was.

"The latter, most likely," she muttered. She crumpled the note and threw it across the room. "Liar," she said. "It was all lies. I knew it. How could I be such a fool?"

Because Mr. Bates had not asked her to dance, and she'd watched him whirl Lady Susan Morris, Lady Bartham's daughter, about the floor. Lady Susan was petite and dark and pretty, and next to her Clara always felt ungainly and awkward.

Then what?

A moment's hurt. Then Lord Adderley was at her elbow, with a glass of champagne, and a perfect remark, sure to make her smile.

Irish blarney, Mama would have said.

Maybe that's what it was. Or maybe it was like the beautiful words he wrote, stolen from gifted writers. False, either way.

Champagne and waltzing and flattery, and Clara had taken the bait.

And now . . .

What to do?

She rose and walked to the window and looked out. In the garden below, the rain was beating the shrubs and flowers into submission. If she'd been a man—if she'd been Harry—she'd have climbed out and run away, as far as she could go.

But she wasn't a man, and she had no idea how to run away.

Time, she thought. Her only hope was time. If they could drag out the engagement for months and months, a new scandal would come along, and everybody would forget this one.

Davis entered with the tea. "I put in a few extra drops, but you'll need to drink it quickly," she said. "Lady Bartham's called, and Lady Warford said you're to come straightaway."

"Lady Bartham," Clara said. "That wants more than a few drops. That wants a bottle."

She swallowed her brandy-laced tea, put on her company face, and went down to the drawing room.

The visit was even worse than anticipated. Lady Bartham was so sympathetically venomous that she left Clara half blind with rage and Mama with a sick headache.

The next morning, Mama announced that she was sick to death of this ghastly engagement and everybody's insinuations. They would consult the calendar and fix a date for the wedding.

"Yes, of course, Mama," Clara said. "In the autumn, perhaps. Town won't be so busy then."

"Autumn?" Mama cried. "Are you mad? We've not a moment to lose. You must be married before the end of the Season—before the Queen's last Drawing Room at the latest."

"Mama, that's only three weeks!"

"It's sufficient time to arrange a wedding, even a large one—and a small one is out of the question. You know what people will say. And if those wicked French dressmakers Harry took you to can't finish your bride clothes on time, it is too bad. It is not my fault if my children disobey me at every turn."

Chapter Four

Now, thanks to steam-presses, steam-vessels, and steam-coaches, the prolific brain of a French dress-maker or milliner has hardly given a new cap of trimming to the Parisian élégantes, before it is also in possession of the London belles.

—*La Belle Assemblée*, March 1830

Friday 5 June

Longmore transferred the reins to one hand and with his other took out his pocket watch. He flicked it open.

Eleven o'clock, she'd said. *In the morning*—because the fashionable aristocrats shopped in the afternoon, and she had to get there before they did.

"It's important to arrive before Dowdy's favorite customers do," Sophy had told him. "Shopkeepers like that will fawn over the great ladies with the heavy purses and pass off dull rustic misses to lowly assistants. It would be truly useful to see the pattern for your mother's dress, since she's one of their most important customers. That means I can't be passed off to an assistant. It has to be Horrible Hortense herself or her forewoman."

It was exactly eleven o'clock. Longmore looked up at the sky. Cloudy, but not threatening rain as his tiger, Reade, had insisted. Reade had not been happy about having to remain behind. If it rained—as he assured his lordship it would surely do—his lordship would need help raising the curricle's hood.

Well, then, they'd simply have to get wet, Longmore decided. While convenient for minding horses and helping one wrestle temperamental hoods, on the present occasion a groom would be very much in the way.

Longmore put the watch away and reverted to staring at the shop door. She'd told him to collect her, not at Maison Noirot, but at the ribbon shop farther down St. James's Street, near St. James's Palace. To Allay Suspicion.

She was hilarious.

"Cousin?" said a familiar female voice.

He blinked. It was Sophy's voice and it wasn't. He knew this had to be her but his eyes denied it. The woman standing on the pavement next to his carriage was so nondescript that he'd probably been looking straight at her without actually seeing her.

The murky brown cloak concealed her shape. The muddy green bonnet and lace cap underneath concealed most of her hair. What was visible was limp, dull, and stringy. She'd sprouted a mole to one side of her perfect nose. And on that nose she'd planted a pair of tinted spectacles, which dulled her brilliant blue eyes to cloudy grey.

He was aware of his jaw dropping. He quickly collected himself. "There you are," he said.

"You'd have seen me sooner if you hadn't been woolgathering," she said, as shrewish as Gladys— and in the same graceless accents. She climbed up into the vehicle as clumsily as his cousin would have done.

If he didn't know better, he'd have been sure this was his cousin, playing a trick on him.

But Cousin Gladys didn't play tricks. She had no imagination.

"How did you do it?" he said. "You can't have met her. She hasn't left Lancashire in ages."

"Lady Clara is a fair mimic," she said, "and it was easy enough to classify the type. We do that, you know: We size up a woman when she walks into the shop. Broadly speaking, they tend to fall into certain categories."

"Gladys is a type? I'm sorry to hear it. I'd always thought her one of a kind, and that one more than sufficient."

He gave his horses leave to walk on, then he had to keep his attention on them. Though he'd driven them through Hyde Park to work off their morning high spirits, they were still excitable. Apparently they were as little used as he was to traveling the shopping streets in the early hours with ordinary folk. Whatever the reason, they were looking for trouble: They tried to lunge at other vehicles, run onto the pavement, take aim at passing pedestrians, and bite any other horses who looked at them the wrong way.

Normally, he'd find this entertaining.

Today it was inconvenient. He had a campaign

to conduct with the woman beside him, and she was tricky and he needed his wits about him. At present, however, he had to concentrate his wits on getting them to Piccadilly alive. Then he had to wrestle his way through the great knot of traffic approaching the quadrant into Regent Street.

"What the devil are all these people doing out in the streets at the crack of dawn?" he said.

"They heard the Earl of Longmore would be up and about before noon," she said. "I believe they mean to mark the event with illuminations and fireworks."

He'd been driving since childhood, and he couldn't remember when last he'd had to work so hard at it.

"I think you're frightening the horses," he said.

"I think they're not used to busy streets in daylight," she said.

"Maybe it's the mole that's bothering them," he said. Or maybe it was her scent. It wasn't Gladys's. This was so faint as to be more of an awareness than a fragrance: Woman and jasmine and something else. Some kind of herb or greenery.

No, the scent wasn't bothering the horses. It was getting him into a lather he couldn't do anything about at the moment. That wasn't the only disturbance. He was extremely aware of her swollen skirts brushing against his trouser leg, and he could hear the petticoats rustle under the skirts. It was as clear as clear to him, above the street's cacophony of animals, vehicles, people.

He was primed for tackling her and he couldn't, and the horses sensed the agitation.

It was so ridiculous he laughed.

"What is it?" she said.

He glanced at her. "You," he said. "And me, up at this hour to drive to a dressmaker's shop."

"I know you rise before noon on occasion," she said.

"Not to shop," he said.

"No. For a race. A boxing match. A wrestling match. A horse auction. I'm not sure I can offer equal excitement."

"I expect it'll be exciting enough when they find you out," he said. "Which they're bound to do. You'll need to get undressed to get measured. What if the mole falls off while you're taking off your clothes? What if your spectacles get tangled in your wig?"

"I've put on several extra layers of clothing," she said. "I don't plan to allow them to get beyond the first one or two. And it isn't a wig, by the way. I put an egg mixture in my hair. People say it leaves a shine after you wash it out, but it does the opposite."

It would be quite a job, washing her hair. It was thick and curly, and unless she added false pieces to it, as some women did, it must be long. To her waist? He saw long, golden hair streaming down a bare, silken back.

There was something to look forward to.

"You promised me bullies," he said. "I was looking forward to the fight. It's the only thing that got me out of bed. Do you have any idea how long it's been since anybody did me the courtesy of hitting back?"

"If I were a gentleman, and I saw you coming at me with fists up, I'd run in the other direction," she said.

"Bullies aren't gentlemen," he said. "They won't run."

"If you get desperately bored, you can always pick a fight," she said.

"If they exist," he said. "I've never heard of hired ruffians in a dressmaking shop."

"You've never noticed because you never think about how a shop is run," she said. "You only notice whether the service is good or bad. But they can be useful in an all-woman shop. One has to deal with drunken men knocking over things or pawing the seamstresses. But the worst for us is a pack of thieves. They'll come in small groups of twos and threes, all dressed respectably and seeming not to be together. One or two will keep the shopkeepers busy while the others fill their pockets. They've special pockets sewn into their clothes. They're very quick. You'd be amazed at how much they can make off with if you look away, even for a second."

"Where do you hide the muscled fellows who work for you, then?" he said.

"We don't need ruffians," she said. "We started in Paris, you know, and it was a family business, so we started young. Let me see. I think Marcelline was nine, so I was about seven or eight, and Leonie was six. When you're absorbed in a trade from childhood, every aspect of it becomes instinctive. Drunks, thieves, men who think milliners' shops are brothels—we're perfectly capable of dealing with such matters ourselves."

He remembered the hard look that had flashed across her face so briefly, when she'd told him she'd dealt with messy situations. He hadn't time to pursue that train of thought, though. As they were turning into Oxford Street, two boys ran out in front of the curricle. Swearing violently, Longmore turned his pair aside an instant before they could trample the children.

His heart pounded. A moment's delay or distraction, and the brats could have been killed. "Look where you're going, you confounded idiots!" he roared above the neighing horses and the other drivers' shouted comments.

"Ow, you ugly bitch!" a voice shrieked close to his ear. "Let go of me, you sodding sow!"

"Oh, no, I don't think so," Sophy said.

Longmore glanced that way.

A ragged boy half hung over the back of the seat. Sophy had him by the arm, and she was regarding him with amusement.

Longmore could spare them only a glance. His team and the traffic wanted all his attention. "What the devil?" he said. "Where did he come from?"

"Nowhere!" the boy snarled. He wriggled furiously, to no avail. "I wasn't doing nothing, only getting a free ride in back here, and the goggle-eyed mort tried to take my arm off."

This, at least, was what Longmore presumed he said. The Cockney accent was almost impenetrable. *Nothing* was "nuffin," and aitches were dropped from and attached to the wrong words, and some of the vowels seemed to have arrived from another planet.

"And you were trying to keep your hand warm in the gentleman's pocket?" she said.

Longmore choked back laughter.

"I never went near his pocket! Do I look like I'm dicked in the nob?"

"Far from it," Sophy said. "You're a clever one, and quick, too."

"Not quick enough," the boy muttered.

"I wish you could have seen it, *Cousin*," she said. "The two who ran in front were meant to distract you while this one jumped on and did his job. The little devil almost got by me. It took him two seconds to leap onto the groom's place. Probably he would have wanted only another two to get your pocket watch—perhaps your seals and handkerchief as well—while you had both hands busy with the horses. I daresay he thought I was a gently bred female who'd only stare or scream helplessly while he collected his booty and got away."

She reverted to the boy. "Next time, my lad, I advise you to make sure there's only one person in the vehicle."

Next time?

Longmore nearly ran down a pie seller.

"What next time?" he said. "We're making a detour to the nearest police office, and leaving him to them."

The boy let loose a stream of stunning oaths and struggled wildly. But Sophy must have tightened her hold or done something painful, because he stopped abruptly, and started whimpering that his arm was broken.

"As soon as I get out of this infernal tangle, I'll give you a cuff you won't soon forget," Longmore said. "*Cousin*, will you give him a firm thump or something to stifle him in the meantime?"

"I don't think we should take him to the police," she said. "I think we should take him with us."

Longmore and the boy reacted simultaneously. The boy: "Nooooo!"

Longmore: "Are you drunk?"

"No, you don't," the boy said. "I ain't going nowhere with you. I got friends, and they'll come any minute now. Then you'll be sorry. And I think my chest's got a rib broke from being bent like this."

"Stifle it," Longmore told the boy. He needed a clear head to find his way through Sophy's rabbit warren of a mind. He couldn't do that and translate the boy's deranged version of English at the same time.

To Sophy he said, "What exactly do you propose to do with him?"

"He's wonderfully quick," she said. "He could be useful. For our mission."

Occupied with horses and traffic, Longmore could give the urchin no more than a swift survey. He looked to be about ten or eleven years old, though it was hard to tell with children of the lowest classes. Some of them looked eons older than they were, while others, small from malnourishment, seemed younger. This boy was fair-haired under his shabby cap, and while his neck was none too clean, he wasn't an inch thick with filth as so many of them were. His clothes were worn and ill-fitting but mended and only moderately grimy.

"I don't see what use he'd be to anybody, unless someone was wanted to pick pockets," he said.

"He could hold the horses," she said.

"Could he, indeed?" he said. "You suggest I put my cattle in charge of a sneaking little thief?"

The boy went very still.

"Who better to keep a sharp eye out, to watch who comes and goes, to give the alarm if trouble comes?" she said.

The mad thing was, she had a point.

"You don't know the brat from Adam," he said. "For all we know, he's a desperado wanted by the police, and due to be transported on Monday. He tried to steal my watch. And climbed up behind the carriage to do it! That wants brass, that does—or something gravely amiss in the attic—and if you think I'm leaving a prime pair of horseflesh in the grubby hands of Mad Dick Turpin here, I suggest you think again. And take something for that brain injury while you're about it."

"Oy!" the boy said indignantly. "I ain't no horse thief."

"Merely a pickpocket," Longmore said, egging him on.

"What's your name?" Sophy said.

"Ain't got one," the boy said. "Saves trouble, don't it?"

"Then I shall call you Fenwick," she said.

"*What?*"

"Fenwick," she said. "If you don't have a name, I'll give you one, gratis."

"Not that," the boy said. "That's a 'orrible name."

"Better than nothing," she said.

"I say, mister," the boy appealed to Longmore. "Make her stop."

Longmore couldn't answer. He was working too hard on not laughing.

"That is not a mister," she said. "That's an actual lord whose pocket you tried to pick."

"Yer lordship, make her stop. Make her stop breaking my arm, too. Which this is a monstrous female like nothing I ever seen before."

Longmore glanced at Sophy. She was regarding the ghastly little foul-mouthed urchin, her expression speculative—or so it seemed. He couldn't be sure. For one thing, he could spare only a glance. For another, the spectacles dimmed the brilliance of her eyes.

But he saw enough: the smile playing at the corner of her mouth, and the angle at which she held her head as she regarded the boy, like a bird eyeing a worm.

"Now you're really in trouble, Fenwick," he said. "She's *thinking*."

Sophy's father had been a Noirot and her mother a DeLucey. Neither family could be bothered with charity, being too busy keeping one step ahead of the authorities.

Although Cousin Emma had taken in Sophy and her sisters and taught them a trade, they'd bounced back and forth for a time between parents and cousin. Their early life had not been sheltered. They'd learned how to survive on the streets. Among other skills, they'd learned to size up others quickly.

Sophy had seen and heard enough in a few minutes to understand that the lad was a rare find. With a very little training, this boy could be extremely useful. She was not going to let him be thrown into prison with ordinary criminals.

"We're quite close to the Great Marlborough Street police office," she said. "It would be no trouble to drop you there, Fenwick. Or, if you prefer, you could continue with us to our destination, and watch his lordship's horses, and keep a sharp lookout."

"And what would I be looking out for, I want to know," the boy said.

"Trouble," she said. "Do you think you can recognize it?"

"I haven't the smallest doubt of his abilities in that regard," Longmore said.

"If you do the job properly," she went on, "I'll see that you have a good dinner and a safe place to sleep."

"Where, exactly, did you have in mind?" Longmore said.

"Don't fret," she said. "I wasn't intending to foist him on you."

"You certainly won't foist him on yourself," he said. "You don't know a damned thing about him. He's probably crawling with lice—"

"That's slander, that is!" the boy cried.

"Sue me," said Longmore.

"Don't think I won't," the boy said. "There's no more vermin on me than on you, yer majesty. I had a bath!"

"At your christening?" Longmore said. "But no, I forgot: You don't have a name."

"Fenwick'll do," the boy said. "She can call me Georgy Pudding Pie if she wants, if she gives me dinner and a bed like she says. But she won't, will she?"

"Have you heard of the Milliners' Society for the Education of Indigent Females?" Sophy said.

The boy narrowed his eyes at her. "Yeah," he said in wary tones.

"You know someone there, it seems," she said.

"Yeah," he said.

"I'm closely acquainted with the women in charge," she said. She could hardly be more closely acquainted: She and her sisters had founded the organization last year. "If you know of that place, you know we don't make empty promises."

They'd reached Bedford Square. "Look here, Fenwick," she said. "There's the shop his lordship and I mean to visit." She nodded toward Dowdy's. "Do you know the place?"

"They makes clothes for the nobs," he said. "A girl I know used to work there, but they was all let go for no reason."

Sophy hoped the girl had gone to the Milliners' Society. She and her sisters had better look into what had happened to Dowdy's discharged seamstresses.

But one thing at a time.

"While his lordship and I visit the shop, you'll mind the horses as well as the business of everybody about you," she said briskly. "Give a long, sharp whistle to let us know if we're about to be interrupted. Do the job satisfactorily, and I'll do as I promised. Have we a bargain, Fenwick?"

"No tricks?" the boy said.

"No tricks?" Longmore echoed. "The brass of the brat!"

"Do I look like the tricky sort to you?" Sophy said.

The boy gave her a long, searching look. He spent some time peering into the tinted lenses. "Yes," he said. "Not to mention you got a grip like a manacle."

She smiled. "There, I knew you were a sharp one. But no tricks."

She released his arm. He made a great show of massaging it, and checking for broken bones. He muttered about "mad gentry morts" and "bruiser lordships."

"Never mind the grumbling," Longmore said.

"I don't mean to spend all day shopping with a female. Either you'll do it or you won't. Make up your mind. I don't have time to dawdle here, palavering about it, all day."

"Be yourself," Sophy told Longmore when he joined her on the pavement after a lengthy conversation with Fenwick—about the horses, she supposed, and what would happen to the boy if he failed his assignment.

"Myself?" he said. "Are you sure?"

"I need you to be you," she said. "Lord Longmore, Lady Warford's eldest son. The son of Dowdy's favorite customer." That was why she'd had to pursue and enlist him. She had to save her shop, and that meant going into enemy territory, to find out what Maison Noirot was up against. The easiest and most effective way was to use him as part of her disguise. "No pretending required. Simply be you."

"I need to pretend you're Gladys."

"I'll seem so like her, you won't have to pretend. Leave everything to me."

"And if they chuck you out?"

"Be yourself," she said. "Laugh."

"If you were you, yes," he said. "But Gladys is another story." He frowned. "This is going to be confusing."

"Not at all," she said. "All you have to do is be you. Don't think about it. It doesn't need thinking."

She marched toward the door in the determined way certain gauche misses did.

He moved smoothly ahead and opened it for her. In her mind she became Cousin Gladys—plain and awkward and sensitive to slights. She marched inside. Mouth set, she looked about her, making it plain that she wouldn't be easy to please. At the same time, though, she was still Sophy Noirot, evaluating her surroundings with an expert eye, and more than a little surprised . . . and troubled . . . at what she discovered.

Though no one could match Maison Noirot's flair, someone had tried. The walls had been freshly painted pale peach, the trim a creamy yellow, and someone had given thought to a variety of colorful accents. That someone had taken the trouble to arrange the fabrics artistically. Some hung on large rings near the display windows. Others lay on counters, looking as though they'd only a moment ago been unfolded for a customer. A book of fashion plates lay open on a table, inviting perusal. Comfortable chairs stood in small clusters about the room, giving it the snug air of a private parlor. Tables next to them held men's as well as ladies' magazines.

The showroom, while not as obsessively clean as Maison Noirot's, was much neater and less dingy than it used to be.

The explanation, Sophy saw, stood behind the counter.

Dowdy had hired a Frenchwoman. She was pretty and elegant and graceful. Her fair hair was arranged becomingly under a splendid lace cap.

Her poise didn't falter although her welcoming smile did, a little, as she took in Sophy/Gladys. The woman's light brown gaze turned with obvious relief to Longmore.

Subtle as the rebuff was, it wouldn't be too subtle

for a sensitive soul, as Sophy imagined Gladys to be. The Frenchwoman shouldn't have given any sign of dismay. She should have looked as delighted to see her as she would be to see Queen Adelaide.

Many specimens as unpromising as the faux Gladys came into dressmakers' shops. How one served them made all the difference in the world. The Frenchwoman seemed to see Lady Gladys Fairfax as an ordeal to endure, rather than as an exciting challenge, as Sophy and her sisters would view her. Their faces would have lit up when she stepped through the door.

"Mrs. Downes?" Sophy said.

"I am Madame Ecrivier, mademoiselle," the Frenchwoman said. "Madame Downes is occupied at the moment, but I—"

"Occupied!" Longmore said, startling Sophy as well as Ecrivier. "Where in blazes would she be occupied if not in her own shop? This *is* her shop, I presume? It had better be. I had the devil's own time getting here. Accident on Oxford Street and everybody stopping to gawk and slowing travel in three directions."

Sophy was too experienced in deceit to show her feelings. She didn't gawk at him, except in her thoughts. He'd said he was confused, and she'd had a moment's alarm, that subterfuge was beyond his intellectual abilities.

But whether by accident or not, he'd created a beautiful opening, and she knew how to play along.

"Did Lady Warford not tell Mrs. Downes to expect family members this week?" she said. "Her daughter, Lady Clara—my cousin, you know—is getting married. Surely my aunt must have informed you. I don't see how she could have failed to do so. She told me she'd ordered a dress to wear to the wedding. She ordered it from this shop. On Monday, I believe."

And she'd thrown a spectacular fit, according to Lady Clara, when she learned that the latter hadn't gone to Dowdy's.

"Oui, mademoiselle—milady. And most certainly—"

"Here's my cousin, come to be fitted out for my sister's wedding," Longmore said. "The first wedding in the family, I might add. And where's the proprietress? I say, this is a fine way to treat clients. Well, Gladys, we'd better be off. Who was that other milliner Clara mentioned? French name, wasn't it? On St. James's Street. If I'd known we'd get the cold shoulder here, I could have saved myself a bothersome journey."

Madame Ecrivier was all but dancing with panic. "Oh, no, oh, no, milord. There is no coldness of the shoulder. Only a moment, if you please. I will send someone to inform Madame. A thousand apologies. Certainly Madame will attend the young lady. If you will pardon me for a moment, I will arrange this."

The Frenchwoman glided away and vanished through the door behind the counter. Though she closed the door behind her, Sophy could hear her voice, high, communicating via the speaking pipe to somebody somewhere.

Longmore strode to the window and looked out. "The carriage is still there," he said in a low voice. "Fenwick hasn't sold the horses yet."

When he lowered his voice, it became husky,

and the sound made Sophy go still, like an animal catching the scent of danger. It took her a moment to shake off the feeling.

"Your cattle couldn't be safer," she said. "He's thrilled."

"It doesn't show."

"He's learned to hide important feelings," she said.

He gave a short laugh and left the window. He wandered the showroom. He fingered a length of muslin. He turned pages in the pattern book. He moved with careless grace, but his wasn't the usual lazy ease of an idle aristocrat.

Her skin prickled with awareness. He was a man, merely a man, she told herself. Yet an aura of danger surrounded him, and it seemed as though a wolf prowled the room.

She detected footsteps and voices approaching the door to the shop's back rooms.

"If I'd known this was the way London shop-keepers treat their best patrons, I should have had my dress made in Manchester," she said more audibly. "To be kept waiting endlessly—when there isn't another customer in the shop! I'm sure I should have something quite as elegant made at home as anything on offer here. And at a fraction of the price."

Dowdy burst through the door. She was a pain-fully thin woman of medium height. An elaborate pelerine of embroidered cambric, extending over the wide *à la Folle* sleeves of her printed muslin dress, helped create the illusion of a fuller figure. Large, round dark curls framed her face under the lacy tulle cap.

The ensemble was handsome, one must give her

that. It was a shame she didn't dress her ladies as carefully as she dressed herself.

"My lady, my lord, my apologies," she said breathlessly. "I never expected you so early in the day."

"The shop opens at ten o'clock," Longmore said. "Or so I was told."

"The sign in the window says so," Sophy said.

"You are quite right, miss—my lady." Dowdy bustled out from behind the counter. "I was called away. A—erm—a little difficulty in the workroom. But we are all in order now. A dress for the nuptials of Lady Clara Fairfax, is it not? Would her ladyship care to peruse the pattern book? We have all the latest styles from Paris, and a splendid selection of silks."

Judging by the crumbs on the pelerine, she must have been enjoying a leisurely breakfast.

"My aunt says I'm to place myself in your hands," Sophy said.

"And mind you do her up well," Longmore said. "None of your fobbing off that putrid green you bought too much of on account of seeing it in the wrong light."

Sophy strangled a laugh.

"My cousin may be a rustic," he said, "but—"

"I! A rustic!"

"My dear girl, your idea of sophistication is attending a lecture on stuffed birds at the Manchester Museum."

"England's finest mills are in Manchester!" she cried.

"Certainly, your ladyship," Dowdy said. "But I must say a word for our Spitalfields silks, you know. And as to that, I do believe we have exactly the thing for you. Madame Ecrivier, kindly show her ladyship the silk I mean."

Ecrivier gave Sophy a swift survey, then glided away to a drawer. She withdrew a length of blue silk.

"Blue!" Sophy said. "But I never wear blue."

"With the greatest respect, milady, perhaps it is time, yes?"

"What color is my aunt wearing?" Sophy said. "I can't wear the same color, and I know she likes blue."

Dowdy smiled. "I regret that we cannot divulge that information. Her ladyship—"

"Not divulge it!" Longmore said. "See here. I won't have my cousin trifled with. And I don't mean to hang about having my time wasted. You can deuced well show us what my mother is wearing to the wedding. By gad, do you think we'll report it to the newspapers?"

He slanted one incinerating black glance at Sophy.

"Do you know, Cousin, I'm finding this shop exceedingly tiresome," Sophy said. "Aunt assured me we'd receive every attention. But first we're made to wait, and then they're suddenly coy about my aunt's dress, when it's of the utmost importance that my own complement hers."

"I do beg your ladyship's pardon, but Lady Warford expressly forbade us to share the details," Dowdy said. "She was concerned that copies might be made, in advance of the matrimonial occasion, which I am sorry to say has happened in the past. Other dressmakers, you see, send their girls into the shop to spy, and—"

"Do we look like dressmakers' spies to you?"

Longmore demanded. "I vow, this is the most aggravating experience. Come away, Cousin. I've had a bellyful of this dithering and delaying."

He started for the door.

Ye gods, he was *perfect*.

Sophy followed. "I cannot think what I'll say to Aunt," she said. "You know she'll ask me why I went to that other place—the French dressmakers on St. James's Street. What is it?"

"Maison Noirot," he said. He opened the door.

Sophy heard a muttered oath behind her.

Then, "You heard his lordship, Madame Ecrivier. Show the lady the silk Lady Warford selected."

Longmore closed the door. He turned toward the two shop women. "And the pattern," he said.

"The pattern?" Dowdy's beady eyes widened.

"You heard me," he said. "Here's my cousin, fresh from the country. She's not at all comfortable with London ways, and the treatment she's received here this day has done nothing to reassure her. Show her the pattern. If she likes it, we'll stay. If she doesn't, this will be the last you see of us."

She was Gladys, through and through. Never slipped out of character, even for an instant.

Longmore didn't slip, either. Well, how could he, when he was only required to be himself, a role he could perform admirably.

She, on the other hand . . . but guile came to her so naturally.

She reacted to whatever he said in the same way Gladys would have done. She had the same mingled arrogance and uneasiness that made Gladys so tiresome. And the same vulnerability.

Cousin Gladys was disagreeable company, yet he always felt a little sorry for her.

There were moments when he almost forgot she wasn't Gladys. But the scent reminded him who she was.

It was all great fun while he and she played off each other. When she went into another room with the two dressmakers, though, he grew uneasy. She hadn't told him what he was to do if she was unmasked. She'd dismissed the possibility.

But when they undressed her how could they help but find out she wasn't shaped like a potato?

She'd said she was wearing numerous layers. How many?

How long would it take him to get them all off?

That would depend, wouldn't it?

His mind painted images that made him smile. He indulged himself for only a moment, though. He was expecting trouble—looking forward to it, in fact.

Best to keep his mind on what went on about him.

He leaned his stick against a chair, picked up a ladies' magazine on the table nearby, and put it down again. He went to the shop window, folded his hands behind his back, and looked out.

With all the colorful bits of cloth and ribbons and things hanging on display, it wasn't easy to see what was going on outside, but he found a position that allowed him to keep an eye on Fenwick.

The carriage still stood on the opposite side of the street, next to the fenced-in oval of greenery at the center of the square. Longmore had left it there because the place was shady and the vehicle would be out of the way of anybody collecting or dropping off passengers.

He heard the interior door open.

He turned quickly away from the window.

But it was only a tired-looking girl. She carried a tray bearing a glass of wine and a plate of biscuits. After a moment's hesitation, she set it on the table nearest the chair where he'd left his walking stick. She hunted up some sporting magazines and arranged them next to the refreshment tray. She took away the ladies' magazine and placed it on a table farther away.

She asked if she might get him anything else.

"Nothing," he said. "How long is this going to take?"

"Not long at all, your lordship," she said. "It's only the one dress. But since her ladyship is a new customer, they'll want a few minutes to measure."

She said something else, but a shout from outside yanked his attention back to the window. He saw two big men hurrying round his curricle toward the greenery. He couldn't see Fenwick.

Longmore slammed out of the shop.

Chapter Five

The baths of London are numerous and commodious, and are fitted up with every attention to the convenience of visiters. The usual price for a cold bath is 1s., or a warm bath, 3s. 6d.; but if the visiter subscribe for a quarter of a year or a longer time, the expense is proportionably diminished. The sea-water baths are 3s. 6d. each time, or if warm, about 7s. 6d.

—*Leigh's New Picture of London*, 1834

The street, unlike the commercial thoroughfares leading here, was nearly empty. Longmore crossed quickly—in time to see the two men come out from behind the curricle, a squirming Fenwick between them. The taller fellow was nearly as tall as Longmore, but wider. The smaller one was not much smaller, but thin and wiry. Both had scarred faces. Both needed shaving. Both were expensively but flashily dressed.

Brute One, the burlier one, had caught a fistful of the back of Fenwick's ragged coat collar.

"I warned you not to make me chase you," Brute One said. "Now you've gone and made me mad.

You ain't gettin' off this time, you dirty, thievin' brat."

"I ain't dirty!" Fenwick snapped. "You take your filthy mitts off of me!" He struggled, but Brute One must have caught hold of more than the collar alone. The boy could have wriggled out of his clothes otherwise. "I got friends, I have, and they'll make you sorry!" He looked up and spotted Longmore. "There!" he said. "There's one of 'em!"

"What the devil is this?" Longmore said. "The boy was minding my horses."

"With respect, sir, you been took advantage of. This little bastard here ain't to be trusted no farther 'n you can throw a house."

"I'll be the judge of that," Longmore said. "Let him go."

"Beggin' pardon, sir, but I better not," said Brute One. "There'll be the devil to pay, then, won't there?"

"We warned him again and again he wasn't to hang about the premises," said Brute Two. "Missus don't want him. Brings down the tone of the neighborhood. How many times we warned him off?"

"Well, I couldn't go, could I?" the boy said. "His worship'd have me hanged, he would, for deserting my post. He said so, didn't you, yer majesty?"

"You'll be hanged anyway, one of these days," said Brute One.

"Let him go," Longmore said.

"With respect, sir, don't you be feelin' sorry for this one," said Brute Two. "He's overdue for a trip to the workhouse, he is, and that's if he's lucky, 'cuz this here's penitentiary material, you ask me. Loiterin' and malingerin' when he's been told—"

"I told him to stay," Longmore said. "I'm growing tired of this conversation. Let the boy go and take yourselves off."

Brute One looked at Brute Two. They both looked down at the boy, then across the street at the shop.

"I'll tell you what, sir," said Brute One. "Missus don't like bein' contradicted."

"Funny," Longmore said. "Neither do I."

"Why don't I escort the boy out of the square, where she can't see the little bugger," said Brute One. "Farley here'll look after your horses, sir. And you can go on about your business—"

"You ain't taking me nowhere! I won't go!" Fenwick kicked his captor.

Brute One cuffed Fenwick's head, knocking his grimy cap off.

Longmore launched himself at the bully.

A muffled shriek came from the showroom.

Sophy, whose ears had been straining to detect signs of trouble outside, pulled on her cloak and ran out of the dressing room.

Dowdy and Ecrivier ran after her. "But your ladyship, your bodice," Dowdy said.

Sophy ran to the window, where the seamstress stood, her hand over her mouth.

Sophy was in time to see a burly fellow take a swing at Longmore, who dodged the blow, and hit back hard enough to make the brute stagger.

"I do apologize for Farley and Payton, your ladyship," Dowdy said. "But it's that horrid little boy again, making trouble. I'll send the girl out to—"

Sophy waved her away and looked about for a weapon.

Longmore's walking stick leaned against a chair nearby. She grabbed it and ran out.

She heard Dowdy call after her.

She raced across the street.

Having knocked down the bigger one, Longmore was starting for the other one. Then Fenwick decided to help, and flung himself at the smaller one, a mad little dervish, all flailing fists and kicking feet.

Ignoring his protests, Sophy dragged the boy out of the fray.

Longmore immediately picked up the thinner fellow and threw him into the fence. He bounded back, and started for Longmore. At the same time, the bigger one pulled himself up off the ground, gave a roar, and started running at Longmore.

Sophy thrust the walking stick in the ruffian's way. He tripped and went down hard on the pavement.

Longmore grabbed the thin one and threw him into the fence again. This time the ruffian folded into a heap at the bottom of the fence.

"Time to go," Longmore said.

Sophy climbed into the carriage. Fenwick hesitated.

The brutes were stumbling to their feet.

"You, too, Mad Dick," Longmore said.

The boy leapt up onto the groom's place.

Longmore quickly settled the agitated horses, and gave them office to start.

As they drove away, Sophy called out, "Tell your mistress to cancel my order. I don't care for the people she employs."

Bedford Square and its adjacent byways, well away from the hubbub of the major shopping streets, were practically deserted. It took Longmore only a moment to get out of the square and into Tottenham Court Road.

The area was quiet enough for him to hear his passengers breathing hard.

Even he was more winded than he ought to be.

But then, the fight had turned out less straightforward than usual.

"Good grief," Sophy said. "I can't leave you two alone for a minute."

"I was bored," Longmore said. "Didn't you advise me to pick a fight if I got bored? I was beginning to enjoy myself, too, when you and Mad Dick had to get into it. How the devil am I to have a proper set-to, when I've got to look out for a pair of interferers, and make sure I don't trip over them—or they don't get killed accidentally?"

That had certainly added interest and excitement to what could have been a mundane mill.

"You can't think I'd hang about the shop when you'd given me a perfect excuse to make a hasty exit," she said. "And then another fine excuse to cancel the order for that ugly dress. Really, it couldn't have worked out better if I'd planned it."

"What're you saying, Miss?" Fenwick piped up from the back. "We went to all this bother, and I nearly got drug to the workhouse—and you didn't even want a bleedin' dress?"

"She's the tricky sort," Longmore said. "You said so yourself, as I recall."

The street being less chaotic than those they'd traveled previously, he was able to give her more than a cursory glance. She was completely disheveled, her ugly cap hanging crookedly from one side of her head, her stringy hair falling down in back and clinging stickily to her forehead and cheeks. And her bodice was hanging loose.

"Your clothes are falling off," he said.

"Oh," she said. She reached under the cloak to refasten her dress. After a moment's struggle, she muttered under her breath. It sounded like street French.

More audibly she said, "That fool woman missed a hook. I don't know what she's done, but I can't get the wretched thing undone. Fenwick, you'd better unhook it for me."

"Not on your life," the boy said. "There's things I'll do and things I won't and getting tangled in females' personal hooks and buttons and such is where I draw the line."

"Don't be so missish," said Sophy. "You can't expect Lord Longmore to stop the horses and do me up."

"Better him than me," Fenwick said. "I won't touch them things with a pitchfork."

"Coward," Longmore said. The day simply kept getting better and better.

He turned into the nearest side street, and halted the carriage. He sent Fenwick down to hold the horses' heads. Then he faced Sophy.

"Turn sideways," he said. "I'm not an acrobat."

She unfastened the cloak and shrugged it from her shoulders. It slid down to her waist. Then she turned and lifted her hair out of the way. She bent her head.

And he became aware of the air changing, humming with tension.

Her neck lay bare before him. Smooth, perfectly creamy skin, and a trace of golden down where the hairline tapered off.

He could almost taste her skin. His head bent, and all he could think of was licking the back of her neck the way a cat licked cream.

"You were brilliant in the shop, by the way," she said.

"You told me to be myself," he said, his voice thick. He could smell her skin, tinged with lavender and . . . pine?

He could barely focus on the hooks. He stared at her soft neck.

"I think it's somewhere in the middle," she said.

"What is?"

"The hook she fastened to the wrong bar. It's a stitched bar, you see? Not a metal eye."

He hauled his attention to the dress. The fabric was bunched up near the middle of her back. Above the place where the dress was crookedly fastened, a small gap had opened. He could see a bit of undergarment. Fine muslin. Embroidered. With tiny flowers.

He swallowed a groan.

"You got right into the spirit of the thing," she said. "You were brilliant."

He cleared his throat. "I was being myself."

He told himself not to rush his fences.

He wasn't easy to persuade. Resisting temptation had never made any sense to him. But there was nothing to be gained by giving in now, in a public byway. Even a dolt like the Earl of Longmore could understand that.

Do the job and be done with it, he told himself.

Certainly it was no onerous task. He was used to doing and undoing women's clothing. He'd done it wearing gloves, more than once. He'd done it in the dark. He'd done it at speeds that might be records for the Northern Hemisphere, while the female hissed, "Hurry, for heaven's sake—he's coming!"

He set to work.

It should have taken seconds. But there was some sort of tangle, and he was fumbling, and getting nowhere. His fingers felt like sausages. No matter how he tried to get at the hook, he failed, and with each failure his temperature climbed another degree.

"What's wrong?" she said.

"These hooks," he said. "They're the very devil."

"That fool must have bent them," she said. "They ought to be easy to manage. We haven't a retinue of servants, and one can't always count on having a sister on hand. One needs to be able to dress without help, if necessary."

"You must be deuced flexible," he said.

Wrong thing to say.

She went quiet and his mind started painting pictures. Just in case he wasn't heated enough already.

He wasn't used to behaving himself for long stretches. And she was . . . flexible . . . and his mind wouldn't let go of the idea. And she smelled like a woman and lavender and greenery. And he could see a bit of her underthings.

His head was going to explode.

"Lord Longmore?" she said.

He gathered what was left of his wits. "The hook is either mangled or tangled," he said. "I can't see what the problem is." Because he was going cross-eyed, from the scent and the warmth of her body and the consciousness of his hands and how he needed to keep them at their job.

His pulse was racing, sending heat flooding downward.

Christ.

"She caught it in the seam stitching, probably," she said. "She was in a fearful hurry. Couldn't wait to be done with me. I'm surprised she didn't leave it to the Frenchwoman. Ecrivier. You saw what that was all about, I don't doubt."

"I should have made the boy do this," he said. "His hands are smaller."

"Go ahead and pull, and don't worry about breaking the thread," she said. Her voice sounded shaky. "We can easily mend it. Or better yet, leave it. All you need to do is fasten enough to keep the bodice in place."

"It's only one confounded hook," he said. "I'm not surrendering to a bit of metal—especially not with Mad Dick looking on, composing Cockney mockery."

He squared his shoulders.

He peeled off his gloves.

This time, when he touched the back of her dress, she shivered.

His palms were sweating.

He bent closer, squinting. He found the bit of thread the hook was tangled with. He pulled it free.

He let out the breath he hadn't realized he was holding.

He heard her suck in air.

Well, then.

She'd *noticed.*

And not in the way of noticing a fly landing on her skin, or a dog thrusting his nose into her hand but in that special *feminine* noticing way.

The siege machinery had advanced.

At great sacrifice. But still.

He cheerfully did up the other hooks and buttons, pulled the cloak up over her shoulders, and turned away to pull on his gloves.

He'd fought a terrific battle with himself, with his very nature, and he'd emerged victorious.

He'd advanced.

"You can come back, you little coward," he said to Fenwick. "She's decent again."

Lord Longmore drove back to St. James's Street at death-defying speed.

As they plunged into knots of traffic, Sophy heard people scream and curse, but they got out of the way.

She only clung to the side of the carriage and wished he could go faster.

She could still feel his hands at her back and his warm breath on her neck. She could still hear his voice, so low and husky, at her ear.

Her willpower had oozed away.

She'd actually felt her brain melting, and her muscles going the same way, and she had very nearly leaned back into his hands and let him do whatever he wanted to her.

He hadn't, apparently, wanted to do anything, luckily for her.

Luckily, too, she was done with him. He'd served his purpose, and she hadn't done anything catastrophic, and now all she had to do was get home and pour herself a glass or four of brandy and tell her sisters what she'd learned.

When they reached the shop, she practically leapt from the curricle.

She turned to run into the shop when she remembered the boy. Good grief! How could she forget *him*?

She turned back. "Well, what are you waiting for? Come along, Fenwick."

He eyed the shop warily, but he started to climb down.

"No, you don't," Longmore said.

The boy paused, looking from her to him.

"You'll come along with me," Longmore said. "I'll see that you get fed and find a berth. There's a fine pie shop over—"

"Absolutely not," Sophy said. "I was the one who made the promise."

"She did, yer highness," Fenwick said.

"Would you trust her before you'd trust me?" Longmore said. "You know what that is?" He nodded toward Maison Noirot. "A dressmaker's shop. All *women*."

"Maybe I better stay with him, miss," said Fenwick. "He's bigger than you."

"No, you won't," she said. "I found you first." She strode toward the curricle. The boy drew back to the far corner of the seat.

"No offense, miss, but he saved me from being drug to the workhouse," said Fenwick. "Not to mention he could squash me like a bug if he took it into his head."

"*I* saved your life by pulling you out of that fight before one of them accidentally stepped on you," Sophy said. "And if his lordship was meaning to squash you, he would have done it right after you tried to rob him. Now come along, and stop being ridiculous."

She reached up to grab Fenwick's arm. He shrank back.

"I don't have time for this nonsense," Longmore said. "Good day, Miss Noirot."

Then she had to back away because he signaled the horses and they started eagerly.

He drove away. Hands clenched, she watched him go.

Longmore knew it wasn't a good idea to leave her fuming on the pavement. It was a far worse idea, though, to let her harbor young felons. Who knew who the boy's confederates were? Who knew how hardened in crime he was? Hardened or not, he could be intimidated by more calloused individuals, and unlock the shop's back door to a gang of thieves and cutthroats.

After a moment, Fenwick spoke. "I thought her name was Gladys."

"She has a hundred names, as suits her convenience," Longmore said. "Don't try to keep track of them. You'll only hurt your head."

He heard a high-pitched cry.

He looked in that direction. Sophy/Gladys was trotting alongside the vehicle. "You give that boy back!" she cried.

"Go home!" he shouted.

She let out an unearthly shriek. Then she swayed and sank into a heap on the pavement.

Instantly, people hurried to the spot.

Longmore stopped the carriage, threw the reins to Fenwick, and thrust through the rapidly gathering crowd. "Get out of the way, confound you! Are you trying to trample her?"

He scooped her up. She lay completely limp in his arms.

He told himself not to panic. Women always

fainted. They were used to it. It hardly ever killed them.

Yet he knew she worked long hours, and she'd been in a fight only a short time ago—a fight that had left him winded. She'd thrown herself into the fray and she'd done splendidly, demonstrating unusually quick thinking, especially for a female.

His conscience smote him. As smitings go, it wasn't much, his conscience being in poor fighting condition.

"Damn me, damn me, damn me," he muttered.

He carried her down St. James's Street, a small parade following, and turned into Bennet Street. At that point he looked over his shoulder at the gawkers. "Be off," he said.

The parade melted away.

He carried her into the narrow court and kicked the private door.

One minute.

All Sophy had needed was one more minute, and she would have been able to get Fenwick away. As soon as she shrieked, people got interested. The onlookers would have taken her side because she'd play the helpless mother whose child had been torn from her. And she could make herself so piteous that the boy would have felt sorry for her and come, she knew.

But Longmore, curse him, hadn't given her the minute, or even an instant to think. He'd scooped her up as easily as if she'd been a packet of ribbons.

And now she was crushed against his big, hard, warm torso, one muscled arm under her knees, the other bracing her back.

She opened her eyes. "You can put me down now."

She felt him tense. Then a narrowed black gaze met hers. "How hard?" he said.

He didn't let go of her.

"You're not taking that boy," she said. "I found him. You would have taken him to the police."

"I should have done," he said. "He's no use minding horses, what with being wanted by the authorities. I'll wager we'll find handbills seeking his capture."

His body was *very* warm and her muscles were softening and her body wanted to melt itself all over his big, hard one. "Put me down or I'll scream," she said.

"That's playing dirty," he said.

"That's the way I play," she said.

He let her down, but not hard and not quickly. He made a show of taking excessive care, easing his grip only a bit at a time, so that she slid down slowly against his body, traversing a large expanse of wool and linen and silk, all imbued with the dizzying scene of male, before her feet quite touched the ground.

She'd known he was dangerous. He had that reputation.

She'd assumed he was dangerous merely in the obvious way: big and wild and reckless.

This wasn't *merely*. This was deadly.

"I recommend you save yourself a great deal of bother and stop fighting me," she said. "I want that boy, and I will stop at *nothing*."

She watched while he took this in and mulled it over, his dark gaze growing distant.

After a moment, he said, "Do you know, I don't find that hard to believe."

"We need a boy for the shop," she said.

"You told me you don't need them. You said so a moment before he crashed into our lives."

"We don't need *bullies*," she said patiently. "But we do need a lad to run errands and carry messages and packages. He's not too young or too old to train. He's quick and clever and well-looking. With a bath—"

"And de-lousing—"

"And proper clothes and a little instruction, he'll be *perfect*."

Longmore grimaced with what she had no doubt was the pain of cogitation.

She waited, aware of sweat trickling between her breasts. If she hadn't been a Noirot, she would have clenched her hands and gritted her teeth to keep herself from doing something fatally stupid.

Given that she was a Noirot, it was amazing that she could keep her mind on the boy at all.

But thanks to Cousin Emma, Sophy and her sisters were made of sterner stuff than many of their kind. She stood and waited, and wondered why the devil no one came to the door. She could use some sisterly reinforcement about now.

"Very well," he said gruffly.

His voice had dropped a full octave, and the sound made her head thick.

"I'll admit it's not a completely lunatic idea," he said. "But you'd better let me break it to him. I'll feed him first and soften him up. Then I'll bring him back."

"This had better not be a trick," she said.

He gave her an exasperated look.

"What?" she said.

"Trickery is *your* department, Miss Noirot," he said. "Mine is knocking people about. But I'm flattered that you imagine I'm clever enough to trick you."

He gave a short laugh and left.

"Tell my sisters I'm back," Sophy said, moving quickly past Mary, the maidservant who'd finally opened the door.

She hurried up the stairs and on to her room. She needed to wash and change. She needed to wash in *cold* water.

She tore off the ugly cloak and the ugly dress and then had a struggle with the corset strings. The struggle reminded her of that endless, tormenting time while Longmore had been working on her dress hooks.

She didn't need reminders.

She stomped to the chimneypiece and pulled the bell cord.

She moved away and filled a bowl with water. She peeled off the mole and scrubbed her face.

She hadn't time to wash her hair. That was a time consuming project. But she needed to get out of these clothes. Where the devil was Mary?

The door flew open. It wasn't Mary but Marcelline.

"My dear, are you all right?"

"No. Undo me, will you? I hate these clothes. They're nothing but trouble. When I get them off, I want them to go straight into the fire."

"Sophy."

"I need to get out of this corset," Sophy said. "I've three extra layers underneath and I think I'm going to suffocate."

"Sophy."

"I'll talk when I get these blasted clothes off," Sophy said.

Marcelline went quickly to work on the corset. A moment later, Sophy flung it to the floor.

"I take it that matters didn't go well," Marcelline said.

"Matters went beautifully," Sophy said.

She told herself not to be a nitwit. Longmore didn't matter. He was a means to an end. What mattered was the shop.

She started pulling off her clothes. While she removed layer after layer with Marcelline's help, she told her sister how splendidly Longmore had been himself: the thickheaded, overbearing aristocrat. She explained how, thanks to him, she'd had a good look at the pattern as well as the silk Lady Warford had selected. She told Marcelline about Dowdy's refurbishment and the French modiste.

"That's not good," Marcelline said.

"It isn't what I'd hoped for, but it could be worse," Sophy said. "Our furnishings are still superior to Dowdy's. All we need to do is make them even more beautiful and exciting. Maison Noirot needs to look different. It needs to look ten steps ahead of Dowdy's. People don't notice subtle differences."

That would take money they didn't have. But Leonie would think of something. She had to. Sophy couldn't think of *everything*.

"And the patterns?" Marcelline said. "Lady Warford's dress?"

"We'd give it to the girls at the Milliners' Society to pick apart and remake," Sophy said. "Of course, Lady Warford won't see its flaws."

"How can she stand next to her daughter and not see the difference?"

"She's the way Lady Clara was before we took her in hand," Sophy said. "Her eye is untrained. And at the moment, I don't see a way to train her. I'm thinking I need to give my attention to Lady Clara's problem first. Right now, she's all that stands between us and failure. If she continues to shop with us, we have a prayer. If she marries Adderley, she can't shop with us."

Marcelline paced for a few minutes.

"Leonie would say we need to set priorities," Sophy said. "We've three problems, and rating them from simplest to hardest, I'd put Lady Warford as the hardest nut to crack, Lady Clara's difficulty as next hardest, and Dowdy's as the most manageable. Do you agree?"

Marcelline nodded, still pacing.

"We know what to do about Dowdy's—at least for the moment," Sophy said. "So I'm tackling Lady Clara next."

Marcelline paused in her pacing. "It would help to know what's going on in her head."

Lady Clara had come by on Wednesday, to order another riding dress and two more hats, but Sophy had been busy with Lady Renfrew, one of their earliest and most loyal customers of rank.

"Can we bring her in for a fitting tomorrow?" Sophy said. "If I can get her to myself, I'll get her to talk."

"We can send a seamstress with a message," Marcelline said. "But I hate to remind anybody at Warford House that she's patronizing her mama's enemies."

"We can ask Lord Longmore to take the message," Sophy said. "He's supposed to come back in an hour or so."

Marcelline's eyebrows went up.

Sophy told her sister about Fenwick, and about Longmore's attempt to make off with him.

"How sweet of him!" Marcelline said with a laugh "He's trying to protect you from the dangerous criminal. If only he knew."

Fenwick was a little innocent, compared to them. Not that they'd ever picked pockets. But there wasn't a game or a trick of the streets they didn't know. In Paris, they'd had to deal with every sort of knave and villain, from minor to major. For a time, during the cholera, Paris had been almost completely lawless. But they'd survived.

"I wasn't thinking of that," Sophy said. "I was too furious with his highhandedness. So angry that for a moment I couldn't even think what to do. But it was only for a moment. Then I made a scene, and fainted. Unfortunately, I had to faint on the pavement, which is vile."

Marcelline smiled. "I can picture it. But couldn't you have thought of a less disgusting measure?"

"Maybe, but I hadn't time. I was afraid he'd get away. He drives like a drunken charioteer, headlong, and never mind what might be in the way."

Marcelline kicked to one side the heap of ugly clothing on the floor. "I agree we'd better burn them. And I'll send Mary to run you a proper bath." She eyed Sophy's stringy tresses. "We ought to wash that mess out of your hair."

"That will have to wait until tonight," Sophy said. "I've left you and Leonie on your own all day, and I have a customer expecting to see me this afternoon. I'll pin it up tight and put on a pretty lace cap, and no one will notice."

"You're not going out tonight?"

"There's only Lord Londonderry's party, and no one there will be wearing our dresses."

"Good," Marcelline said. "You could use a proper night's sleep."

What Sophy could use was some big hands on her body, leading her into temptation.

One of these days, she promised herself. But they wouldn't be Longmore's hands. Nothing but horrible consequences there.

She told herself she had enough difficult matters to deal with, and she ought to deal with the ones that weren't completely impossible.

All she needed to know about Longmore was whether he'd bring the boy back or force her to take drastic measures.

She cheered herself up by devising the measures.

More than two hours after making off with Fenwick, Longmore returned to the rear entrance of the dressmakers' shop. He told the maidservant Mary who answered the door to tell Sophy Noirot that he'd brought back her "young ruffian."

The maid led them into a room on the ground floor. It was more Spartan in appearance than the parlor upstairs, being reserved, the numerous cupboards and drawers told him, for more commercial uses.

Though this wasn't a room customers would enter, it was as scrupulously clean as every other part of the shop he'd seen.

Fenwick kept looking the floor as though he'd never seen one before.

He'd probably never seen a clean one before.

They had only a few minutes to wonder what was in the cupboards and drawers before Sophy appeared.

She'd completely shed her Lady Gladys persona.

Fenwick didn't recognize her at all. For a long time he stood uncharacteristically silent, staring at her.

"Yes, it's the same lady," Longmore said impatiently. "As I mentioned, she has a hundred names, and becomes a hundred different people. And this," he told her, "is your dear Fenwick."

"What did you do to him?" she said.

"We removed some layers of dirt," he said.

"It looks as though you removed some layers of skin as well," she said.

Fenwick found his tongue. "His worship made me have a baff," he said. "I told him I had one last week. I fink they rubbed my face off."

"Bath," Longmore said. "Not *baff*. *Think*, not *fink*. You put your tongue between your teeth, as I showed you."

"*Th*ink," Fenwick said with exaggerated care.

"My head got tired, translating from whatever language it is he speaks," Longmore told her.

"I had pie," Fenwick said. "A meat pie big as my head." He gestured with his hands. "We went to some shop and he found me these fings."

Longmore looked at him.

The boy put his tongue between his teeth. "*Th*ings."

"We called on a dealer in readymade clothing near the baths," Longmore said. "I know you mean to stitch him into wildly gorgeous livery, but it made no sense to have him scrubbed clean, only to put him back into those—what he was wearing."

She looked up at him. Her eyes wore a softer expression than usual.

Was that approval? Good gad.

He'd inched forward another step.

"Fenwick and I talked the matter over at length," he said. "We concluded that he was likely to be happier in your service than anywhere else I could think to place him. He'll have a roof over his head, regular meals, unusually fine clothing, and a place to sleep where he's unlikely to be robbed or assaulted or dragged off to jail or the workhouse."

"I couldn't have said it better myself," she said.

"Perhaps not, but you would have used more adjectives," Longmore said. "In any event, I couldn't ascertain his real name or where he came from or who he belongs to, if anybody. It's more than possible he truly doesn't know."

London's streets teemed with abandoned children who weren't sure what parents were, let alone whether they had any.

"I daresay you can ferret out his deep, dark secrets," Longmore went on.

Her sisters entered before she could answer.

Fenwick stared at them.

Longmore couldn't blame him. One Noirot woman was stunning enough, with all the lace and the great ballooning sleeves and skirts, and ruffles and ribbons. Three of them, in all the colors of the rainbow, all rustling as they moved, made for a hallucinatory experience.

"This is Fenwick," Sophy said.

All three women regarded the boy with the same expression of polite interest.

Longmore wondered what was going on in their heads. No, the truth was, he only wondered what was going on in *her* head.

Fenwick said, "I had a bath."

"With soap," Longmore said. "Well, do you mean to keep him or not?"

The Duchess of Clevedon smiled. "I think he'll do very well."

Miss Leonie said, in her usual brisk way, "Yes, come along, Fenwick. Our maidservant Mary will take charge of you for now. We're rather busy today. But we'll talk later, after closing time." She put a hand on the boy's shoulder and steered him through the interior door.

"How very good of you to have him cleaned and re-upholstered," said the duchess, still smiling.

"I thought it would be easier to simply take him to the baths and let them do a thorough job with him," he said. "But now he's yours, and I shan't keep you any longer from your customers."

He bowed, and was turning to leave when he heard the noise. The room wasn't far from the back door, which someone seemed to be trying to batter down.

He remembered Dowdy's hired ruffians.

He remembered Fenwick talking about his friends. Young thieves usually traveled in packs led by an older criminal.

He blocked Sophy from going out ahead of him, strode quickly down the short passage, and flung open the door.

His brother Valentine stood with fist upraised, about to thump on the door again.

"What the devil?" said Longmore. "Does *every-body* know about this door?"

"I've been looking everywhere for you," Valentine said. "I tried your house, then White's, then I went to Clevedon House—but they hadn't seen you and he wasn't in and nobody knew where he'd gone. Then I thought maybe you'd made a long night of it, and so I came back, to look in at Crockford's, and someone there told me he'd seen you turn into Bennet Street a while ago. I came here and saw your carriage. I tried five doors in this curst court. What is this place?"

"Never mind what it is. What the devil do you want?"

Valentine glanced past him.

Longmore turned and discovered that Sophy had followed him into the passage.

"I'd rather talk to you outside," Valentine said. "Something's happened."

"It's Lady Clara," Sophy said.

Valentine's eyes widened. "How the devil—"

"What's she done now?" Longmore demanded. "Has she killed her fiancé? Our mother?"

"Does *she* know everything?" Valentine said, his glance flicking to Sophy.

"This is Clevedon's sister-in-law, you nitwit. She's practically family."

"Not *our* family," said Valentine.

"Don't be pompous," Longmore said. "Makes you look constipated. What's Clara done now?"

"Will you not come outside? I'd rather the world didn't know."

"This world," Longmore said with a nod at Sophy, "finds out everything anyway."

Valentine muttered under his breath, let out a sigh, then stepped into the passage, closing the door behind him.

"Clara's bolted," he said.

Chapter Six

Some persons think the sublimest object in nature is a ship launched on the bosom of the ocean: but give me, for my private satisfaction, the Mail-Coaches that pour down Piccadilly of an evening, tear up the pavement, and devour the way before them to the Land's-End!

—William Hazlitt, *Sketches and essays*, 1839

D on't be an idiot," Longmore said. "Clara would never—"

"My lords," Sophy cut in. "This isn't the best place to discuss the matter. People coming and going. Doors opening and closing."

"What the devil is there to discuss?" Longmore said. "You can't possibly take this seriously."

Her expression was all too serious. "I recommend you do so," she said. "But a quieter place would be better."

She walked away, back to the room Longmore had just left. She didn't wait to see whether they followed. For a moment he watched her hips sway. Then he noticed that his brother was watching the same thing.

"Don't stand there like a lump," Longmore said.

"You're the one who wants to make a great secret of this."

They followed her into the room. She closed both doors.

"This is a typical Fairfax family tempest in a teapot," Longmore said. "Clara's incapable of running away. She can't dress herself. She barely knows how to feed herself. She has no money. Where could she go?"

"She took Davis," Valentine said.

"You can't be serious."

"What sort of joke do you imagine I'm playing?"

"A lady can't keep secrets from her personal maid," Sophy said. "She'd have to tell Davis. Though Davis must have been extremely unhappy about it, she'd never tattle or let Lady Clara go alone."

True enough. Davis was a bulldog of a maid, ferociously loyal and protective. As well, she had— or so Longmore had always assumed—both feet planted firmly on the ground.

"Clara drove out in her cabriolet near midday," Valentine said. "She had a lot of parcels she said were old clothes she was taking to one of her charities. Then she was going to visit Great-Aunt Dora in Kensington and spend the night. She's done that before. No one gave it a second thought. We might not have known the truth until tomorrow, if Great-Aunt Dora hadn't come to see Mother today. Then we had a to-do, as you can imagine."

Longmore was amazed he couldn't hear the screaming from here. Warford House was only a few streets away, overlooking the Green Park.

"Did Lady Clara leave any message?" Sophy said.

Valentine got all stiff. He took off his hat and made an extremely correct bow. "I don't believe I've had the honor," he said.

Pompous ass.

Longmore said, "Miss Noirot, will you allow me to present my brother, Valentine Fairfax."

Another excruciatingly polite bow from the nitwit, who said, "Miss Noirot, perhaps you'd be so good as to allow me to speak to my brother in private."

She curtseyed. It wasn't remotely correct. Down she went in a great flurry of bows and lace and muslin whispering like scandalized playgoers when a notorious tart appeared in her theater box. And up she came again, graceful as a ballet dancer. Then she looked up at Valentine, all wide blue eyes. "I'm not good at all," she said. "Ask Lord Longmore."

"I'm still undecided in that regard," Longmore said. "I will say it's no good trying to keep secrets from her."

Valentine, now gazing raptly into the great blue eyes, didn't hear a word.

"A message, Valentine," Longmore prompted. "Did our sister leave a message?"

Valentine shook himself out of his trance and dug out from the recesses of his waistcoat a piece of notepaper. He gave it to his brother.

The message was short enough:

I will __not__ marry that man. I'd rather be disgraced for the rest of my life and live as a beggar.

C.

"Oh, good," Longmore said. "That's what we need: drama."

Yet he remembered the way Clara's face had crumpled last week, when he'd brought her here. She'd said . . . What had she said?

Something about their mother harassing her. Something about the marriage. The hasty marriage.

The marriage she wouldn't have had to face had he done the one simple task even he'd understood was necessary: keep Adderley away from her.

Sophy held out her hand. He gave her the note.

She scanned the few lines quickly. She turned the paper over. On the outside Clara had written "Mama."

"As soon as Mother realized that Clara hadn't gone to Aunt Dora's, she ran upstairs and ransacked Clara's room," Valentine said. "The note was tucked into Clara's jewel box. She'd taken everything else out of it. Not that she'd much of value there. Usually our mother lends her jewelry—and she keeps the good things under lock and key."

"She could sell her clothes," Sophy said. "Her maid could do it for her. That's why she took all the parcels."

Both men looked at her.

"They'd fetch a fair sum, each of her dresses, especially the ones we made," she said.

That was when Longmore felt the first stirrings of alarm.

Clara. On the road. With nobody but her maid to look after her.

He felt sick.

"I daresay our mother's worked that out by

now," Valentine said. "She'd have found the wardrobes and such empty."

"Has she stopped screaming long enough to work anything out?" Longmore said.

"She didn't scream at all," Valentine said. "First she fainted, then she started crying, then she locked herself in Clara's room. She won't let anybody in and she won't speak to anybody."

"Oh, no. The poor woman." Sophy put her hand to her mouth and closed her eyes. It was only for an instant. One hint of emotion. Longmore realized at that moment how rare a sight it was: true emotion. He didn't know how he knew it was true, but he knew it in the same way he knew her, no matter what disguise she wore.

A glimpse of feeling, then it was gone, and she became brisk. "One could wish she'd left larger clues. But she did take her maid. And clothes and trinkets to pawn. So she planned, to a degree. But first things first. We need to discover which direction she's taken."

"We?" the brothers said simultaneously.

Lord Valentine Fairfax, whom Sophy had seen many times before, resembled his eldest brother only in size. His coloring was like Lady Clara's. Yet it was obvious they were brothers. Both men regarded her with the same rapid succession of expressions: surprise, confusion, annoyance.

They were aristocratic men. Their brains were not over-large and definitely not attuned to subtlety.

She donned a look of confusion. "I assumed you'd wish to help me."

"Help *you*?" said Lord Longmore.

Lord Valentine remembered his manners. "It's very—er—kind of you, Miss—er—"

"*Noirot*, you idiot. I told you. Clevedon's sister-in-law. And if she—"

"Yes, of course," said Lord Valentine. "I dare-say we can call on Clevedon to assist in organizing a search."

"Ah, yes?" she said. "Where do you propose to begin looking?"

"Why . . ." Lord Valentine frowned and looked at his brother.

"Because I'm baffled where you'd start," she said. "Perhaps I'm wrong, but it seems to me that you'll need a prodigious large search party, to search every way out of London for a sign of her, and then all possible routes to . . . well, everywhere."

They looked at each other, then at her.

"I can't help wondering, too, how you'd do this without calling attention to the fact that Lady Clara Fairfax has run away from home, with no companion but her maid," she said. "Perhaps I'm wrong—I'm merely a shopkeeper—but I'd always thought that gently bred girls were not allowed to simply dash off by themselves. I'd supposed that if a girl did such a thing, her family wouldn't want it known."

"Well," said Lord Valentine.

Longmore uttered a vehement oath.

Sophy could have added several equally vehement ones, in two languages. This was so bad, on so many counts. A gently bred girl, traveling unchaperoned and unprotected, except by one maid. She might as well paint a big red target on her

back. And front. And if the Great World found out
. . . after what had happened with Adderley . . .

Nothing could mend her reputation then.

One could only hope the girl had had second
thoughts and was even now on her way home.

But Sophy knew better than to rely on hope.

Thanks to a lifetime's practice, nothing of what
she felt inwardly showed outwardly.

"I've a large network of acquaintances I can
call upon in a situation like this," she said. "Even
better, we have Fenwick. I suspect he'll be able to
call on his own associates as well. Among the two
groups, someone will have noticed two women in
a vehicle of such-and-such description, going in
such-and-such direction."

She waited for arguments. The two men only
stood and listened, both wearing the same intent
expression. She supposed they were both thinking
hard about what she'd said. One couldn't expect
them to do anything else at the same time.

"All I need from you is a description of the vehicle and its distinguishing features." She took up
the little pocket watch that hung from her belt
and opened it. "It's nearly half past four o'clock.
With any luck, we'll hear something before nightfall."

"Nightfall!" said Lord Valentine. "My dear girl,
she's already been gone for hours. By nightfall she
could be in Dover or Brighton or even on a vessel
traveling to the Continent."

"Miss Noirot is not your dear girl, you pretentious half-wit," Longmore said.

"She'll need papers to travel to the Continent," Sophy said. Unlike the Noirots, Lady Clara
wouldn't know how to go about obtaining forged

passports and letters of credit and such, or how to forge her own.

"That merely leaves all of Great Britain," Lord Valentine said.

"Thank you for stating the obvious," Longmore said.

"I only meant—"

"Never mind what he means, Miss Noirot," Longmore said. "He doesn't know what he means, and being high-strung, like the rest of our lot, he flies into a panic over everything."

"I think there's some reason to panic," she said. "This isn't good."

"You said a moment ago that we might be of use," he said. "What do you want me to do?"

"Or me, of course," said Lord Valentine.

There was no choice.

Sophy couldn't do it alone. She'd never traveled outside London. She needed help.

"Lord Longmore, I suggest you go home and tell your valet to pack for a journey of several days," she said.

"Several days!" Lord Valentine dragged a hand through his hair. "Traveling with only her maid! Clara will be ruined past mending!"

Lady Clara's ruin was the least of Sophy's worries at the moment. She could only hope the girl wasn't assaulted. Raped. Murdered. She was completely vulnerable. She didn't know a damned thing. Look how easily Adderley had taken advantage of her.

"Please pack for several days," she said. She kept her voice low and calm, her expression tranquil. She didn't wring her hands. Lord Valentine needed quieting, and Longmore needed to believe that she knew what she was doing. "The instant I have news, I'll send to you, and we'll set out."

"We," said Lord Longmore.

"I'm used to you," she said. "I hardly know Lord Valentine and he hardly knows me."

Longmore at least understood—to a point—what she was capable of. He knew about her work for the *Spectacle*. She wouldn't have to waste time explaining every little thing. They'd worked together well enough at Dowdy's.

She'd used him then and she'd use him now. An instrument. That's all he was, she told herself.

She turned to the younger brother. "My lord, I advise you to return to Warford House. What you need to do is help your family memorize a simple excuse for Lady Clara's not being at home to visitors. A severe cold or some such—the sort of thing that makes people keep a distance."

He looked at his older brother.

"Have you any better ideas?" Longmore said. "Do I need to point out to you that Miss Noirot has a good deal at stake in this? Clara's the shop's favorite customer. Everything they make for her is special for *her*. If she comes to harm, they'll have her confounded trousseau on their hands, and they'll go all to pieces—because *no one* can wear those clothes as Lady Clara can." He mimicked Sophy as he said the last bit. "Not to mention they've hopes to sell her more, once they devise a scheme for disposing of Adderley."

"It's so like you to make jokes at a time like this," said Lord Valentine.

"I'm not joking—as you'd know if you were the one blackmailed and browbeaten into escorting our sister to buy her curst clothes."

"It's no joke," Sophy said. "My sisters and I want Lord Adderley out of the picture. We want your beautiful sister to marry someone with a massive income. She truly is our best customer, and we truly will go all to pieces if she can't wear the beautiful bride clothes we're making for her."

No joke. Horribly true. Truer than they could guess.

Longmore turned away from his plainly bewildered brother. "Miss Noirot, you said you wanted a description of the cabriolet. I suggest you find a pen and writing paper. I ordered that vehicle specially for her, and I recall every last detail. And if I happen to miss anything, Valentine will let us know. He believes I ought to have bought a carriage for *him*."

A short while later, the three Noirot sisters were in Sophy's bedroom, helping her pack. She'd told them about Lady Clara and her plan—such as it was—for finding her. She'd hoped they'd come up with a better solution. Hers, she felt, was far from satisfactory on numerous counts.

But Marcelline and Leonie, who saw the problems as clearly as she did, hadn't anything better to offer.

"I don't see an alternative," Marcelline said. "It's not only dangerous to her reputation to advertise this disappearance, but it's physically dangerous as well. Any number of scoundrels would start looking for her, too. She could be held for ransom—and that's the best case." She paused in the act of folding a chemise. "*Mon dieu*, her poor mother."

Marcelline had a daughter she'd nearly lost.

Twice. She knew what Lady Warford was enduring at this moment.

They all understood why the marchioness had locked herself in her daughter's room.

Lady Clara was no more than a customer, yet Sophy was sick with worry.

"Speaking of scoundrels," she said as she rolled up stockings, "I'd like to know what Adderley did to set her off."

"Does it matter?" Leonie said.

"I wish I'd known before she bolted," Sophy said. "It might be ammunition."

"You can find out when you find her," Leonie said. "And you *will* find her. You have to."

"Of course Sophy will find her," Marcelline said. "But my loves, what the devil am I to tell Clevedon? He'll be frantic. You know how dear Lady Clara is to him."

He'd lost a sister at an early age. When the Fairfax family had taken him in, Lady Clara had become a sister to him. They'd always been close. Though they'd had some turbulence a short time ago, Lady Clara had attended his wedding to Marcelline, and she seemed to have accepted them as family . . . as sisters, almost.

"Give him something to do," Sophy said. "I told Longmore I'd dispose of Adderley. But I can't be in two places at once. Ask Clevedon to find out quietly all he can about Adderley. I need as much information as I can get."

"What can Clevedon find out that isn't public knowledge, such as Adderley's gaming habits and the state of his finances?" Leonie said.

"That scene on the terrace was not one reckless act of passion," Sophy said. "I knew something was wrong. I'm positive it was planned. Adderley should have fought desperately for the woman he loved, but he let Longmore hit him, and he let Lady Clara protect him. Let Clevedon get to the bottom of it. He can find out as much over a casual game of cards as I can eavesdropping at parties and talking to demireps."

She took up the hat she planned to wear, and sat down to attach a veil to it.

"Maybe I can look more deeply into Adderley's financial affairs," Leonie said.

"You and Marcelline will have enough to do, running the shop while I'm away," Sophy said. "I'm sorry to leave everything to you."

"Don't be ridiculous," Leonie said. "You have to find her. That's the priority."

"Lady Clara's part of our family now, whether her mother likes it or not," Marcelline said. She frowned at the hat Sophy was working on. "Speaking of families, love, we need to have a little talk before you go."

Though he'd made good time crossing London after Fenwick came to summon him, it was nearly half past eight o'clock when Longmore drove his phaeton to the Gloucester Coffee House in Piccadilly. The sun was setting.

As happened every night at this time, an atmosphere of drama and excitement prevailed. The seven western mail coaches were about to depart, and everybody here was either part of the show or part of the audience.

Longmore knew that the commotion had been worse a few years ago. Then, all thirty-five Royal Mail coaches left London at the same time—eight o'clock—along with a number of stagecoaches.

While having the western coaches leave half an hour later had reduced the congestion somewhat, it did not make this an ideal time and location for meeting "Cousin Gladys." Finding a nondescript female wasn't easy in a crowd, and at this time of night, there was always a large audience watching the mail coaches' departure.

Then he noticed more than the usual flurry in one group of onlookers. Men were shoving one another out of the way, tripping over their own feet, and coming perilously close to falling under hooves and coach wheels.

In their midst stood the explanation.

Instead of her usual camouflage, Sophy this evening flaunted the latest in insane styles from Maison Noirot. The color of her dress was a muted lilac. Nothing else about it was muted. A wide collar spread out over her shoulders. Under that was another collar or cape sort of thing that reached to her elbows. Beneath it bulged sleeves the size of ale casks. Yards of black lace dripped from the collars of the dress and along the front. Green stuff meant to look like sprouting leaves sprang up from the crown of her white hat. Green bows and white lace lined the brim's interior front, framing her face—or what you could see of it, past the alluringly draped black veil.

It was completely ridiculous.

It was oddly fetching.

"By gad," he said. "By gad."

She spotted him then, and walked unhurriedly toward his carriage, hips swaying more, he thought, than altogether necessary amongst this rowdy crew. An inn servant followed, carrying her portmanteaux.

"That's her," Fenwick said from his place in the back.

"So I see," Longmore said. Before he could get down to help her, a herd of men surged toward the vehicle. One, who'd managed to shove ahead of the others into prime position, held out a hand to help her up, but Longmore leaned out and offered his. She grasped it, and his big, gloved hand nearly swallowed up her smaller one, encased in soft kid. There was the slightest pause before she sprang up into the carriage seat.

The men stood silent during this process, admiring the rear view. A sigh went up when she settled—with a great deal of tantalizing rustling—into the left section of the divided seat, and more or less disappeared under the hood.

Then two men tried to wrestle her bags from the inn servant, but he quickly heaved them up into the back, where Fenwick stowed them alongside Longmore's.

Since a riot seemed imminent, and Longmore hadn't time for one, he gave the horses leave to start. He had no choice but to fall in line behind the mail coaches.

"Not the ideal time to depart London," he said. "All the western mail coaches take the same route at the same time through Piccadilly to Hyde Park Corner. We'll have to follow them until we reach the Brompton Road. The Portsmouth coach turns off there, as we'll do."

"I prefer leaving in the middle of a busy throng," she said. "With so much going on, one set of travelers attracts less attention."

"And how did you propose not to attract attention in that rig?" he said, nodding at her attire. "Is this supposed to be a disguise?"

"Yes," she said. "I'm your newest light o' love."

He wasn't sure he'd heard aright. They were traveling on granite stones, following a long and noisy parade of vehicles. Scores of hooves clacked against the stones, chains tinkled, and wheels clattered and hummed.

He looked at her. "You're my what?"

"I'm a demirep," she said. "My sisters and I agreed that no one who knows you would think twice if they saw you with a female of dubious morals—and I'm much less likely to be recognized than you. Even the women who shop at Maison Noirot don't take much notice of our faces."

She was out of her head. No one with working vision could fail to recognize her deceptively angelic face—the very slight uptilt of her shockingly blue eyes—the pert nose—the invitingly full lips.

"We're not quite as invisible as servants, but nearly so," the lunatic went on. "Too, people tend not to recognize a person when she's outside her usual sphere. I chose this dress especially, because it makes me look very expensive—and it's more dashing than respectable Englishwomen wear. I'm a merry widow, you see." She touched the alluring veil. "And no one would find it odd if the woman with you chose to veil her face in public."

"You've appointed yourself my mistress," he said, swallowing a smile. "That's sporting of you."

"It's no sacrifice," she said. "Most of my other guises are uncomfortable and not at all pretty. Even my usual clothes aren't terribly exciting."

"By whose standards, I wonder," he said. "I recall a hat with some sort of windmill arrangement at the back and ribbons and flowers and feathers and who knew what else exploding from it."

"One can be more dashing with hats," she said. "But one can't wear this sort of ensemble in London. It frightens the customers. Marcelline's the only one who gets to wear her most daring creations, usually, because she's the one who goes to Paris. And don't forget, married women are allowed more leeway, here as well as there."

He was well aware of this fact. Men were allowed more leeway with them, too.

She wasn't a married woman, but she was a slightly French milliner. Practically the same thing.

"Even if I went to Paris, I couldn't wear quite what she does," she went on. "Unwed women there make even more of being virginal than they do here, you know. Simple frocks. Hair pulled back tight. I'm not sure what the men find appealing about that—but then . . ." She trailed off and gave a short laugh. "What do you care? What matters is, this way, no one will get over-curious about you or about me and what we're doing. The added advantage is, people will be so busy staring at my clothes, they won't pay close attention to my face."

A virgin?

She could *not* be a virgin.

It was completely impossible. With that body and that walk and—and she was a *milliner*!

"Speaking of virgins," he said, "let's talk about my sister."

According to the note she'd sent with Fenwick, Sophy had good reason to believe Clara was traveling the Portsmouth Road. Now she gave him the details. Some of Fenwick's associates had spotted the cabriolet at Hyde Park Corner. After that, the vehicle had been noticed on the Knightsbridge Road, heading for Kensington. But according to a post boy, some time later, at an inn in Fulham, a woman who looked like a bulldog had asked for the best route to Richmond Park.

"She made it appear that she was traveling to her great-aunt's house, then turned about and headed, apparently, southwest," she said. "Does Richmond Park hold any significance for her?"

"None I know of," he said. "If I'd had to guess, the only place I'd have thought of would be Bath. As a girl, Clara traveled with our paternal grandmother to Bath sometimes. The were very close. Grandmother Warford died some three years ago, and Clara took it hard. She'd always liked the old ladies, my grandmother's friends." He shook his head. "I can't think of anybody she might take refuge with in Richmond Park."

"Maybe she doesn't know where she's going," Sophy said. "Something happened and she couldn't bear whatever it was, and so she ran away. Blindly. She simply ran away."

They'd reached the Hyde Park turnpike. Unlike the mail coaches, their vehicle had to stop, and he had to pay.

He took advantage of the pause to check on Fenwick. The boy sat in the rear seat, arms folded in the approved posture for tigers, looking up at the rapidly darkening sky.

Longmore looked up, too. Thick clouds swarmed overhead. He wasn't concerned. The hood was up, and if they faced a heavy rain, he could put up the apron. The back seat hadn't a hood, but Fenwick would be all right. Olney had packed an umbrella, and Reade—deeply unhappy about being left behind—had been made to donate one of his older cloaks.

Longmore drove on, through the turnpike. They passed the White Horse Inn and the Foot Barracks.

"I don't understand what's got into my sister," he said. "She always used to be so sensible."

"Sensible but ignorant," Sophy said.

He heard a wobble in her voice. It was very slight, but he was acutely attuned to her voice, in all its changes. Sometimes, in a crowd, he knew her by her voice alone, even when she adopted one of her provincial accents.

He looked at her. She had her hand to her forehead. The veil was in place, making it impossible to read her expression, yet even he could tell she was upset.

"Now what?" he said sharply.

"She doesn't know anything," she said. "Even for a girl of one and twenty, she's lamentably naïve." She took in a deep breath and let it out.

He watched the rise and fall of her bosom. It was crass in the circumstances, he supposed, but he was a man, and it was nighttime and she was dressed like a fashionable impure.

They passed the Westbourne conduit and approached the Rural Castle Inn. The mail coaches' horns sounded. They were sending the Portsmouth coach on its separate way, down the Brompton Road. Where he'd soon follow.

"She has three brothers," he said. "She's not

that innocent. She knows what men are like. She should have known better than to encourage any of that lot of loose screws."

"A woman might think she knows about men, but until it happens—until a man touches her, she doesn't *know*."

He remembered this woman's reaction when he'd breathed down her neck.

Was it possible she didn't know what he'd assumed she knew?

But that was ridiculous. She was no schoolroom miss. She'd grown up in Paris. She was a milliner. And she walked the way she walked.

He passed Sloane Street and turned into Brompton Road. No parade of mail coaches now. Only the lone one, not very far ahead.

"Maybe that's it," she said.

"What is?"

"Maybe she's had even less experience than other girls her age. It's—what?" She counted on her gloved fingers. "A month since she told my brother-in-law to go to the devil. Only think what it's been like for her. Imagine spending most of your life assuming you'll marry one person, and then realizing he or she isn't what you want. I'm sure she felt liberated and exhilarated after rejecting the Duke of Clevedon—but afterward . . . She had to find herself. She had to do what other girls do at seventeen or eighteen, in their first Seasons."

"Yer worship!" Fenwick's high-pitched voice broke into a very difficult piece of cogitation. "I say, your highness!"

"Your *lordship*," Sophy corrected. "I explained that to you. How hard is it to remember?"

"Yer lordship!" Fenwick said more forcefully.

"You better close up the front the best you can. East wind coming about."

"What is he, a weathercock?" Longmore said.

That was when the rain started pelting down.

"Better hurry, yer majesty," the boy said. "Weather's going to turn ugly in a minute."

Chapter Seven

On Putney heath, to the south of the village, is an obelisk, erected by the corporation of London, with an inscription commemorating an experiment made, in 1776, by David Hartley, Esq., to prove the efficacy of a method of building houses fire-proof, which he had invented, and for which he obtained a grant from parliament of £2500.

—Samuel Lewis, *A Topographical Dictionary of England,*
1831

The weather did turn extremely ugly, very quickly. The wind picked up speed, driving the rain sideways at times, so that even the apron couldn't fully shield them.

Still, any driver could manage a team in rain. This weather wouldn't slow the Royal Mail, let alone stop it. Mail coach drivers continued through thunderstorms, floods, hailstorms, sleet, and blizzards. At present Longmore had only a bad rainstorm to contend with. No thunder and lightning to agitate the horses.

He drove on.

The storm drove on, too, with increasing intensity, the rain pouring straight down sometimes and at other times pelting sideways at them, depending on the gusting wind.

Though the waxing moon wouldn't set until the small hours of morning, the storm swallowed its light. Rain poured off the hood, obscuring Longmore's view of the horses as well as the road ahead. It dimmed what little light the carriage lamps threw on the road. The farther he drove, the darker grew the way ahead. He slowed and slowed again, and finally settled to a walk.

By the time they passed Queen's Elm he was driving half blind and trusting mainly to the horses to keep to the road. Luckily this was a major coaching route, wide and smooth, which lowered the odds of his driving into a ditch.

Still, he needed to keep his mind on driving. Talking was out of the question. In any case, with the rain thumping on the roof and the wind whistling about their ears, they'd have to shout to make themselves heard.

They drove on through villages distinguishable mainly thanks to the lights in a few windows. Not many lights. It was bedtime in the countryside. The inns and taverns were awake, but not much else.

He glanced to his left. Only Sophy's gloved hand, clenched on the curved arm of her seat, hinted at fear.

Though he quickly brought his gaze back to the road ahead, a part of his mind marveled at her. He couldn't think of another woman who wouldn't be shrieking or weeping right now, and begging him to stop.

He was starting to argue with himself about whether he ought to stop.

Though their creeping pace made it seem they'd

been on the road for hours, he knew they hadn't gone far. They hadn't yet crossed the Putney Bridge, and that was only four miles from Hyde Park Corner.

Through the lashing rain he made out flickering lights ahead. Gradually, he began to discern the rough outlines of houses—or what seemed to be houses. Finally they reached the quaint old double tollhouse, with its roof spanning the road. The roof diverted some of the downpour while they waited for the gatekeeper to collect his eighteen pence and open the gate. Though he wasn't inclined to prolong the encounter, he did answer Longmore's question.

Yes, he remembered the cabriolet. An exceptionally fine vehicle and a prodigy of a horse. Two women tucked under the hood. Couldn't properly make out their faces. One had asked for directions to Richmond Park.

When pressed for more detail, the gatekeeper said, "I told them to keep on this road up to the crossroads, then watch for the obelisk at the corner of Putney Heath, and go that way, rightish. I told them what to look for. It's not hard to keep to the main road, but for some reason, there's them that go astray there, and end up in Wimbledon." He hurried back into the shelter of his tollhouse.

"Richmond Park," Longmore said. He had to raise his voice to make himself heard over the wind and drumming rain. "What the devil's there?"

"I read that Richmond Park was beautiful," Sophy said.

"You think she's gone *sightseeing*?"

"I hope so. It might calm her."

He had to stop talking to negotiate the bridge.

An old, narrow, uneven structure, it bulged up unexpectedly here and there. At this time of night, in this weather, the only way to proceed was cautiously.

Caution wasn't Longmore's favorite style.

He was grinding his teeth by the time he got them safely to the other side of the Thames. Thence it was uphill to Putney Heath and the obelisk, about two miles away.

The horses trudged up the road while the rain went on thrashing them, torrents cascading from the hood's rim. The wind, howling occasionally to add atmosphere to the experience, blew the wet under the hood. It dripped down Longmore's face and into his neckcloth.

Though he knew her glorious monstrosity of a traveling costume involved layers and layers, the wet would eventually penetrate to skin, if it hadn't already.

He threw her a quick glance. She'd turned her head aside so that the back of her hat took the brunt of the wind-driven rain. That was the only sign of discomfort. Not a word of complaint.

He went on wondering at it, even while he watched the road and argued with himself what to do.

When at last they reached Putney Heath, the wind abruptly died down. In the distance a bell tolled. An ominous rumbling followed. He turned his head that way in time to see the crack of lightning.

The wind picked up again, coming from the same direction.

It was driving the thunderstorm straight at them.

* * *

Sophy was petrified.

Her heart had been pounding for so long that she was dizzy. She was terrified she'd faint and fall out of the carriage and under a wheel. If she fell, Longmore might not even notice at first, between the darkness and the rain's incessant hammering.

Safe at home, the sound of rain drumming on a roof, even as fiercely as this, could be soothing.

This was not soothing.

She was city bred. If she'd ever spent time in the country, it must have been in her early childhood. She vaguely recalled traveling across the French countryside when she and her sisters had fled cholera-ravaged Paris three years ago. But they'd traveled in a closed vehicle, and not at night in such hellish weather.

Intellectually, she knew she wasn't in any great danger. While a famously reckless man, Longmore was a highly regarded whip, too. In a carriage, one couldn't be in safer hands. He drove with the magnificent calm the English deemed *de rigueur* in whipsters. The horses seemed tranquil and absolutely under his control. Traveling on the king's highway, she knew, one could count on smooth, well-maintained roads. Hostelries lined them at short intervals. Help was rarely far away.

All the same, she didn't feel very brave.

She'd started out concerned mainly about Lady Clara. The difficulties of travel, even at night, hadn't crossed Sophy's mind. For one thing, at this time of year, a sort of twilight prevailed rather than full darkness. For another, this evening had promised to be a pleasant one: When she set out from home for the Gloucester Coffee

House, she'd assumed the moon would brighten their journey.

Instead, within minutes they were pitched into a streaming Stygian darkness, which feeble lights here and there only seemed to emphasize. The world about her felt too empty.

Breaking in on an unexpected silence, the crack of thunder, distant as it was, made her jump. Longmore's head turned sharply that way, and in the faint glow of the carriage lights, she saw his jaw muscles tighten.

He turned to her. "Are you all right?" he said.

"Yes," she lied.

"The horses won't be, in a thunderstorm," he said. "I've decided not to chance it. With a broken neck you won't be much help to my sister. We'll have to stop."

She was only half relieved. As alarming as she found it to travel at present, she was impatient at delay. Back in London, after Fenwick had reported what his friends had told him about the cabriolet, she'd looked up Richmond Park in a road guide. It wasn't very far from London. Still, near as it was, if even Longmore didn't want to risk traveling on, no sane person would try it.

Though they seemed to be crossing an endless uninhabited wilderness, it wasn't long before he turned into the yard of an inn. White flashes lit the sky, and the thunder rumbled oftener and more loudly, nearer at hand.

While the ostlers rushed out to take charge of the horses, Longmore practically dragged her from her seat and swept her along under his arm to the entrance, calling over his shoulder, "Look after the boy. If he isn't drowned, dry him off and see that he's fed."

A short time later, she was shaking off the wet from her carriage dress, and Longmore was treating the landlord with the same imperious impatience he'd shown Dowdy and her accomplice: "Yes, two rooms. My aunt requires her own. And you'd better send a maid to her."

"Your aunt?" Sophy said after the landlord had hurried away to see about rooms.

Amusement lit Longmore's dark eyes and a tiny smile lifted the corners of his mouth. "I always travel with my aunt, don't you know? Such a dutiful nephew. Luckily, I've scads of them."

That was all it took: one rakish glint in his dark eyes and a ghost of a smile. Her heart gave a skip and pumped heat upward and outward and especially downward. She had to fight with herself not to rush to the nearest window and pull it open, storm or no storm. She needed a sharp dose of cold water.

She told herself to settle down. He'd used that look on hundreds of women, probably, with the same effect. And she was a Noirot. She was the one who was supposed to slay men with a glance.

In any event, she supposed she ought to be glad he owned at least a modicum of discretion.

As *fille de joie* euphemisms went, "aunt" was probably more useful than "wife." Half the world would probably recognize him, and that half would know he wasn't wed or likely to be anytime soon, if ever.

He took out his pocket watch. "This is ridiculous. We haven't covered eight miles and it's nearly half past ten o'clock."

"She wouldn't travel in this weather, surely?" Sophy said in a low voice, though they were alone in the small office. "If she did visit the park, wouldn't she stop at an inn nearby when it grew dark?"

"I hope so," he said. "But who knows what's in her mind?"

"She has Davis," Sophy said. "She wouldn't let her mistress endanger herself."

"Clara can be obstinate," he said. "My hope is the horse. Wherever she tries to go, she'll have the devil of a time changing horses. The cabriolet only wants one, but it needs a powerful one. Inns reserve those for the mail and stage coaches. She'll probably find it easier to keep the one she set out with. Which means she'll need to stop at intervals—and stay for a good while—to give the creature food and drink and rest."

Sophy knew little about the care of horses. She and her sisters had had enough to do in learning not only their trade but a lady of leisure's accomplishments as well. This was no small feat for girls who had precious little leisure. But it was unthinkable merely to learn a trade. While the DeLuceys and Noirots might all be greater or lesser rogues and criminals, they never forgot they were blue bloods. Too, they knew that refined accents and manners vastly improved the odds of luring unsuspecting ladies and gentlemen into their nets.

Learning dressmaking and learning to be a lady—not to mention acquiring other less virtuous Noirot and DeLucey skills—left no time for the finer points of horsemanship. Sophy could distinguish general types of vehicle, and she could appreciate a handsome horse, but for the rest she had to trust Longmore's judgment.

"I think I'll send Fenwick to insinuate himself among the stablemen," he said with a glance at the door through which their host had departed. "They'll have noticed the cabriolet if it passed, or they'll have heard about it from post boys. We'll get more detailed gossip from them than from any tollgate keepers."

The innkeeper reappeared then, a plump maidservant following. While she led Sophy up to her room, Longmore stayed behind, talking to the landlord.

Meanwhile, less than ten miles away, in Esher's Bear Inn, Lady Clara sat by the fire, studying her copy of *Paterson's Roads*.

"Portsmouth," she told Davis. "We're already on the road, and it's only a day's journey." She calculated. "Not sixty miles."

"It's not twenty miles back to London, my lady," Davis said.

"I'm not going back," Clara said. "I won't go back to *him*."

"My lady, this isn't wise."

"I'm not wise!" Clara jumped up from her chair, the guidebook clattering to the floor. "I declined a duke because he didn't love me enough. Poor Clevedon! He at least *liked* me."

"My lady, everybody who knows you loves you."

"Not Adderley," Clara said bitterly. "How could I be so blind? But I was. I believed all those romantic words he'd taken out of books."

"Some gentlemen can't express themselves," Davis said.

"I'd almost got myself to believe that," Clara said. "But that wasn't the point, was it? That wasn't

the real problem. How humiliating that I needed
Lady Bartham to point out the simple fact: If he'd
truly loved and respected me, he would never have
done what he did."

Her ladyship hadn't said it quite so baldly as
that. But Lady Bartham never insulted or hurt anybody plainly and honestly. She'd slither about the
subject like a snake, and every so often, when you
weren't expecting it, she'd dart at you, tiny fangs
sinking in, so tiny you barely felt them . . . until a
moment later, when the poison seeped in.

There was a moment's silence, then, "Portsmouth is a naval town, my lady. Very rough. Sailors and brothels and—"

"It's near," Clara said. "It's a port. I can get on
a ship and sail far away. It can't be so very dangerous. People go there to tour and sightsee. I'm
ruined. Why shouldn't I see the world? I haven't
even seen England! Where do I ever go? To our
place in Lancashire and back to London and back
to Lancashire. Since Grandmamma Warford died,
I don't go anywhere. She used to take me away, and
we had such fun." She swallowed. She still missed
her grandmother. No one could take her place.
Clara had never felt more in need of her counsel
than now.

"She used to drive her own carriage, you know,"
she went on, though Davis knew perfectly well.
But Clara needed to talk, and her maid wouldn't
shriek at her, as Mama did. "She was an excellent whip. We'd drive out to Richmond Park and
visit her friends there." They would go out to Richmond Park and Hampton Court for a day's outing.

Clara had driven to the park today, hoping
somehow her grandmother's spirit would find her,

and tell her what to do. She'd left the park no wiser, and gone on to Hampton Court. None of Grandmamma's wisdom came to her there, either, and even a living person, Grandmamma's great friend, Lady Durwich, had no advice but for her to turn back and stop being such a ninny.

Clara wasn't sure where she was going. To Portsmouth, to start with. After that . . . somewhere, anywhere. But not back to London. Not back to *him*.

Sophy's room was small but clean, and the maidservant was as eager to please as Sophy expected her to be. People of every social degree judged by externals. While an upper-class accent and fine clothes were sure to win attentive service, generous tips and bribes could raise the quality of service to unadulterated obsequiousness.

Not only was Sophy expensively dressed but she had ready money. Marcelline had made Leonie provide funds for tips and bribes, and Sophy wasn't stingy with her coin. She wanted supper and a fire and a bath and she was happy to pay for them.

She got all three quickly, without fuss, despite the hour and the sudden influx of storm refugees.

As it turned out, she was in too much turmoil, about Lady Clara and about the shop, to do more than pick at supper. Since she was, at the best of times, a light sleeper, she knew she was in no state to attempt sleeping until after she'd had a bath. That would quiet her. Certainly she'd feel better once she washed the ghastly egg mixture out of her hair. She'd brought her favorite soap, scented with lavender and rosemary.

Though the inn servants had brought a very

small tub, she'd bathed under more primitive conditions. And no, it wasn't the easiest thing to wash her hair without help, but she managed it.

And so, in time, thanks to the hair washing and the bathing and the soothing scent of her soap—and a glass of wine—the turmoil began to abate.

She donned her nightgown, wrapped herself in her dressing gown, poured another glass of wine, and settled into a chair near the fire to dry her hair.

The old inn's walls were thick. She heard little of what passed outside her own room. The thunder grew more distant as the storm traveled on. The rain continued, beating against the window, but now that she was safe and dry indoors, the sound soothed her. She'd always liked the sound of rain.

She remembered rainy days in Paris, and the misty rain last week, when she'd strolled up St. James's Street to lure Lord Longmore from his lair. While pretending to be gazing elsewhere, she'd watched him saunter across the street to her . . . such long legs in his beautifully tailored trousers . . . the finely cut coat, sculpted to his upper body, emphasizing his broad shoulders and lean torso . . . the snowy white neckcloth tied with elegant simplicity under his strong chin . . . he moved with the easy grace of a man completely at home in his body and completely sure of himself . . . such an odd combination he was . . . part dandy, part ruffian . . . so tall and athletic . . . she'd like to be his tailor . . . oh, she'd like to fit him in something snug . . . no harm in dreaming . . .

. . . What was burning?

Longmore tried not to think about his sister, out in the storm.

She wouldn't be out in the storm, he told himself. She wasn't that stupid. Even if she was, Davis wouldn't stand for it.

But wherever Clara was, he wasn't likely to catch up anytime soon. And wherever she was, he couldn't protect her.

While his mind painted ugly scenes featuring his sister in the clutches of villains, he wasn't altogether unaware of what passed in the next room. He'd caught the muffled sound of voices when Sophy talked to the maid, and the tramp of feet in the room and a thump of something heavy being set down and then the splashing.

She was taking a bath.

That was a much more agreeable image than the ones of his sister in peril.

He told himself that worrying about Clara wasn't going to help her, and it would only wear on his nerves, already frayed after the slog through the storm.

He had another bottle of wine sent up and he gave his coat to the inn servant for drying and brushing.

Since his trousers were still damp, he drew a chair up before the fire. There he sat, drinking.

By degrees, he grew calmer. Clara might be out of her head, but she wouldn't endanger her horse, he reminded himself. She'd have taken shelter. She'd go to a respectable inn because Davis wouldn't let her go into one that wasn't—and respectable inns lined the Portsmouth Road.

The wine and more optimistic thoughts calmed him enough to make him grow drowsy. He was putting his booted feet up onto the fender when Sophy screamed.

He sprang from the chair to the door between their rooms. He yanked the handle. It wouldn't open. He stepped back a pace and kicked.

The door flew open, crashing against the wall.

She was making little sounds of distress and dancing about and trying to pull off her dressing gown. Smoke rose from the hem. He saw a tiny flame lick upward.

In two quick strides he reached her, ripped the ties she'd been struggling with, pulled the dressing gown off her, and threw it into the bathtub.

"Oh!" she said. "Oh!"

"Are you all right?" he said. Without waiting for an answer, he turned her around, his heart racing while he looked for signs of incipient fire. He spied some brown spots and holes at the bottom of the garment, but no signs of active burning.

"What the devil were you doing?" He turned her around again. Though festooned with frills—at the neck and wrists and down the front opening—her nightdress was a flimsy nothing. Tissue-thin muslin . . . through which one could easily make out the outlines of her . . . naked . . . body.

A haze entered his mind. He shook it off. No time for that now.

No rushing fences. Not the time and place.

A part of his mind said, *Why not?*

He ignored it. "Are you drunk?" he demanded. "Did you fall in the fire?"

Someone beat on the door to the passage. "Madam! Madam!"

She ran to her portmanteau and began rummaging.

Longmore strode to the passage door and

yanked it open. An inn servant stood there. "What the devil do you want?"

"Sir—your lordship—I beg your pardon—but someone screamed—and one of the guests smelled smoke."

Sophy drew on a shawl. "Yes, I screamed," she said. "I thought I saw a bat."

"A bat, madam? But the smoke?" The servant sniffed. "I do smell smoke."

The fellow was trying to peer round Longmore, who advanced to the threshold to block his ogling half-naked females who didn't belong to him.

"That was the bat," Longmore said. "I caught it and threw it into the fire. Do you fancy a bite? It's not quite cooked through, I'm afraid. No? Well, then, off with you."

He shut the door in the servant's face.

He turned back to Sophy, whose most interesting parts the shawl now enveloped.

At first, he'd checked mainly to see whether she was on fire. After that he'd discovered how flimsy her nightdress was. Now he noticed that her hair was damp, streaming down her shoulders. It fell over her breasts. It was long and thick. In places, long tendrils had started to dry, and as they did, they were brightening from a pale brown to gold . . . and they were curling. All by themselves.

His breathing quickened, and that instantly got his breeding organs excited.

Not now.

Why not?

"What the devil happened?" he said. He spotted the wine bottle on the little table near the fire. "How much have you had to drink?"

"I'm not drunk!" she said. "I—I was too agitated to sleep. I had a bath."

"I heard," he said.

Her eyes widened.

"I would have looked through the keyhole," he said, "but that method isn't all it's cracked up to be. One can only see a small part of the room, usually, and in my experience, it's the wrong part. In any event, I was by the fire, drying out, and it seemed a great bother to leave the warmth and the bottle to crouch at a door, all for the chance of not seeing much."

She looked at the doorway between their rooms, then at the bathtub, then at him.

"You didn't think it was worth the *bother*?" she said.

He shrugged. "I don't know what came over me. And I still don't know how you proceeded from being wet to being on fire."

There was a pause, then she said, "I not only bathed, but I washed my hair to get that nasty egg mixture out. It was getting rancid. I was sure if I put my head on the pillow, any vermin in the vicinity would come running to feast on it."

"It wasn't that bad," he said.

"You say so because it wasn't on *your* head," she said. "And so I washed my hair. And then I had to dry it at the fire, didn't I? Which is what I was doing. But I must have dozed—and when I woke, my dressing gown was burning. I must have slumped in the chair and got too close, and a spark caught it. And then I couldn't get the stupid ties undone, to get the blasted thing off." She blinked hard. "Thank you for saving me. I'm sorry I caused so much t-trouble."

"Well, it was exciting," he said.

"I don't like to be exciting in th-that w-way," she said.

"Good gad, you're not going to cry, are you?" he said. "You can't be upset because I ruined your dressing gown?"

"N-no. Of c-course n-not."

"Because I didn't look through the keyhole?"

"Don't be r-ridiculous."

"Then what are you crying about?"

"I'm not crying!" She blinked again. "I'm perfectly well."

"No, you're not."

"Yes, I am. It's only . . . I keep thinking I should have stayed with your sister when she came to the shop last Saturday. I told you we'd deal with Adderley, but I didn't tell her. I had other things on my mind. Your mother. And Dowdy's. And now . . . it seems my priorities were wrong."

"What rot. You didn't know Clara was going to act like an idiot."

"I wasn't paying attention! And now she's in danger. She hasn't the slightest idea how to survive. She wouldn't know a scoundrel if he wore a badge announcing it. She trusted Adderley, of all men! I should have done something!"

"What are you talking about? What could you have done?"

She waved her arms. "Something. A diversion."

He stomped back to her, grasped her shoulders, and gave her a little shake. "Stop it," he said.

"I'm so worried," she said.

He took her face in his hands and tilted it up so that he could look down into her eyes. They were filling. It was like looking into the Adriatic Sea through a mist. A tiny bead of moisture trickled down the side of her nose. Her lower lip jutted out in a pout. It trembled.

It wasn't the time and place.

He oughtn't to rush his fences.

But she'd waved her arms, and that made her womanly parts jiggle and he could only keep one idea in his head at a time, and in any case, *oughts* never went down smoothly with him.

He was who he was, and that wasn't a good boy. And so down he went, and crushed her sulky little mouth under his.

He'd never done things by halves. He wasn't likely to start now.

He kissed her firmly, fearlessly, recklessly, the way he did everything. It never occurred to him to be cautious.

Not much occurred to him, in fact. He simply did it, in the way he did everything, without thinking or worrying.

And then he walked off a cliff.

Down he went, as though there were a sea below, and he was falling straight into it.

He was falling into her somehow. He tasted the sea—a hint of salt tears—and there was a hint of the wine she'd drunk, too. He breathed in the fresh scent of her. Where he was sinking, the world was warm. Lavender and something else scented the air and the scent brought back a moment: the sun of Tuscany and a villa framed in lavender and jasmine. He felt the same inexplicable, soaring happiness he'd felt a few years ago, far away from England.

He wrapped his arms about her. It was instinctive to hold on to something too wonderful to understand.

And her mouth simply melted under his, so soft and welcoming. Her body melted against him, too, as though it was the most natural thing in the world. Her arms came up and wrapped about his neck. Her breasts pressed against his waistcoat. She was so warm and so softly curved and he was warm and warmer still, his pulse racing while he drank in more deeply: the sweetness of her mouth and the clean scent of her and the way her soft curves fit against him.

He slid his hands down and grasped her bottom and pressed her close—and she made a choked little sound against his mouth—and small as it was, it was a jolt, and all the signal he needed.

He lifted his hands away from her bottom.

He lifted his mouth from hers.

He took one unsteady step back, and another.

Her great blue eyes were dazed, and she swayed a little. The shawl lay in a puddle on the floor.

"My goodness," she said breathlessly. "My goodness."

She tipped her head to one side and studied him in the manner of a drunk trying to focus.

Hell.

It was her first time.

She'd never been kissed before.

That was completely impossible.

No, it wasn't.

Yes, it was.

Never mind. There was nothing for it but to bluster his way out of it, whatever it was.

"Don't," he said. "Do. That. Again."

"Yes," she said with a dazed little smile.

"I can't abide hysterics," he said firmly.

"Yes," she said.

He was dizzy, too, but he could see her clearly enough. He could see far too much of her . . . or not nearly enough. He could see the bed as well, only a few steps away, so inviting.

Well, then, why not accept the invitation?

Because . . . he didn't know why. Or why not.

He turned his back, on her, on the bed, on everything, and stomped out.

In a kind of haze, Sophy watched him go.

She watched *all* of him go: his black hair disheveled as though he'd dragged his fingers through it—or had she done that? . . . the broad shoulders and the motion of his shoulder blades under the waistcoat . . . the muscles of his arms, tantalizingly visible under the fine linen of his shirt . . . the back of his waist and the upside down V of the waistcoat where it gathered at the base of his spine . . . and on down over his hips and the long legs . . . and all of that big body moving so smoothly and as gracefully as a thoroughbred.

He walked to the door and closed it behind him, with a sharp thud that made her jump, and jolted her out of the daze.

She shook her head. She closed her eyes and opened them. She drew her tongue over her lips . . . the way he had done.

She moved to the table, refilled her wineglass, and drank it down in a gulp to strengthen her resolve.

She marched to the door connecting their rooms and pushed it open.

He froze, a wineglass halfway to his mouth. That wicked, dangerous mouth.

"No," she said. "Absolutely not."

"What are you saying?" he said. "Are you insane?"

"I was for a minute," she said. "But you can't do that again. You can't be such an idiot."

"Go away," he said. "Do you know you've almost no clothes on?"

"Never mind. I need—"

"*Never mind*? Listen to me, Miss Innocence. There are many things a man can 'never mind.' A nearly naked woman isn't one of them."

"*Taut pis!*" she said. "There wasn't time to dress. I have to say it while I know why I'm saying it, while I'm still under the influence."

He dragged his hand through his tangled hair. "You don't have to say anything. You have to go away."

"I can*not* get involved with customers," she said. "It's bad for business."

"Business!"

"And do *not* tell me you're not a customer."

"I'm not, you nitwit. When was the last time I bought a dress?"

"Any man who has the means to pay our bills is likely to acquire, sooner or later, a woman we want in our dress shop," she said. "She won't patronize us if we have a reputation for poaching the men."

"Business," he said. "This is about the *shop*."

"Yes," she said. "Which means I couldn't be more serious. If you kiss me again, I'll stab you."

She turned and marched out, slamming the door behind her.

She poured herself another glass of wine, but this one she drank more slowly. Her heart was pounding so hard it hurt. She couldn't remember when last she'd done something so difficult and terrifying and so completely the opposite of what she wanted to do.

No wonder Marcelline had lost her head over Clevedon.

No wonder she'd insisted on explaining to Sophy, for the hundredth time, how babies were made.

Lust was a dangerous force.

Like any Noirot, Sophy liked danger, risk, a gamble.

But she could not, would not, gamble with Maison Noirot. If she let the dangerous force sweep her away, it would sweep away everything they'd worked and suffered for.

She rose, walked to the bathtub, and took out the dressing gown he'd drowned there. She wrung it out and draped it over the chair—near the fire but not too near. It wasn't completely unsalvageable. The girls at the Milliners' Society could take it apart and make something of it.

The dressing gown wasn't important. It was the shop Sophy needed to save—and that meant saving Lady Clara. That was all she had to do, and it wasn't going to be easy.

She smiled. But she was a Noirot, after all, and if it were easy, it wouldn't be much fun.

Chapter Eight

Richmond-park is eight miles in circumference, and contains 2253 acres, of which scarcely one hundred are in this parish; there are 650 acres in Mortlake, 265 in Petersham, 230 in Putney, and the remainder in Kingston. The ground of this park is pleasingly diversified with hill and vale; it is ornamented also with a great number of very fine oaks and other plantations.

—Daniel Lysons, *The Environs of London*, 1810

Warford House
Saturday 6 June

"Well?" Adderley said. "It's nothing . . . serious, I trust?"

Clara was as healthy as a horse. A cow. She was anything but weak or sickly.

"We hope it isn't," Lord Valentine said. "She might have caught a chill last night, at Great-Aunt Dora's. Drafty old house. Wet night."

"A chill," Adderley said. He felt chilled, too. Gloom hung in the air of Warford House today.

More than the usual gloom, that was to say.

He'd found the atmosphere frigid at best. Toward him Lady Warford had been strictly polite while contriving to look as though she smelled something good manners did not permit her to mention. Clara had started out warm enough—or as warm as she knew how—but had grown a little more distant every day.

Not that their feelings mattered. Clara had to marry him, and everybody knew it. They might kick all they wanted, and Lady Warford might lose no opportunity to remind him—with scrupulous politeness—of his low origins, but he was not going to go away, and they couldn't let him go away.

The one thing he hadn't reckoned on was Clara's falling ill.

Gravely ill, judging by the signs.

Lord Valentine's face was positively funereal.

Alarm stirred in Adderley's gut.

She couldn't die. Not before the wedding.

"Is there anything I can do?" he said.

Lord Valentine shook his head sadly. "Sorry. Nothing to be done. Our mother is with her. Hasn't left her bedside."

"You've sent for a physician, of course?"

"I assure you, my sister is being well looked after. I daresay she'll be right as a trivet in a day or two."

Lord Valentine did not say this with much conviction.

Anxious and angry, Adderley left.

He'd devoted months to cultivating her. Months he could have devoted to someone else.

She'd better not die.

It would be deuced inconvenient. He knew of no other well-dowered female who'd be nearly so easy to win over. And he'd have to win the alternate over in a hurry. His creditors wouldn't even wait until the funeral.

By the time they were seated in the carriage again, Longmore was wondering what had possessed him last night, not to take advantage of a perfect opportunity.

It was the surprise, he decided. He'd been completely taken aback to discover Sophy was so inexperienced.

Normally, he rebounded quickly from shocks. But it had been a trying day. His sister had bolted, and it was the first time in years he'd needed to worry about her. Then Sophy had set herself on fire.

No wonder his wits had scattered.

After some tossing and turning—no doubt on account of his parts getting all primed for a woman for nothing—he'd slept well enough. The day had dawned fair. And his wits were back in working order. He could see the thing clearly now.

Perhaps she wasn't greatly experienced. That didn't mean she'd had none. She was French. She had taste. She was simply a discriminating girl who hadn't had much practice in the amorous arts.

Someone was going to advance her education, one of these days. Why shouldn't it be him?

True, he'd never had to teach anybody before, but there was a first time for everything, and he was always open to new experiences.

True, too, she'd told him to keep off.

But that was *after*.

Until he'd made the imbecile mistake of returning to his room, she'd been enthusiastic enough.

She'd greeted him cheerfully at breakfast today.

He saw nothing sulky or subdued in her appearance, certainly.

Today's fashion extravaganza was a greyish-pinkish traveling dress. One of those capelike things women doted on these days spread itself over stupendously swollen sleeves. At the neck of the capelike item fluttered a collar of white lace, below which marched the line of bows, all the way down the front of the cape, which ended in a point below her waist—as though a man needed any directions there. The bows continued down two sides of the skirt, along an inverted V—yes, pointing to the same area. Today's hat sported flowers all around the inner brim that framed her face, and more flowers sprouting up from the back. Green ribbons quivered among the flowers.

It made a man giddy, simply looking at it.

He preferred her mostly naked, but this was certainly entertaining.

Since the prospect of searching Richmond Park lay ahead of them, entertainment was sorely needed.

They'd scarcely left the inn when Fenwick, at the back of the carriage, started sniffing loudly.

Longmore glanced back. "You'd better not be sickening," he said. "We haven't time to nurse chills."

"I was only smelling somefing," Fenwick said.

Longmore scowled at him.

"Some*th*ing," Fenwick said. "What's that smell?"

"What smell?" Longmore said. The only scent he was aware of was Sophy's lavender and the something else that underlay it. He doubted that

Fenwick, from his seat well behind the folded-down hood and the pile of luggage, could detect a fragrance that was more not there than there.

"I believe he means the air," Sophy said. "That's country air you smell, Fenwick." She inhaled deeply, and her bosom rose and fell. It was easy to ascertain the degree of rise and fall because of the bows.

Undoing them was definitely something to look forward to.

What Sophy saw of Richmond Park appeared beautiful. Although city bred, she could understand the appeal of a broad expanse of nature, and this was an immense area, some five times as large as Hyde Park, Longmore had told her. She could easily imagine Lady Clara looking out from the summit of a hill and seeing London, a haze hanging over it, stretching out in the distance. She would feel she was a safe distance away from her troubles.

But she wasn't safe. She hadn't the first idea how to look after herself, and one maid wasn't enough.

Since it wouldn't help matters to let the world know an innocent was on the loose, the search team had to be careful what they said when questioning people. To avoid giving anybody else ideas of looking for Lady Clara, they'd devised a simple story: The cabriolet's driver had left behind at an inn her pocketbook, containing a little money and some papers, and they were trying to return it.

They didn't attempt to search the park itself. That would take days, Longmore said. Instead, they asked at the various hostelries near the gates. Even so, hours passed, and they'd made nearly a complete circuit of the park, as well as a detour to Richmond Hill, before they learned anything.

It was mid afternoon when they finally found an inn where Clara had stopped. There she'd asked for the best route to Hampton Court Palace.

"So much for hoping she'd return to London," Longmore said, when they were on their way once more.

"At least we have news," Sophy said.

"Yes. Back to the Portsmouth Road we go— after a prodigious wild goose chase. When I get my hands on her—"

"It's so easy for you," she said.

"Easy? What the devil do you mean?"

"If somebody offends or insults you, you punch him or call him out. If you're wronged, you can act. What can your sister do?"

"She isn't supposed to do anything. She's a girl."

"So she should simply endure? Has it occurred to you how humiliated she must feel? I'll wager anything her so-called friends have been slyly tormenting her. How is she to strike back? It's impossible. Meanwhile, she's painfully aware that all the men who once admired and respected her now think she's a dirty joke. Can you imagine how that feels?"

"*Feelings*," he said in that mocking tone that made her want to punch him.

"Yes, feelings," she said. "Why not? She can't hit back. She can't make them stop. It must have been horrible for her. And so she ran away. It was that or run mad, I don't doubt. I'm worried about her, and I wish she hadn't done it—but I have to admire her risking everything, rather than passively suffering."

There was a long pause. She didn't try to fill it, only looked straight ahead, waiting for her ire to die down.

Insensitive clodpoll. She knew she'd wasted her breath, but really it was too much—

"You admire her," he said.

"Yes," she said. "She was brave."

"Reckless is more like it. Stupidly reckless."

"Like her brother."

Another pause.

"You have a point," he said.

The rant was a surprise, and it wasn't the only one.

Longmore still hadn't fully digested her astonishing speech about Clara when, a while later, as they were crossing the Thames again, Sophy spotted the old palace.

"Oh, how wonderful!" she cried out. "Oh, look!" She laughed, a throaty sound that tickled his ears and set off odd, warm feelings in his chest.

"I was about to say that Lucie would love this," she said, "but I must be six years old, too, to be so excited."

He looked at the sprawling building and back at her. "You've never seen Hampton Court Palace before?"

"When would I?" she said, still smiling. "My world's been London, for three years. I'll admit, it's seemed large and interesting enough for me. But I've never been outside it."

This was another Sophy altogether, an almost childlike Sophy. She practically bounced in her seat with excitement.

"No river jaunts?" he said.

"I own a *shop*," she said. "It's open six days a week. We're at work from nine to nine."

She worked longer than that, he realized: into the night and early morning, spying for Tom Foxe.

No time for pleasure jaunts into the country.

He'd never thought of that. Why should he? He'd never worked. He knew nothing about it.

Didn't know much about his sister, either, apparently.

That was another surprise. He wasn't sure his brain could contain any more of them.

"It's odd, isn't it?" she said.

It certainly was.

"I've only to step out of the shop and look down St. James's Street to see St. James's Palace," she said. "I know it's from Tudor times as well. But it's got buildings and streets around it. Carriages going back and forth. Omnibuses and carts and such. To me, it's merely another building. It's more or less the same with the other palaces. They all look grand enough but"—she made a sweeping gesture—"this sprawls over the countryside. It *looks* like a castle."

"It's one of the more decrepit ones," Longmore said. "For ages none of our monarchs have wanted to live here. Not the present king. Not the last one or the one before. It's bachelors and spinsters and war heroes' widows . . ." He trailed off as comprehension dawned, finally.

Richmond Park. Hampton Court. Of course.

"Spinsters and widows?" Sophy said.

"In the grace and favor apartments," he said. "Awarded to those who've served the Crown in some special way. Or whose fathers or husbands or brothers did. It's mainly single women, mostly elderly. And I know why Clara came here."

Though Longmore hadn't called on his grandmother's crony in a while, the palace officers recognized him. Yesterday they'd recognized his sister, too, as they quickly let him know, volunteering the information before he had to ask.

They must be wondering why Lady Durwich was so popular with the Fairfax family in recent days. Longmore let them wonder. He hurried Sophy through the maze of passages toward the grace and favor apartment Lady Durwich had occupied for the last twenty-five years.

That was to say, he tried to hurry Sophy. She wanted to gawk at the quaint old turrets and such and peer down passages into the courtyard. It was like trying to lead a child along.

"One would think you'd never seen a lot of crumbling Tudor brick before," he said.

"I own a *shop*," she said.

"Right," he said. "Six days. Nine to nine."

"Sometimes one of us would take Lucie to the zoo or to Astley's Amphitheater or to a fair or such. But we've never made a day's jaunt outside of London. This is so interesting. Lucie would love it."

"Well, then, Clevedon ought to take her sometime while the rest of you are blowing up your competition," Longmore said. "Today we haven't time for a tour. I'll take you at another time. There are some fine paintings and statues, and the gardens are agreeably odd. But for now, the only sight for us is Lady Durwich."

"I understand," she said.

"Don't play any parts," he said. "For this you have to be yourself."

"A dressmaker?" she said.

"Lady Durwich is a thousand years old," he said. "I doubt there's anything left on earth that can shock her. Still, I'm an old-fashioned fellow—"

"Backward, I'd say."

"And a little shy—"

"That's the first thing I noticed about you," she said. "Your shyness. When you burst into the Duke of Clevedon's house ranting about—"

"Quite shy, in fact about introducing you to my grandmother's friend as my *chère amie*—most especially when you're not." A fraction of a pause. "Yet."

"And never will be, but I can pretend so beautifully you'll believe it's true," she said.

"The point is, I can't deal with her and an imaginary female at the same time."

She considered. "You're right," she said.

Not very long thereafter, a manservant ushered them into Lady Durwich's drawing room.

The dear old thing had acquired a few more wrinkles and shrunk somewhat, but she was remarkably well preserved, considering she was in the region of ninety. She'd always been the plump, comfortable sort, not in the least high-strung— the antithesis of his mother—and today she was as well-groomed as always. Once upon a time, she and Grandmother Warford had formed, with the Dowager Countess of Hargate and some others, one of London's most dashing sets.

"Longmore, I haven't seen you this age," she

said, putting out her plump, beringed hand, which he gallantly kissed. "Your family has been unusually busy visiting lately. Clara yesterday. But that's why you've come, of course. She told me she'd bolted, the silly chit. I told her to go straight home. What nonsense! 'Doesn't love him,' she says. She should have thought of that before she went out to the terrace and allowed him to take liberties. Really, I was amazed. I always thought Clara had more sense—" Her sharp brown gaze fell on Sophy. "But who's this?"

The old lady took up her quizzing glass and made a slow inventory of his companion, from the top of the ridiculous hat to the toes of her stunningly impractical silk half-boots. "Looks familiar—but not one of you, I know. No Fairfax, this one."

"No, indeed, Lady Durwich. Please allow me to present Miss Noirot, a famous dressmaker."

Sophy sank into an excessive curtsey, exactly like the one she'd treated Valentine to—ribbons and bows fluttering and flowers quivering.

"My, my, one seldom sees that anymore," said Lady Durwich as Sophy rose. "A dressmaker, is it? What do you call that color, Miss Noirot?"

"*Cendre de rose*, my lady."

"Pink ash?" he said.

Both women gave him the same what-a-moron look.

"Miss Noirot is Clara's dressmaker," Longmore said. "She's deeply worried about Clara's trousseau."

"Stop talking rubbish," said the old lady. "I know it's difficult for you, but make an effort. I haven't a great deal of time left to waste—ten or twenty years at most. Perhaps it would be better to let the young woman speak for herself." She let the quizzing glass fall to her lap and bent a bright, expectant gaze upon Sophy.

"Not to put too fine a point on it, my lady, it occurred to me that Lord Longmore, for all his many fine qualities—"

"Oh, you've discovered some, have you?" he said.

"For all his many fine qualities," Sophy went on, with a little toss of her head, which set the ribbons fluttering. "For instance, a prodigious uppercut, an air of command, and excellent tailoring. These are merely a few examples. In these and many other matters, one cannot fault his lordship. However, I believe it is not unreasonable to declare him less than overburdened with the gifts of tact and persuasion. I strongly suspect Lady Clara will need a good deal of persuasion."

"You may well think so," said Lady Durwich. "I began to believe she was all about in the attic."

A maidservant entered then, with tea. A hiatus followed, while Lady Durwich performed as hostess. Though they had no time to lose, Longmore supposed that the lady didn't often have guests—or young ones, at any rate. Though he was wild to get his information and be gone, he knew it would be churlish to hurry matters.

The trouble was, she found Sophy much more interesting than Clara's difficulties. And no wonder, with Sophy pouring on the charm.

When Lady Durwich, making small talk over tea and sandwiches, asked if she'd toured the palace before, Sophy instantly reverted from sophisticated French milliner to excited English girl.

"Lord Longmore could barely get me to move

along," she said. "I kept stopping and gaping like the veriest child. How wonderful it must be for you, to live here. I hadn't realized anybody did—that is, apart from the staff, you know."

"Good heavens, where has the girl been?" said Lady Durwich. "You'd never heard of the grace and favor apartments?"

"Miss Noirot lived in Paris until quite recently," Longmore said. "She's rather French."

"My parents were English," Sophy said. "But yes, I spent the better part of my growing-up time in Paris. I'm a city bumpkin, you see."

"Miss Noirot has told me this is the first time she's ever been so far from London since she came," Longmore said.

"And now that I've seen the countryside, I wonder at Lady Clara's temerity, in driving out on her own," Sophy said. "The roads are all well enough, but one must stop to eat, and deal with ostlers and such. One must pay the tolls at the gates, and be careful not to make a wrong turning. It isn't at all like traveling about London. She must have felt desperate, indeed, to run away."

"She always was a headstrong girl," Lady Durwich said. "People think she isn't."

"The angelic beauty," Longmore said. "Her beaus write the most idiotish poems about her. Don't know her at all."

"They underestimate her," Sophy said. "Because she's so beautiful, they think she can't have any brains."

"She's a woman," Longmore said. "What does she need brains for?"

"For dealing with men who haven't any," Sophy said. "It isn't easy." She reverted to Lady Durwich.

"Perhaps, my lady, if you would tell me as much as you can recall of your conversation, we might find a clue to her intentions."

This was going to take forever.

Longmore left his chair, and went to the window. Since the apartment comprised an extensive set of rooms on the ground floor, and this window looked north into the court through which they'd come, he hadn't much of a view to distract him: a cobblestone walkway below and rose brick walls climbing another three stories and blocking the daylight.

Old ladies were garrulous and forgetful. They rarely told a tale in its proper order, instead taking detours here, there, and everywhere. In a few hours the light would be gone. Still, he and Sophy could travel by night, as long as the weather didn't betray them again.

He listened as well as he could to the women's conversation.

No easy job. His mind wanted to wander into twisted byways and nooks and crannies, like the ones in this, the oldest part of the palace.

He thought about his sister and what Sophy had said about her. That hadn't been pleasant.

He thought about Sophy's hair streaming down her back, and over her breasts, the long locks curling and turning gold as they dried . . . the outlines of her breasts under the thin muslin nightdress . . . the outlines of her thighs . . . the place between them, the triangle he knew would be dusted with gold.

That was much more agreeable.

Still, he felt stifled. The room was too cozy and warm. The apartments in Hampton Court were notoriously ramshackle, dark, and dank. Her ladyship had a fire going, against the damp. The accumulated bric-a-brac of decades filled the place. Behind him the women's voices were low as they conversed like old friends.

He was of no use here, obviously. He might as well go out. While the females gossiped, he could question the officers. He could find Fenwick and get his report. He'd just decided to excuse himself, when Lady Durwich cried, "But there! I knew you looked familiar. Now I have it! Those eyes. Those are DeLucey eyes. I'd know them anywhere."

Sophy was aware of Longmore turning away from the window, his gaze sharpening.

She smiled politely at Lady Durwich. "Your ladyship is not the first to say so."

"And small wonder," said the old lady. "One doesn't forget those eyes. It took me a moment, though, to recall the connection. But the previous Earl of Mandeville was a great friend of my husband's, you know. And then there was Eugenia, the Dowager Lady Hargate. Her eldest son, Rathbourne, married a girl from the cadet branch—the wild set. Lady Rathbourne's daughter was a great favorite of Eugenia's. I saw the girl at Eugenia's funeral. You recall meeting Lady Lisle, do you not, Longmore? Pretty red-haired girl. Are those not the DeLucey eyes?"

His expression changed very little but it was enough for Sophy. She noticed the slight widening of his dark eyes and the change in his stance: a degree more alert, like a wolf catching a scent.

"Ah, yes, the wild set of DeLuceys," Sophy said, her voice amused. "I've been told that most of them lived abroad. It's not entirely impossible that one of my ancestors was born on the wrong side of the blanket."

From the time they'd arrived in London, she and her sisters had been aware of the risk they ran. Marcelline could get by easily, having taken after Papa. But Sophy and Leonie had inherited Mama's DeLucey eyes, and those large, vividly blue eyes were, as even a lady near or in her ninth decade could see, all too distinctive.

The "wild set" of the DeLuceys—more commonly known in England as the Dreadful DeLuceys—were still, and with good reason, mistrusted at best, loathed at worst. Marcelline, Sophy, and Leonie were the last of the lot, so far as they knew. The cholera had killed everybody else.

"Most of us could say the same," Lady Durwich said. But she took up her quizzing glass and scrutinized Sophy again. Sophy met the scrutiny calmly. She'd had years of practice playing cards—not to mention waiting on extremely trying customers.

"Not to cut short the fascinating gossip about olden times," Longmore said, "but the day is wearing away, and we seem not to have discovered where Clara went after leaving here."

"The impatience of youth," Lady Durwich said. "That's what I told Clara. She wouldn't say what possessed her to wander out unchaperoned with Adderley, of all men. I suspect it was nothing to do with him at all."

"How can it have nothing to do with Adderley, when he was the one who got half her clothes off?" Longmore said.

"Actually, he didn't," Sophy said. "He'd pushed

her neckline down about an inch or so, and spoiled the delicate folds of the bodice."

Knowing that arcane dressmaking detail would drive Longmore wild and take his mind off DeLuceys, she continued, "The corsage was quite low, you see, my lady, the drapery crossed on the front in narrow folds. We embroidered a wreath of moss roses, with buds, stems, and leaves, to go round the bottom of the skirt and up the front. She had a brooch—emeralds, to set off the embroidered foliage. We fastened it low—so." She indicated the area between her breasts corresponding to the spot where Lady Clara's brooch had been placed. "This allowed a pretty display of a bit of her chemisette, of a very fine blond—"

"Yes, yes, I daresay Lady Durwich read the infinity of dressmaking details in the *Spectacle*," Longmore cut in. "As did we all."

"I was merely pointing out that Lady Clara may have appeared to your brotherly eyes to be in a greater state of dishabille than was objectively the case," Sophy said.

"What difference does it make, whether it was a little or a lot?" he said. "She was alone with him and he'd disarranged her dress and pretended to be gallant by trying to hide the fact when he knew it couldn't be hidden."

"Ah, but if he'd truly been gallant, he wouldn't have needed to hide anything," said Lady Durwich. "If he truly cared for her, he wouldn't have led her out to the terrace in the first place. Naturally I didn't say so, not wanting to upset the child further. But she knew already. That was what threw her into such a tizzy, you see. She told me that wretched Bartham woman had said it to her face—or hinted it broadly enough. And Clara said it was bad enough to bear the humiliation—but to bear it for a man who despised her was intolerable. I tried to reason with her, but you know how she takes things to heart. Her grandmother might have persuaded her. She always knew the way. But I might as well have talked to the chimneypiece. I don't see how this matter can be put right. She certainly doesn't believe it can—and so I can only fear for her."

Chapter Nine

HAMPTON COURT is a royal palace, thirteen miles from London, erected by Cardinal Wolsey, and presented by him to his royal master, Henry . . . The palace and grounds, which are well worth the attention of the stranger, are very accessible, on polite request to one of the officers of the establishment.

—Cruchley's Picture of London, 1834

Some eternity later, Longmore was trying to lead Sophy out the way they'd come. She loitered, gawking up at windows and down narrow passages and staring at closed doors as though looking hard would let her see through them.

"You'd have stayed the night if I'd let you," he said.

"I was only trying to learn as much as I could," she said. "Persuading your sister to return to London isn't going to be easy. I need to understand as much as possible."

He hadn't wanted to understand any more. Lady Durwich's revelation, coming on top of Sophy's speech about Clara, had left him seething. He'd had to get out of that cozy apartment or break something.

He no longer wished he'd killed Adderley. Death was too good for him. He needed to be beaten to a pulp, all his beauty smashed away forever. He needed to hurt for the rest of his days, for the way he'd hurt Clara.

"I was better out of it," he said. "Women discussing *feelings*. Not my favorite thing. More useful to talk to the palace officers and servants. Clara seems not to have been very confiding, except with Lady Durwich. But Davis talked to a gardener about local inns, and he recommended the Bear at Esher. We need to be on our way."

"I know," she said.

"Well, then," he said.

"I'm coming."

"You're dawdling," he said.

"I'm thinking," she said.

"You can't walk and think at the same time?"

"Are you always so impatient?" she said. "But why do I ask?"

"We've lost hours," he said.

"Not much more than your sister has," she said. "She couldn't travel in the storm. She spent the night at an inn. She has to rest her horse, you said."

"She has a day's start of us!" he said.

"I don't think we should set out when you're so upset," she said.

"I'm not upset," he said. "And even if I were, it wouldn't affect my driving."

"You're *extremely* upset," she said. "It's what I said about Clara, isn't it? And what Lady Durwich said. And now you want to kill somebody. Or hit somebody. And we can't afford your picking fights, because if you're arrested—"

"I'm not going to be arrested," he said.

She moved to get in front of him, forcing him to stop. She grabbed his lapels. "Listen to me," she said. "I'm going to take care of your sister's problem."

"You!" he said. "This can't be fixed. I was deluded to think it could be. That blackguard ruined my sister deliberately. It wasn't even lust, confound him. It was cold-blooded—"

"I'll take care of him," she said.

"You're a female! A shopkeeper! What the devil do you think you can do?"

"You've no idea what I'm capable of," she said.

"Lying, yes. Acting, yes. Spying, yes."

"You are a spoiled, aristocratic blockhead," she said. "You know nothing about me. You don't know what I've lived through. You're a child. An infant. A spoiled, temperamental overgrown baby who hits people when he can't get his own way. You—*oof*!"

He'd wrapped his arm about her waist, pulled, and brought her up hard against his chest.

"A child, am I?" he said.

Sophy squirmed, but it was like struggling with a brick wall. He ducked his head under her hat brim and his mouth found hers, and by the time she remembered to draw back, it was too late, because he was kissing her. This time he was doing it more determinedly than before.

She could feel it all the way down to her toes.

She clenched her hands. She could do this. She could fight it. She could fight him. She made herself hit him. She beat on his chest, but it was pathetic, and even if she'd put more force into it, she doubted he'd feel it.

And then, his hard, cynical mouth was so warm on hers, and he was so big and warm and hard and . . . safe.

And she could smell him. She could smell his skin and his maleness, and it was like smoking opium. His big body and the smell and taste of him killed her willpower and her brain.

Everything gave way. Her body molded to his and her lips parted. The kiss turned dark and deep and dangerous, and everything went away except feelings. Sensations she couldn't name swirled in her heart and made it pound and pound, then eddied lower, to the danger area, to make her hungry in a way she'd never been hungry before.

Her hands unclenched only to grasp his upper arms, to hold on because her knees were gone and she was fainting. She was conscious yet she was fainting, over and over.

He pushed her against the wall, his mouth still holding hers captive while his tongue taught her every kind of sin. She let go of him, and let herself go, letting the wall hold her up, her hands flat against the cool brick while everything else was so deliciously warm. He brought his hands up and rested them on the wall, too, on either side of her head, boxing her in, and she felt the tilt of his head change, tipping to one side as he taught her another hundred sins of kissing: the changing slant of his mouth, the press of his tongue.

She heard something but it was far away, not important.

Then it was louder.

Someone clearing his throat.

Her eyes flew open at the same moment Longmore lifted his mouth from hers and, barely raising his head, turned his gaze toward the sound.

"Beggin' your lordship's pardon," a gravelly voice said.

Longmore lifted his head another few inches, but only to send a warning look toward the voice. "Can you not see I'm busy?"

"Yes, your lordship," the voice said. "But—"

"Aaargh!" Sophy pushed at Longmore's chest. "Curse you!" She pushed again. It was like pushing at the castle wall.

He looked down at her gloved hands, his dark eyes glinting and a corner of his mouth—his wicked, wicked mouth—turning up.

"Get off!" she said.

Longmore inhaled and exhaled slowly, then slowly backed away. It wasn't nearly enough time for his arousal to subside, although that was the easier part. The difficult part was the thinking, because his head was pleasantly thick and warm, and he'd much rather remain in that state than return to the one he'd been in only moments ago.

Through narrowed eyes he regarded the author of his disturbance. Sophy was a very little disheveled, but it was enough. Her hat was askew and her lips were swollen and she regarded him with wide, dazed eyes.

She looked delicious.

"I was only saying farewell," he said, his voice lower and huskier than normal.

"Is that what you call it?" she said.

"I'm leaving you here," he said. "With her lady-ship. You and she can talk about feelings to your hearts' content."

She yanked at the bow under her chin, and it came undone. She pulled the hat off and hit him with it. She hit him in the chest and on the arm and then on the chest again. Then she flounced away. The hat, dangling by the ribbons from her hand, bounced against her skirt as she walked, hips swaying.

"You'll get lost in this place without me," he called after her.

"I think not," she said without turning around.

He shrugged and was straightening his own hat when he noticed the palace officer was still there. He stood stolidly expressionless a few feet away.

"You wanted something?" Longmore said.

The man glanced up toward a window. A dark shape was visible through the wavy glass.

"Lady Flinton's a bit of a stickler, my lord," the officer said apologetically. "Gets in a state about what she calls immoral goings-on. She told me to put a stop to it."

Longmore tipped his hat to the figure in the window.

Then he went after Sophy.

She had, as he'd expected, taken a wrong turn. He found her in the Clock Court, slapping her hat against her skirt and staring up at the Astronomical Clock.

"You said you were going to stab me if I kissed you again," he said.

Her blue gaze, no longer dazed but cool and sharp, came down from the clock to rest upon him.

"I was looking for a weapon, but they all seem to be taken."

"Shall I take you up to the Guard Chamber?" he said. "All sorts of pikes and spears and other stabbing sorts of things hanging on the walls."

"Yes, by all means," she said.

"Sadly, we haven't time," he said. "We have to find my sister." He took her arm. This wasn't as easy as one would think. The upper part was like a large cushion. He had to take hold of the lower part . . . near her wrist. He was tempted to clasp her hand but he suspected that would set him off again, and they'd wasted far too much time already.

Not a waste, really, but still . . .

He clasped her lower arm firmly and led her away. She came easily enough. Too bad. He wouldn't mind another tussle.

But no, they needed to be on their way.

"I thought you were going to leave me here," she said.

"You talked me out of it . . . a moment ago . . . when you were against the wall, under Lady Flinton's window."

"Oh, yes—and speaking of that—"

"Oh, good," he said. "We're going to *discuss* it now."

"We certainly are," she said. "I had all my clothes on this time, so don't try to use any excuses about my being mostly naked."

"I don't need an excuse," he said. "But it might be that you have too many clothes on."

She gave him a look of pure exasperation. He was familiar with that look. People turned it on him all the time. Her version, though, was precious.

"The only part uncovered was your face," he said. "And your mouth kept moving. And so I had to stop it."

"Why has no woman stabbed you before now, I wonder?" she said.

"I have quick reflexes," he said.

She looked away, up at the clock again. "If that's what Lord Adderley did to Lady Clara, it's no wonder she got into trouble," she said. "It's extremely unsporting of a man who possesses worlds of experience to take advantage of a young woman who has no experience whatsoever."

That was the last answer he expected.

It stung, too. "I didn't take advantage of you," he said. "It was only kissing."

"Only," she said.

"I didn't even touch your clothes, let alone try to take them off." He'd put his hands on the wall—some part of his brain must have been thinking, to do that, to keep his hands off her. "Of course, taking them off does look like a two-hour job. At any rate, now that you've had some practice, and I was . . . productively occupied instructing you . . . that means it'll be much harder for unsporting men to take advantage of you in future . . ."

Belatedly, what she'd said sank in. "What do you mean, it's no wonder Clara got into trouble?"

"I'm not a sheltered lady," she said. "I grew up in a shop in Paris. I run a business. I'm supposedly clever. She's an innocent girl who's always had others protecting her. If Adderley kissed her like that, she hadn't a chance. It's so *unfair*."

Longmore wasn't taking unfair advantage. She wasn't a gently bred girl who'd been protected from the real world since childhood. She was a milliner—from Paris!—whose sister had turned the Duke of Clevedon into a dithering idiot. It couldn't be unsporting to kiss her. Could it?

"Do you mean to hit me with that millinery extravaganza again?" he said. "Or should you like to make yourself presentable and put it back on before we return to the carriage?"

She hit him with it. He snatched it from her and walked quickly ahead.

He could hear the leather soles of her frivolous boots tapping on the cobblestones behind him and the rustling of her petticoats as she hurried after him. He didn't look back.

He let her catch up with him near the main entrance.

Her face was flushed and she was panting. She put out her hand. "Give me my hat," she said.

Ignoring her outstretched hand, he planted the hat backward on her head and took her arm to lead her out. She pulled away and hurried to the nearest window. It gave back a distorted image.

"You look like a gargoyle," he said.

She stepped nearer to the window and stared for a moment.

Then her shoulders shook, and she giggled. Then she laughed fully, and the ribbons danced and the bows fluttered, and he thought he'd never heard anything so wonderful as that sound.

He felt as well as heard it. It seemed to dart deep inside him and touch a long-hidden place, and it was a sharp feeling, as though she had stabbed him to the heart.

A moment later it was over. The laughter dwindled to a smile. She shook her head. Then she took off the hat and put it on straight, trying to see in the unhelpful glass.

He came behind her, and arranged it correctly.

She turned and looked up at him, her great blue eyes shining with an expression that alerted some instinct and made him wary.

He didn't stop to work out what it was. He simply heeded the instinct.

He tied the ribbons. Then he stepped away, out of reach of that shining blue.

"Well, then," he said. "We'd better be off."

No one had to tell Sophy that kissing her meant nothing special to the Earl of Longmore. He was a man, and one not famous for celibacy or even constancy.

For her, though, it had been a shocking learning experience. For whole stretches of time, she hadn't had even a wisp of a thought about Maison Noirot, or clothing, except for feeling there was too much of it. In the way.

If this sort of thing happened all the time with men, she'd never be able to afford a love affair: She wouldn't have any mind left for the shop.

How on earth did Marcelline manage it?

A stronger mind? Or was it marriage? Maybe matrimony had a quieting effect.

It was hard to imagine a more horrifying prospect than marrying Longmore. It was bad on so many counts that her mind shrank from contemplating it.

She'd have to quiet herself somehow. Yet even now, fully aware he was simply doing what men did, she had to work very hard to get her mind back on Lady Clara and the simplest part of that problem: where she was headed.

The answer came only a few miles down the road from Hampton Court, at the Bear Inn at Esher.

It was a large, busy coaching inn. When they arrived, several coaches were either entering its yard or leaving it. They were bound for London, Longmore told her. "The down stages will all arrive at about the same time," he said. "You might have noticed them when you were waiting for me at the Gloucester Coffee House. Or maybe you didn't notice, being surrounded by men trying to attract your attention."

"Don't fret about those men, my lord," she said. "I had eyes only for you."

"At least you have taste," he said.

And that was the end of that exchange, because he had to make his way past the other vehicles. When he drew the carriage to a halt, Fenwick promptly jumped down and went to the horses' heads.

It dawned on her that the boy—a street urchin—had done this, again and again, from the start.

"He does it so easily," Sophy said as she alighted. She looked up at Longmore. "You trusted him with your team yesterday, at Bedford Square. Is that usual?"

"There are always boys loitering about, willing to hold one's cattle for a coin," he said while hustling her toward the inn. "But you said yourself how quickly and smoothly he leapt up onto the back of my curricle to rob me. It would seem he's had experience in a stable or a coach house. Not that one can extract from him any sort of information. That'll want thumbscrews, I daresay."

"I'm glad, for this journey's sake," she said. "But

you're not to imagine you can poach him from me."

"Wouldn't dream of it," he said. "My man Reade would murder him in his sleep. Very possessive fellow is my tiger. Even now, I daresay he's plotting against the boy for usurping his place."

The conversation broke off as they entered the inn, to be jostled by various parties coming and going. In a very few minutes, though, the London-bound coaches were gone, the flurry had ceased, and Longmore was able to corner the landlord and tell the story of the forgotten pocketbook.

As busy as the place was, the innkeeper had no trouble remembering the cabriolet and the two ladies. He even showed the entry in the guest book: They'd signed as Mrs. Glasgow and Miss Peters. Sophy recognized Lady Clara's elegant handwriting. Davis, who probably wasn't in the habit of signing anything, had written her false name in tight, square letters that looked as disapproving as letters could look.

"They left midmorning," the innkeeper said. "Bound for Portsmouth."

"Damnation," Longmore said.

"Portsmouth, of all places," he said when they were once more in the carriage. "Naval town. Bursting at the seams with brothels and drunken sailors and every sort of pimp and bawd looking for pigeons to pluck. And ships bound for everywhere. The Continent. Ireland. America."

This was worse, far worse than Clara's simply being on the road alone.

He was aware of panic welling up and trying to swamp him. He beat it down.

"She can't leave the country," Sophy said.

"She doesn't know that," he said. "She'll try. In a place teeming with cheats and scoundrels happy to take advantage of an ignorant female. They'll see her coming from a mile away, a sheltered miss and thorough greenhorn."

"She isn't on her own," Sophy said. "She has Davis. Anyone who wants to get to Lady Clara will have to get past the maid. Davis may have to yield to her mistress's whims, but she went with her in order to protect her."

"One female," he said.

He didn't have to look. He felt the stiffening, the something in the air that told him he'd got her back up. Again.

"Why do you assume all women are weaklings?" she said.

"Because they are," he said. "I can pick you up with one hand. Can you pick me up, even using both hands?"

"That's not the only kind of strength," she said.

"She's a lady's maid," he said. "She's at the top of the female servant ladder. No heavy lifting necessary."

"She's up at all hours and out in all weathers," Sophy said. "When she isn't dancing attendance on her mistress, she's mending and cleaning and taking things out and putting them away. If milady falls ill, it's her maid who does the dirty work of nursing her while doctors and mothers give orders. The maid runs up and down stairs all day and night, fetching and carrying. She's keeping an eye on the lower servants, making sure everything done to or for milady is done properly. No weakling would survive for half a day."

Longmore stared at the horses' heads. He'd never thought about the woman who looked after his sister, beyond noting that she was plain and her expression reminded everybody of a bulldog.

"I'll give you that she's strong," he said. "The fact remains, she's only one female."

"A formidable female," Sophy said. "Lady Clara was in more danger from Lord Adderley than she is from naval Lotharios in Portsmouth."

"Clearly, you've had little to do with naval men," he said.

"How little you know," she said.

So it seemed.

"Enlighten me, then," he said.

"I'm a dressmaker," she said. "A milliner. Everybody knows we're fair game."

"You don't seem to know that," he said. "You're deuced uncooperative."

"I spoke ironically," she said.

"Better not," he said. "Goes right over my head."

"Furthermore, I have powerful reasons for being uncooperative, which I explained to you last night. Don't tell me you didn't understand."

"I wasn't completely listening," he said.

"You're going to make me hurt you," she said.

"You'll need a brick," he said.

"My aim is excellent," she said.

They passed through the Cobham Gate, where they learned—in case they'd any doubts—that the cabriolet had passed the day before.

The sun was lowering toward the horizon. It would set near eight o'clock. They had a long drive to Portsmouth, more than fifty miles. Thanks to the time of year and the moon, it wouldn't be an altogether dark journey, if the weather didn't turn on them again.

He wasn't going to stop this time, even if a hurricane blew their way.

He looked at her. Her hat had deflated somewhat. The ribbons were limper and the flowers not as sprightly as before. No wonder, after she'd tried to beat him with it. He smiled, remembering.

She was an amazing antidote to gloom.

"Tell me about the naval men," he said. "Did you spill hot tea on them? Trip them over their own swords?"

"Did you know you could kill a person with a hatpin?" she said.

"I did not," he said. "Do you speak from experience? Have you murdered anybody? Not that I'd dream of criticizing."

"I've only ever wounded anybody," she said. "It's amazingly effective. There was a captain who screamed like a girl and fainted."

"A pity you hadn't the training of my sister," he said.

"A few tricks wouldn't do her any good," she said. "She'd need a lifetime's experience—and even then she might have fallen into the trap. Adderley is a beautiful man, and he has a winning manner. But Lady Durwich thought your sister was trying to make another man jealous—that, or she was upset with somebody. Maybe *she* was jealous—and it was a case of 'I'll show you' or 'Two can play that game' or—"

"Is it always like this?" he broke in. "Does your busy mind never rest?"

"If not for imagination, Marcelline, Leonie, and

I wouldn't be where we are today," she said. "You don't need to think of such things. Men rule the world, and the world is made for the convenience of aristocratic men. But women need to imagine, to dream. Even Lady Clara. We taught her to dream a little and to dare a little—and I refuse to feel guilty for that—but I was a sort of Pygmalion, wasn't I? And I should have—"

"Classical allusions," he said. "Clevedon does it all the time. Now you. Which one was Pygmalion?"

"The sculptor who created the beautiful statue, and—"

"That one, right. She came to life."

"Yes."

"How do you know these things?" he said. "Where does a shopkeeper find time to learn who Pygmalion was? Where does she learn to write overwrought prose?"

She turned the politely interested look upon him: the look that made a blank of her almost-beautiful face. "It's not marvelous to you when a gentleman can speak, read, and write three or six languages, make speeches in Parliament, perform chemical experiments, write botanical papers, and found or help direct half a dozen charities? Don't you ever wonder where any gentleman finds the time to do all that? I certainly do. Take Dr. Young, for example."

"Never heard of him."

She enlightened him.

The fellow had died a few years ago. He'd been a prodigy. A physician at St. George's Hospital. Active on the Board of Longitude, the *Nautical Almanac*, the Royal Society. Wrote about geology and earthquakes, about light and life-insurance calculations and musical harmony. Even helped decipher the Rosetta Stone.

Longmore's mind returned to the conversation with Lady Durwich and what she'd said about the wild DeLuceys. He remembered Lady Lisle, who'd spent most of the years since her marriage traveling in Egypt with her husband. A charismatic female, too, who exuded a similar energy . . .

He turned to study Sophy . . . and discovered Fenwick hanging over the hood.

Longmore scowled at him. "What do you think you're doing?"

"Listening," the boy said. "The fings you nobs talk about."

"Things," Longmore said automatically.

"*Th*ings," Fenwick said. He rested his folded arms on the hood, making himself comfortable. "It's like listening to stories. What was the one about the pig man?"

"Pygmalion," she said. She went on to tell the story, not sparing adjectives and adverbs. The telling took several miles. Then she launched into other tales: Atalanta and the apples, Icarus and his wings, and thence to Odysseus and his wanderings.

Listening to her now was a different experience from reading her stories about clothes. When she spoke, she took on the characters' personalities. She held spellbound not only the boy but Longmore as well, and he forgot Lady Lisle altogether.

No one would ever mistake Lord Longmore for an intellectual prodigy. Still, being a simple man, he could take hold of a notion and not let go of it.

Sophy had dealt with Lady Durwich's reference to the DeLuceys easily. Distracting Longmore wasn't difficult, either.

She knew he wouldn't care at all about her being a Dreadful DeLucey. He wouldn't care that the Noirots were equally disreputable. The trouble was, since he didn't care, he mightn't think it important enough to keep to himself. If she could drive it out of his mind—where, she reasoned, there wasn't overmuch room—he was less likely to speculate aloud to any of his friends.

The *Odyssey* got them through the next two changes. Then Longmore decided she looked tired and hungry. As they consumed a hasty meal at an inn, he told her to rest. "The moon's been up since early afternoon," he pointed out. "It'll set in the early-morning hours. I need to concentrate on driving—and the fantastical adventures of Greek heroes are too distracting. And Fenwick needs to sleep."

He kept the horses to a steady clip, and let them gallop on the flat stretches. Now and then he'd point out sights along the way, some ghostly in the moonlight, like the Devil's Punchbowl, or gibbets on the side of the road.

But for a good part of the journey they drove in an easy silence. Twice she woke, and discovered she'd fallen asleep on his shoulder. This was no small feat. Even with excellent springs and scrupulous maintenance, no carriage ride was perfectly smooth.

The second time she woke, and hastily drew away, he laughed and said, "I knew you were tired."

"It's the rocking," she said.

"You might as well sleep if you can," he said. "We've a distance to go. I only hope we can reach Portsmouth before the moonset. I'm not looking forward to navigating streets I don't know in the predawn dark."

Chapter Ten

Happy, indeed will the visitor be who is so fortunate as to be on the Platform when a first-rate man-of-war is sailing out of the harbour. He will then enjoy one of the grandest sights in the world, in beholding the majestic castle gliding along the water, and hearing the astounding sound of her guns, when in passing she salutes the garrison flag.

—*The new Portsmouth, Southsea, Anglesey & Hayling Island Guide*, 1834

The moon was setting by the time they reached Portsmouth. Still, all Longmore had to do was keep to the main thoroughfare. Along the High street were many prosperous-looking establishments. For lodgings he had a choice between the Fountain and the George, the two major coaching inns. He decided on the George, because the Royal Mail set out from there. Too, it was the one recommended to Clara's maid.

After sending Fenwick to gossip with the servants and stablemen, Longmore took Sophy into the inn.

He was sure he'd be relying mainly on Fenwick at this point, since the landlord of a busy town's busy inn—still awake and bustling even at this hour—probably wouldn't remember the two women. If Clara behaved as she'd done previously, she'd have kept in the background, letting Davis hire the room and arrange for meals and such. Plain women tended not to make an impression.

The innkeeper had no recollection of two ladies traveling together, and his guest ledger confirmed this.

Longmore moved away, to talk to Sophy. "We might as well stop," he told her. "There's little we can do at this hour."

"But you said the sun would be up soon, near four o'clock," she said. She took up the pocket watch that dangled from the belt of her carriage dress. "It's only half past two."

"And you look like the very devil," he said. "You need to sleep."

"I slept in the carriage," she said.

She'd slept against his shoulder, her hat's absurd decorations tickling his chin now and again. She'd sink lower and lower, then, at a certain point, she'd wake with a start.

He thought it was adorable—an odd thought to have about Sophy, but there it was. She was a complicated girl. That was what made her so interesting. That and the delicious mouth and smell and perfect figure.

"It wasn't proper sleep," he said. "The fact remains, you look like the devil." Ignoring her protests, he hired a room for her and ordered a meal as well. And a maid. Someone needed to get her out of her clothes and into bed. It had better not be him, or no one would get any rest.

* * *

Sophy had only the dimmest memory of what had happened after they reached the inn. Weariness had welled up, a massive wave, which must have been building for weeks. It had simply swamped her. She could barely keep her eyes open, let alone continue arguing with Longmore.

She did remember his fussing over her and ordering everybody about. He'd insisted on a maid for her, and she dimly recalled the maid chattering at her as they went up the stairs to the room he'd hired. He'd had a light meal sent up and Sophy had eaten it, surprised at how hungry she was. She'd washed and undressed with—considering the hour—the maid's extremely cheerful and patient help. Longmore must have given the girl a large gratuity.

Tired as she was, Sophy hadn't expected to sleep. The longer they'd searched, the more anxious she'd become about Lady Clara. She'd persuaded Longmore that his sister was safe with Davis watching out for her, but Sophy hadn't persuaded herself.

Yet sleep she must have done, since the noise woke her. She was so groggy that it took a moment to realize someone was beating on the door.

She bolted upright, heart pounding, to see early-morning sunlight streaming in through the window. How long had she slept?

She stumbled out of bed, found her dressing gown on the chair nearby, and was pulling it on when she heard Longmore's voice. "Where's the confounded maid?"

Sophy ran to the door and flung it open.

Longmore stood in the corridor, fully dressed

in the same clothes he'd been wearing when they arrived. Had he not slept? He hadn't shaved, certainly. The shadow along his jaw made him look more dangerous than ever.

"Clara's here," he said.

"Here? In the inn?"

"No," he said. "That is, if she has, nobody's told me. But she hasn't left Portsmouth yet. I shouldn't have wakened you—"

"You shouldn't have let me sleep," she said.

"Never mind that. I need your help. People get suspicious when a man seems to be hunting a young woman. They become less than candid. Fenwick lacks your charming methods of extracting information from the unwilling, and I'm having trouble holding onto my temper."

"You've been searching, without me," she said reproachfully.

He stepped over the threshold and she took two steps back. He looked down at her feet. She did, too. They were bare.

"Where are your slippers?" he said.

Without waiting for an answer, he strode to the bed, found the slippers, and gestured at a chair. She sat. "I can put on my own—"

"You're not even awake." He knelt and took her foot and slid it into the slipper. He paused, his hand still on her foot, and stared for what seemed a very long time.

"I'm awake," she said. "I can do that."

He came out of his trance and put the other slipper on, then stood. "You shouldn't run about barefoot in public hostelries," he said.

"I wasn't running about—and you shouldn't have been searching without me."

"You needed sleep," he said. "You've needed it this age, I'll wager anything. You keep ridiculous hours."

"I'm a working woman," she said.

"You ought to give it up."

"*What?*"

"The whole thing's absurd," he said. "Your sister married a duke. I told Clevedon . . ." he trailed off.

"What did you tell him?"

"Never mind that now," he said.

"I certainly will mind it now," she said.

"Do you want to find Clara or do you want to quarrel?" he said.

"Preferably both," she said.

"Don't aggravate me," he said. "I haven't time to throttle you. Fenwick and I were up at dawn's crack—"

"Without me."

"Without you," he said. "Some infernal gun went off. I'm informed that it does so twice a day, sunrise and sunset. After that I saw no point in trying to sleep. I took Fenwick to the docks. It took a while for me to find the area we wanted, but we did eventually. We found out which passenger ships had left since the earliest time Clara could have arrived. We're reasonably sure she wasn't aboard any of them. But I can explain all that later. I only came to tell you to make haste."

"Very well."

She rose from the chair and stumbled to the washstand. In spite of the abrupt awakening, she was still muddle-headed. She filled the bowl with water and washed her face. That improved matters. She was drying her face when she saw his, behind her, in the mirror.

"Can't you go any faster?" he said.

"It will take me at least half an hour without a maid's help," she said.

"I don't know where she went or what she's doing," he said. "All I know is that when I asked for one a moment ago, I was told, 'Straightaway.' That could mean hours from now. The place is a madhouse. Most of the servants seem to be in the dining room, running frantically hither and yon, serving breakfast."

He waved at the carriage dress she'd worn yesterday, which the maid had hung carefully over a chair. "Just throw it on, can't you? We're not going to a fashion parade."

"I can't just throw it on! How can you be so obtuse?"

"Easily," he said. "It wants no effort at all."

Later, when she had time, when she could see straight, she was going to hit him with something bigger than a brick.

She found her chemise and petticoats and corset, and laid them out on the bed. Tired and cross—and maybe because she was who she was and couldn't resist playing with fire—she pulled off her dressing gown, then the nightdress.

She would have done the same thing had she been with her sisters and in a great hurry to be gone from somewhere. She was well aware she wasn't with her sisters.

"Damnation!"

She glanced back at him as she pulled on her chemise. He'd turned his back on her nakedness.

That was funny. Her mood lightened a degree. "You could try sending for the maid," she said.

"Not for worlds," he said.

"Then look," she said. "I don't care. I'm not modest."

That was no lie. Merely because she made clothes for a living didn't mean she was shy about being unclothed. Even in front of him. Or, rather, *especially* in front of him. She was a Noirot, after all.

"I'm not looking," he said. "I'm not modest either, but I need to keep my wits about me. By Jupiter, you're the very devil."

She stepped into her drawers and tied the tapes at the waist. She donned the petticoat and tied it. She arranged the corset on the bed and started lacing it.

"What's taking so long?" he said. He turned. "What in the name of Satan and all his minions are you doing?"

"It's one of the new corsets Marcelline invented," she said. "One can do it up oneself. But the maid didn't understand how it worked, and I was too tired to explain clearly enough, it seems. She untied the lacing, and I need to—"

"I can do up the lacing," he said. "Actually, I'm quite good at it."

"This doesn't surprise me," she said. She slid the corset over her head and slipped her arms through the straps. She tugged the corset down and snugged it over her torso.

As she was adjusting the straps, Longmore came up behind her.

"One leaves it knotted at the bottom and laced," she explained. "Then one need only put it on and pull it tight in front."

"Ingenious," he said.

"But she untied the knot and undid it in the usual way."

"I see that," he said.

She was aware of his hands at the base of her spine, knotting the tie. She felt him drawing the lacing through the eyelets, smoothing the narrow tape as he worked his way steadily up her back, tugging with precisely the right degree of firmness.

He certainly had the knack of it. How many women had he undone?

His hands were warm against her back. His breath was warm, too, at the back of her neck. The tiny hairs at her nape rose.

When he'd finished, he didn't move away immediately. His hands rested on her hips. He stood so close that she could hear his quickened breathing. She could feel the heat of his big body—or was that her own heat? He stood so close that she had only to lean back a very little . . .

Her heart was racing, and the devil in her was clouding her mind, urging her to lean back that small distance. *Don't you want those deft, capable hands on you, on your skin?* it seemed to whisper. *Don't you want that powerful body on yours? In yours?*

Then the tiny voice, the one Cousin Emma had instilled, argued: *And what happens to your power, if you succumb to this?*

She'd already given in to her inner demons and played with fire: She'd thrown off her nightclothes and given him an eyeful. It was madly irresponsible—even for her—to forget why she was here.

Lady Clara.

Everything depended on her. The shop. Their future. Success or a mortifying failure. Dowdy triumphing over them, laughing at them.

Grimly she summoned her willpower.

He turned her around and pushed her hands away from the corset. He gave another firm tug, then swiftly tied the lacing in front.

She stepped away from him and took up one of the sleeve puffs.

"Gad, must you?" he said. His voice was low, the dark, dangerous voice that made her mind thick.

She looked up. He was dragging his fingers through his hair.

She wanted to tear her hair out. But she was a Noirot. "Have you noticed the size of my dress sleeves?" she said calmly. "Without the puffs, it'll look as though I have skirts hanging from my shoulders." She slipped her arm through one of the puffs. "You said people were suspicious of you. Have you had a good look at yourself in the mirror? One of us at least oughtn't to look disreputable. And it won't take long. Leonie invented these."

"You're all so inventive," he said.

She started tying the upper tape to her corset strap.

"Why did you wear this complicated rig?" he said.

"This is what one of your fashionable *chères amies* would wear," she said patiently. "Although I don't doubt their clothes wouldn't be quite so well made. Nor would they be made at the farthest, dangerous edge of the latest fashion."

"Let me do that," he said. "You might be unusually flexible, but I can see better what I'm doing."

While he tied the sleeve puffs, she adjusted the arm bands over the sleeves of her chemise, and smoothed the edge of the sleeves.

When she took up a stocking, though, he backed away.

But he didn't turn away. Sophy was shakily aware of his dark gaze fixed on her as she quickly drew on the stockings and tied the garters.

As soon as that was done, he grabbed her dress and flung it over her head. He tried to stuff her arms through, and swore. "There's no room, dammit! It's like trying to push a pillow through a keyhole."

"You squeeze the puffs through," she said. "They're filled with down. They'll compress quite a bit. But you need to do it carefully."

"I have never seen a more idiotish fashion garment in all my life."

"It's not that difficult," she said. "Just calm down."

"Easy for you to say," he said.

It was easy to say. Feeling it was another matter. She wasn't at all calm. No man had ever helped her dress or undress. The intimacy was almost painful. "I'll do the left and you do the right."

They worked quickly, in silence. Once the sleeves were dealt with, he knew what to do with everything else. He even went so far as to crouch to smooth the skirt, and tug it straight.

Then he sprang up, grabbed her hat, thrust it on her head, tied the ribbons, and pushed her at the door.

"My boots," she said. "My boots."

He looked down at her slippered feet. "This is diabolical," he said.

He found her boots, pushed her onto a chair, drew on the boots, and fastened them. Then he grabbed her hand and pulled her upright, so abruptly that she fell against him.

His arms went round her. He let loose a few more oaths and jerked away as though she were contaminated.

"I vow, you're doing this on purpose to drive me mad," he said.

And what of me?

She had been kissed by other men, and he had shown her there was another entire world of kissing.

But that intimacy was nothing to this, to his touching her undergarments, her dress, everything that touched her person. She was shaking inside.

Outside, she was a Noirot. "You could have sent for the maid," she said.

He stomped to the door and pulled it open. While he stood there, breathing hard, vibrating impatience, she found her gloves and her reticule. When she passed through the door, he said something under his breath. It sounded, strangely enough, like French.

Longmore took Sophy to Broad Street, from whose hostelries travelers could obtain passage to various destinations.

It was a wonder he could find his way, considering she'd destroyed his brain. What remained of it.

He wasn't a man who was easily shocked.

She'd shocked him.

She'd simply thrown off her nightwear and calmly tossed a chemise over her naked—completely, splendidly naked!—body.

He'd seen her in profile, and the image was seared into his mind: soft, creamy skin and perfectly formed breasts and the most beautiful bottom he'd ever seen in all his life—and he had seen a few.

Then to have to help her get dressed . . .

That evil corset. By the time he'd finished, his hands had been shaking from the fight with himself not to undo all he'd done.

He would rather have fought a tavern full of drunken sailors.

Then those curst sleeve puffs—to be reaching through her neckline to bash the damn things into place.

He was going to throttle his sister. And Adderley.

Sophy, meanwhile, calmly perused a guidebook to Portsmouth he'd bought at the George some hours earlier.

"This was an excellent idea," she said, sounding surprised.

"I have them now and again," he said. "I'm not the sort of traveler who wants guidebooks, but I've rarely been to Portsmouth. To the races at Goodwood or Soberton often. Here, almost never. I thought the information would be more reliable than what a harassed innkeeper would offer, and I knew it would be a great waste of time to wander about aimlessly, asking at every inn and ticket office for Clara. That book, as you see, narrows the possibilities."

"Only two steam packets leave on Sundays," she said, drawing her finger down the appendix page listing the packets: "One to Ryde."

"I doubt the Isle of Wight is far enough away for her," Longmore said.

"There's a packet to Ireland on Sundays, too," she said. "From here to Plymouth to Cork, thence to Liverpool." She looked up at him. "The book says it arrives here in the morning."

"Can you wonder at my hurrying you?" he said. "But the earliest steam packets don't leave before seven, and we've nearly half an hour until then. The one to Ryde doesn't leave until eight. Yet I can't believe she's so addled as to come all the way to Portsmouth, only to travel to Ryde. And if she did, why get up at dawn's crack for the purpose, when the Ryde boats leave several times a day? Clara is no more of an early riser than I am."

"She'd be awake early if she couldn't sleep," she said. "In any case, we ought to start with the Sunday packets. The one to Ireland leaves from a place called the Blue Posts. Shall we start there?"

"I thought Ireland or the Continent might be her first choice," he said. "Still, in the event she does decide to make for the Isle of Wight, I've sent Fenwick to the Quebec Tavern. I described her to him, and told him to create a scene if she turned up and was headed for a boat. I don't doubt he'll think of something. He offered to play the starving boy and faint at her feet—which, he made sure to point out, would be easy, since he hadn't had his breakfast."

"He hadn't had much sleep, either," she said. "I can't believe you took him with you but left me at the inn."

"He slept in the back of the carriage," Longmore said. "It was probably the most comfortable berth he's had in a long time." Then he realized he'd dragged her away without breakfast, either. "We'll find you something to eat at the Blue Posts," he said.

Sunday brought visitors to Portsmouth, to tour the sights listed in the guidebook Longmore had given Sophy: the fortifications, churches, and ships— above all the *Victory*, Lord Nelson's famous ship. However, Sunday was a slow day for shipping, and at this early hour, one didn't have to compete so much for attention against crowds of eager or worried travelers.

Sophy and Longmore soon learned that Clara hadn't booked passage for Ireland. Yet. No pair of women appeared on this morning's passenger lists.

She'd tried and failed to get a berth on the American Line, bound for New York.

"I didn't like the look of it," the agent explained to Sophy. "Anyone could see she was a lady, couldn't they?—same as they could see the other one wasn't. I knew something wasn't right. Hardly any luggage. It was easy enough to put her off. She hadn't any travel papers, had she? She wouldn't get past the customs officers, and so I told her. I told her, too, whatever the trouble was, she was only going to find worse, being a stranger in a strange place. Well, I ask you, madam. It was plain as plain to me she was a gentlewoman, and the other one wasn't no aunt. I wasn't born yesterday, was I? I hope you find her, before she gets into any trouble she can't get out of."

Lady Clara had met with a similar rebuff when she tried to book places on the packet bound for Havre.

Sophy and Longmore were proceeding to the

next ticket office on their list when a ragged boy ran toward them and stopped short.

"You the ones lookin' for the two females?" he said. "One tall and pretty and one plain and looks like a bulldog?"

"Yes," said Sophy.

"I fought it was you," the boy said. "You look like what he said—tall, dark gentleman and the lady with big blue eyes and lots of fancy clothes. I was to tell you as Mad Dick says he found 'em, and hurry along to the Quebec Tavern, as he don't know if he'll be able to keep 'em. Too many officers and such about, givin' him dirty looks."

Sophy and Longmore found Clara on the wharf, pacing, while her maid stood guard over their piti-ful pile of belongings. The day was warm, but a stiff breeze blew, and she seemed to be huddled against it, her arms folded. Now and again she looked out over the water. To Sophy she looked pale and ill.

The maid noticed them first, but Longmore put up a hand, signaling her to be quiet.

Fenwick sat on a crate, chin in hand, watching Clara pace. As he'd reported, there were a number of naval officers about. They were all keeping an eye on him, and not making much effort to pre-tend they weren't. He did look the worse for wear. Two days' travel had restored much of his grubbi-ness and his general appearance of being up to no good.

Longmore neared and then, "Ah, there you are, Clara," he said, and she started at the sound of his voice. "I've been all over the town, looking for you."

She rushed toward him and he opened his arms, but instead of accepting comfort, she started hitting him in the chest. "No," she said. "No, no, no."

"What the devil?"

"I won't go back," she said. "You can't make me go back."

"Then where do you mean to go?" he said.

"I don't know," she said. "Anywhere. Anywhere but here."

The scene promptly attracted attention.

Sophy decided it was time to intervene. She advanced toward the nearest sturdy-looking officer, gave a little shriek, and fainted.

It was a strategic swoon, Longmore noticed. She'd made sure to do it where she could fall into the arms of a muscular, good-looking fellow. For a moment, even Longmore was taken in. He knew she was fatigued to a dangerous degree—even he was tired, and he hadn't been working long hours before he set out—and he'd hurried her and dragged her from the inn at an unholy hour.

But then Clara hurried toward her, crying, "Oh, Miss Noirot, are you ill? You poor thing. My brother is such a brute."

At that, the deep blue eyes fluttered open. "My dear, is that you? We've been so worried." She gracefully disentangled herself from the entirely too-handsome naval officer she'd landed on.

"Are you sure you're all right, miss?" he said.

"Oh, yes, merely dizzy for a moment," she said in a faint voice.

Longmore advanced. "She's quite all right," he said. "She hasn't had her breakfast yet, that's all."

The wind gusted then, and the two young women clutched their hats, while their skirts flew up, treating the onlookers to an exciting vision of lacy petticoats and well-turned ankles.

The naval officer's gaze darted from one pair of ankles to the other.

"Fenwick, help the maid with the bags," Longmore said. "Ladies, we've entertained the audience sufficiently, I believe."

Clara's face took on a familiar, mulish expression.

Sophy said, "Do be reasonable, my dear. You can't go on a voyage with only *that*." She waved at Clara's woefully small pile of belongings. "You won't have a thing to wear."

To Longmore's amazement, it worked. Clara looked at the bags and at her maid and then at Sophy.

"What you need is a brandy," said Sophy.

"Yes," Clara said.

"Let's go back to the hotel," Sophy said.

Clara's lower lip trembled.

"I promise you, everything will be all right," Sophy said. "Let's talk about it in a comfortable place."

"Talking won't do any good," Clara said.

"Yes, it will," Sophy said with so much confidence that even Longmore believed her.

They returned to the George, where Longmore procured a private dining parlor. He ordered brandy first. If getting his sister drunk would make her cooperate, he was happy to do it.

It didn't take much. After half a glass, Clara seemed to calm a degree. She sat close to Sophy.

"Are you feeling a little better?" Sophy said.

"I can't bear to go back," Clara said. "Isn't there another way?"

"We're going to fix this," Sophy said. "My sisters and I will fix this, and we'll do it beautifully, the way we make your clothes. But I need to understand everything that happened. Think of it as my taking measurements, and trying colors next to your face."

"It's easy enough to tell," Clara said. "I was angry."

"About what?"

"Something stupid. It isn't important."

"A man?"

Clara met her gaze.

"Very well," Sophy said. "Not relevant."

"Why not?" Longmore said.

"Because," Sophy said. She gave him a look. The message was as clear as if she'd grasped his lapels and said, *Don't say anything. Don't do anything.*

He subsided. Not happily. But they were women, and he was wary of setting off his sister again.

"Go on," Sophy told Clara.

"I was angry," Clara said. "And there was Adderley, with champagne. I drank too fast and we danced and I was dizzy."

"You were drunk," Longmore said.

Clara glared at him. "Don't you dare lecture me."

"I wasn't—"

"And don't tell me I oughtn't to have gone out onto the terrace with Adderley. I've seen you slip away with women—even at St. James's Palace! At a Drawing Room!"

"I'm a man," Longmore said. "And I don't do that with innocent girls."

He looked straight at Sophy.

He hadn't got her drunk. And she wasn't innocent.

She might be a trifle inexperienced with some of the more intimate aspects, but he was very sure she knew more about men than Carlotta O'Neill did.

In any case, innocent girls didn't throw off their nightclothes in front of a man.

Well, perhaps dressmakers did. Dressing and undressing were business, after all.

And perhaps he'd instigated it . . . inadvertently. He'd woken her from a sound sleep and barged into her room and expected her to get dressed in no time.

Maybe she'd done it to spite him.

Maybe. Maybe. Why the devil was he obliged to think at this hour?

"I thought he was going to talk," Clara was saying. "I thought he was going to tell me how wonderful I was, and I wanted to hear that, because I didn't feel . . . pretty. I felt big and clumsy."

"You aren't that big," Longmore said.

"Lady Clara isn't big or clumsy, but this is the way she *felt*," Sophy said.

"Feelings," he said.

"Yes."

He sat back and drank his brandy.

"I thought Lord Adderley might steal a kiss," Clara said. "And I was cross and feeling . . . I don't know."

"Defiant," Sophy said.

"Yes. But then it wasn't like stealing a kiss at

all. It was something else completely. I wasn't sure I liked it, but it was exciting, because I knew it was wrong. But then things happened so quickly—and then there were all those people. And then Harry came, and I knew he'd kill Adderley."

"I would have tried," Longmore said. "But I suspect Miss Noirot would have come after me with a chair or a potted plant—or she would have shrieked and fainted."

Clara looked from him to Sophy.

"Absolutely," Sophy said. "I knew he wasn't thinking clearly. Or at all. I was prepared to let him hit Lord Adderley. But that was all. If I couldn't find something to hit him with, to get his attention, I was prepared to create a diversion."

"I wish I'd known," Clara said.

"Then you weren't trying to protect him," Sophy said. "I knew it wasn't quite . . . true."

"The tears were true enough," Clara said. "I was terrified for my brother."

"For me? Against that limp—"

"You never think of consequences. You'd lose your temper and kill him, and then you'd have to run away to the Continent. But you'd never run away, from anything. They'd try you and hang you for murdering a defenseless man."

Longmore stared at his sister.

"You were protecting *me*?"

"Someone had to," she said.

"For God's sake, Clara."

"How was I to know Miss Noirot understood, and knew what to do? I didn't even know she was there." She looked at Sophy. "Where were you?"

"It's better not to know," he said. "Are we done talking about our feelings? Because I've had enough revelations for one day. You look as though you've had enough, too, the pair of you. Looking seedy—"

"Harry!"

"You both look like the devil," he said. "I recommend a dose of beauty sleep for the rest of the morning. If we leave by midday, we ought to be able to make London tonight."

Chapter Eleven

> A Cabriolet . . . is in reality a regeneration of the
> old One-horse Chaise . . . It carries two persons,
> comfortably seated, sheltered from sun and rain,
> yet with abundant fresh air, and with nearly as
> much privacy as a close carriage, if the curtains be
> drawn in front. It can go in and out of places where
> a two-horse carriage with four wheels cannot turn.
> —William Bridges Adams, *English Pleasure Carriages*,
>   1837

"This is maddening," Longmore told Sophy,
as they left yet another posting inn. "We
haven't a prayer of reaching London before dawn."

His sister drove ahead of them, and set the pace.
Glaciers moved faster.

"You did say she'd travel slowly," Sophy said.
"You said she'd need a powerful horse, and the
inns kept those for the stage and the Royal Mail."

"It never dawned on me that she'd refuse to
change hers," he said. "Seventy miles and some
from Portsmouth to London. I was prepared to
bribe the ostlers to get her the horses she'd need. A
day's journey, I reckoned. I hadn't reckoned on her
insisting on keeping her own."

Men took pride in being able to handle any sort of beast. But Clara didn't fancy herself a whipster. She wanted the beast she was familiar with. That meant extended stops to give the creature refreshment and rest.

"I can understand her dragging her heels," Sophy said. "Before, she had emotion driving her. It's probably like being in a fight. You don't think much, then, about getting hurt, do you?"

"Certainly not. All I care about is demolishing the other fellow."

"She wasn't thinking much, either, of danger or difficulties," she said. "She swam out over her head. Now the shore looks to be a long way away. And all she sees there is trouble."

"I know she's unhappy," he said tightly. "But there isn't a bloody thing I can do about it at the moment."

"No one can do anything at the moment," Sophy said. "I only wish I knew how to drive. She and I could trade places now and again."

He shook his head. "Even if you knew how, you'd hate driving the cabriolet. It's a fine, handsome vehicle to take a lady about London, but it isn't built for long journeys. Gets uncomfortable very quickly. Before, she might have been too wrought up to mind it, but now I reckon she's noticing the shaking her innards and bones are getting."

"How much farther is it?" Sophy said.

"We're not even halfway to London," he said. And the sun was sinking ever closer to the horizon.

"Do you think we ought to press on?" she said. "I know nothing about driving, and you know everything. I'm not concerned about traveling the entire distance this day—but from what you tell me, it's different for your sister."

"Completely different," he said. "The cabriolet is made for short jaunts about Town, not for long-distance work." He went on to explain the vehicle's design, its advantages and drawbacks, concluding with, "I bought it for her to drive herself about London. I never meant for her to take off across the country—and without her tiger, of all things!"

"She managed," Sophy said.

"I'm amazed, I must say," he said. "I didn't think Clara even knew how to put on her own stockings."

"I don't think she does," Sophy said.

"Did she tell you how she managed it?" he said.

"No."

Clara had shared Sophy's room. They'd slept in the same bed. Like sisters.

So strange. But Clara trusted her. Or was charmed by her.

Not that it made any difference.

"Did she happen to say anything more coherent than what she told us this morning?" he said.

"I thought it was coherent enough," Sophy said. "I don't need to know any more. I understand perfectly now. In any case, I thought rest would do her more good than talking. She seemed in better spirits after she slept."

"And you?" he said. "Are you in better spirits?"

She'd seemed a trifle blue-deviled.

"I'm relieved we've found her," she said. "I'm relieved she came to no harm. I'm only waiting for a brilliant solution to her problem."

* * *

No brilliant solution had presented itself by the time they stopped at the King's Arms at Godalming. By then, the sky was darkening, and they were, according to Lady Clara's road book, thirty-three and a half miles from London.

"We'll stop in Guildford," Longmore told them. "It's well supplied with inns, and I know we can count on a good dinner and decent rooms at any one of several." He eyed his sister, who looked worn out and deeply unhappy. 'It's only four miles, Clara. We'll find better lodging there than here. Thence it's a shorter drive to London tomorrow. Can you manage?"

She lifted her chin. "Of course I can. I drove to Portsmouth, didn't I? I can jolly well drive h-home."

The wobble at the end told Sophy all she needed to know. It must have told Longmore something, too, because his brow furrowed. But he said, briskly enough, "I'll take the lead this time. If you encounter any difficulties or feel unwell, signal to Fenwick, and he'll tell us."

He turned away to tell the boy he'd have to sit facing backward, to keep a sharp eye for trouble with the cabriolet. "And you're not to be sick with traveling backward," Longmore said.

"Sick?" Fenwick said scornfully. "From a little thing like that?"

Sophy didn't doubt he'd have a fine time amusing the women by pulling faces and attempting various tricks liable to land him on his head in the road.

That, at least, would give Lady Clara some distraction from her misery.

A little while later, when they were on their way again, Longmore said, "When we reach Guildford,

I'd better send an express to Valentine. That way the family won't be up all hours, waiting for her. They'll know she's safe, and they can go to bed and rest easy."

Sophy looked at him.

"What now?" he said.

"She's lucky to have you for a brother, and your parents are lucky to have you for a son," she said.

He laughed.

"It's true," she said. "To a point."

"To a point."

"So many other men would not be understanding at all," she said.

"I don't understand," he said. "I don't understand anything about it."

Yet he was kind, unexpectedly kind. Men weren't, always. They didn't necessarily mean to be unkind. But they were so accustomed to the world rolling on according to their desires that they never noticed when it rolled over women and crushed them.

"You understand that your sister needs help, not judging," she said. "That's a great deal."

He laughed. "What a joke. Who am I to judge anybody, I wonder? If not for Clevedon, I should have been ejected from school a hundred times. As the eldest son and heir, I make a deuced poor show."

She thought he made a fine and exciting show, but she wasn't like the members of his class. She was a Noirot, and drawn to daring and rule-breaking. By the standards of his world, he was primitive, she knew.

"I abhor politics," he said. "Philanthropy means

a lot of tedious dinners with bad food and pompous speeches. No fun there. You'd think the military would be promising, since it offers so many happy opportunities for fighting. But no. Even an officer must follow orders. Intolerable."

"The church isn't appropriate for the eldest son, I know," she said. "Otherwise, it would be perfect for you, would it not?"

He stared at her.

"Yes, let me think about it," she said. "Lord Longmore in holy orders. Now there's a picture."

He laughed, and the worry lines in his handsome, piratical face went away.

"What appalling choices you aristocrats have," she said. "I almost begin to feel sorry for you. You can't become a pugilist or a sword swallower in the circus—"

"The circus!"

"Or a buccaneer or a highwayman or a charioteer."

"Indeed, it's a deadly dull life sometimes, Miss Noirot, and my father doesn't care for my ways of livening it up. He gave up on me long ago. I'm no paragon. But you know that."

"You're a paragon of a brother," she said. "As to the rest, you're simply the sort of man who chafes at rules. Your sister does, too. The trouble is, it's nearly impossible for a lady to get away with breaking them."

"It's easier once she's wed," he said. "If Clara ends up married to that swine, I'll encourage her to break them. I'll offer suggestions."

"It won't come to that," Sophy said.

"You're so sure."

"Utterly sure," she lied.

At the moment, she had no idea what to do. All she knew was, everything depended on her doing it.

White Hart Inn, Guildford
That night

"I've had so much time to think, and I can't think how to get out of it," Lady Clara said.

Lord Longmore had sent his express message to London as soon as they'd arrived. He'd hired rooms, placing his sister in the one between his and Sophy's. Davis had a cot in her mistress's room, and a greatly surprised and gratified Fenwick had been given his own little room—the type of cupboardlike space usually allotted to a manservant—adjoining Longmore's.

After washing off the dirt of travel, Longmore, Lady Clara, and Sophy had dined. Following that, Longmore had told the women to get a full night's sleep, and had retired to his room.

But Lady Clara had invited Sophy to stop in her room first, to drink tea.

It wasn't tea Sophy discovered on the tray, though. It was brandy, a clear sign that her ladyship was more rattled than she'd seemed at dinner.

The night was by no means cold, but she'd complained of feeling chilled to death, and ordered a fire. They sat before it, their chairs close together.

"If I were less of a catch," she went on, "and if it hadn't happened so publicly, with all those people seeing me half undressed, there would be an easier way out."

"You weren't half undressed," Sophy said. "Your bodice was a little disarranged, that was all."

"Not that it makes any difference," Lady Clara said bitterly. "Ruined is ruined."

"We're going to un-ruin you," Sophy said. "Don't worry about it. Let me worry. All we need at present is a tale, in case anybody's recognized you at any point on the journey."

"That's not very likely."

"You truly believe that, don't you?" Sophy said. "How you contrived to survive a journey to Portsmouth is beyond me."

"It was more complicated than I thought, I'll admit," Clara said. "I'd no idea what things cost. But I knew we'd need money. I sent Davis to sell some of my dresses before we left London. She was the one who dealt with the innkeepers and such. We pretended she was my aunt. I kept in the background as much as possible."

"You, in the background." Sophy smiled. "That must have been a prodigious trick."

"I wore my plainest clothes and one of Davis's bonnets while we traveled."

"But you weren't so plain in Portsmouth," Sophy said. "Someone there might have recognized you. I think we'll say that Lord Longmore took you to Portsmouth to collect an old friend who was coming to the wedding."

The amusement faded and her ladyship's beautiful face set into the stubborn expression Sophy had seen before. "There isn't going to be a wedding."

"It's what we'll *say*," Sophy said. Her insides churned. There could not be a wedding. But she still had no idea how to stop it. Shedding an unwanted fiancé was simple enough. But to do it in a way that restored Lady Clara's good name? Was it even possible?

Meanwhile, time was running out for Maison Noirot.

Sophy bent over Lady Clara and set her hands on her shoulders. "Listen to me," she said. She spoke firmly. Her expression was confident and reassuring. She could persuade anybody of anything, and she'd persuade this girl. "This is a tricky situation, as you've said. You're the fly who's stepped into the spider's web. It's a sticky one, and unsticking you with your reputation intact is going to be a delicate business."

"It's bad," Lady Clara said. "I knew it was bad."

"It is," Sophy said. "But I've made you my mission, my only mission for the present. You need to be patient, though, and trust me."

"I'll try to be patient," Lady Clara said. "But we have so little time."

Sophy kept the confident and reassuring expression firmly in place while her heart sank. "How much time?" she said.

"Less than I'd thought." Lady Clara explained what had happened on the Wednesday and Thursday before she'd run away.

"Before the Queen's last Drawing Room of the Season," Sophy repeated when the tale came to an end. She hoped she hadn't heard correctly. She knew it was too much to hope.

The last Drawing Room was scheduled for the twenty-fourth of the month. Quarter Day. Doomsday.

"That's why I bolted," Clara said. "That was the last straw. I'd been counting on having months.

Mother was so opposed, I was sure she'd put it off for as long as possible."

It made no difference, Sophy told herself. The shop needed to recover lost business by Quarter Day, no matter what.

"More than a fortnight, then," she said calmly. "Plenty of time."

"Are you sure?"

"Of course."

Lady Clara looked up at her, and the hope and trust in her eyes made Sophy want to cry.

"Leave it to me," Sophy said.

Dammit, *now what?*

Sophy closed the door of Lady Clara's room behind her and stood for a moment staring blankly at the wall opposite.

She'd helped hunt the girl down.

She was taking her back to London.

Then what?

Only a little more than a fortnight—at most—to work a miracle.

If she failed . . .

"What ho!" a male voice called. "Look what's turned up, lads."

Sophy looked toward the sound of the voice.

Oh, perfect. It only wanted this. A quartet of drunken gentlemen. Worse, *young* drunken gentlemen, some of them still sporting spots.

"A miracle, an angel, most fetching," another of them said. "An angel dropped down from heaven."

"Whither, fair one?"

"Don't mind him, madam. That one's a clod-poll." The last speaker made a drunken attempt at a bow.

Sophy treated them to one of the special Noirot curtseys, the kind that took actors and dancers years of practice to perfect, and the kind that took onlookers completely by surprise. It made an excellent distraction. While the boys were trying to decide what to make of it, she reached into the concealed pocket of her skirt and unpinned the hatpin she kept there for emergencies. With luck, she wouldn't need to use it. The question was, Retreat to Lady Clara's room or continue on to her own?

"A ballet dancer, by Jupiter," one boy decided.

"Won't you dance for us?" said another. He lurched toward her, and stumbled. He grabbed her for balance, making her stagger and drop the hatpin.

She pushed. He held on. "Yes, let's dance," he said, blowing alcoholic fumes over her face.

"Get off," she said.

"That's right, get off," another one said. "She wants to dance with me." He pulled her away from his friend.

She thrust an elbow into his gut. He only laughed, too drunk to feel it, and pulled her against him, grabbing her bottom.

She stumbled back and he pushed her against the wall. The smell of drink was making her sick.

"I saw her first," one said.

"Wait your turn," said the one on top of her. "First I get a kiss."

He thrust his face at hers, lips puckered. She kicked him in the shin. He fell back, but someone else was there, grabbing her arm.

Panic welled, ice forming in her gut. They were merely boys, drunken boys, but there were too many of them. She had no weapon. She saw nothing in the corridor. Only an empty pair of boots, a long way away, awaiting cleaning.

She twisted her head, but she was trapped. They were all around her, too close. She kicked and struggled, but it was all a drunken game to them. Women didn't matter. Women were for fun.

She opened her mouth to scream. One of them fell onto her, knocking the wind out of her.

Panic swamped her mind. She struggled blindly, couldn't think. She pushed at the boy and started to scream.

A roar drowned her out.

She looked toward the sound.

Longmore was bearing down, face dark, eyes glittering with rage.

"What the devil?" said the one who'd fallen on her.

Longmore reached out and picked him off her and flung him aside.

"No fair!" his friend cried. "We saw her first!" He tried to pull Sophy against him.

Longmore knocked him aside. Another came at him, and he backhanded him. The boy staggered backward and fell.

Another tried to take a swing at Longmore. He stepped out of the way. The fist kept going, taking its owner with it, through an awkward turn. Momentum carried him to the top of the stairs, where he collided with the head post, and sank into a heap.

The corridor fell quiet.

"Anybody else want to play?" Longmore said.

He could barely see them. The world was a red glare, and he could barely hear above the blood pounding in his ears.

His fingers flexed, primed for violence. Itching to break and crush.

He waited.

There was a flurry and a scuffling and they were gone.

"Cowards," he said. He started after them.

That was when he heard it.

Thud.

Thud.

Thud.

He looked that way.

Sophy stood, her forehead resting on the door. He heard a catch and a sob, and another.

He saw her fist rise and go down on the door.

Thud.

Sob.

Thud.

Sob.

He forgot about the drunken gang.

He went to her. He turned her around. Tears streamed down her face. She was shaking.

"Are you all right? Did those bastards hurt you? I know they're boys, but if they hurt you—"

She hit him. "You idiot!"

She set her forehead against his chest, the way she'd done to the door. She sobbed, and she beat on him, in the same way. *Thump. Thump. Thump.*

"What?" he said.

"Don't help me!"

"Are you insane? Did they give you a concussion?"

Clara's door opened and her nightcapped head appeared. "What on earth is going on?"

"Nothing," Longmore said. "Go back to bed."

"Harry, are you brawling again?"

"It's over," Longmore said. "*Go to bed.*"

"Harry."

"Leave it alone," he said between his teeth.

Clara glared at him. But she drew back into her room, and the door closed.

"We need to get out of the corridor," Longmore said. "We've attracted enough attention."

"I don't care," Sophy said. She still trembled.

He picked her up.

"Put me down," she said.

"Stop it," he said. "You're hysterical."

He shifted her to take most of her weight in one arm, and opened the door to her room.

When they were inside the room, he kicked it shut behind him.

"I hate you," she said, her voice clogged with tears. "Stupid, drunken aristocrats. I didn't know what to do."

"I know," he said.

"I hate to be afraid."

"I know," he said.

He carried her to the bed. He was still shaking, too, with rage.

And fear.

If he'd fallen asleep, he mightn't have heard.

The doors were thick. Sounds from the corridor were muffled. And it was an inn. Drunken voices were only to be expected.

If he'd fallen asleep, he wouldn't have known.

They would have shamed her. Hurt her.

His gut knotted.

He sat on the bed, still holding her. "Why didn't you scream?" he said.

"I thought I could deal with it."

"Four of them?"

"They were drunk. Easily unbalanced. Easily diverted. But . . . I was slow."

"You were tired," he said.

"Don't make excuses! I'm not helpless!"

"I know," he said. He wasn't sure what he knew, except that she might have been hurt and she'd surely been afraid, and she had every reason in the world to be wild and unreasonable.

A lot of boys, down from Oxford or wherever, drunk and looking for fun. And she'd looked like fair game: an expensive tart—the disguise she'd adopted to help him find Clara. He felt sick.

"I went for my hatpin," she said. "But they were all jostling me. So many of them, the clumsy oafs. I dropped it."

"You should have screamed for help, straight off," he said.

"I never had to scream for help in my life," she said.

What hellish kind of life had she led? She was a dressmaker. By the sounds of things, the profession made war look like a tea party.

"There's always a first time," he said.

"I was going to scream," she said. "But that numskull fell on me, and he knocked the wind out of me."

"Yes, well, I'm sure you could have got out of that on your own," he said. "But the bumping and bumbling and such had already roused me from a pleasant doze, and I wasn't about to stand idly by when a fight was on offer."

"Yes." She clutched her head.

He brought his hand up and covered hers and gently pressed her head against his shoulder. "You had a bad moment," he said.

"I don't know what to do," she said. "I always know what to do. It's a horrible feeling, not knowing. Being helpless. I hate it."

"You're not helpless," he said. "You're too unscrupulous to be helpless. You're temporarily at sea, that's all." He paused. "Not only about those oafs."

"No."

"About Clara."

"Yes. She's one passenger. On my boat—the one that's tossing on the sea, rudderless and doesn't know where it is."

"What else?" he said.

"You know," she said. "Your mother. How to bring her round."

"Hopeless cause," he said. "Throw her off the boat."

She pushed his hand away and lifted her head. "She's making our life so difficult," she said.

"She does that to everybody," he said. "Tackle something you can manage. Adderley, for a start. Fix your busy mind on him. Forget about my mother. Forget about those spotty boys. They don't know how easy they got off. Another minute, and you'd have thought of something, and they'd *wish* some big fellow would come along and knock them about."

She was looking up into his eyes, and he saw something change. A flicker, a light, like the first star of evening.

Then her mouth slowly curved upward.

And while he watched that slow smile, the tension he hadn't known he was holding began to ease.

He saw the devil lurking in her eyes and in the

edges of the smile, where it lifted the corners of her lips.

He was so tempted to touch his lips there.

Too crass, probably.

But he was a man, and she was in his lap, and she was warm and soft. And now that her distress was sliding away her body relaxed, too. Now he was acutely aware of every curve and exactly where each part of her touched a part of him.

She bent her head and lifted his hand and held it against her cheek.

His breath caught.

"You're impossible," she said softly. "Just when I want to strike you with a blunt instrument . . . you say things . . . do things."

"It's all part of my cunning plan," he said. He'd said whatever came into his head. If it happened to be the right thing, that was an accident.

"You don't give up, do you?" she said.

"Obstinate," he said. "It runs in the family."

"Yes. Things run in my family, too." She sighed.

She turned her face into his hand and kissed the palm.

The touch jolted through him like a lightning bolt.

"Thank you for saving me," she said. "No one ever did that before."

"Why the devil not?" he said.

"They weren't you," she said.

She came up off his lap and onto her knees, straddling him. She rested her hands on his shoulders and leaned in as though about to tell him a secret . . . and she kissed his cheek. It was the lightest touch, like a butterfly, but it was a shock again, and then his heart was beating too hard, pumping blood everywhere but to his brain.

Great Zeus.

She kissed his earlobe.

She thrust her fingers though his hair.

"Oh," she said. "This is intolerable."

"What is?" he said thickly.

"Self-restraint."

"Then throw it off the boat," he said.

"All right," she said.

And she grasped a fistful of his hair and held him while she kissed him, firmly, determinedly . . .

Exactly the way he'd kissed her.

Exactly the way he'd taught her.

Only better.

Chapter Twelve

In examining their own conduct, analysing motives and correcting errors, repressing those faults to which they know that they are prone, and resolving to cultivate virtues in which they have proved themselves defective,—females, at all ages, are, it is evident, exceedingly well employed.

—*The Young Lady's Book*, 1829

She'd been too demented before to take any notice.

But a few minutes in his arms, listening to his low voice sort out the world in a way only he could do . . . that had brought her back.

To him.

He'd taken off his coat and neckcloth, and his black hair was tousled. The lamplight made his shirtsleeves almost transparent, revealing the outlines of the muscled arms holding her. Her cheek had lain against his silk waistcoat. She could smell him and she could feel him: the big shoulders and lean torso under waistcoat and shirt. Her gaze had drifted downward, over the fine embroidery, glimmering in the soft light.

She was aware of his strong thighs under her

and below them the long legs in tight trousers that left one nothing to imagine.

Her insides were vibrating.

She'd been so wretched and wild.

But he'd rescued her and he'd said things, and her mind had come back and her confidence, too.

And desire.

She wanted him. She'd wanted him from the moment she'd first seen him storming through a corridor of Clevedon House, looking like murder.

And now she wanted him with a craving fiercer than anything she'd known before in all her life. Even the shop dimmed in her mind, next to him.

How long was she supposed to wait?

Why did she have to be good?

She was a Noirot.

She threw self-restraint off the boat.

She kissed him fearlessly and deeply, the way he'd taught her. And while she kissed him, she let her hands rove over his big shoulders, where his shirt's thin linen allowed her to feel his skin's warmth and his muscles' tensing under her touch.

The pleasure of it was almost unbearable. It was as though her insides held a sea of feelings, all in a beautiful storm, rocking her this way and that.

She rocked, too, in his lap, letting the wonderful feelings carry her along. She felt him stiffen and start to draw away.

"Wait," he said. "Wait one . . ."

"Wait for what?" She nibbled his ear.

"You need to tell me . . ." his voice trailed off.

"What shall I tell you?" she said.

"Never mind. I forget."

He wrapped his arms about her, and kissed her

back. No waiting, no hesitating. Bold and straight to the point, as direct as a blow to the head.

She was dizzy, but she knew what to do. He'd taught her.

They kissed like a dance and like a duel: advancing, retreating, circling, in a world that grew steadily darker and hotter while thought drifted beyond reach.

She found the button of his shirt and unbuttoned it. She slipped her hand into the opening to touch his skin, and it was a shock, feeling his throat and collarbone under her palm. It was a shock to him, too, making his body go rigid. But he didn't push her away. He tightened his hold, bringing her closer. She could feel his arousal under her. She knew what that was. She would have understood even if her sister had never explained it. He wanted her.

She wanted him.

That was all.

Dangerous. Wrong. Reckless.

Irresistible.

She pushed, and he loosened his hold and looked at her. His eyes were so dark, black as midnight, black as the sin they promised.

She pushed again, hard, leaning into the push. He finally got the hint and gave way. He fell back onto the bed with a choked laugh.

"Sophy—"

"*Oui*," she said. "*C'est bien moi.*"

"Sophy," he said, in the low, lover's voice. Tingling sensations traveled up and down her spine. They set off things inside. Heat. Impatience.

She crawled over him. "What do I have to do?" She started unbuttoning his waistcoat.

"You devil," he said. "Come here."

Her pulled her down and kissed her, but this was different, more tender. He kissed her forehead, her eyebrows, her nose, her cheeks, her chin. He kissed her ear and then her neck, in the sensitive place under her ear. She shivered.

He kissed her in this way until she was trembling and dizzy. Then he brought his big hand flat against her back and rolled her onto the bed, changing their positions. He was on top, looking down at her, and all she saw were fathomless black depths, hot and promising sin and sin again.

Her heart raced like a mad thing.

He drew his hands down from her shoulders and down, slowly, deliberately, over her breasts, and she went hot everywhere, down to her toes. She let out an aching sigh that sounded like a moan in the quiet night. So quiet it was. They might have been far away, only they two, and no one else in the world.

They were quiet, too. Nothing broke the night's silence but sighs, murmurs of wanting and pleasure, and the rustle of clothing and bedclothes.

Lower his hands slid, over her belly and down to the place between her legs. She stretched and moved, seeking more, as a cat did when petted, though no cat could feel like this. His hands—cunning, capable hands—tracing the shape of her, learning everything about her, all the private places her beautiful dresses hid.

Then he was turning her onto her side, and she felt his hands moving over her back, over the fastenings. She remembered this morning, and a wave of heat flooded her.

In a moment he'd loosened her bodice. There

was a flurry of movement, and she was aware of tapes coming undone while he kissed her neck and shoulders. He drew away to pull the dress over her head, moving her this way and that, as if she'd been a doll. He threw the dress aside and she heard the whooshing noise it made as it slid to the floor.

Her shoes went next. The sleeve puffs flew away. He quickly undid her corset, which came undone easily, as it was made to do. With a few flicks of his fingers and a twist of his body, he shed his waistcoat.

His shirt hung open where she'd undone the button. She slid her hands over the fine linen, tracing the warm ridges and planes of his chest and belly. Under her touch, his muscles tensed and flexed.

She touched, and he answered. She wasn't helpless. She'd never be helpless again.

She had power, over this big, dangerous man.

She was dimly aware of her petticoat sailing away, and her chemise following it. Her garters came undone and her stockings slid down. She didn't care. She was wrapped up in him. She'd watched him fight. She'd watched him drive. She'd watched him walk. She'd watched him move. Whenever he was in the vicinity, she'd never been able to look away. And now she couldn't stop touching, and wondering at him, at his strength and beauty, at everything that made him what he was and who he was.

Like all her family, she'd always dared and gambled and risked. She dared now, running her palm over his trouser front, over the fascinating ridge there, hot and pulsing against her hand. Cousin Emma's voice sounded in her head, but the warning was too faint, stuck in a distant corner of her mind.

There was too much of him, overpowering reason. To much rampant masculinity overwhelming her senses. Too much wanting, overruling her good sense.

He bent and kissed her, and the kiss made her ache. It blotted out cousins and Paris and London and every ordinary thing.

She cared about nothing but this moment between them. All the world shrank to him: the taste of him and the feel of his mouth . . . the way he was rough and gentle at the same time . . . the weight of his body when he pressed against her.

He kissed her everywhere: her face, her neck, her shoulders, her breasts—and that made her want to cry again, and laugh, too. Down farther he went, kisses like little fires over her belly, while she tangled her fingers in his hair. And down farther still he went, to the place between her legs.

She felt his hands gripping her thighs while his tongue did to her most private place what he'd done to her mouth. Then nothing made sense anymore . . . and everything did, finally.

Everything changed. The world was another place, a great black lagoon on a sultry night. The air was thick, intoxicating. Pleasure grew and grew and an ache grew with it, for something she couldn't name but needed to find, to reach.

She was aware of the movement and the rustling as he shed the rest of his clothing. Then he brought his nakedness against hers as his mouth covered hers again, and the kiss was so deep, so tender, and so endlessly sweet—

And he thrust into her, shocking her out of the

lust-drunken stupor. The fog in her mind lifted
and her eyes flew open. She was aware of the size
and heat of his phallus . . . inside her. It was strange
and uncomfortable and she felt trapped. And *What
have I done?* she thought.

But he was kissing her still, and his mouth moved
from her lips to her cheeks and throat, and her tension melted under the tender caresses. Shock faded,
and her body eased, slowly accepting his. Then it
was strange and wondrous, to be joined so intimately. She slid her hands over his back, relishing
the feel of his skin and the pulse of muscle under
her hand.

The scent of a man filled the air and filled her
nostrils and her head. She was drunk on it. She
was drunk on her power over him and his over
her. When he began to move inside her, she moved
instinctively, catching his rhythm in the same way
she'd learned his way of kissing . . . as though
somehow she'd always known and had simply been
waiting for the signal to begin.

He played her gently and slowly at first. She felt
like a violin, and the feelings were music. Then,
when he had every string of her being vibrating,
the music grew more intense. The slow, deliberate
thrusts came faster and harder. The world grew
darker and wilder, and she moved in that world as
though she was, finally, in her element. She moved
with him at the same hectic rate, racing recklessly
to some unknown destination.

And all that was in her heart was *Yes, take me
with you.*

He took her, and after the feverish hurry and
ferocity, it was a shock again when something
seemed to burst inside her, and pleasure broke out,

wave upon wave of it, until everything went away, and only happiness remained. She drifted there, in happiness, and a strange quiet filled her, a delicious, unexpected peace.

How long Sophy hung in that nothingness, she wasn't sure. She was dimly aware of his easing away from her and drawing her up against his warm body, her back to his front. She felt so comfortable and safe and warm.

Perhaps she'd slept. Or maybe she'd simply hung suspended, in a trance, for a time. She wasn't sure.

All she knew was that the world came back abruptly, her eyes flew open, and her mind came back with painful clarity and, "Oh, no!" she said.

She jerked out of his arms and sat up. "I can't believe it. How could I? No, no, no! Please let this be a dream."

"Sophy." His voice was thick, sleep-clogged.

"It's not your fault," she said. "It's mine. I did it on purpose. I can't believe it. I did it on *purpose*—when I *knew*—" She writhed in agony. "Oh, how could I be so stupid?"

"Sophy," he said.

"Why not simply blow up the shop?" she said. "Why not set fire to it? What better way to destroy the business than this?"

"Sophy," he said. "Go to sleep."

"I can't sleep at a time like this!"

He reached up and wrapped one muscular arm around her and pulled, and down she went.

"Be quiet," he said.

"We're ruined!" she said. "And I did it! Why didn't I simply go to work for Horrible Hortense? I couldn't have done her a bigger favor."

"Sophy, go to sleep," he said. "No talking. We're not *discussing* this now. Go to sleep."

Then he brought one big, warm hand up to cup her breast. She sighed. She snuggled back against him. She fell asleep.

When next Longmore woke, it was on his own. The level of light told him the morning had advanced, but not very far.

He felt her stir next to him.

"Oh, no," she said. "Oh, no."

He swallowed a sigh.

"What am I going to—"

"Wait one minute," he said. He turned her toward him and kissed her neck. He'd discovered it was a weak spot, one of many.

"Oh," she said, in the way that made his cock come to rigid attention.

He went on kissing her because he liked the feel and smell and taste of her skin and the way she reacted, all instinct, no playacting. In lovemaking, she was completely honest.

He went on kissing her because he liked doing it and because he was a reckless man who had never formed the habit of worrying about consequences.

He ran his hands over her naked body, and she wriggled with pleasure.

"Not fair," she said thickly. "Not fair."

"I don't play fair, either," he said, echoing what she'd said the other day. He kissed her everywhere his hands had gone. He lingered at some of the most delicious places—the spot behind her ear and the inside of her elbow. He kissed her breast with special appreciation before taking the perfect pink bud into his mouth and gently sucking. Her legs moved against his and her belly tautened. She thrust her hands into his hair—and that possessive gesture sapped his control.

Still, as unthinking a man as he was, his basic instincts were strong. Those simple instincts told him he might not have another chance like this, and he'd better make the most of it.

He paid the other, perfect, perfect breast the same homage, and worked his way down. He lingered for a time in the silky golden triangle between her legs, letting his tongue flick over her until she was moaning helplessly, murmuring in French some nonsense and some exceedingly sweet endearments. Then he continued down along the route he'd envisioned countless times: along the beautiful curves of her leg and down to the finely-turned ankle and the elegant instep and down to her perfect toes. He kissed each one.

Then he started all over again, working his way down the other side.

And when he was done, he turned her onto her belly.

"My lord," she said.

"Harry, I think," he said. "We needn't be formal at present."

"Harry," she said breathlessly.

He was not sure any woman who wasn't a near relative had ever uttered his Christian name. She even made it sound . . . French.

He was sure it had never before seemed so fine and desirable a name.

He kissed the nape of her neck, and let his hands follow his mouth, over every inch of her back. Such a back this was: straight and silky smooth . . . and at its base the beautiful curve and rise of her perfect bottom.

He kissed it, reverently.

She giggled.

He wedged himself between her legs and brought his hand up to stroke her. She caught her breath and arched up, moving against his hand. She was damp against his fingers, and that, in an instant, made him impatient. He pulled her up against him and guided his cock into her from behind.

"Oh, oh, oh," she gasped.

"Yes," he said. He nuzzled her neck.

Yes yes yes yes yes.

All his mind and body said it. With one hand he held her against him and with the other he held the silky mound between her legs while he moved inside her with slow strokes.

He wanted to make it last for hours, but his control wasn't strong enough. He eased out of her and brought her down gently and turned her over.

He entered her again, in the usual way, a splendid way, because he could see her face and because she put her hands on him in that wonderful way she did, as though it was the most natural thing in the world and she'd known him forever and he'd been hers forever.

She stroked over his belly and down to the place where they were joined, and pushed against him, her rhythm matching his, then driving his.

He saw her face change as she neared her peak, and he gave one hard, deep thrust, and she cried out. Then he spent, and his body went on vibrating for a time after, until at last he sank down, and buried his face in her neck.

* * *

They'd slept again, and the light streaming in told Sophy it was mid morning, long past the time she'd normally rise. She wasn't eager to rise now.

It was so very comfortable, sleeping in a man's arms, and Longmore kept her snuggled close.

He likes women, she thought.

But then, what did she know? Only what she'd heard: women complaining of men turning away and going to sleep. Or making abrupt departures.

He hadn't departed yet, and that was going to be a problem, given that his sister was next door.

She felt his body change position behind her.

Behind her. She remembered what he'd done. *That* had been interesting.

"You have to go," she said.

"Not yet," he mumbled.

"Your sister," she said.

"Won't be awake for hours."

"You can't be sure."

"She doesn't keep a shop. You get up at the crack of dawn. Clara sleeps like the dead and never rises before eleven."

Sophy sat up.

"Oh, good," he muttered. "We're going to *discuss* it now."

"No discussion," she said. Her mind was quite clear now, as though a fire had blazed through it, burning away all confusion. "It's perfectly simple. *No One Must Ever Know.*"

He came up onto one elbow and looked at her. "Do you know," he said, "I can hear those five words in italics. Capitalized."

"I mean it," she said. "If nobody knows, nobody knows. You must promise to tell nobody."

"I'd like to know where you get the idea that I'm the sort of fellow who confides my amorous affairs to my friends," he said. "Do you think I'm the sort who boasts of deflowering virgins?"

"Who said I was a virgin?"

"No one had to say anything. I worked it out for myself. Eventually."

"Because I didn't know what to do," she said.

"That and your extremely snug little lady part."

"I didn't have time!" she said. "I never had time for men."

"I wasn't criticizing," he said. "It was a bit of a shock, but . . . actually . . ."

"You like being the first."

"Yes," he said. "I do. It's odd. I never was the type who cared for that sort of thing. But in your case, I'll make an exception."

She liked his being the first, too. The world was filled with philanderers and false men. Marcelline had married one. Lady Clara had got into trouble with one.

But whatever Longmore's faults might be, he was exactly what he seemed to be. Himself. Always.

It was reassuring.

"Well, then, as long as you keep silent, there's no problem," she said.

"What about you?" he said. "Will you keep silent?"

"I don't propose to advertise it in *Foxe's Morning Spectacle*, if that's what you mean."

"That isn't what I mean. What about your sisters? Do you or do you not tell them everything?

"Ye-e-es."

"Well?"

"They're not going to tell anybody."

"They're women," he said.

"Who would they tell?" she said. "Clevedon's aunts? Our customers? Do be sensible."

"Why should I start now?"

"I promise you, we've enough troubles with Marcelline's having trespassed on aristocratic territory," she said. "If it gets about that I've seduced Lady Warford's eldest son, she'll do more than blackball Maison Noirot. She'll crush us. Permanently. Even I won't be able to revive the shop. My sisters know that."

"Very well," he said. "As long as we understand who seduced whom."

"That part is painfully clear," she said.

"You couldn't help yourself," he said.

"Actually, I couldn't," she said. "If I hadn't the opportunity—if you hadn't been so shockingly understanding—and tempting—"

"I worked damned hard at that. The tempting part. I wasn't sure you were paying attention."

"Apparently, I was doing little else but."

"Good. I had a whole strategy laid out."

She looked at him. "You *thought about it*?"

"I had to, didn't I?" he said. "You're complicated."

"Simpler than you suppose," she said. "I'm not a good girl."

"And I'm not a good boy," he said. "It's unsporting to chase inexperienced girls. But I couldn't resist."

"Of course not," she said. "I can't be resisted. So you mustn't blame yourself."

"That's one thing I never do," he said. "Still . . ."

He frowned. "We might have made one of those . . . you know . . . little squirmy pink things that howl."

"A baby," she said. "I know."

"In that case—"

"Let's not cross that bridge until we come to it," she said, ignoring the icy panic in her gut. "Right now, I have a more pressing problem. Your sister's wedding is only a fortnight away."

Longmore had simply lain there, lazily letting Sophy's fascinating view of the world entertain him while he gazed at her wonderfully naked body. There were her breasts, in plain view, and a magnificent view it was.

It took a moment for the last sentence to sink in. Then he came completely awake. He sat up. "You're roasting me."

She shook her head, and the blonde curls tumbled this way and that.

No wonder she'd fallen apart last night. "I didn't realize," he said. "I'd thought my mother would delay the inevitable as long as possible."

She told him what his sister had told her about Lady Bartham and his mother.

"I've sworn to make that wedding not happen and to restore your sister's reputation," she said. "I told her she was my mission, my only mission. I'm sorry . . ."

She closed her eyes briefly. "Wait." She opened them, all brilliant blue. "I'm *not* sorry about all this." She gestured at him and at the bed. "It was stupid of me—but it was exciting and wonderful, and I can't imagine a more thrilling end to maidenhood. But I need to concentrate on business."

"Right." He folded his arms under his head. He'd have to do something about her. He wasn't sure what.

Whatever it was, he'd have to work it out on his own.

She wasn't going to help, and he wasn't going to ask anybody's advice.

The very thought of confiding his amorous doings to anybody made his blood run cold.

In any case, he was Sworn to Secrecy.

Even when he thought it, he pictured the words as Sophy would write them, capitalized.

No One Must Ever Know.

She'd infected him with her melodramatics.

He gazed fondly at her for a long moment.

"Business," she said.

"Right," he said.

She let out a sigh, and he watched her bosom rise and fall. "You need to go now," she said. "Your sister mightn't be up for hours, but Davis could already be stirring."

"Right."

He left the bed and began unearthing his clothes from the chaos of mingled outer and undergarments, hosiery and shoes.

Sophy left the bed and, as naked as a newly made Eve, helped him dress.

When he was at the door and about to leave, she gave a little sigh, and ran up to him and grasped his lapels. He bent his head.

She rose on tiptoe and kissed him hard on the lips.

Then, "Go," she said. "Go . . ." Her voice trailed away, her hands slid from his lapels, and her head tipped to one side. Though she was looking at him, he knew she didn't quite see him. He could see her, though, every pink and white and gold inch of her.

"Wait," she said.

"Yes," he said. She was thinking. He could almost see the wheels turning, satanic mills at work.

"Oh," she said. "Yes."

Her eyes widened, her blue gaze sharpened to sapphire brilliancy. "I've got it," she said.

She rested her head on his chest. He let his hand slide up to ruffle those golden curls. He manfully resisted the other hand's itching to clasp her breast.

"You splendid man," she said. "I've got it."

"Got what?" he said dimly, lost in the scent of her hair and skin, the summery scent of a far away place where he'd been happy. "And what makes me—"

"I've got the idea," she said. "I know how we're going to save your sister."

Warford House
That night

The family had risen from dinner and were in the library when Longmore brought his sister home.

Their mother instantly jumped up from her chair. "Oh, Clara how *could* you?" she cried.

Longmore saw his sister brace herself for the onslaught of recrimination, accusation, and other verbal assault that was Lady Warford's idea of affectionate motherly advice to her eldest daughter.

Longmore opened his mouth to say something undutiful.

Then Lady Warford rushed at Clara and wrapped

her arms about her, and wept, "Oh, my dear girl, I'm so happy you're home. You must never, never run away again. Whatever the trouble is, you must tell me, my love. Promise. Promise me, please."

It was, he thought, the first *please* he'd ever heard issue from his mother's lips.

"I'm sorry, Mama," Clara said. Her voice, muffled against her mother's shoulder, sounded shocked.

"This has been a dreadful business for you," their mother said. "Traumatic to a young girl's sensibilities—but of course you knew nothing of what men can be like. You trusted him, foolish girl. But how could you know? It's ever the way. They are never what we think them to be." She gave Clara another crushing hug and stepped away. "I must say that Harry has surprised me. He's surprised us both, has he not, Warford?"

Longmore's father said, "So he has. Good work. Looking after your sister. Made a muck of it the first time—"

"Warford," said his spouse.

"But you found her and brought her back. A good thing, too. Thanks to your clever ruse, we've learned that Adderley might not be entirely the blackguard we thought him to be."

"I need a drink," Longmore said, and made his way posthaste to the nearest decanter. It was sherry, not his first choice, but it would do. He poured himself a generous glassful and drank.

"He has called every day," said Lady Warford.

"Heard of Clara's indisposition," Lord Warford said. "Very solicitous he was."

"Flowers, my dear," said Lady Warford. "He brought flowers for you. And fruit from his greenhouses. He seemed quite distraught with worry, did he not, Warford?"

"Most solicitous," said Lord Warford.

"He said that he understood that the circumstances leading to your betrothal were not what one could hope—but he said—he said . . ." Lady Warford trailed off. "I can't remember exactly what he said, but it was all it ought to be. There's no changing the fact that he's a bankrupt, and his mother is not what one could wish for. But she is dead, and he does seem to care about you, Clara, and I do believe that with a little work, you can make something of him."

Though Clara was clearly taken aback, she caught Longmore's warning look, and contrived to appear to be seriously taking this in.

He didn't try to hide his incredulity. Not that anybody would expect him to. He was sure Adderley's worry about Clara was genuine: If she sickened and died before the wedding, he'd need to find another fortune in a hurry, and dowries like Clara's weren't thick on the ground.

"If anybody can make a man of him, it's Clara," he said. "In any event, I've said before that we need to make the best of matters. There'll be less talk if we all seem pleased with the arrangement. It does no harm for the world to see that we've belatedly discovered that Adderley isn't quite so bad as everyone's assumed. For my part, I promise to be civil to him when next I see him." He drank the rest of his sherry and set down his glass. "May I go now?"

Chapter Thirteen

To secure the honour of, and prevent the spreading of any scandal upon peers . . . by reports, there is an express law, called scandalum magnatum, by which any man convicted of making a scandalous report against a peer of the realm (though true) is condemned to an arbitrary fine, and to remain in custody till the same be paid.

—*Debrett's Peerage of England, Scotland, and Ireland,*
1820

Exclusive to Foxe's Morning Spectacle
Wednesday 10 June

It has come to our attention that a Mysterious Stranger from France has arrived this week in London with a considerable retinue. The trunks containing the lady's wardrobe, we are informed, were so numerous as to require the hire of a private vessel. This portends a lengthy stay on our green and pleasant isle. As to where, specifically, in these domains the lady will reside, to what purpose, and—most especially—her identity, we hope to inform our readers with our usual alacrity.

The Queen's Theatre
Wednesday night

All of London was aware that the Duke of Clevedon had met Madame Noirot at the opera in Paris. This night was the first, however, that she'd appeared in any theater in London, and the occasion left no one in the audience—the masculine part of the audience, certainly—in any doubt as to why the duke of Clevedon had succumbed to the lady.

This was the first time any gathering of Those Who Mattered had ever seen her. While the handful of Maison Noirot's clients present knew her, these were primarily ladies of the gentry classes and aristocracy's lower ranks. In the great scheme of things, they counted, but not very much.

To all intents and purposes, this was Fashionable Society's first look.

The men looked very hard, indeed, because His Grace had escorted into his box not one dashing woman but two: his duchess and a fair-haired stranger.

Across the theater, in the Warfords' box, Lady Warford gazed resolutely at the stage, refusing to acknowledge the new Duchess of Clevedon's existence.

Clara, however, stared for all she was worth. To Lord Adderley, who sat dutifully beside her, acting the part of attentive spouse-to-be, she said, "Do you know who that lady is with the Duchess of Clevedon?"

Adderley, who'd been staring as hard as everybody else, turned a surprised look on her. "Don't you know? I thought she must be one of the sisters. Isn't one of them a blonde?"

"The sisters are unwed, and this lady is wearing the dress of a married woman," Clara said. "A married Frenchwoman, I should say."

Longmore, who sat behind the engaged couple, said "French? You can tell that from this distance? And without employing an opera glass—as the other ladies are doing, I notice."

"One can always tell," Clara said. "We Englishwomen can wear exactly what Frenchwomen do and yet somehow we always look English." She turned round to meet her brother's gaze. "You were in Paris, Harry. Don't you agree?"

Their mother made a harrumphing noise and sent a frigid glare their way. Both of her offspring pretended not to notice.

"What I can be sure of is that she's got the theater in an uproar," Longmore said. "One can hardly hear the performers—not always a bad thing, although I'd rather she'd done it at a long, boring German opera instead of during *The Waterman*. But a little stimulation for the performers to outdo themselves won't come amiss. I believe I'll toddle round at the interval and make Clevedon introduce me. Then I can tell all of you what the fuss is about, a few hours in advance of the *Spectacle*, for once."

Knowing that a great many other fellows would be traveling to the same destination, he left his family's box some minutes before the interval began, and entered Clevedon's ahead of the pack.

His nod in Clevedon's general direction passed for polite greetings.

"Beat the other fellows by a furlong," he said.

"I thought you would," Clevedon said. "You can be quick enough off the mark when you choose."

Longmore turned to Her Grace. "Before the hordes descend, Duchess, would you be so good as to make me known to the lady?"

"Madame de Veirrion, will you permit me to introduce Lord Longmore, a very good friend of my husband," the duchess said.

Her friend looked blank.

Her Grace repeated the introduction in French.

"Ah, yes," said Madame. "Thees friend of a long time. *Comme un frère, n'est-ce pas?* Lord Lun-mour." She gave a little nod, and the brilliants artfully arranged among the plumes of her headdress sparkled and danced.

Her English was comically dreadful. To spare her, Longmore carried on their exchange in French. This gave him a small advantage over the mob of males who stampeded into Clevedon's box a moment later. While most of them spoke correct French, as a properly educated gentleman ought to do, it was like Clevedon's—correct French spoken by an Englishman. It was the conversational version of dress, as Clara had described it: They had all the right words, but they still sounded English.

Longmore, the world's worst scholar, had, for some reason, an aptitude for languages. The Latin-based ones, at any rate.

"But Monsieur de Lun-mour speaks my language like the *parisiens*," said Madame. "How is this? Me, my English, he is stupid. I cannot be taught. *Hélas*, they try. *Mon mari*—my 'usband so dear—" Her blue eyes grew dewy. A lacy handkerchief appeared in her beringed and braceleted hand, and she dabbed gently at the tears. "*Ce pauvre Robert!* He try and try to teach me. But what? I am the dunces."

All the gentlemen begged to differ.

Longmore said, when they'd quieted down, "But you are a charming and beautiful dunces, madame. And," he continued in French, "a charming and beautiful woman can get away with murder. Can you imagine that any man here would prosecute you for assassinating our language?"

Longmore left Madame and her coterie shortly before the interval ended, and returned to his family's box.

His mother was looking daggers, and no wonder: Lady Bartham had joined her, and had undoubtedly been rubbing salt in as many wounds as she could find. Or inflict.

"A French lady, as you deduced," Longmore told his sister, not troubling to lower his voice. The two older women stopped talking. "Madame de Veirrion. A friend of the duchess from her Paris days. A widow—of some means, I'd say. I bow to my sister's knowledge of dress, but the lady's looked deuced expensive to me. The jewelry's easier to judge, and it isn't paste, I assure you."

Lady Bartham put her glass to her eye and proceeded to inspect the French lady.

After the briefest hesitation, Mother did the same. "A widow, did you say, Longmore?"

She always took care to use her eldest son's title with Lady Bartham, who had two marriageable daughters, both dark-haired little fairies, too bony for his taste.

"Quite a young widow," Longmore said. "Speaks the most appalling English."

"That presents no problem to you," Clara said.

"No, indeed," Adderley said. "Always was your forte, language. That and the punishing uppercut." He smiled ruefully, and stroked his jaw. The bruise was still visible. "Served me right, too," he said in a low voice.

It was exactly what a man ought to say if he wanted to make peace with his in-laws-to-be. He did it so well that a less cynical man than Longmore might have believed it.

"You were there a good while," Clara said.

"She's pretty, and she mangles English in a most charming manner," he said.

"Clearly, she's charming," Lady Bartham said. "She seems to have enthralled all the gentlemen."

"Frenchwomen so often do," Lady Warford said darkly.

"I thought the duke would be obliged to summon the attendants to control the crowd," Clara said.

"She's undoubtedly caused a commotion," said Lady Bartham. She turned her sharp hazel gaze upon Longmore. "But who *is* she?"

Exclusive to Foxe's Morning Spectacle
Thursday 11 June 1835

Who is she? That is the question on every-one's lips since last night, when the Myste-rious Stranger made her appearance at the Queen's Theatre, wearing a black satin dress, the corsage à la Sevigné, ornamented with a row of black bows. The sleeves, which were topped with nœuds de page, were very full, with double sabots of white satin. What appeared at first to be a robe was in fact an artful illusion created by a front panel of gold brocaded satin.

Your correspondent has it on the very best authority that Madame de V_____ is the descendant of a French count whose family was long associated with the court of the House of Bourbon, and who perished, tragically, as did so many members of the ancien regime, under the guillotine blade. Given the present unrest in Paris, we cannot be surprised that the lady, bereft in this last year of the protection of a devoted husband and acting no doubt on the sage advice of her counselors, has determined to place herself and her considerable fortune (rivaling, we are told, that of the Duke of C_____) in the peaceful realms of His British Majesty. We are told that the lady has determined to seek a permanent residence in London. In the meantime, she has taken a suite of rooms at one of those hotels described in Cruchley's Picture of London *as having* "sheltered the incognito of foreign grandees and potentates." *We are reliably informed that the lady was one of the Duchess of C_____'s premier patrons during Her Grace's long sojourn in Paris, and that both Madame and the late Monsieur de V_____ were among His Grace's numerous acquaintance during his time there.*

Following the usual court news, general gossip, commentary on the Sheridan-Grant elopement, and amusing anecdotes, there appeared at the end of the last column preceding the page of advertisements, this note:

> *We observed last night a certain lord in the company of the lady he is to wed in a fortnight. We are pleased to report that the lady appears fully recovered from her recent alarming illness. We cannot claim to be pleased to inform our readers that later in the same evening—or it would be more accurate to say, in the early hours of the following morning—his lordship was observed to enter a gaming establishment of dubious reputation, from which he did not emerge until some hours after dawn. For all of those—and we count ourselves among them—who have wished her ladyship, in spite of the distressing circumstances that precipitated her engagement, a happy future, this is a most disheartening turn of events. We had hoped that, having obtained the hand of this beautiful lady, his lordship would show his gratitude by resolving to go and sin no more. We had hoped that, having left his errors behind him, he would reflect upon the errors of his forbears, and resolve—for the lady's sake if not his own honor—to restore dignity to the family name. As our readers are no doubt aware, his lordship's father was awarded a barony for services rendered to a royal personage. These included considerable loans, one of which was the loan of his*

*beautiful wife for an indeterminate time. The
fortune having long since been dissipated at
the gaming tables, we must wonder at the
motives and mendacity of any person who
encourages his lordship to further folly by
extending him credit for such a purpose.*

Drawing room, Warford House
Thursday afternoon

Like most of the ton, Lord Adderley had read
the *Spectacle* with his morning coffee. He
swore a great deal, and abused his valet and every
other servant who had the misfortune to cross his
path this day. Having put his household into a state
of seething resentment, he'd hastened across town
to present himself to his intended. There he proceeded to lie through his teeth—that was to say,
issue a suitably indignant denial.

He'd taken the offending document with him.
After being shown into the drawing room, where
his bride-to-be awaited him, he'd flung it down on
a table with a fine show of righteous outrage.

"I don't know how those curs of the *Spectacle*
get away with printing these filthy falsehoods," he
said. "They need to be taught a lesson. It's long
past time they were prosecuted for these slurs. If
Tom Foxe were a gentleman, I'd call him out. Since
he isn't, I'll insist he be arrested."

Lady Clara drew in a deep breath, let it out, and
said, "People can be so unkind. They will take the
most innocuous circumstance, and twist it into
something shameful. They exaggerate everything

they hear and see. But the *Spectacle* never name names, do they? In any case, surely anybody who reads that won't believe it refers to you."

"They won't?" He frowned at the paper. Though he'd never thought Lady Clara Fairfax particularly clever, he'd supposed she could put two and two together.

"Certainly not," she said. "Harry said that even a man of the meanest intelligence would know better than to game there. The place is as crooked as Putney Bridge, he said."

His face heated. "Longmore was here—about this?" He nodded in the direction of the scandal sheet.

"Oh, he often collects a copy of the *Spectacle* on his way home from wherever he goes after the theater or a party," she said. "He came by a little while ago. He was on his way to call on Madame de Veirrion. He was going to try to persuade her to drive out with him. Is she respectable, do you think?"

Not if she's driving out with your brother, he thought.

He said, "I've heard nothing to the contrary."

"I think she must be," Lady Clara said. "She's a friend of the Duchess of Clevedon, and the duke apparently made her acquaintance as well, when he was in Paris. I can't imagine their taking her to the theater if she wasn't."

"Clevedon seems to care nothing about what others think of him," he said.

He didn't say, and she was too tactful to point out that, with an annual income numbering in the hundreds of thousands, the Duke of Clevedon could afford not to care.

"He cares what's said of his duchess and her daughter," Lady Clara said. "The King and Queen have accepted her. I don't think she'd wish to jeopardize her position by associating with improper persons."

"It would be foolish, I agree."

"If she *is* respectable, Mama will be in alt," Lady Clara said. "Madame's husband left her everything. Mama won't mind her being a widow. She's always been terrified that Harry would end up marrying a ballet dancer or a barmaid."

Adderley's face burned. His mother was a sore spot. Still, she hadn't been a barmaid but an innkeeper's daughter. She'd been a royal mistress, as had scores of "respectable" women. Unfortunately, she'd become one after he was born. No one cared if one was a bastard, if one was a *royal* bastard. It's no small thing to be descended from kings. He, alas, was descended from an innkeeper and obscure country gentlemen. Not a drop of royal blood trickled through his veins.

"Marry?" he said, bewildered. "Longmore?" That was inconceivable. "Has it gone so far as that already?"

Clara shrugged. "Who can say? But he seemed quite taken with her. And you know Harry, always plunging headlong into—" She broke off, coughing. She put her hand to her forehead.

It was a small, involuntary gesture, but it was enough to remind him that she'd recently been ill—ill enough for the house to be closed to all but a very few visitors, for three days. He hurried to her, and knelt by her chair. "My dear, are you unwell?"

She let her hand fall. "No, a little . . . oh, it's

nothing, only I've been indoors forever, it seems. What I need is a dose of fresh air. I think I'll order the cabriolet, and take a turn about the park."

"Nonsense," he said. "If you wish to take the air, I'm happy to drive you. You've only to send a maid for your bonnet and shawl."

The fashionable hour of promenade hadn't yet arrived when Lord Longmore turned his curricle into Hyde Park's Cumberland Gate. He was listening to his fair companion. She was prattling in a fractured English so ridiculous that he couldn't help but smile, though he wasn't in the most cheerful frame of mind.

"You have too much in your head," said Madame. "One part of milord attends me. The other part of him rests in another place. I am compelled to demand to myself, Do I cause to him the ennui?"

"I begin to wish, oddly enough, that you were some degrees more boring," he said. "It's almost more excitement than I can bear. Last night . . ." He shook his head.

"But how calm you seemed! Not in the least fearful."

He looked at her. "You've deceived the ton with breathtaking ease. I vow, women who must have looked straight into your face countless times while you adjusted their bows and such ought to have recognized you, even from across the theater. Several men who came into the box last night were at White's on the day you stood in the rain on St. James's Street, generously offering them a view of your petticoats and ankles."

"People see what they expect to see," she said. "In the shop, one is the modiste. When one isn't in the shop but in a place where she isn't expected to be, she merely seems vaguely familiar."

Her false voice, the false accent, the mangled English slipped away, and he marveled at that, too: the ease with which Sophy shed one personality and assumed another.

"Shopkeepers are like servants, invisible," she went on. "Outside their proper sphere, their customers don't recognize them. If one pretends, boldly and confidently, to be someone else, the observer simply accepts."

Servants were another matter. No one was invisible to them. If that hadn't been the case, Madame would be residing at Clevedon House, and Longmore would have one less worry. But that was out of the question. One couldn't expect a large household to keep such a secret—or any secret, for that matter. She'd gone out in one of her guises and hired French servants from one of the agencies she knew and trusted. These made up the retinue attending her at her hotel. In time, the *Spectacle* would explain the circumstances under which she'd fled France. That, he had no doubt, would be a bloodcurdling story of treachery and betrayal and flight under cover of darkness and harrowing escapes from Enemies.

He shook his head. "It's still hard to swallow: the same men who gawked at you through White's bow window, all competing now to be witty and charming in French."

"Because the scene was so beautifully set," she said. "All we needed was for you and Lady Clara to pretend not to recognize me."

"Clara contrived to do it without telling an outright lie, I noticed."

But Clara had had only a small part to play. It was Sophy who'd had to take center stage. It was she who'd had to adopt another identity—with every single eye in the theater on her.

She'd done it with a flair and assurance that took his breath away. She'd seemed thoroughly at ease, and he'd thought, *She's in her element*.

"You played your part splendidly," she said. "So well, in fact, that you almost threw me off-stride. I'm still not over the shock of your perfect French."

He shrugged. "That won me some flattery from Adderley. He even had the temerity to compliment my uppercut—and to say he deserved it."

"He'll say anything," she said. "He's in very bad trouble."

And that was one of the many matters worrying Longmore's brain. "He'll do anything, too," he said. "Kindly remember that. And remember as well that he's not stupid. You'd better have a care."

She stiffened. "I can't believe you're giving *me* acting advice. Have you forgotten our day at Dowdy's?"

"This is different."

"It's the same thing," she said. "I'm pretending to be somebody I'm not. I do it all the time. I pretend I don't want to slap a customer. I pretend she isn't an idiot. I pretend I like changing the ribbon fourteen times because she doesn't know what she likes or wants until thirty of her friends have all given their opinions."

"This isn't women in a shop," he said.

"I'm well aware of that," she said. "Have you forgotten whose idea this was? Have you forgotten that you said it was a *perfect* plan?"

"You were stark naked when you told me," he said. "At the time, *any* plan would have struck me as perfect."

"Well, then. It ought to be imbedded in your brain."

"Well, nothing. That was before Clevedon gave us the nasty details about Adderley."

While they'd been hunting for Clara, Clevedon had been doing his own sleuthing. He'd learned that Lord Adderley's debts were considerably greater than rumored—and rumor had named a very high figure. He was in so deep that some of his creditors were keeping a close watch on him. He wouldn't be the first gentleman to decide to flee his obligations via a packet to Calais or other continental parts.

"He's dealt with some unsavory moneylenders," she said with a dismissive wave. "I know about them."

"Their methods aren't always sporting," he said.

"I know what they're like," she said.

"They're not harmless oafs like Dowdy's hired ruffians," he said.

She let out a huff. "I told you: I *know*. You've no idea what we dealt with in Paris."

"I don't," he said. "It grows clearer and clearer how little I know about you."

. . . except that her breasts were perfect, and her bottom was beyond perfect, and when she made love she was completely honest.

. . . and that he was spending far too much time working on the problem of how to get her back into his bed.

"We'll have to indulge in reminiscences another time," she said. "There they are."

He looked up. Adderley's carriage was approaching.

"I only want you not to be overconfident," he said. "I don't want you to get into trouble."

"You don't know what I'm capable of," she said. "I'm not your sister. I never had a sheltered life. You don't know what it takes to establish a successful shop. You have to stop fretting about Adderley's creditors and unsavory moneylenders, and leave him to me. You need to trust in me to know what I'm doing, so that you can concentrate on doing your own part. You have to be Longmore, who's taken a fancy to Madame de Veirrion. Look at me. I'm *Madame* now."

And she changed.

It was a marvel to him, to watch her. As the other carriage approached, her demeanor changed completely: her posture and the way she moved—even her face wasn't quite the same face. This all happened in a way too subtle for one to put into words.

Unlike her stint as his cousin Gladys, she wore no disguise this time: no tinted spectacles to dull the brilliant blue of her eyes, no artificial blemishes to spoil her perfect skin, no noxious mixtures to dull the gold of her hair. She was dressed more expensively and extravagantly than usual—and that was no small accomplishment—but her face was in plain view.

Yet she became someone else, as though she had a hundred souls at her disposal, and could become another person as entirely and as easily as another woman changed hats.

In some way, through the sheer force of personality, she made the world believe the illusion she created.

But she was right, or at least partly right: He had to stop thinking about the delicious and troubling puzzle that was Sophia Noirot and concentrate on the allure of Madame de Veirrion.

He'd driven into the park through the Cumberland Gate, at the park's northeast corner, in order to "accidentally" meet up with the other couple. Most of London's fashionable set typically entered at Hyde Park Corner, making a great crush at the southeastern edge of the park. The aim was for Longmore and his companion to seem to be on their way out of the park when the encounter occurred.

Once abreast of each other, the two vehicles halted, and Longmore made the introductions.

Clara showed exactly the right degree of feminine curiosity about Madame.

Adderley was doing the masculine version: trying to size up Madame's assets under the capes and gigantic sleeves of her carriage dress without being obvious about it. But of course it was as plain as plain to Longmore, as it would be to any man, that Adderley had discerned her splendidly rounded figure, and dwelt on it rather longer than he needed to. He made a valiant effort not to appear interested—one must give him a little credit, as little as possible—but Madame kept his attention. He was the hapless fish, swimming into her nets without realizing the nets were there.

Longmore had watched her captivate his friends last night. This afternoon he watched her casually throw the bait: a sidelong glance at Adderley, a tilt of her head, a gesture here, a fleeting smile there. In five minutes, she had him. A speculative gleam came into Adderley's eyes, and a silent dialogue went on between them—and Longmore was developing a headache from the effort it took to pretend not to notice.

All the while, Madame was talking mainly to Clara. She made it seem that she was eager to win Clara's approval. And all the while Clara listened to Madame's mangled English with a perfectly sober expression, seeming completely oblivious to the silent byplay between Madame and Adderley.

"I am too much—oh, what is the word I want?" Madame frowned prettily. "To go ahead too much. Ah, *forward*. I am too much forward, yes? Too bold."

"Not at all," Adderley said, gallant fellow. Conceited, sneaking swine.

Madame feigned not to notice, her attention apparently given to Clara. "But my Lady Clara, this I demand: Who knows what arrives? Today we are content, so 'appy. The day after this, the one we love so much—*poof!*—he is gone. This is what arrives in my life. One day all is content and peace. The day that succeed, all is agitation. *Mon époux*, he die. Then Paris go mad. Who can say what will pass?"

"Not I, certainly," said Longmore.

"The time, he run away from us," she said. "One cannot attend." She closed her eyes. "That word is not correct."

"The word you want, madame, is *wait*," Longmore said. He'd learned her trick of using English words that sounded similar to French but whose meaning was not quite the same. *Demand* when she meant *ask*. *Succeed* instead of *follow*. "I believe you meant that because time does not wait for us, you will not wait for time."

"This is so true," said Madame. "I make haste. My Lady Clara—*la très belle sœur* of Lord Lun-mour—let us make an acquaintance with each other. Let us encounter again." She sent a fleeting glance Adderley's way. "Tomorrow, yes? We attend the exhibition of the paintings at—What is the place, Lord Lun-mour?"

"The British Institution," he said.

"That place," said Madame. "I persuade Lord Lun-mour to accompany me to regard the art."

"Oh, yes, I should like that above all things," Clara said. She did not break into hysterical laughter or mention how many times her brother had said he'd rather have his eyes put out with hot pokers than join a mob shuffling about, gaping at paintings and making pompous, and inevitably wrong, comments about them.

She simply turned to Adderley and donned a sympathetic look and said, "But perhaps you'll find it dull, Lord Adderley? If so, there's no need to try your patience. My brother can easily escort two ladies. He can borrow Papa's landau."

"Milord does not enjoy to regard the paintings?" said Madame, looking up at Adderley, her mouth turning down in an adorable little pout.

"In the company of two such beautiful and charming ladies, I should enjoy looking at paving stones," Adderley said.

Exclusive to Foxe's Morning Spectacle
Friday 12 June

A Curious Coincidence? An intriguing piece of information has been brought to this correspondent's attention. We recently learned that, mere days before the King's Birthday Drawing Room on the 28th of May, a certain gentleman was denied further credit at a number of establishments where he has large accounts substantially in arrears. As we are all aware, many of our tailors, purveyors of furnishings, vintners, tobacconists, boot makers, &c, often find themselves obliged to wait months, sometimes years, for their patrons to attend to accounts. His late Majesty, it may be recollected, left debts amounting to many tens of thousands of pounds. To what extremity a merchant must be driven, to refuse one of his lordly patrons further credit, we can only speculate. We need not puzzle our minds quite so much, perhaps, regarding the close proximity between this turn of events and the one leading to the same lord's hasty engagement, a consequence of his luring to her disgrace a certain lady. The lady concerned, as everybody knows, will bring to her marriage a dowry reported to be in the vicinity of one hundred thousand pounds.

That afternoon

It was the British Institution's annual summer exhibition of old masters, featuring works from the collections of everybody who was anybody, from His Majesty on down through a selection of dukes, marquesses, earls, lords, ladies, and sirs. A privileged few had attended a private viewing on the previous Saturday. On Monday, the exhibition had opened to the public.

In spite of his aversion to pretentious mobs shuffling past fusty works of art, Lord Longmore might have found some entertainment in paintings of battle scenes and grisly deaths.

He wasn't in the mood. Within a very short time of their arrival, Adderley and Madame had begun trailing behind Longmore and his sister. Now they'd moved out of hearing range though still within sight. Adderley stood quite close to Madame as they ostensibly discussed No. 53, Rocco Marconi's "Woman Taken in Adultery."

"You saw the *Spectacle*, I suppose," Clara said, drawing him out of a darkly enjoyable fantasy whose highlight was the breaking of Adderley's teeth.

"Like the rest of the world," he said.

"Adderley was furious," she said. "We had another scene when he came to collect me. He's threatening to have Foxe arrested for *scandalum magnatum*. I feigned sympathy, but pointed out that the week before our wedding seemed not the ideal time to get involved in legal wrangles. I told him that Papa said they couldn't hope to prosecute Foxe, since he named no names. Papa pointed out that if the previous king hadn't been able to arrest every man who wrote scandal about him, a nobody like Adderley hadn't a chance."

" 'A nobody like Adderley,' " Longmore said. "You said that to his face."

She turned an innocent gaze on him. "I was only repeating what Papa said."

"How unfeeling of you," he said.

"Yes. I daresay he's telling his troubles to Madame." Clara threw them a glance. "She looks *very* sympathetic, don't you think?"

Madame was gazing up at Adderley, listening for all she was worth, one gloved hand resting over the center of her extremely tight bodice.

"She missed her calling," Longmore said. "She belongs on the stage."

"I'm amazed you can watch them with a straight face," Clara said. "She's so funny, is she not? So clever while seeming so thoroughly bubble-headed. I quite love her."

"Which *her* do you mean?"

"Both," Clara said. Her gaze came back to her brother. "You don't seem to be enjoying yourself."

"I'm not supposed to," he said. "The fellow's poaching on my preserve. That's the scene. I'm supposed to be sending suspicious looks their way." This had turned out to be extremely easy. "Then, after running out of patience, I'm supposed to have a blazing great row with Madame."

"Perfect," she said. "She'll run into his arms for comfort."

That ought to be very funny. It wasn't.

"Yes," he said. "That's the plan."

He started toward them.

Chapter Fourteen

British Institution. As pilgrims approach a hallowed shrine in adoration mingled with fear and trembling so do we ever regard the summer exhibition of the works of the old masters at the British Institution . . . Here are 176 pictures . . . and there is hardly one amongst them the possession of which might not be coveted as a gem.
— *The Court Journal*, Saturday 13 June 1835

Though one would have thought it impossible for Adderley to look more conceited, he managed it. He wore a provoking smirk while he took his time about drawing away from Madame, into whose ear he'd been whispering.

"Lord Lun-mour, Lady Clara," said Madame with a too-innocent smile. "We are too slow for you, I think."

"No hurry," Longmore said. "The paintings will be here for some time. We merely grew curious as to what you find so fascinating about this one."

"*Eh bien*, it gives me a memory of another thing, and so I tell Lord Add'lee a little anecdote." She blushed.

She actually blushed.

Longmore knew she possessed astounding acting skill. She'd demonstrated time and again. He knew she could weep on command. She could even let her eyes fill with tears that didn't fall. He'd never heard of anybody who could blush on command.

"I should like to hear it," he said.

Adderley glanced at Clara. "I'm afraid it isn't suitable for an unwed lady's ears," he said.

"But it's perfectly suitable for a bridegroom-to-be?" Clara said, eyebrows aloft, eyes chilly. It was a look their mother had perfected.

"I pray, *ma chère*—my dear lady—you will take no offense," said Madame. "It is only a naughty little joke. Lord Add'lee will tell it to you after you marry."

Clara turned her icy gaze to the painting. "It's interesting, is it not, what a vile crime adultery is when a woman commits it. But with men, it's practically a badge of honor. I daresay this is a fine painting, but it is not to my taste."

She walked away, spine stiff, chin aloft.

After a moment's hesitation, Adderley went after her.

"I should have a care, madame, if I were you," Longmore said. "Some might misinterpret your— erm—friendliness."

"A care must I have?" she said. "You English. So stiff in the neck. I flirt a little. What is the harm? It is a privilege of the married woman."

"In the circumstances, it might be misunderstood as more than flirtation."

She waved a hand. "English ways are so strange. Here, everyone attends to the unmarried girls.

They flirt and dance, and all the men chase them. In France, these mademoiselles sit tranquil with their chaperons. They must be quiet and modest, like nuns. It is the married ladies who have the flirtation and the *affaire*, but very discreet."

"You're not in France anymore, madame."

"You do not approve of me, milord? You find my manners not amiable?"

"On the contrary, I find your manners rather too amiable," he said.

"But what does this mean? In what regard am I too amiable? To converse with your friend?"

"With my sister's betrothed," Longmore said.

"What then?" she said with a careless laugh. "You have fear I will take him from her? And if I do this thing, perhaps it is best for her. If I were the girl betrothed, I would not desire a man who goes so easily to another woman. And this to happen only a few days before the wedding! Ah, well. Perhaps it is a great favor I do for her."

Clara's voice—not loud enough to be understood but vehement enough to convey her displeasure—drew their attention thither.

Whatever she was saying was making Adderley stand very stiffly. A dull red darkened his fair skin and he didn't look so angelic and poetic.

"But there, you see?" said Madame. "Already they quarrel."

"So it would seem."

Clara was gesticulating and her chin was up. She started away from Adderley, her walk radiating anger. Adderley went after her. They disappeared through a door.

"To make a jealous scene is not wise," said

Madame. "She makes him angry. So soon before the marriage, this is foolish. This is how to chase the man away." She shook her head.

"Maybe he's too dashed eager to be chased away," Longmore said.

She gave that laugh again, that distinctively Gallic laugh, and followed it with a distinctively Gallic shrug. "*C'est la vie*. What one loses, another gains, yes?"

If he didn't know—if he didn't remind himself he knew—he'd think she was an adventuress, experienced in the ways of men, in the ways of the world. He'd believe she'd had a raft of lovers.

But no, only me.

He knew that. He knew he'd been the first.

And maybe that was the trouble.

Had he created a monster? Had he opened the floodgates? Had he—

Gad, what was he thinking? He was thinking like *Sophy*.

The attendant who appeared at his elbow ejected Longmore from his lunatic reverie. "I beg your pardon, my lord," the man said, "but Lord Adderley has asked me to express his regrets to the lady and to you. I am to tell you that her ladyship your sister is unwell, and has expressed a wish to go home."

Longmore glanced about him. The quarrel with Madame, quiet though it was, was attracting attention.

The performance isn't over, he told them silently.

Madame was shaking her head. "They are not suited," she said. "At once I saw this."

"Did you, indeed?" Longmore said. "And to whom did you think he might be better suited?"

She regarded him with narrowed eyes. "It is strange, Lord Lun-mour, but I myself discover that I am not so well. It is the air in this place, I believe. It oppresses me. Or perhaps it is the company. I think I would prefer to return to my hotel."

Exclusive to Foxe's Morning Spectacle
Saturday 13 June

The British Institution's annual summer exhibition has drawn a number of distinguished visitors. Those attending yesterday, however, might have observed, as well as works of art, a drama unfolding under the paintings. A certain recently engaged couple, mentioned previously in our pages, made their appearance. With them were the lady's brother and the French lady his lordship has escorted on so many occasions since her arrival in London. We are sorry to report that discord has arisen between the couples. While we will not say the green-eyed monster appeared on the scene, certain visitors might have noticed a frosty atmosphere between the two ladies prior to their early—and separate—departures. The chill in the air might have arisen as a result of one gentleman's paying more marked attention to his future brother-in-law's companion than to the lady he is to marry in a matter of days. We would be remiss if we failed to add that, when the future bridegroom departed the scene, it was not his intended who cast a languishing eye after him.

Maison Noirot
Sunday afternoon

"No," Longmore said. He crumpled the note and threw it into the empty grate.

"I was not asking your permission," Sophy said.

They stood in the room on the second storey where, he'd discovered, the sisters worked according to their individual talents. Here Her Grace of Clevedon designed her exuberant creations. Here Miss Leonie labored over her ledgers. And here Miss Sophia composed her fashion dramas for the *Spectacle* and devised schemes for keeping Maison Noirot in the front of Fashionable Society's mind.

Longmore had found her hard at work. She had ink on her fingers and a spot on her cheek. A curly golden tendril had escaped its pin to dangle against her left eyebrow.

"You have ink on your face," he said.

"Don't change the subject," she said. "That invitation is *perfect*."

"It's a perfect opportunity for you to get into trouble," he said.

According to the note Longmore had thrown away, Lord Adderley wished to seek Madame's advice on a private matter. Would she do him the honor of dining with him this evening at the Brunswick Hotel?

"No, he's saved us trouble," she said. "Now you can break into his house."

He stared at her. "Are the ink fumes rotting your brain?" he said. "You never said anything about housebreaking. Why on earth should I do such a thing?"

"To find Incriminating Evidence."

In his mind's eye he saw the words writ large and Capitalized.

"Haven't you found enough?" he said. "All the reports you get from Fenwick and his numerous criminal associates? The gossip Clevedon's passed on, from the clubs and his aunts? The private financial reports Miss Leonie obtains, I will not ask how. What more do you need?"

"Letters from the physicians attending his wife, who's locked up in a madhouse against her will," she said.

"*What?*"

"It would be useful to find that he already has a wife," she said. "Preferably well and living in Ireland, but mad will do."

"That would be useful," he said. "But it's highly unlikely. Those sorts of things happen in horrid novels—the mad wife in the attic—the long-lost true heir to the title he's kept locked in a dungeon for twenty years. Not likely in his case, I'm sorry to say."

"We need something powerful," she said. "It's nothing to Society when a gentleman is up to his ears in debt, or games, or chases women. It's not enough to counteract Lady Clara's heinous crime of letting him kiss her in a less than brotherly manner and disarrange her clothing."

"What about that last bit in the *Spectacle* dealing with the creditors and the curious coincidence?" he said. "It made my blood boil. It's sure to put him in bad odor with some of the high sticklers." He hadn't known of that interesting detail until it appeared in the scandal sheet.

"That was quite good, but I'd like something stronger," she said. "Letters from the creditors or the moneylenders. Interesting promises—such as, 'You'd better marry quickly, my lord, or expect severe bodily harm.' That sort of thing."

He had to take a moment to make his mind calm enough to consider what she was saying. She had a way of sweeping one into the raging current of drama that filled her teeming brain.

He quickly sorted matters and said, "Sophy, what kind of idiot would put something like that in writing? And what kind of imbecile would keep it?"

"You'd be amazed," she said. "Most criminal types don't have very large brains. They have little squirrel brains that think of nothing but nuts, nuts, nuts and how to get more nuts. The unsavory moneylender, for instance, doesn't need to be a financial genius. He merely needs to be good at amassing large piles of nuts. Ask Leonie. Now, hers *is* a great financial mind. But most of them—"

"Sophy."

"Adderley isn't very clever, either," she said.

"Neither am I," he said. "But I'm perfectly capable of seducing a woman if I put my mind to it—and he—"

"You're much cleverer than he is," she said. "I can't believe he's so great a moron as to invite a woman to dine with him mere days before his wedding. And to invite her to a hotel he not only can't afford but one where he's sure to be recognized? It grows very clear to me how he got himself into such shocking debt. He's one of those men who assumes everything will turn out in his favor: the next throw of the dice, the next deal of the cards. In short, he's a dolt, and he hasn't a prayer of seducing me. I'm seducing *him*, remember?"

"No. I never agreed to your seducing anybody."

She smiled, advanced on him, and took hold of his lapels. "Listen to me," she said, looking up into his eyes, hers all brilliant blue.

"No," he said. "You talk mad talk."

"I'm not Clara," she said. "I can look after myself."

"Not always."

"Always," she said. "And certainly in this case. Adderley is in far more danger from me than I am from him. I'm going to dine with him, as he asks, at the Brunswick. I'll keep him there for two hours at the minimum. That ought to give you plenty of time to search his house. It isn't a big one."

It wasn't. Adderley had had to sell off most of his property. What he couldn't sell he'd mortgaged. The family estate was let to a military gentleman and his family. At present, Adderley leased a small townhouse near Leicester Square.

"It's a private property," he said. "A house. With servants—though everybody wonders how he pays them. My career hasn't been the most reputable, as you know, but one thing I've never done is break into a gentleman's private house."

"It's not very different from breaking into lodgings," she said. "Or breaking out of school after curfew. You've done that, I'm sure."

"How do you know?" he said. She was standing too close. Her scent drifted in the air about him. It drifted into his brain and acted on it the way honey would act on a clockwork mechanism.

"You went to public school," she said, "and I know you didn't win prizes for good behavior."

"I mean, how do you know the two things aren't different?" he said. "How do you know these things, Sophy?"

She released his lapels and stepped back a pace.

"Oh, for heaven's sake, it's obvious. They're *buildings*. With doors and windows. Housebreakers either pick locks or pry open unlocked windows or smash locked ones." She waved a hand. "I'm not sure which is the best method—but Fenwick will know."

"Then let Fenwick do it," he said. "He's small and less noticeable. He can wriggle in and out of tight places—and being an experienced desperado, he's much less likely to get caught and have to answer annoying questions. If he does get caught, we can easily arrange to get him out of trouble."

"He can't read," she said.

She tipped her head to one side, studying him, thinking, thinking, thinking. That busy little brain.

"I thought you'd relish the prospect of breaking into Adderley's house and discovering his evil secrets," she said.

"I would relish it, if he were in his house at the time. While you were elsewhere."

"Do try to be logical," she said. "Nothing is going to happen to me. It can't. If Adderley gets what he's after from me, he'll lose interest."

"Or maybe not." Longmore hadn't lost interest. On the contrary, he was far too interested for his peace of mind. He couldn't remember spending as much time thinking about a woman as he'd done thinking about her.

Not enough amorous activity, that was the trouble.

"If I succumb to him, he won't be so eager to please," she said. "He won't be watching for an opportunity to get me alone. He won't be on the prowl. He won't be in a high state of excitement.

He needs to be thwarted a little—not enough to discourage him, but enough to increase his zest for the chase. Why must I explain this? You're a man. You know how men think."

"Actually, we don't really think all that much."

"You know what I mean."

"I know these situations can get out of hand." He remembered the drunken boys. His mind painted images of her at Adderley's mercy.

"I should like to know how it could possibly get out of hand with a man one finds repellent," she said. "Or do you imagine that all women are slaves to desire, and all men have to do is kiss and fondle them to make them lose their minds?"

"He is *not* going to kiss and fondle you," he said.

"And I am not going to lose my mind," she said.

"You weren't completely rational with me, I recall."

"That was *you*," she said. "That was completely different. I know the difference—and really, I find it disheartening that you don't. Are all women interchangeable to you? But no—don't answer that question. I find, on the whole, that I'd rather not know. I prefer to keep some girlish delusions."

"Girlish delusions? Have you got any, by Jupiter? Because it seems to me . . ." He trailed off. It dawned on him then that women had always been more or less interchangeable. Except for her. "Never mind. I don't know what I think anymore."

"Don't think," she said. "All you need to do is get into his house and find Incriminating Evidence. I'll keep him occupied."

She was going to go and he couldn't stop her—short of tying her to a chair and locking her in a room—and she'd find a way to wriggle out of that, he had no doubt.

"Very well," he said.

She came close again. She put her hand on his chest. "Thank you," she said. "I know you're worried about me, and I know you'd tell me to go to the devil, if it weren't for your sister."

That wasn't exactly true, but he didn't argue. Instead, he cupped her face and kissed her once, firmly, possessively, on the mouth. He held her so and looked into her brilliant blue liar's eyes and said, "I should like it if you would try not to be kissed or fondled," he said. "By him."

"Trust me," she said softly.

He wanted her and thought about her too much and he worried about her to an extent that made him slightly ill. But he didn't trust her.

And so he didn't trust her not to do what she'd made up her mind to do, whether he cooperated or not. Seeing no alternative but to cooperate, he might as well look on the bright side: It would be great fun to break into Adderley's house and find something that would wipe the smirk off his face permanently.

And if that didn't work, one could always shoot him.

That night

Getting into Adderley's house was easy enough. After reconnoitering, Fenwick reported that the staff had gathered belowstairs, where they were smoking, drinking, and playing a noisy game of cards.

Fenwick's mode of entry was perfectly straightforward. He climbed up a drainpipe, thence into the house through one of several unlatched windows. He made his way inside to the front of the house and opened the door to Longmore. Anyone watching would have supposed a servant had let in one of Lord Adderley's friends.

After that, the main difficulty was making one's way through an unfamiliar, poorly lit house without running into furniture or knocking over breakables. After a few heart-stopping creaks and bumps, Longmore relaxed.

He took his mind off Not Getting Caught and set it on Finding Something.

This turned out to be much less straightforward.

The rooms they searched bore all the signs of a discouraged if not outright hostile staff. That explained the party belowstairs and the unlatched windows.

He and Fenwick found a great deal of paper: heaps of newspapers and sporting magazines and racing sheets and *Foxe's Morning Spectacle*. Piles of invitations. Mounds of unsorted correspondence. There were tradesmen's bills aplenty, but none held any secrets that Leonie and Clevedon hadn't already uncovered.

Longmore took special care in searching the study desk, looking for false bottoms and hidden compartments. It hadn't any. Not without distaste, he proceeded to Adderley's bedroom. He searched the writing table, the bed stand, the wardrobe, and under pillows and mattress. He found a great deal of rubbish and evidence of bad housekeeping. It was tedious work, and it seemed as though he and Fenwick had hardly begun when a clock somewhere in the house began to strike. In the same moment,

Longmore heard church bells in the neighborhood tolling the same long count: ten strokes.

Ten o'clock.

Already.

Fenwick, who'd been charged with guard duty, said, "They're stirring down below, yer majesty." A pause. Then, "Somebody's on the stairs."

A moment later Longmore heard the voices approaching.

"You, into the wardrobe," he said.

The boy instantly vanished into the wardrobe.

Lord Longmore dropped to the floor and crawled under the bed.

Unlike Clevedon's aunts, many nobles who came to London for short stays put up at one of the West End's many luxury hotels. The Clarendon in New Bond Street, like others of its ilk, was accustomed to accommodating its guests' requirements, and doing so discreetly.

Madame de Veirrion had taken one of the largest suites. If she chose to regard her rooms as private apartments, the Clarendon's staff were happy to support that vision. It was not for them to question, and certainly it would have been as much as their positions were worth to tattle about what she did there or whom she saw. This was why Clevedon had chosen it for the scheme.

Late as it was when Madame returned, her entrance brought guests and staff alike to rapt attention. She wore a spectacular dinner dress, for which she'd already provided the *Spectacle* a detailed description, to appear in Monday's edition. It was one of Marcelline's more glorious creations, and Maison Noirot would receive full credit in the paper.

In Paris, black taffeta mantelets were all the rage, worn usually with a contrasting softer textured dress, made of *mousseline de laine* or muslin. But Marcelline had paired a deep rose satin with the black taffeta mantelet, which created a rich, sensuous rustling as one moved.

Every woman who'd seen Madame de Veirrion this night had regarded the dress with the kind of lustful expression one observed more usually in a man's face.

Lord Longmore never looked at her in that way.

But he was different, Sophy told herself. His card-playing face could be as good as hers. One had to study him closely to catch the way his dark eyes glittered when he was noticing her in a more intent way than usual . . . and there was a certain slant of his mouth or tilt of his head . . .

She shivered, recalling when last he'd regarded her that way, only a few hours ago, an instant before he'd kissed her.

She was in a very bad way.

If she hadn't had to rescue Lady Clara, with almost no time at all to do it, Sophy could have easily made a great fool of herself over him. She could have wept into her pillow at night. She could have written sickening poetry about Lovers Torn Apart by Fate. She could have quoted whole scenes from *Romeo and Juliet*, and sobbed because those young lovers hadn't had it so bad, compared to her.

But she hadn't time to act like a sentimental moron.

She was obliged to play Cleopatra to Adderley's Mark Antony—and really, she'd never thought Mark Antony worthy of the Queen of Egypt. A bit dim, she'd always thought.

She was contemplating the role of wicked seductress and thinking it mainly took patience, when the footman standing outside the door of her suite informed her, as he opened the door, that Lord Longmore awaited her in the drawing room.

Her heart sped up.

She'd thought she'd have time to rest and compose herself before Longmore arrived. Being calm with him wasn't as simple as it ought to be. Too often she felt he was looking straight into her brain and seeing what he ought not to see. It was like being undressed, with the difference being that she didn't mind his seeing her body unclothed. She minded very much his seeing inside her head.

Keeping her guard up was not going to be easy, after a draining evening with Lord Adderley.

His mind was slow. She'd had to slog through their conversation while keeping him, not at arm's length, but not too close, either. She'd had to work carefully, to bring his mind to the right position. It was like dancing with a man with two left feet. He'd tried to be subtle, and it had been difficult to pretend she didn't understand what he was trying to ascertain.

It was hard work, and it sapped one's energy— and the project had taken longer than she'd planned.

Still, she'd had success, and that was what she set at the front of her mind. And that was what animated her when she sailed into her drawing room, the picture of confidence.

A maid hurried out, but Sophy ignored her.

Longmore stood by the window, a glass in his hand. His dark hair was rumpled and so was his neckcloth. She couldn't tell whether he'd been in a fight or had slept in his clothes. He looked thoroughly disreputable, and his dark eyes held a dangerous gleam.

She waved the girl away. "Go to bed," she said. "I'll ring if I need you."

When the door had closed behind the maid, Sophy stripped off her gloves. "I hope they've looked after you well," she said. She noted a decanter, three-quarters empty, on one of the room's elegant tables.

"They fed me and they kept my glass filled," he said. "Where the devil have you been?"

She dropped the gloves on the nearest chair, unfastened her mantelet, and carelessly flung it on top of them. Dressmakers neatly folded garments and put everything in its proper place. Great ladies left that job to servants.

"How much have you had to drink?" she said. "Have you forgotten that I was dining with Lord Adderley?"

"For five hours?"

"Certainly not. It can't be—what time is it?"

He slanted her a look, took out his pocket watch, and flicked it open with a sharp click. He said, in a too-quiet voice, "It's half past midnight."

"That's not five hours," she said.

"What the devil have you been doing for all this time?"

"Keeping him occupied."

"Two hours, you said."

"I said I could give you at least two," she said.

"That isn't what you said."

"What difference does it make?" she said. "Or are you vexed because you had to cut short your search, thinking you had only two hours?"

"Never mind my search."

"Never mind? That was the whole point of this exercise."

"Apparently not," he said. "Apparently, you found a good deal to occupy you."

"Well, I did, rather," she said.

"I'm eager to know what that was," he said.

She was not about to describe to him the various maneuvers and counter-maneuvers she'd had to use. She had no intention of instructing any man— and most assuredly not this one—in the arts she used to manipulate males.

"You ought to know what it *wasn't*," she said. "I can't believe you stand there glowering at me as though I'm a wayward sister. How many times do I have to tell you? I'm not Lady Clara, who doesn't know better than to let herself be led out onto dark terraces by bankrupt lords. I'm not Lady Anybody. I'm not naïve."

"All the same—"

"Nothing was supposed to happen," she said. "I know better than to let anything happen. *Nothing happened.*" She wanted to shake him. How could he think she was so stupid? How could he believe she was so *undiscriminating*? "Considering the foul mood you seem to be in, I can only conclude that nothing happened on your mission, either. Or did you find something worse than one could imagine? Grisly remains in the cellar or—"

"Dust clumps under the bed," he said. "And what may or not have been a dead rodent. I didn't touch it. I'm judging only by smell. It might have been your would-be beau's stockings."

"You searched under the bed?" she said. "Why didn't you make Fenwick do that? He's smaller and less likely to bump his head . . ." She trailed off, as the image rose in her mind of Longmore squeezing his big body under a bed. "Oh, no! Did you bump your head?" She moved toward him. "Let me see. You should have told the servants to get ice. I'll send for ice."

He took a step back. "I did not bump my head," he said. "I know to keep my head down. I've been under beds before, though not in recent memory. I remained there utterly still and quiet while a pair of servants made good use of the master's absence by fornicating against his wardrobe. In which Fenwick had secreted himself." He turned away, walked to the decanter, and refilled his glass.

She watched him while her imagination painted the scene he'd described. She knew about these things. She'd seen pictures. But she'd looked at them coolly, feeling mainly curiosity.

She tried to make her mind detached, but it made its own exhibition, of lurid pictures of him, naked, pushing into her and making her feel things she'd never felt before, such wild emotions, so pleasurable as to hurt, almost.

She went hot everywhere, remembering. She wanted to run across the room and open a window and lean out of it.

But no, that wasn't quite true.

She wanted to run to him and make him do it again, make him touch her and kiss her and love her and possess her and wipe out the memory of

Adderley's insinuating voice and double entendres, and his face and body too close to hers.

She made herself look sympathetic but amused. "But you weren't detected," she said.

"I could have started singing *God Save the King*, and I doubt they'd have noticed," he said. "Luckily the position isn't easy to maintain. They weren't long about it. They had a good laugh after, and went out—maybe to repeat the performance in the next room. I didn't stay to find out. I unearthed Fenwick and we made ourselves scarce." He drank.

She said nothing, only watched his hands, and the motion of his shoulders and the way the light played on the bones of his face.

"I had to climb down the drainpipe," he said, into the silence. "After which Fenwick administered a critique of my mode of descent."

She found her tongue. "I do think he—"

"It was a complete waste of time!" He slammed the glass down on the tray, making the decanter bounce. "Adderley has nothing in his house that we don't already know about. It was exactly as I told you it would be. The sorts of things you hoped to find are the things imaginary people find in stories. In make-believe. This isn't bloody make-believe!"

Chapter Fifteen

Whenas in silks my Julia goes
Then, then (methinks) how sweetly flows
That liquefaction of her clothes.

Next, when I cast mine eyes and see
That brave vibration each way free;
O how that glittering taketh me!
—Robert Herrick, *On Julia's Clothes*, 1648

Her head went back as though he'd struck her. Then Longmore wanted to hit something, preferably himself.

He was behaving like an idiot because he'd let himself get into a maddened state—and for that he'd only himself to blame.

He was the one who'd insisted on their meeting here after they'd completed their respective assignments. This way, he'd reasoned, if Adderley tried to make a nuisance of himself by following Madame to her rooms, Longmore would be on the spot to send the swine about his business.

Longmore was on the spot, and had been for what had felt like months. By Society's standards, the hour wasn't late. It seemed very late, though, for a woman to return from a dinner engagement that was supposed to last two hours.

Then, to return looking like *that*.

She'd sailed in, hips swaying, smile confident—the smile of a woman who knows she's desired and believes desire is her due. She'd made her entrance as a queen might do, or some mythical being, a goddess borne on a cloud or a zephyr. And she'd seemed to walk in a cloud in that dress, a mad confection of layer upon shimmering layer, deep pink and black and satin and lace. In the gaslight's glow the rose silk took on the cast of a stormy sunset. But not an English sunset. It called to mind a wild, magical sunset in the Tuscan mountains, when the mountain breeze had wafted about his head, carrying the intoxicating fragrance of lavender and jasmine.

He'd watched her strip off her gloves, and he'd felt his pulse accelerate. He'd watched her unfasten the black mantle that hung over her shoulders, the lustrous fabric moving sinuously and sounding like a hundred voices whispering. Its lace trim veiled the rosy front of her dress. In his mind's eye he saw what lay underneath and underneath and underneath, all the way to her skin, and he knew what that felt like. He knew what it was like to feel the velvety curve of her belly under his hands.

He'd watched her drop the little mantle, and he'd caught his breath. The dress's neckline was shockingly low, barely containing the silken swell of her breasts.

All that.

Adderley had seen all that.

And the realization had made him wild. Then he

was furious with her for making him wild and with himself for letting it happen. He was behaving like one demented and like a brute besides—oh, and a schoolboy, too.

"Confound it, Sophy," he said.

Pink washed her cheeks. "I can't believe what a fuss you're making about this," she said. "You're the man who cares nothing for what anybody says. You're the man who laughs at convention, and thrives on risk, the more dangerous the better. This is the sort of thing you'd do as a practical joke."

"It wasn't a joke."

"Well, then, I should like to know what happened to your sense of humor," she said. "I should like to know what happened to your sense of adventure. I should like to know—"

"You tell me," he said. "What the devil do I care what you do? Why should I care?"

"You're making no sense," she said.

"No, I'm not, and most especially not to myself. I've never been so . . ."

Never been so what? What was he if not himself? What was this?

But his mouth went on talking, lagging behind the thinking, as usual. "I let myself be drawn into these mad schemes of yours . . . and it's amusing. Then it isn't. Then I can't enjoy myself. I couldn't even enjoy housebreaking with the Infant Felon Fenwick because the entire time, every minute while I read the lecher's boring bills and all the pitiful dunning letters from his creditors—all that time I was thinking what a two-faced cur he was, and how desperate he had to be, to trap my sister, of all women . . . and there you were, so sure you could manage him—"

"I can!" she said. "I did! How can you be so thick?" She kept her voice low, but the throbbing vehemence in it was clear enough. "I know he hasn't any conscience. I know he cares nothing about women: They're sport. Even snaring a wife in the most underhand way isn't unsporting to him. It's part of the game. To him it's no different than dice or cards or horse races. I know all of that. I can see him more clearly than you can. And you think I'm in any danger from him—from *him* of all men? You think I would let *him* seduce me? How can you be such an *idiot*?"

"That's what I'd like to know," he said. "How can I be such a fool as to ruin a perfectly good evening worrying about you? And now—when there's plenty of perfectly good evening remaining, I waste more of it quarreling with you."

Her color rose, and her blue eyes narrowed to angry blue slits. She launched into low, furious French: "It's true. A great waste of time for both of us. Well, let me detain you no longer, my lord."

She marched to the door, the satin whispering furiously, the very bows seeming to tremble with rage. She pulled it open, much to the surprise of the footman who'd been leaning in, trying to listen at the keyhole.

"*Bonsoir, monsieur,*" she said, snapping out each syllable.

"*Bonsoir, madame,*" Longmore said. He collected his hat and gloves and stalked to the door.

She stood, chin aloft, gazing up defiantly at him. Blue fire lit her eyes. Hot color burned her cheeks and neck. The fire tinged her creamy bosom, rising and falling fast.

Longmore reached past her and slammed the door in the footman's face.

He threw down his gloves and hat.

He scooped her up in his arms.

"Oh, no, you don't," she said. "You won't play the masterful male with me, you wretched man." She hit his chest. "Put me down." Her voice was cold and hard.

"Make me," he said, his voice colder and harder.

She wriggled. "I'll scream."

"No, you won't." He kissed her, and not gently, but with all the frustration and anger and fear that had been roiling inside him all this day and night.

She went on squirming and struggling—and not gently, either—but he felt her mouth give way long before her body did. The rest was only pique. He was piqued, too, and that wasn't the half of it.

He carried her to the sofa. He broke the kiss and said, "I'm leaving now."

"Good," she said. "It's about time."

He dropped her onto the sofa, and the satin whooshed and hissed at him as she struggled to pull herself up to a sitting position.

"Goodbye," he said.

"Good riddance," she said.

He peeled off his coat. "I'm never coming back," he said.

"Never is too soon," she said.

He untied his neckcloth. "I'm done with you."

"I was done with you ages ago."

He started to unfasten his trousers. He kept his hands very steady. He didn't hurry. One. Button. At. A. Time.

She watched him through narrowed eyes.

"You're dreaming," she said. "Never. Never in a million years."

"I'm not even going to take off your clothes," he said. "It's too much bother."

"You don't *deserve* to see my beautiful body," she said.

"It's not that beautiful," he said.

"Yes, it is—and much more beautiful than yours—which I never want to see again, ever— especially *that* part." Her gaze slid to his trouser front, where his excited cock throbbed against the flap. It didn't know the difference between fighting with a woman and rogering her. Neither did he, at the moment.

She edged back on the sofa.

He took hold of her feet and pulled her back down. He crawled over her and stuffed a velvet cushion under her head.

She said, "I won't put up with this." Her mouth turned down, all petulance. "You're abominable, the worst, thickest, most insensitive cretin to contaminate the earth by being born."

He bent and kissed each down-tilting corner of her mouth. Then he kissed her full on the lips, deeply and hungrily. He was still in a turmoil, but that mattered less and less. He was tired of thinking, worrying.

He'd made her lose her temper, and she was heated and aggravated, as he was. He wasn't at all sure what their trouble was, but that didn't seem very important.

She brought her hands up and grabbed his shoulders and tried to shake him, which was absurd. She did such ridiculous things, like trying to manhandle him. She might as well try to wrestle a house.

He felt her hands move upward, closing about his throat, as though she thought she could choke him. But then she rose a little, and her arms went round his neck, and she pulled, and down he went, without a fight.

Down he went, into a rich atmosphere of Sophy: her scent and the feel of her soft, curving body under his and the taste of her and the sound of her, satin whispering against lace, petticoats rustling, the delicious music of her dress.

He drew his hand down along the curves of her neck and shoulders and down over the ripe swell of her breast, barely contained behind the low neckline. She arched back with a sigh and a "damn you." He slid his hand under the neckline and squeezed and kneaded one perfect, silken breast. Then the other. She writhed under him, her hips moving in undisguised enjoyment.

Undisguised.

Honest.

He slid his mouth from hers and made a path of kisses along the way his hand had gone, over the curve of her throat and shoulder and breast. He tugged the bodice down and suckled, and between moans she told him in French that he was despicable, a wicked man, and she would never, never succumb to him, no matter how much he begged and pleaded.

He dragged up her skirts and petticoats and murmured in French that she was impossible, intolerable, and he wanted nothing to do with her.

"I'm leaving and I'll never come back," he said as he knelt between her legs.

"Good," she gasped. "I can't wait to see the last of you."

He slid his fingers under the bottom of her corset, and up past the slit of her drawers to the tape at the waist. "I won't miss you at all," he said as he untied them.

"I've forgotten you already," she said.

He pulled down her drawers, slowly, down past her knees. Her garters were the same pink as the dress. He untied them. He caressed her velvety thighs, moving upward to the soft mound. That beautiful all-woman place glinted gold in the gaslight. When he put his hand there, she sucked in her breath. "Ah, that's mine," he said.

"Never," she said.

"Oh, yes, *madame*," he said. "Oh, yes, Miss Noirot. Sophy."

Whoever you are.

He stroked her, and she quivered and a sibilant sound escaped her. It sounded like *yes*.

She moved against his hand, encouraging, seeking more. "Stupid man," she said.

"Yet I know exactly what to do in this situation," he said, and it was all he could do to put the words together. She was damp, ready. His mind was so thick that he could barely speak. It was scarcely speech, hoarse and breathless. But hers was no better. They were heated, maddened. Still, he caressed and pleasured her. It was a kind of punishment for him. Yet he liked it, too, so much: the way she moved and the way her breath caught at each jolt of pleasure, and the way her breath came faster and harsher as he stroked her.

Her warm hand closed over his cock and she slid her wicked fingers along his length. Her hold was firm, possessive. "Now," she said, and it was a little kitten growl. A tiger kitten. "*Now*, my lord, you awful man."

He felt the blood racing through his veins, with the same flooding urgency that drove him to fight and kept him fighting. Instinctive. Unthinking. He entered her, and laughed—for the rush of sensation, for the triumph. He grasped her bottom, her beautiful bottom, and thrust again and again. No finesse. Only heat. Desire. Possession.

Mine, with every thrust. *Mine. Mine. Mine.*

She took him in the same way: primitive, simple, unfeigned, greedy desire. She took him and gave herself to him unstintingly and unsparingly. They fought a lovers' battle, a sort of war that wasn't a war at all. Even while the rhythm of their coupling built and built, faster and fiercer, the world was darkening and softening and gentling. Thought drifted far away. There was nothing but *now*.

He felt her hands tighten about his upper arms, and he felt the tremors as she reached her peak. And then she was rising up, dragging her hands through his hair as she kissed him. He tasted something in that kiss and in his answer or the combination. He had no words for it. The sensation was overpowering and white-hot and new. Then she was pulling him down to her, and he was kissing her, like a man starved, and all the world was this, he and she, joined. The world heaved, shuddered, exploded.

He lay sprawled on top of her, and Sophy was sprawled, too, in a most undignified manner, one leg dangling over the edge of the sofa, her stocking drooping about her ankle.

He hadn't even taken her shoes off.

It had been such great fun and so . . . exciting. So much feeling: sensations that nothing else in one's life offered.

She lay for a moment while her breathing quieted, relishing his weight and his warmth and the indescribably wonderful feeling of a man's body—this man's body—entwined with hers.

For this moment, she simply indulged herself, pretending she was Madame, who need think only of the pleasures of the moment. Madame, who had no responsibility but to enjoy herself, to lure men into her nets and revel in her power over them and the pleasure they could give her.

His weight shifted. "Well, then, let that be a lesson to you," he said.

She indulged herself again, running her fingers through his thick, black hair. He turned his head into her hand, like a dog wanting his ears scratched. He was a man of great sensuality, she realized—and that ought to come as no shock. He was so utterly physical, so fully at home and confident in his body.

"Are you not so crazy now?" she said.

"My mind is wonderfully clear," he said.

In a smooth series of movements, he eased his long body up and over her and off the sofa entirely. He bent and kissed her knee, then put her clothes to rights, as easily as though he'd been dressing and undressing her for years. She knew it was only practice, years of practice with women, but it felt like more than that. There was a familiarity, as though they'd been lovers forever. It was almost . . . domestic.

This was what it was like for her sister and

Clevedon. They were together and their lives had joined and they had moments like this, all the time. They had breakfast together.

Longmore pulled up his trousers and fastened them.

"You're not going to tell me to go to sleep?" she said.

"For some reason I don't feel at all sleepy," he said.

"Then I can tell you what I accomplished this evening, and you'll listen without acting like a crazy, jealous man," she said.

"Can't think what the devil I was jealous about," he said. He moved away to the tray the servants had brought him. He filled a glass for himself and one for her and brought them back. After giving her a glass, he straightened and stood back a pace. He drank. He closed his eyes.

She waited.

He opened his eyes and turned their gaze upon her bodice. "That," he said. "You at dinner, and that oily lecher ogling your splendid breasts."

She drank in the words as though they'd been the most precious compliment or even a declaration of eternal devotion. Yes, he'd fondled and caressed and suckled—but "splendid," coming from him, was practically poetry. He was not the sort of man who flattered women. He was so straightforward.

And she was so . . . *not.*

"Marcelline cut it especially low on purpose," she said. "We needed to give him something tempting to look at while I set out my other temptations: my vast wealth, which I spoke of so casually. And my loneliness. And how much I missed having a *husband.*"

She watched understanding dawn in his dark eyes. He sat down sideways on the edge of the sofa, his hip against hers.

Really, he was not nearly as unintelligent as people thought.

"You see?" she said. "You see why I didn't have to deal with his trying to seduce me?"

"You tempted him with a bigger prize," he said. "You made him think he was dreaming too small. He thought only to bed you—but you tempted him to play for higher stakes."

"Madame's fortune rivals the Duke of Clevedon's, according to the *Spectacle*," she said.

"Makes Clara's dowry seem paltry," he said. He sipped his wine thoughtfully. "Still, a bird in the hand, you know."

"I know. That's why I had to make myself so irresistibly delicious."

"And a fine job you did." His voice had deepened. He took her wineglass from her and set it and his down on the floor. He leaned in and kissed the top of her breast. Then the top of the other one. Then he drew his tongue along the neckline.

She sucked in air. His tongue was doing strange things at the place where her neckline met the shoulder of her dress and those things were stirring restless feelings in the pit of her belly. She grabbed a fistful of his hair. "We have only a few days left," she said.

He lifted his head and regarded her with half-closed eyes. "We know what we need to do," he said.

"We have a general plan," she said. "We need to refine it, in light of recent developments."

His eyes were like midnight, and she saw the special glint there, like some devil star.

"Let's do that *later*," he said.

Later

This time, not being nearly so mentally unbalanced or in so great a hurry, Longmore had carried her through the more public apartments to the privacy of her bedroom.

This time, after the lovemaking, he did sleep. He might have slept on until afternoon if he hadn't rolled toward the place where she was supposed to be and found cold bedclothes instead of warm Sophy.

After feeling around, he opened his eyes and came up on his elbows and looked past the bed curtains. Early-morning light filtered into the room through half-drawn window curtains. The light showed no signs of Sophy.

He rose and, deciding that stalking about the place naked probably wasn't intelligent, he pulled on his trousers. He had no idea who else was about at this hour, but while some maids had seen everything and were not easily shaken, others could screech and carry on. That might bring in busybody hotel officials. What Madame didn't need was to get embroiled in a scandal with the Marchioness of Warford's eldest son.

He found Sophy at a writing table in the sitting room, scratching away.

"What the devil are you doing?" he said. "The sun's barely up."

"I need to write my report for today's *Spectacle*,"

she said. "It won't be much good if Tom can't print it today, and he should have had it half an hour ago." She set down her pen. "But it's done, and I'll only be a minute sending it off. We have a little system for getting these things to the *Spectacle* undetected."

She'd donned a frothy dressing gown over what appeared to be an equally frivolous nightdress, judging by the ruffles peeping out from under the dressing gown's hem.

She went out of the room in a cloud of fluttering ribbons and muslin.

He remembered her jumping about, her night-dress on fire, that night of the storm, when they'd stopped at the inn. He felt a tightening in his chest, and a stab. He felt happy and upset at the same time.

He walked to a window and looked out, trying to ignore the sensations.

Some few minutes later, she returned, brow knit, carrying a letter.

"This is interesting," she said. "It was delivered only a moment ago."

He glanced at the letter, looked away, then came back for a closer study. The handwriting seemed familiar. Hadn't he seen it recently?

She sat at the writing table and broke open the seal.

Yesterday. That's when he'd seen it. He'd crushed the message in his hand and thrown it away.

She scanned the letter and smiled. "Oh, my," she said. She read it again, this time more slowly, giggling now and again.

Longmore stood and waited, the remnants of his good humor slipping away.

"Is it a great secret?" he said. "Or may I share the joke?"

She held out the letter to him. He didn't take it, only glanced at the bottom, at the signature. Adderley. As he'd thought.

"Do you want to read it?" she said. "Or shall I? I do think it needs to be read aloud for the full effect.

"Go ahead," he said. "Read it."

" 'My dear Madame de Veirrion,' " she read, " 'I find I cannot sleep. Indeed, I cannot rest at all. My heart is too full for rest, my mind too agitated. To sleep were impossible until I had unburdened my heart to the celestial creature who has stolen it utterly. E'en now I hear your voice, like a haunting melody. I close my eyes and all I can see is your beautiful—' "

"Breasts," Longmore said. "All he can see is your beautiful breasts, the oily blackguard."

"Eyes," she said, stabbing the place with her finger. "My beautiful eyes, 'like twin oceans, of fathomless depths and mystery.' "

"I'm going to be ill," he said.

"Shall I stop reading?" she said.

"No, go on. I have an irresistible need to hear it, rather in the way one can't help gaping at a carriage accident, or bodies being carried out after a building collapse."

" 'I'd always thought myself immune to love's pangs and raptures,' " she read on. " 'I'd always believed those feelings were for schoolboys and poets. Then I met you. Please forgive me, madame—I hardly know what I write. I'm distraught, confused. I know only that I couldn't rest without penning some few words, however inept'—"

"He got that part right, at any rate."

"—'some few words, however inept, to express

my feelings. You are so kind, so understanding, my very dear lady. Pray be kind to this, your humble supplicant.' "

"What a ghastly assault to commit upon an innocent piece of paper."

She giggled again and went on, " 'Only send me a word or two, enough to keep me from utter despair. A little hope is all I seek—let me know when I may see you again. In pity's sake, pray make it soon. I am yours, devotedly, A.' "

She looked up at Longmore. "Isn't it wonderful?" she said.

"Wonderful? Have you taken leave of your wits? The effrontery of the fellow! Plague take him, I knew he was low, but each day proves my estimation grossly flattering. This passes anything! Engaged to my sister and making love to my—my—what-you-call-it."

Her eyebrows went up. "Your what-you-call-it?"

He frowned at her. "You know what I mean."

"Your 'aunt,' perhaps."

"Not an *aunt*, Sophy. Not that. Never that." How could she be so thick? "Nothing like that."

"What then?"

He waved a hand at the letter. "He knows I've been escorting you everywhere. He knows I've an interest. A gentleman doesn't poach on another's preserve."

"Will you listen to yourself?" she said. "You act as though Madame is real. This is all a sham, remember?"

"That isn't the point."

"It's the entire point," she said.

"The point is, he has no damn business writing you love letters," he said. "If I can dignify this turgid spew by that title, which I'm sorry to do, as it gives love letters a bad name."

"Longmore."

"I thought I was Harry by now," he said. "Or is that a sham, too?"

"Which part?" she said. "I'm not sure what you mean."

He wasn't sure what he meant, either. He stared at the letter in her hand. Her hands, her soft hands. She'd raked her hands through his hair, and made as if to strangle him and held his cock and told him she wanted him.

"How dare he?" he said. "How dare the cur be haunted by your voice? How dare he presume to be distraught and confused? He doesn't even know you. It's a damned insult."

She was studying him, her head tipped to one side, thinking, thinking, trying to make him out. "What is the matter with you?" she said. "He's only *saying* those things."

"Yes," he said. "He's saying the things women want to hear. That we're thinking about their *eyes*, not their breasts. Their voices, not the place between their legs. Their conversation, not the quickest way to get under their skirts."

"But he's trying to get me into bed," she said. "That's the point. What on earth has possessed you? You said your mind was clear. I thought we'd settled that matter. How many times do we have to fornicate for you to—"

"We don't fornicate," he said between his teeth.

"It isn't ladylike to say the shorter word," she said.

"We make love," he said.

He snatched the letter from her, crushed it into a

tight little ball, and threw it across the room. "You and I. We *make love*. There's a difference. Worlds of difference. And he has no business making love to you in his illiterate, idiotish letter. And just because I don't write you illiterate, idiotish letters that make one gag—and just because I don't say . . ."

He trailed off, aware of the feeling, the strange feeling, of being stabbed and of being happy and wretched at the same time.

He looked at her for a long time.

Her hands were folded. She had ink on her fingers again. But not on her face this time. She watched him so intently, her eyes piercing, trying to bore into his thick, so very thick skull, trying to understand what he scarcely understood himself.

"Just because I don't say . . ."

He walked back to the bedroom.

She followed him.

He collected his garments from the floor and everywhere else they'd landed, flung them in the general vicinity of one of the room's three chairs, and started to dress. In a growing, increasingly taut silence.

Finally, "It's a sham," she said. "You're not used to pretending, and it's troubling you and making you . . . disoriented."

He pulled on his shirt, unbuttoned his trousers, and stuffed the shirt inside.

"The trick is to believe it while you do it," she said, "but to step back into yourself as soon as you're off stage."

He pulled on his waistcoat and buttoned it. He sat and put on his stockings and shoes.

"He's playing into our hands," she said.

He stood, took his neckcloth off the back of the chair, and threw it round his neck. He knotted it quickly, in a fashion that would give his valet a seizure.

"Adderley's the pigeon," she said. "He's the dupe. He's the mark. It isn't *real*."

He twisted himself into his coat. "Yes, it is," he said.

"No, it—"

"Yes, it is," he said. "You and I: That's real. I love you."

He heard her quick, sharp inhalation.

"That's my trouble, imbecile me," he said. "I love you."

She stood very still, for once—for once—too shocked to pretend she wasn't, too shocked for the tell-nothing face. Her blue eyes were enormous, a great, endless surprise.

He bent and kissed her, full on the lips. "I'm going now," he said. "This is much too shocking. I need to—drink, I believe. Or fight. Something. I love you. That's what it is. That's what's happened. Yes."

He turned away and shook his head. Then he laughed and went out.

Sophy stared at the door he'd gone out of.

"That didn't happen," she whispered. "I imagined it."

Her gaze traveled the room, now bereft of all signs of him.

He couldn't have done it. He was the last man on earth who'd make a declaration.

But her mouth still tingled from the passion of that last kiss, and she remembered the wry look of his mouth and the odd note in his laughter in the instant before he turned away.

She ran out, through the door, and into the next room and the next . . .

And stopped short when she reached the door to the corridor.

What was she doing?

She couldn't run out into the corridor in her nightdress. And to accomplish what, exactly?

As it was . . .

But no. She'd taken care. It was not entirely shocking, she knew, for a widowed foreigner to entertain a gentleman until the early morning hours. Most of the ton was only now returning home after their entertainments, and her apartments, like those of a foreign ambassador, were designed to entertain guests. Those who heard of Longmore's early morning departure from here might speculate, but they wouldn't have a story, unless she gave them one in the *Spectacle*. The servants were well paid not to gossip about Madame, in any language.

If she ran out in her nightclothes into the corridor after his lordship, others would see—and that would most definitely be a story.

She returned to her sitting room.

"Wouldn't make a whit of difference in any event," she muttered. What would she get if she ran after him? More cryptic remarks, no doubt.

She sat at the writing table and stared at the pen she'd set down only a short time ago.

Her heart was still pounding. The words he'd uttered were not too cryptic for it. Her heart understood *I love you* well enough.

"It seems I love you, too, Harry, imbecile me," she whispered. "Much good will it do us."

She sat for a time, contemplating the hopelessness of the situation, even while a part of her mind hunted and hunted for a scheme, as was its nature to do. But no scheme existed that would make everything come out right.

She couldn't be his mistress: It was bad for the shop.

As to marriage . . .

That was laughable. Even if he were mad and reckless enough to ask, she couldn't accept. Society still seethed over Marcelline's conquest of Clevedon. Another misalliance would finish Maison Noirot forever. And Lady Warford would be leading the annihilation army.

At least Marcelline had had the good sense to fall in love with an orphan.

Sophy contemplated the Fairfaxes, all of them allied against her. Even Lady Clara. After all, it was one thing to be fond of one's dressmaker or one's maid. It was quite another proposition to accept that person as a sister.

And then, there was the thorny matter of her antecedents.

No, it was ridiculous and hopeless, and really, she hadn't time to mope and dream mad schemes. She already had one scheme in hand, and that wasn't mad at all. But she'd need all her wits to carry it out.

Chapter Sixteen

The Marquess of Hertford has invited a large party of the fashionable world, on Monday next, to his first fête during the season, at his mansion in the Regent's Park . . . We understand upwards of five hundred invitations have been issued.
—*The Court Journal*, Saturday 13 June 1835

Exclusive to Foxe's Morning Spectacle
Monday 15 June

In light of the recent incident at the British Institution's annual summer exhibition, we can only shake our heads in wonder at a certain gentleman's persistence in folly. This lord has won—whether by fair means or foul, we leave to our readers' judgment—the hand of London's premier belle, a diamond of the first water: a title which even our most hardened misogynists cannot begrudge her. A lady of rank, incomparable beauty, and grace, she ought, we should have thought, to arouse feelings of purest devotion in any masculine heart not hardened into adamantine obduracy by years of self-indulgence and callous disregard

*of obligations. True, the gentleman's depreda-
tions upon the once prosperous family estate
left to him by a loving father have reduced his
dependents to beggary. True, London has not
in many years seen so shameful a case of financial recklessness and disregard, even of the
unwritten code which permits a gentleman
to ignore the clamor of his creditors yet requires him to pay promptly all debts of honor
to his friends. Indeed, to find a case compa-
rable in egregiousness, we must look back to
the date in 1816 when Beau Brummell fled
these shores in the dead of night, leaving his
friends responsible for some thirty thousand
pounds in a mutually raised loan, in addition
to sums owed to divers parties who were not
his friends.*

*At present, we hardly know what to think.
We can only present to our readers a singu-
lar incident: On Sunday night, the gentleman
in question was observed in a quiet alcove of
the Brunswick Hotel. Admittedly, it is nothing out of the ordinary to discover groups
of gentlemen enjoying the hotel's fine food
and drink. Yet no other gentleman joined his
lordship. His only companion at table was a
young French widow last seen on the arm of
his affianced bride's brother.*

*Maison Noirot
Tuesday afternoon*

N o, no!" Marcelline cried. "What are you
thinking, Sophy? It's essential that Lady

Clara wear the white. And you must wear the blue."

"I thought you made the plum expressly for this party," Sophy said.

Marcelline waved her hands near her head, dismissing the plum dress and her plans for it. "That was before I saw the two dresses together, and you and Lady Clara standing together. No, no, it will never do. It's out of the question. The contrast is too strong."

A trio of mannequins wore the dresses at the moment. They were part of a set, twelve in all, and represented an extravagance Leonie hadn't enthusiastically endorsed. But the mannequins made a splendid show, and impressed the customers. Dowdy's had only two antiquated specimens.

"Of course there's a contrast," Sophy said. "I'm a dashing young widow. Lady Clara is an unwed young lady."

"I know that," Marcelline said impatiently. "But if Lady Clara wears the white and you wear the plum, the difference will seem too extreme, and you'll seem fast by comparison. Dashing is all very well. It's exciting. But *fast* is a judgment. And you're not the one we want judged." She turned to Lady Clara's brother. "I appeal to you, Lord Longmore."

He retreated a step. "Ah, no, thank you. When it comes to ladies' clothes, I'm like Mad Dick. He refuses to get near their hooks and buttons and such, and I refuse to enter disputes about style."

He, Lady Clara, Marcelline, and Sophy stood in the private consulting room on the first floor, away from the hubbub on the ground floor—a much greater hubbub than they'd anticipated for the Season's remaining ten days.

The ton liked to end the Season with a series of lavish events, rather like the concluding explosions of a fireworks display, and hosts competed to make the biggest explosion. Likewise, the women's competition for envy-arousing dress was as grim and fierce as preparations for war.

On Thursday, Lady Bartham would hold her annual ball. Her intent, as always, was to cast into the shade, if not the void, all other end-of-Season events, including the Marquess of Hertford's fête in Regent's Park yesterday, the Duke and Duchess of St. Albans's ball and supper this evening, and the Duke and Duchess of Northumberland's *fête champetre* at Sion House on Friday.

Outdoing everyone else was the obvious reason Lady Bartham had invited not only the principals of the exciting Adderley scandal, but a couple who had appeared on precious few guest lists: the Duke and Duchess of Clevedon.

When the Great World learned that both Lady Clara Fairfax and her rumored rival for Lord Adderley's affections, Madame de Veirrion, patronized Maison Noirot, half a dozen of the female members of that world abandoned their own dressmakers and made posthaste for No. 56 St. James's Street. Doubtless they hoped to get a glimpse of the two women, preferably trying to scratch each other's eyes out—not to mention a closer look at the glamorous new Duchess of Clevedon.

But these were lesser motives. The greater was to outdo everyone else, including the Parisian sensation, Madame de Veirrion. It seemed that having a dress made at Maison Noirot was the only way to achieve this aim—even if it meant getting put on the Marchioness of Warford's enemies list.

Since a delighted Leonie gave Sophy full credit for the influx of desirable customers, she'd been more affectionate and less tiresome about accounts than usual. Today, she was taking advantage of Sophy's being on duty at Maison Noirot by visiting the linen drapers. Leonie's eye for fabric was as sharp and discerning as her eye for numbers.

Still, Marcelline was the acknowledged design genius. Had Leonie been present, she would have told Sophy, "But of course you'll wear the blue. Didn't Marcelline say you must?"

Lady Clara, who'd moved to study the dresses, now added her opinion. "You'll be divine in the blue," she said. "It's the perfect shade for your eyes. And it will set off the diamonds splendidly."

"Diamonds?" Longmore said.

"Of course," Lady Clara said. "Madame must be dripping diamonds, to whet a certain gentleman's appetite."

His dark gaze swung to Sophy. She had not seen him since early Monday morning. This was the first time he'd actually looked at her since he'd arrived with his sister. She thought the glint in his eyes was humor.

Perhaps he wasn't in love after all. Perhaps he'd had the ailment for a moment, then recovered, much in the way he'd recover from a morning after too much carousing.

A man in love ought to seem at least a little troubled, perhaps pale and ill. He ought to feel *love's pangs*, as Lord Adderley so tritely put it.

But maybe it was trite of her to expect a man like Longmore to fret over a minor thing like being in love. He wasn't high-strung. One couldn't accuse him of excessive sentiment. He wasn't emotional. He wasn't sensitive.

And she rather loved that about him.

And so many other things about him.

Never mind never mind never mind.

She concentrated on *now*, and getting through this encounter with her poise and dignity intact.

"It's not a time for Madame to be subtle," she said.

"Oh, no one's subtle at Lady Bartham's ball," Lady Clara said, oblivious to currents between her brother and one of her dressmakers. "Women empty their jewel boxes on themselves."

"But not you, Lady Clara," Marcelline said. "You'll wear very simple jewelry. Your beauty requires no adornment in any event, and neither does the ball dress. A great dress should not require mounds of jewelry to make it great. But most important, we want to emphasize your purity and innocence."

"And we want to pretend that I have any purity and innocence," Sophy said. "That is to say, that Madame has any."

Longmore moved to the mannequins and examined the blue dress. "What is it you object to?" he said. "This blue will enhance the color of your eyes—your celestial eyes—or was it your lips—or your soul that the Puff Adder proclaimed celestial?"

"*I'm* celestial," she said. "My entire being."

"Did Lord Adderley say that, really?" Lady Clara said.

"He put it in writing," Longmore said. "Has Madame not told you?"

"When would Madame tell her?" Sophy said.

"Lady Clara and Madame are not on warm terms these days, remember?"

"I'm losing track of who is whom and what they're about," he said. "Too much subtlety and hidden meanings for my little brain box. Too much subterfuge."

It was second nature to her, Sophy thought. Or perhaps first nature.

With a fine show of good humor she told Lady Clara about the love letter. She saw the lady glance at her brother—looking for a reaction?—but he didn't notice. He was walking back and forth in front of the mannequins, hands folded behind his back. He put Sophy in mind of a general inspecting his troops.

In a way, that was what he was doing. Two of those dresses were part of Sophy's and Lady Clara's arsenal.

"I'm so glad I didn't know about it," Lady Clara said when Sophy had, with suitable pathos, conveyed Lord Adderley's closing plea. "I should never have been able to keep my composure yesterday when he called." Her smile was thin. "He was furious about the piece in the *Spectacle*. Once again he threatened to sue them. He ranted about slander. I sat with my hands folded and waited for him to finish carrying on. I thought Mama would explode, but she only sat very upright and stiff and disapproving. He must have caught on that he was using the wrong tactic, because after a while of getting no sympathy he quieted. Then he assured me the incident was perfectly innocent."

"I'm sorry I missed that performance," Longmore said while closely inspecting the blue dress.

"I had to put in an appearance at the Marquess of Hertford's fête."

He'd gone to that party after he'd told her he loved her, Sophy thought. After he'd told her he loved her and then looked as though it was a joke or a puzzle . . . and laughed . . . and left.

Marcelline joined him. "Is something troubling you about Sophy's—" She broke off, frowning, and moved to the white dress she'd made for Lady Clara. "Sophy, do you think these sleeves ought to . . ." She looked at the dress, then at Lady Clara. She narrowed her eyes and pursed her lips in that way she did when her artist's eye discerned something amiss that nobody else could see.

"The sleeves," she said. "They're not quite . . . Lady Clara, I must trouble you to try on the dress."

"Oh, yes, of course. That's why I came. And wasn't it good of Harry to take me, when he could have gone to Ascot? The races begin today, you know, and he hasn't missed an opening day since he came back from the Continent."

Marcelline only smiled and led her ladyship into the dressing room. The door wasn't closed, and Lady Clara's light, musical voice was perfectly audible. "It was too bad he missed Lord Adderley's performance," she said. "That might have made up for Ascot. I think Harry would have laughed himself sick. Mama, naturally, doesn't see the humor in it. She was plainly outraged, but she held herself in check. For which I give her credit. It's very hard to sit quietly while one's intelligence is insulted."

Longmore drew near to Sophy. "I should like to see you dripping diamonds . . . and nothing else," he said in the very low voice that melted her spine and her brain simultaneously. More audibly, he answered his sister, "I was curious how the snake would account for himself."

"Oh, he blamed you," Clara said, her voice slightly muffled. Sophy could hear fabric rustling and Marcelline muttering something.

"I?" Longmore said. He leaned in and licked Sophy's earlobe.

Her fingers curled into her palms. She really ought to step away, but it was too delicious. Too naughty.

"He claimed you'd hurt Madame's feelings," Clara was saying. "He said he was simply trying to cheer her. I said I thought that dining *intime* with a lady at a hotel seemed an odd way to go about it. Why did he not suggest she take a brisk walk in the open air? Why did he not suggest she visit Astley's Amphitheater or the zoo or watch a comedy at the theater?"

Longmore was kissing the little bit of Sophy's throat accessible above the ruche of her chemisette. It was extremely difficult to concentrate on Lady Clara. Yet Sophy was too weak-willed to step away. "That's . . . good," she said. "You didn't forgive him too easily."

"Not at all," Lady Clara said. "I know he was annoyed with me. He expected me to smile and accept whatever he said. He thinks that he can do whatever he pleases, merely because he holds the power to restore my good name—the good name he fouled. On purpose."

Longmore left off kissing Sophy and looked deeply into her eyes. "This is too complicated," he said. "I can't do this and think at the same time."

"Then move away," she said.

"Don't want to," he said.

"I know he wanted to break it off then and there," Clara went on. "But he doesn't dare. A bird in the hand, you know—but, my God, what shall I do if it all goes wrong, and—"

"Hush!" Marcelline said sharply. "It's not going to go wrong. Trust us, my dear."

"Trust you," Longmore murmured, still gazing so intently into Sophy's eyes. "What a funny, funny thing to say."

Since it was best for Sophy not to be seen too often in the shop at present, she avoided the showroom. Marcelline was the one who accompanied Lady Clara and her brother downstairs and saw them out—much to the excitement of the customers, no doubt.

Marcelline returned very soon, however, and with a grim look quickly removed the plum dress from the mannequin. She draped the dress over one arm and took hold of Sophy's arm with her free hand and marched her into the dressing room.

"There's no need to throw a tantrum," Sophy said. Marcelline could become temperamental about her designs. "If you say I must wear the blue, I must wear the blue."

"I know why you want to wear the plum," Marcelline said. "It's ravishing. It'll make Longmore swoon."

"It might make him do some things," Sophy said. "But swooning isn't one of them. He's the sort of man who tells a girl he l-loves her—and then l-laughs. As though it's a j-joke."

To her vexation, she started to cry.

"Oh, my dear love." Marcelline threw the dress

over a chair and wrapped her arms about her sister.

That was all. She simply held her for a time while Sophy cried and cried until she was done.

Then Marcelline led her upstairs to the sitting room and brought out the brandy, the Noirot sisters' preferred remedy for all sorts of disturbances.

"You work too hard," Marcelline said after they'd taken their first sips. "You take too much on. Even Leonie says so."

"But I've left you two to manage everything—and you've got a husband now! You're still newlyweds!"

"Leonie and I have sufficient help from Selina Jeffreys and some of the seamstresses," Marcelline said. "Clevedon and I have no trouble finding all the time we need to be together. Just because one is married doesn't mean one must be with one's spouse every waking minute."

"Still—"

"Still, nothing," Marcelline said. "You're overworked. You had quite enough to do, merely looking after our interests. But now you've taken on this trouble of Lady Clara's. And there's her brother, making love to you at the same time you're trying to conduct a delicate, elaborate, and risky scheme."

Sophy met her sister's gaze over the brandy decanter.

Schemes and dodges and subterfuge and other forms of machination were part of the family inheritance. If there was one thing her sisters understood as well or perhaps even better than they did the art of dressmaking, it was the art of deception.

"And there are my sisters," Sophy said, "carrying on the business, slaving over dresses and indulging spoiled ladies—while I'm at the Clarendon Hotel pretending to be the Queen of Sheba at my brother-in-law's expense."

Marcelline laughed. "*Ma foi*, you can't be so mad as to let that trouble you! Clevedon's thrilled to be part of our plot. And do try to remember that he doesn't care about money. He's not like us. He never had to think about it, let alone worry about it—and it's extremely unlikely he ever will. Pray don't fret about the Clarendon and Madame's servants and such. My husband's friends will have won or lost as much at Ascot this week as he's spent on you. And they won't have had nearly so much fun doing it."

A weight lifted.

Sophy grinned at her sister. "It is great fun," she said. "I get so caught up in worrying about Lady Clara that I forget I'm doing what I was born to do—and it makes a pleasant change from waiting on tiresome women."

"That's the only drawback," Marcelline said with a little sigh. "I love designing clothes. I love making clothes. I don't even mind the dreary, boring repetitive parts."

"They're soothing," Sophy said. "One doesn't think. One simply *does*, and takes pleasure in doing it beautifully."

"I love everything about it," Marcelline said.

"Except the customers."

Marcelline laughed. "If only each customer could send a mannequin in her place. Well, not *all* of them. Some are great fun. Lady Clara is a delight—even when she's arguing with me about things of which she knows nothing. But most of them—really, when one thinks about it . . ." She sat for a moment, staring at the decanter. "There must be a way."

"My dear, if you'd rather be a duchess, and design dresses in your private castle purely for yourself and your own entertainment, you know Leonie and I can manage the shop."

"I'd die if I gave it up," Marcelline said. "Something inside me would shrivel. It's too bad, but Cousin Emma did something to us. In spite of Mama and Papa and all the others."

"She inspired us," Sophy said. "We were meant to be knaves like the rest—and we are. But Cousin Emma made us something more. And now we can't be less, that's all."

Marcelline raised her glass, and Sophy did, too.

"To Cousin Emma," Marcelline said.

"To Cousin Emma," Sophy said. They drank.

"And I must wear the blue dress," Sophy said, "because—"

"Because the other will make Longmore swoon, and we need him to keep his wits about him," Marcelline said. "And speaking of Longmore . . ." She raised her eyebrows at Sophy.

We make love, he'd said.

"Yes," Sophy said. "Yes, I did. That. The thing you explained about."

"The family matter," Marcelline said.

"I was waiting for the right time to tell you," Sophy said. "But there hasn't been time. Lately we see each other for such short intervals."

She told her sister now, what had happened on the way to and from Portsmouth.

She knew Marcelline wouldn't be angry or

disapproving. Noirots weren't like other people. There were rules they didn't understand and didn't care about.

She only listened and smiled now and again, and when Sophy had finished, she shrugged a perfect French shrug, which also happened to be a perfect Noirot shrug. "It was bound to happen sooner or later," she said. "Purity and virtue don't agree with Noirots, do they? And you're all of three and twenty. It's remarkable you kept your virtue for so long."

"Lack of opportunity, probably," Sophy said.

"You barely have time to sleep," Marcelline said. "Where is there time for love affairs? Yet we manage to make the time when we have to."

"I'm not sure I had to," Sophy said.

"I am," Marcelline said. "I know it's damned inconvenient, and I don't blame you for crying, considering what an extremely difficult and complicated situation it is with him."

"Difficult and complicated? Impossible, you mean."

"It does seem rather impossible, I'll admit." Marcelline smiled. "But my dear love—*ma soeur chérie*—I really must commend you on your excellent *taste*."

Warford House
Thursday 18 June

"Pray listen to this, Mama," Lady Clara said. She gave the *Spectacle* a little shake, cleared her throat, and began, " 'It would seem that the rift which had opened a few days ago between a certain lord and a young French widow has been bridged, and all is billing and cooing once more. The couple dined at the Clarendon Hotel last night with the duke and duchess who had introduced them, as our readers will recollect, last week at the Queen's Theater. Madame wore a dress of pink *velours epinglé*, the corsage draped in folds across the bosom, the back close-fitting. Very short, full sleeves cut open in front to display . . .'"

When she got to the "billing and cooing" part, Lord Adderley left his chair and walked to the chimneypiece, where he stared at Lady Warford's collection of Murano glass flowers. He paid no attention to the rest of the recital, which consisted of every last pestilential detail of what Madame wore and what the duchess wore.

He'd dutifully called today as he did every day but Tuesday, when the family was not at home to callers. It was rather like going daily to have a tooth pulled, he thought. He wasn't sure he could endure much more of it: Clara's incessant prattling and her mother's icily patronizing politeness.

"Billing and cooing, indeed," Lady Warford said. "I shouldn't be surprised if Longmore broke Tom Foxe's jaw for his impudence."

"Harry's more likely to laugh," Clara said. "But it's interesting, isn't it, Lord Adderley, that all is mended between them."

"I can't help but believe the engagement for dinner must have been made previously," he said. "No doubt the lady didn't wish to inconvenience her friends. The duke and duchess are friends of long standing, I believe."

"Then my brother obviously took advantage of the opportunity to make up to Madame," Clara said. "He can be winning when he wants to be."

"If Longmore wishes to be winning, one can only conclude that he's decided to fix the lady's interest," Lady Warford said. "I had a feeling it would come to this, from the moment I saw him with her in the theater. Ah, well, it might have been worse, I'm sure."

A barmaid or a ballet dancer.

"I think you'll like her, Mama," Clara said. "She seems good-natured. At least she won't make a disagreeable daughter-in-law."

"Daughter-in-law?" Adderley said. "Have you got them to the altar already?"

"I believe it's only a matter of time," Clara said.

"But you seemed to take her in dislike the other day," he said.

"That was before you told me that Harry had hurt her feelings. I know how provoking my brother can be."

"Shockingly tactless," Lady Warford said. "Unfortunately, Longmore can be tactless quite fluently in several languages."

"In any event, Lady Bartham will ask to introduce her to Mama tonight, and it seems we must like it or lump it."

"I see no alternative but to agree to know the lady," Lady Warford said. "One can never be sure with Longmore, but in the event he turns out to entertain serious feelings about this young woman, I prefer to begin the acquaintance amiably. And if it all comes to nothing—" Lady Warford made a dismissive gesture. "No harm done. The Season is nearly over, and one needn't see her again until next year. By then, who knows what will happen?"

"Indeed," Lord Adderley said. "Who knows?"

He came away from the chimneypiece. "I had better not trespass on your time. I know you ladies will wish to rest and prepare for the ball this evening."

They didn't try to keep him.

He made his farewell with great politeness if not great warmth. As he was leaving the room, as glad to be gone as he knew they were to see him go, he heard Clara say, "I can't wait to see what Madame de Veirrion will be wearing."

He swallowed a smile and went out.

Billing and cooing, was she?

The wicked little coquette.

Let the *Spectacle* print what it wished. Let them think what they liked.

He knew the truth about her.

Countess of Bartham's ball
Thursday night

Longmore watched Lady Bartham approach. "Whatever you do," he said in an undertone, "do *not* treat my mother to that curtsey."

"But what curtsey is this?" Madame said.

"You know the one I mean," he said. "The ballet dancer dying swan Queen Mab curtsey."

"This is absurd," she said. "Why should I do these things?"

He hadn't time to answer because Lady Bartham was upon them, all smiles. A moment later she was leading Madame to meet his mother.

He let them go ahead, while he watched everybody watching Madame. The blue dress had been pretty enough in the shop. Now it was breathtaking, Delicate silver embroidery made a twining pattern over the top layer of blue crepe, which floated upon the satin layer beneath. Gossamer lace fluttered and brilliants sparkled in the sleeves. Under the chandeliers, it was like watching sunlight shimmering on a blue sea.

The dress was cut low, the better to display the eleven tons of diamonds she wore—and which, with any luck, no one would discover had been charged to the Duke of Clevedon's account at Rundell and Bridge.

Longmore glanced about the room, casually taking note of Lord Adderley, lounging near the refreshment room, wearing a self-satisfied smirk.

"My dear Lady Warford, may I present Madame de Veirrion," Lady Bartham said.

Lady Warford sat up a degree straighter and a shade more stiffly. Her blue gaze bored straight into Madame as though she were prepared to read entrails, without the usual preliminaries.

For a moment Madame wondered whether Lady Bartham had made a mistake or misunderstood. Ladies were supposed to ask other ladies if they desired such and such an introduction, to avoid awkward moments. Maybe Lady Warford had agreed but had changed her mind.

Mon dieu, *I'm about to be snubbed*, she thought. *The cut direct—at the biggest event of the Season.*

But nothing of what happened inside Madame showed on the outside. Outside she wore enough of a smile to be amiable but not at all fawning.

After all, Madame de Veirrion had a great fortune, and in Paris she was Somebody.

Lady Warford gave a gracious nod. "Madame."

"Lady Warford." Madame didn't return the nod. She sank into a Noirot curtsey, the one Longmore had told her not to perform.

She heard everybody in the vicinity catch their breath.

When she rose, Lady Warford was wearing a speculative look.

Longmore appeared at Madame's elbow. "Good gad, madame, it's my mother, not Louis XIV. You French, always carrying everything to excess."

"What is this excess you speak of?" said Madame. "This is *madame la marquise*, yes? What is wrong in this way I make my courtesy to your so elegant *maman*? Of whom, yes, I beg the pardon." She turned her attention to Lady Warford. "You will pardon, I beg you please, *Madame de*—ah, no. It is Lady Warford I must say. My English is not yet of perfection."

"I'm sure you'll master it in time, Madame de Veirrion," Lady Warford said. "As you seem to have mastered . . . other things." She shot a glance at her son before returning to his companion. "I believe this is your first London ball?"

"Yes, *Madame*—Lady Warford. I make my debut, thanks to the great kindness of your friend Lady Bartham."

"But of course I must have you," Lady Bartham said. "Unthinkable not to have the most-talked-about lady in London at my party."

"Of course you must," Lady Warford said, smiling sweetly.

Lady Bartham said, with a laugh. "And I must have, too, the second most-talked-about, the Duchess of Clevedon."

"Since most of the talk is in English," Longmore said, "Madame is in the fortunate position of not understanding most of it. I daresay she barely comprehends three words in ten of the present conversation. Madame, you're looking a trifle dazed. I think you need a drink. Lady Bartham—Mother—Clara—if we may be permitted to exit your exalted presence?"

He swept her away.

Chapter Seventeen

Had Mr. Brinsley Sheridan been a low, worthless, extravagant profligate, whose marriage was a skilful arrangement with his impatient creditors, we should have been the first to condemn and deplore the step which has been taken.
—*The Court Journal*, Saturday 13 June 1835

They danced.

It wasn't what Sophy had expected. She'd been so fixed on her scheme and playing her part that she'd almost forgotten she wasn't an actor in a stage drama but a lady attending a ball.

The music had started as Longmore was leading her away from his mother. In another moment, Lord and Lady Bartham began to dance, not with each other but with the partners etiquette dictated.

Then Longmore was saying, "Ah, the perfect excuse not to make polite conversation." He led Sophy out among the swirling couples, and his arm went round her waist, and she caught her breath and said, "I'm not sure . . . It's been an age since I—"

"I'll lead," he told her in French. "Leave it to me, Madame. *Trust me.*"

Moments later, he'd swept her into the waltz, and she forgot business and schemes and villains. For this time, there was only this man, and the motion of his athletic, confident body, as sure and thoroughly masculine in dancing as in everything else.

Round and round the ballroom they went, and it seemed she was floating among clouds of silks and satins, whites and pastels and vivid jewel tones and black and grey, all swirling about her, while rainbow stars sparkled among the clouds: emeralds, sapphires, rubies, pearls, and diamonds—above all, diamonds—glittering under another thousand stars in the crystal chandeliers.

It was like a fairyland.

How many such events had she attended, playing a maid? How many times had she described such scenes for the *Spectacle*'s readers?

But always, she described from the outside looking in.

She hadn't danced in ages, as she'd tried to tell him. Not since Paris. And then she'd never attended a gathering like this. She'd never before danced in the arms of a man she . . .

Loved.

She looked up and found him gazing down at her, wearing a hint of a smile while amusement glinted in his dark eyes: amusement and something else she couldn't read.

"You naughty girl," he said in French. "What did I tell you about the curtsey? And why did I imagine you'd pay me the slightest heed?"

"I had a reason," she answered in the same language. It was much easier to converse that way than in Madame's mangled English. French came naturally. Murdering the English language in a believably French style needed thought.

"You always do," he said.

"Firstly, like a ballet dancer's movement, it captivates the eye," she said. "Secondly, it displays the dress in a way that no other movement can."

"Even this?" he said. "Was it not designed to appear at its most enticingly beautiful during dancing?"

"You're learning," she said.

"In self-defense," he said. "Like Clevedon."

He looked away and she followed his gaze. Marcelline and the duke were dancing, and it had to be obvious to all onlookers why he'd broken a cardinal rule of his class and married a shopkeeper. It had to be obvious as well, that he'd married a woman who loved him. Marcelline wasn't wearing her card-playing face. She was herself: a woman deeply, deeply in love with her husband.

She deserved her good fortune, Sophy thought. Marcelline had worked since she was a child. She'd made the best of a bad marriage to a charming philanderer of a cousin. And when the cholera had come and destroyed their world, everyone in it, and everything they'd worked for, she'd gathered what remained of her family and brought them to England, with a handful of coins and a ruthless will to succeed.

Sophy tore her gaze from her sister. "If you understand this much about the dress design, then you know my motives were ulterior," she said. "It's true that this and all our gowns are meant to appear beautiful at rest and even more so in motion. But I ask you to bring to mind my earlier mission—the one that took us to Hortense the Horrible. Do you recall?"

"As though I could forget," he said. "Your mole, in particular, is deeply etched—or should I say permanently sprouting—in my recollection."

"We went there so that I could see whether it was the same old Dowdy's or something different and more of a threat," she said. "I needed to see your mother's dress because they'd do their best work for her. It was better than their usual thing, but it still couldn't hold a candle to ours. But how to make your mother see this?"

"I don't see what this has to do with the curtsey," he said.

"It didn't occur to you," she said, "that at the moment I was being introduced to your mother, she was surrounded by the work of Maison Noirot: Lady Bartham, Lady Clara, and I were all wearing Marcelline's creations. Your mother couldn't fail to notice the difference between what she was wearing and what we were wearing. It may take her a while to fully comprehend, but we've planted the seed."

"Business," he said. "The curtsey was business."

"Advertising," she said.

"You make my head spin, madame," he said.

He drew her into a turn that made her head spin, too. Then she forgot business. How had she ever thought the waltz was merely a dance? To waltz with him was like making love—a kind of tortured making love—touching but not caressing. Holding but not embracing. A feeling of growing urgency and heat with no way to relieve it, no climax possible.

She was close enough to feel the heat of his body and the way his breath came faster. It was so deeply intimate, like the feel of his hand clasping hers, his other at her waist. It seemed as though this was where she belonged and had always belonged. She wondered at the women about her, who could dance in this intimate way with men who weren't their lovers.

How can I stop? she thought. *How can I go back to my life without him?*

Nonsensical questions. He and she played a game, and this love affair of theirs—if that's what it was—was merely a happenstance. Only a complete ninny would turn it into a romantic tragedy.

She hadn't time to be a ninny.

She had a job to do. And if she made a mistake, a young woman's life would be ruined . . . and take three women's hopes and dreams and years of hard work with it.

Yet it was hard to stay detached and calculating while she danced with him.

When the music faded to a close, it was far too soon. Sophy wanted to throw her arms about his neck and kiss him witless and hold on to him because . . .

Because for a short time she'd known what it was to live in his world, rather than trespass in it. For a short time she'd known what it was to be special in that curious way her ancestors had been special: not because they were skilled artisans or inventors or brave soldiers or had in any way contributed anything of value to their fellow men, but because they were simply born special: aristocrats.

Above all, though, she'd imagined—believed—

felt, even in her cynical, black Noirot heart—that she was special to him.

Maybe she was. But she knew how this story had to end.

Time to put an end to the tragi-comedy. Or farce. She wasn't at all sure which it was.

Sometime later

*L*ongmore looked on while Madame proceeded to cut a swath through the gentlemen. At present he stood with his mother, who was watching her, too.

As was Adderley, on the other side of the room.

"Do you mean to let the other gentlemen steal a march on you?" his mother said. "I should not be too sure of her, if I were you, Harry. You might have been first out of the gate, as you would put it, but these others might easily make up time."

For the moment, there was no one else about, except an extremely elderly lady—another of Grandmother Warford's friends—who was profoundly deaf. For a time, they'd had to say everything six or seven times, as well as answer the same question at least that often, but at present, her head was sinking toward her ample bosom and she was snoring.

Even though no one could overhear them, he was surprised. He bent an enquiring look on his mother.

"Don't give me that look," she said crossly. "It only shows how obtuse you are."

"I can't help it," he said. "The lady doesn't strike me as quite what you'd choose for my bride—yet here you are, urging me on to the altar."

"She's nothing like what I'd choose," his mother said. "Still."

He raised his eyebrows.

"Her English is atrocious," his mother said. "She can't have had a proper education."

"Some people simply have no aptitude for languages," he said.

"Apt or not, I'm not at all sure she isn't a complete henwit," she said. "But she is a handsome girl—"

"With a handsome fortune."

"Don't be vulgar."

"If she were penniless, you wouldn't be urging me to chase her," Longmore said. "And I don't see what the hurry is about."

He glanced at the dance floor, on whose fringes Adderley lurked, watching Madame. "Oh, but look, that's Lady Bartham's third son Madame is dancing with. It would be a great pity if he won the lady's heart and her formidable fortune."

"It would be a great pity if you lost any girl to that callow creature," his mother said. "But do as you like, Harry. You always did. Your sister, too. I vow, I have been plagued with the most undutiful children. If she had only listened to me, she would not be in this wretched situation. Every day that passes, I like him less and less—and I despised him to begin with. Look at him. Two dances with Clara and he abandons her. When I think of the men she might have had. Oh, it is too much. And see, even he is ogling Madame. How dare he?"

"They're all ogling her."

"And you're mighty cool about it, I must say."

"I believe it's the sort of thing one must get used to. She attracts attention wherever she goes."

She watched Madame for a time, her brow knitting. "Do you know, Harry, she puts me in mind of somebody."

The dance was ending and Longmore saw Adderley making his way to Madame.

"Oh, no, my fine fellow," Longmore said. "Amuse yourself if you like, but not with my merry widow."

"Why should he not?" his mother said. "She isn't yours. You make no push to fix her interest."

"He has no business trying to fix it when he's engaged to my sister—not to mention that Madame promised this dance to me."

"Don't make a scene, Harry. Not here, of all places."

"Mother, you cut me to the quick. I never make scenes."

He didn't hurry across the room and he didn't push anybody out of his way. Lord Longmore didn't need to. All he needed to do was wear a certain expression, and people hastily moved out of his way.

When Longmore reached them, Adderley was leaning in much too close to say something to Madame.

"So sorry to interrupt the tête-à-tête," Longmore said. "But this dance is mine."

"I believe you're mistaken," Adderley said. "Madame has promised the dance to me."

Madame looked in bewilderment from one to the other. Then her expression became chagrined. "This is too bad," she said. "You must pardon me, Lord Add'lee. Lord Lun-mour speaks correctly. It was this dance I promised to him. My abominable memory—I beg you to forgive. But you will have the next one."

"Next is supper," Longmore said. "Since this is the supper dance, I have the privilege of taking you in. To sup."

"*C'est exact*," she said. "I forget this."

"How easily you forget," Longmore said.

She shot him an unfriendly look, then turned a more affectionate one upon Adderley. "I shall see you after the supper, Lord Add'lee. If I am not too greatly fatigued."

Adderley bowed and left, still smirking.

Longmore watched him go before turning back to Madame. "You expect to find my company fatiguing?"

"That is not what I say," she said. "You turn my words the wrong way."

"And your gaze as well?" he said.

"I cannot comprehend you," she said.

"I noticed the glance you cast his way. I've never claimed to be a genius, but I reckon I know a flirtatious look when I see one."

"And why should I not flirt?" she said. "Why have we this disagreement again and again? Have I the collar around my neck, like a dog? I am not your dog on the leash, Lord Lun-mour. I do not belong to you."

Dream on, he answered silently.

"Perhaps not," he said. "But the gentleman belongs to my sister—as I have pointed out to you. Again and again."

"This is monstrous. Of what do you accuse me? To steal this man from your sister?"

"The other day you seemed to think he needed to be stolen."

She waved this aside. "I was angry, and some things I said were foolish things. But only a little time ago, I met your mother, who was so amiable to me. And your sister has forgiven me my little error. Why should I wish to distress them? Here I am a stranger. Alone. No one protects me. I have only my friends to guard me, and I am glad to make friends." Her mouth turned down.

"I'm glad for you to make them, too," he said. "However, when you grow too friendly—"

"No! I was only amiable." The blue eyes flashed at him. "I flirt with him a little, in the way all the women do. I do not see why you must tell me I am wrong to do this. *You* have not said even one word of special regard for me."

"I said three, as I recall," he said quietly. "What more do you require, madame?"

Pink tinted her cheeks and spread downward, under the diamonds encircling her neck and dripping over her bosom. "I believe you play with me," she said.

"Is that what you think?" he said. "That I'm toying with your affections?"

"You seem to think it is a great joke."

"Is it not?"

Tears shimmered in her eyes, and in that moment he knew they weren't playing—or if they were, they danced on the very edge of truth.

"Yes," she said. "Yes, it is. Hilarious. Ha ha."

She turned away in a flurry of satin and lace, and made her way, hips swaying, chin aloft, across the ballroom.

Sophy had scarcely turned her back on Longmore when Lord Adderley loomed in her path. "I thought you'd promised this dance to Lord Longmore," he said.

"It seems I am *fatiguée*," she said. She snapped open her fan and waved it briskly before her face. "And too hot." He'd think her heated reaction was to him. "I have lost my humor to dance. I have lost my pleasure in this ball."

"As have I," he said in his English-accented French. "And you know the reason."

She eyed him over the top of her fan. "Do I?"

"Have I not told you?" His voice became low and throbbing. "Have I not laid my heart bare to you? Every word I've written to you is torn from my heart. You know I'm in agony. Why do you torture me?"

She looked about her. "You are indiscreet. Someone will hear."

"We must settle this," he said. "Every day you change your mind."

"Every day!" she said. "How many days has it been? Days, milord. Not years or even months or weeks. A few days. A few letters." Ah, yes, she'd answered his. She'd given him reason to hope and reason to despair. She'd encouraged him while seeming to push him away or seeming undecided. But she'd taken care never to write anything undecided enough or rejecting enough to cause him to give up. "You must not press me."

"I haven't time to wait," he said. "If you mean to trample on my heart, do it now. Kill my hope, but do it quickly, for God's sake, and put me out of my misery."

She moved away. He followed her.

"You hurry me," she said. "A woman should not be hurried in affairs of the heart."

"I knew my heart the instant I met you," he said. "I knew we belonged together."

As soon as you heard of my great fortune.

A servant approached, carrying a tray laden with glasses of champagne. She shook her head at the servant and continued toward her destination.

"We cannot talk in this place," she said. "Too much activity. Too many people. Another time we will meet."

"They're going in to supper," he said. "There won't be a better time. And there won't be another time. I must know tonight. You promised me an answer tonight."

"You are too impetuous."

And she'd done her best to make him that way.

"Madame, for me, time is running out."

"Ah, yes, you are to be married."

"That is for you to determine."

"I cannot abide the thought of taking you away from that pretty girl," she said. "To break her heart? I am not that kind of woman." While they talked, she never paused but walked on, at a leisurely pace, letting him follow.

"Break her heart?" he said. "She barely tolerates me, as well you know. You've seen. All her family despise me. If it were not for one foolish moment, I should be free. And then I should wait and wait for you to make up your mind."

"One foolish moment? And how do I know I am not another foolish moment for you?"

"What proof do you want?"

They'd reached the French windows, which stood open to let air circulate through the ballroom on this warm night. Beyond lay a small terrace, bordered by a stone railing. Some light from the ballroom cast its glow over the terrace. To the left, one part of the railing stood in shadow. Beyond the terrace, lanterns lit the gardens. So romantic. She smiled to herself.

She stepped through the French window and walked to the shadowy part of the railing.

"What proof?" he said again

"I will not have an affair," she said in a low voice. "I was true to my husband. I am not a wicked woman. I will not be your mistress. I am not the courtesan."

"I don't want a mistress," he said.

Naturally not. Mistresses were expensive to keep.

She said nothing.

"My intentions are honorable," he said. "I can prove it."

She glanced up at him.

"I can," he said. "Come away with me—now—tonight. We can be in Scotland in less than two days—and we can be wed as soon as we get there."

"To elope?" she said. "You would do this?"

"Why not?" he said. "Sheridan did it not long ago. And unlike him, we needn't worry about being pursued."

She put her hand to her heart and turned away from him.

"Madame?"

She shook her head. "No, stay away. I must think. This is not what I thought. I was not prepared." While she spoke, she made a few quick, covert adjustments to her dress. "I never dreamed you would go so far," she said. "To run away with me—it will anger your friends. This means disgrace for you, perhaps."

"I don't care," he said. "If I have you, nothing else matters. Madame, I beg you." He set his hands on her shoulders and turned her around. She didn't resist. He drew her into his arms. "Come away with me."

"No!" she shrieked. "No! Stop! Help!" As she cried out in French and English, she pushed him away. When she did so, the bodice of her dress slid down, exactly as it had been designed to do, revealing the expensive blond lace of her chemise and a bit of one of Marcelline's elegant Venetian corsets.

At the same moment, right on cue, a small crowd spilled out onto the terrace, Lady Clara in the lead.

Adderley jumped away from Sophy as though she'd broken out in boils. "What the devil?" he said. "What is this?"

"It's quite obvious what it is," Lady Clara said. She marched up to him and slapped him. "You brute. You false, despicable brute."

"For shame!" someone in the crowd said.

"You disgust me," Lady Clara said. "I will not marry you. The world may think what it likes of me—but I wouldn't marry you if you were the last man on earth."

Adderley said, "But I didn't—"

"For shame!"

"Disgraceful!"

Other voices chimed in, to the same effect.

Marcelline made her way through the bystanders and went to Sophy. "*Ma pauvre dame!*" She glared at Adderley. "*Quel monstre!*"

Adderley said, "But I never—"

"Beast!" someone cried.

"Brute!"

"What the devil is going on?" Longmore broke through the crowd. He looked at Sophy. He looked at Adderley. He started for Adderley.

Clevedon pulled him back. "Don't," he said. "Don't dirty your hands."

"Not worth the effort," someone called.

"Let him rot," said another.

"Not on my terrace," Lady Bartham said. She stood in the French window. Beside her stood Lady Warford. With the light of the ballroom glowing behind them, they looked like avenging angels.

"Lord Adderley, I must ask you to leave," Lady Bartham said. "And you are not welcome to return."

Longmore knew what he was supposed to do.

"Don't on any account hit him," Clevedon had counseled, and all the Noirot sisters had agreed with him.

This was Clara's moment, they'd all said. Let her do it. Let all those who'd judged her see.

And so Longmore had let Clara slap Adderley.

But the cur was slinking away, and flames danced in front of Longmore's eyes.

He started after Adderley. He'd not gone three paces when he heard Madame's voice, shaky and tear-clogged. "Lord Lun-mour." He turned. She stood, her sister's arm about her shoulders, her beautiful dress disordered. Tears streamed down her face. "Please return me to my hotel."

The sight of the disordered dress turned his mind black with rage. All he could think was murder, and he almost said, "Clevedon will take you."

But the great blue eyes held him.

He dragged in a lungful of air and let it out. He returned to her. "Of course, madame," he said.

He picked her up and carried her—through the

ballroom, past a lot of gaping and whispering aristocrats and on through the corridor and down the stairs and out of the house.

He held her, her face buried in his shoulder, while a carriage was hastily commandeered to transport them.

Within a very few minutes, their host's carriage arrived. He quickly bundled Sophy into it.

When they'd turned a corner, and were well out of sight of Bartham House, he said, "That went well, I thought."

She had been slumped against him, teary and trembling.

The trembling stopped and she sat up and drew out the world's tiniest handkerchief and briskly wiped away the tears. "Nearly perfectly," she said.

"Nearly?"

"You were not supposed to go after Adderley with murder in mind," she said. "You were not supposed to go after him at all. I explained that to you. We all explained it to you. It would diminish the effect. Have you forgotten how it goes? He assaults your what-you-call-it."

"My aunt," he said, turning his gaze to the window. He was an ass sometimes, a great ass.

"If you hit him, the matter is settled, the problem is solved. We didn't want it settled that way. We wanted him shamed, the way he'd shamed your sister."

He leaned back in the seat and closed his eyes. "I know."

"But you forgot," she said. "One can't forget things like that. You very nearly spoiled it."

"He touched you," he said.

"For three seconds," she said.

"He saw your chemise."

"One inch of it."

"And your corset."

"Another inch. And so did everybody else. That was the point."

"I know," he said. "But I'm a man in love, and a man in love doesn't think in a rational manner."

There was a silence in the carriage.

From outside, the clip-clop of hooves and the clack of wheels were plainly audible. He heard voices in the distance. A bell tolled somewhere.

"Something must be done about you," he said.

"You already did something," she said. "Several times. In two different hostelries. Employing a variety of maneuvers."

We make love.

"I think I have to marry you," he said.

Sophy felt a sob welling painfully in her chest. She willed it away.

"Two proposals in one night," she said. "The blaze of diamonds must fry men's brains."

"That's what I like about you," he said. "So romantic."

She turned to him. "Well, it's a joke, isn't it? On us. And if I don't make a joke I'll cry. I've cried quite enough tonight."

"That was make-believe."

"I don't really know the difference," she said.

"And that, strangely enough, is another thing I like about you. In any event, like you or not, my mother wants me to marry you."

"She wants you to marry Madame, you mean."

"She finds you passably attractive, although not

very intelligent. But she will assume that makes us compatible, since I'm nothing special in the brains department."

"You can't marry Madame," Sophy said. "And you can't marry me."

"Then what do you propose we do?" he said.

"I don't know," she said.

"Well, *think*," he said. "You got my sister out of a situation everyone else deemed completely hopeless. Surely you can devise a scheme for us. You must. Don't you have a cunning plan to make my mother love you?"

"In time, I might lure her to Maison Noirot," she said. "I might persuade her to tolerate me as her dressmaker. But making her love me is out of the question. Only imagine how she'd feel."

"Feelings," he said.

"She's a woman," she said. "She's a mother. Try to put yourself in her place: Clevedon married my sister instead of her daughter. Then you decide to marry me—the sister of the woman who ruined her cherished plans and who is therefore at least indirectly responsible for Clara's difficulties."

"Is it so important that my mother love you?" he said.

You don't understand, she wanted to cry. *My family has done nothing but destroy families. For generations. I'm not good. I'm not virtuous. I'm a knave. But I don't want to be like that.*

She said, "Your parents will cut you off. It's the most powerful weapon they have. Perhaps the only weapon."

"Then I reckon I'll have to take up quarters over the shop and let my wife support me," he said.

"Harry," she said.

He met her gaze.

"You know that's absurd," she said. "You'd hate it. Are you aware that Leonie holds the purse strings? Marcelline and I are not good with money. That is to say, we're good mainly at spending it."

He stared at her for a long moment. Then he let out a sigh. "We're doomed," he said. "In that case . . ."

He pulled her into his arms.

Chapter Eighteen

In most of the principal streets of the metropolis, shawls, muslins, pieces for ladies' dresses, and a variety of other goods, are shown with the assistance of mirrors, and at night by chandeliers, aided by the brilliancy which the gaslights afford, in a way almost as dazzling to a stranger, as many of those poetical fictions of which we read in the Arabian nights' entertainment.

—*The book of English trades,
and library of the useful arts*, 1818

On Friday, the *Spectacle* reported all the details of the incident at Lady Bartham's ball—which did promise to make hers the biggest explosion of the Season's end—along with lengthy descriptions of the dresses worn by the principals in this drama.

On Saturday, the *Spectacle* informed its readers that Madame de Veirrion had disappeared from London as mysteriously as she'd appeared. She'd checked out of the Clarendon Hotel on Friday night, apparently, and driven away in a coach and four. And that was the last the *Spectacle* had been able to discover.

On Sunday, the *Spectacle* reported that Lord Adderley had been barred from all of his clubs.

On Monday, the *Spectacle* announced that Lord Adderley had departed London in the dead of night. His creditors, it said, were in pursuit.

On Tuesday, Sophy sat at her writing table in the sisters' shared work area. She was composing a description of the dress Lady Bartham would wear to Almack's on the following evening. Though the piece wouldn't appear in the *Spectacle* until Thursday, she was trying to get some of this work done in advance, during lulls in the shop. With the increase in titled customers and the flurry of end-of-Season events, she had more dresses to describe than previously.

Thanks to Madame de Veirrion, Maison Noirot would squeak through Quarter Day intact.

Sophy had got to the headdress when Mary Parmenter told her she was needed in the private consulting room.

When Sophy entered the room, she found Lord Longmore, Lady Clara, and Lady Warford all studying the plum dress. At her entrance, they turned simultaneously toward the door, and three pairs of eyes fixed on her.

Sophy didn't take a step back. She didn't let her eyes widen. She didn't exclaim. She showed only her politely interested dressmaker's face.

Lady Warford frowned, then gave a little gasp. "Madame de Veirrion?" she said. "But I thought . . ." She trailed off as her gaze moved downward and she took in Sophy's attire. It was elegant and stylish, as a dressmaker's clothing ought to be. However, as a dressmaker's clothing ought to be, it was nothing like the attire a great lady like Madame de Veirrion would wear.

Sophy curtseyed. It was the Noirot curtsey. It wasn't necessary, but she did it anyway, perhaps to irritate Lord Longmore, who'd had his way with her on the way to the hotel on Thursday night, then at the hotel, and then had left and busied himself with forgetting she existed, apparently.

"Yes, it's Madame," Longmore said. "But it isn't. It's one of those dreadful Noirot women, Mother. This one is Sophia—the one who allowed herself to be assaulted the other night, in order to save Clara from a miserable marriage."

Sophy's heart sped up. She said nothing. She tried to look nothing, too, though it was very difficult, when she was discovering what it was like to have one's heart in one's mouth.

Lady Warford was looking from her daughter to her son to Sophy.

"It was a cunning scheme, which Miss Noirot devised," he continued. "She did it because Clara is their favorite client and they didn't want to lose her. And because they rather love her, it seems." He paused briefly. "I rather love Miss Noirot. But I'm in a difficulty. She won't marry me unless you love her."

"Marry!" One word. One pained cry from his mother.

"She won't marry me unless you love her," he said. "I wish you'd make the effort."

Lady Warford closed her eyes and swayed a little.

"Perhaps you'd better sit down, Mother," Lady Clara said.

Lady Warford opened her eyes. "Nonsense. I'm

perfectly well." Her chin went up. "A dressmaker. Another dressmaker." She looked about her, and Sophy saw the lost look in her eyes.

"My lady," she began.

"Perhaps, after all, I will sit down," Lady Warford said.

Longmore drew a chair forward for her. She sat. After a moment she said, "That scene at Lady Bartham's ball. It was . . . arranged?"

"All arranged, to the last detail," Longmore said. "Arranged by Miss Noirot. It was all her own plan. She devised it while we were bringing Clara back from Portsmouth. That was Miss Noirot's doing, too. Without her, I should never have found Clara."

"Oh, Harry," Lady Warford said.

"She won't marry me unless you love her," he said. "You liked her well enough before."

"Oh, please," Sophy said. "That was different. I was a lady. With a great fortune. Money cures a host of ills, as you know very well. It's bad of you to harrow your mother's feelings."

She turned to the mother. "My lady, perhaps you'd like a restorative." Without waiting for consent, she went for the brandy, which was kept in a cupboard in case of sudden swoons or fits, no uncommon occurrence in a shop catering to ladies. As she poured, she said, "I cannot think what was in Lord Longmore's mind to subject you to such a shock. With no preparation, I daresay."

"If I'd told our mother what I was about," he said, "she wouldn't have come."

"I came," Lady Warford said slowly. "That is, I *believed* I'd come to see what could be salvaged of Clara's . . . trousseau." Her eyes filled. "For that horrid wedding. To that awful man. And you . . ."

"She saved me, Mama," Lady Clara said. "She saved me. Twice."

Lady Warford turned to her daughter. Her gaze was pure love. It made Sophy's heart ache. Her mother had never looked at her in that way . . . when Mama was about . . . when she remembered she had children.

She gave Lady Warford the brandy. She drank. She stared into the glass for a time. No one spoke. Sophy's heart was pounding so, everyone must hear it. It pounded so, she thought she'd faint. But she made herself stand perfectly straight, and kept her expression exactly as it ought to be. Politely interested. Deferential, but not too much so. Dressmakers must always keep the upper—

"I think, perhaps," Lady Warford said. She paused. "I think perhaps I can . . . like her."

Her children said, at the same time:

"Oh, come, Mother!"

"Really, Mama!"

Lady Warford's gaze lifted to Sophy. "It is perfectly unreasonable to expect me to love you on short acquaintance," she said. "However."

They waited.

"However, you have done me . . . a great kindness." She paused and composed herself. "A very great kindness, which is impossible to repay—and really, it's most provoking of you. But you are presentable at least. And your sister is a duchess. That is no small thing. In any event, there's never any stopping Harry when he takes it into his head to do something."

"Will that do, Sophy?" Longmore said. "It's not quite what you wished for, but for the present, I think it's the best she can do."

Sophy swallowed a sob. "Yes, it will have to do," she said. "I shall try to make her love me more—but in the meantime—yes, it will do—I shall make do—because—because I should be so very wretched without you."

She flung herself into his arms.

On Friday, the day after the Queen's last Drawing Room of the Season, Miss Sophia Noirot and the Earl of Longmore were married by special license in the red drawing room of Clevedon House. The party in attendance was rather larger than the group at hand when the duke had been married. This time, along with the bride's sisters and niece and most of Clevedon's aunts, Lord and Lady Warford and their other five offspring looked on.

Sometime later, after the wedding breakfast, after the marquess and marchioness had returned home and were thinking their own thoughts in her sitting room's quiet, Lord Warford said, "Is that a new frock, my dear?"

"Yes, yes, it is," Lady Warford said, surprised. Her husband, to the best of her recollection, had never taken any notice of anything she wore. He noticed the dressmaking bills, and sometimes grumbled about them, but that was all.

"Very becoming," he said gruffly. "Reminds me of the girl I married."

She colored a little. "Does it, indeed?"

"Yes." He rose and closed the sitting room door and locked it.

And then some things happened, which made her forget to mention a curious thought she'd had, to do with her new daughter-in-law's eyes.

* * *

After the wedding breakfast, the newlyweds set out for Lancashire, the sisters having decided Society needed time to forget Madame Veirrion before meeting the new Lady Longmore.

Longmore and Sophy stopped for the night at the Angel Inn, some thirty miles from London.

And it was there and then, after he'd laboriously taken off every stitch she wore, and made love to every naked inch of her, and while he lay defenseless in a state of post-coital bliss, that she disentangled herself from his embrace and sat up and said, "There's something I have to tell you."

"There always is," he said.

"I should have told you before the wedding," she said. "Marcelline was appalled that I hadn't."

"A confession?" He raised himself onto his elbows. "Murder perchance? A mad husband in the attic? But no, you were a virgin."

"That's all the purity you get," she said.

"I'm not a great devotee of purity," he said. His gaze drifted to her breasts. The lamplight made them seem to glow, like two beautiful moons. But not quite full moons. More like three-quarter, with a delicious uptilt, like the uptilt of her nose.

"Look at my eyes," she said.

"In a minute," he said. "I'm admiring your breasts. I think I could write a poem about your breasts. That's how splendid they are. And about your bottom. It's completely perfect. You ought to model for statues of Venus. But I don't want a lot of lechers ogling you. I'd rather keep you to myself."

"I do love you," she said.

"You ought to," he said. "I suit you perfectly."

"You do. You understand me. And that's why I'm sure you won't take this the wrong way."

"This sounds ominous," he said.

"Nothing frightens you," she said. "Look at my eyes."

He looked.

"Well?" she said.

"They're remarkably blue. An uncommon color."

"It's the DeLucey blue."

"Obviously runs in the family," he said. "Funny, how your older sister didn't end up with them, but her daughter did."

The great blue eyes widened.

He stared at her for a moment. "Was that the confession?"

"Yes. You *knew*?"

"Sometimes," he said, "I can put two and two together. All those hints you've dropped about your past. I knew there had to be a story, but I was too busy trying to seduce you to try to squeeze it out of you. But today, it suddenly became clear."

"Today," she said. "Before, during, or after the ceremony?"

"Does it matter?"

"Yes, because Marcelline said I married you under false pretenses."

"Well, that would have added to the fun, but it isn't true. I knew exactly what I was getting into. I've always known, I daresay. I knew you weren't like anybody else. I knew you weren't boring."

"No one has ever accused the DeLuceys of being boring," she said.

"But I didn't see the whole picture until everybody had gathered for the wedding," he said. "Then there you all were: you, the duchess, Leonie, and Lucie. I remembered Lady Durwich talking about the DeLuceys. I recalled the way you answered her, making a little joke of it. I recalled the way you launched into that long, boring description of my sister's dress."

"To put you off the scent," she said.

"It worked," he said. "Until today. Then it became as clear as clear. And I thought, 'By Jupiter, this day just keeps getting better. My marriage is going to give Society a heart attack. They'll think the Revolution is at hand or the Apocalypse is nigh. I've persuaded the most delectable bit of devil in female form to lie about loving, honoring, and obeying me for the rest of our lives—'"

"That wasn't a lie," she said. "Except for the 'obey' part."

"'And she's a *Dreadful DeLucey*. I've married into a gang of them.' My heart soared. And I almost did myself an injury, not laughing."

The corners of her mouth began to curl. "I was fairly certain you wouldn't mind," she said.

"Mind? It's perfect."

"*You're* perfect," she said. "And I think you deserve a reward for not falling down laughing, and breaking the solemnity of the occasion."

"It about killed me."

She slid back down and into his arms. "A *big* reward," she said. "There's just one thing." She stroked over his chest and downward.

"Anything," he said.

"No One," she said, "Must Ever Know."

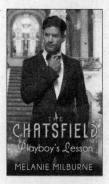

Hot reads!

These 3-in-1s will certainly get you feeling hot under the collar with their desert locations, billionaire tycoons and playboy princes.

Now available at
www.millsandboon.co.uk/offers

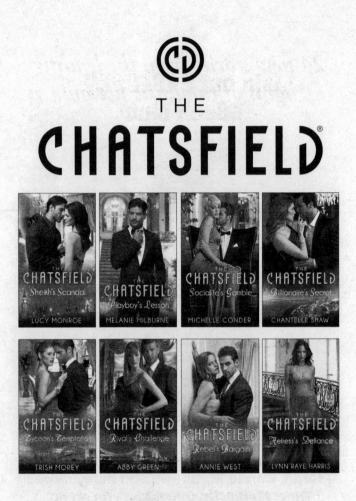

Which series will you try next?